Pr...
The M...

BEN...

"Lush, sexy, and thr...er darkly addictive entry ...maker's Song series. Adrian Phoenix makes her world of vampires, fallen angels, compelling characters, and rich settings come alive. I have two words for Ms. Phoenix: write faster."

—*New York Times* bestselling author Jeaniene Frost

IN THE BLOOD

"Phoenix trips the dark fantastic in this wild, bloody sequel. . . . She keeps the plot thick and the tension high."

—*Publishers Weekly*

"The atmosphere is dark, and treachery abounds, making this story white-knuckle reading in the extreme."

—*Romantic Times*

"Filled with twisting plots, shadowy government agencies, conspiracies, and betrayals, *In the Blood* kept me hooked from page one. This dark urban fantasy is not only action-packed from beginning to end, but at its core, it is also a story of hope and love."

—*ParaNormal Romance*

"Adrian Phoenix is fast becoming one of my favorite authors. Her ability to create a dark, edgy atmosphere so real you can see, hear, and taste it, while maintaining a fast-moving, page-turning plot, is simply amazing."

—Jenna Black, author of *Speak of the Devil*

A RUSH OF WINGS

"Hard-charging action sequences, steamy sex scenes, and a surprising government conspiracy make this debut, the first in a series, engrossingly fun." —*Entertainment Weekly*

"Phoenix's lively debut has it all . . . vampires and fallen angels and a slicing-dicing serial killer . . . Phoenix alternates romantic homages to gothdom and steamy blood-drinking threesomes with enough terse, fast-paced thriller scenes to satisfy even the most jaded fan."
—*Publishers Weekly*

"Sharp, wicked, and hot as sin."
—*New York Times* bestselling author Marjorie M. Liu

"Twisted science and the paranormal collide in this eerie new detective thriller that takes an intriguing slant on the supernatural. Phoenix's gritty and original characters are instantly engaging, and the rapid pace keeps you glued to the pages." —*Romantic Times*

"A thrilling tale of lust and murder that will keep you turning the pages to see what happens next. A *Rush of Wings* joins the vampire romanticism of Anne Rice with the brutal intrigue of *The Silence of the Lambs*."
—*Gothic Beauty Magazine*

"Ms. Phoenix spins a deliciously dark and seductive tale filled with sadistic serial killers, sexy vampires, powerful fallen angels and secret experiments. The fast pace and creative twists make this action-packed read one to remember, and the steamy romance will have readers eagerly looking for more of the same."
—*Darque Reviews*

"A complex, layered story filled with twists and turns . . . a dark, rich treat you won't soon forget."

—Romance Reviews Today

"This one pulled me in from the first page. Heather and Dante are among those rare characters readers so often look for and seldom find."

—*New York Times* bestselling author Barb Hendee

"*A Rush of Wings* is a fast-paced ride, its New Orleans setting appropriately rich and gothic, its characters both real and surprising."

—*New York Times* bestselling author Kristine Kathryn Rusch

"*A Rush of Wings* grabs you from the first sentence and doesn't let go . . . Phoenix is one of the best new talents I have seen coming into literature in decades."

—*New York Times* bestselling author Dean Wesley Smith

"A goth urban fantasy that moves as fast as its otherworldly characters. A bit like *The Crow* crossed with *The Silence of the Lambs* crossed with a voice that is Phoenix's own, *A Rush of Wings* is decadent, glittering fun, wrapped up in leather and latex."

—Justine Musk, author of *BloodAngel*

"*A Rush of Wings* is a dark, rich, sensual treat . . . a perfect blend of suspense, romance, and lyrical prose to keep readers up until late, late at night turning pages. I can't wait to read more."

—Jenna Black, author of *Speak of the Devil*

"If vampires didn't exist, we'd have to invent them. To do that deed, I'd recommend Adrian Phoenix."

—Gerald M. Weinberg, author of *The Aremac Project*

These titles are also available as eBooks.

Beneath the Skin

Book Three of The Maker's Song

Adrian Phoenix

POCKET BOOKS

New York   London   Toronto   Sydney

Pocket Books
A Division of Simon & Schuster, Inc.
1230 Avenue of the Americas
New York, NY 10020

This book is a work of fiction. Names, characters, places, and incidents either are products of the author's imagination or are used fictitiously. Any resemblance to actual events or locales or persons, living or dead, is entirely coincidental.

First Pocket Books paperback edition January 2010

POCKET and colophon are registered trademarks of Simon & Schuster, Inc.

For information about special discounts for bulk purchases, please contact Simon & Schuster Special Sales at 1-866-506-1949 or business@simonandschuster.com.

The Simon & Schuster Speakers Bureau can bring authors to your live event. For more information or to book an event, contact the Simon & Schuster Speakers Bureau at 1-866-248-3049 or visit our website at www.simonspeakers.com.

Cover design by Lisa Litwack
Illustration by Craig White

Manufactured in the United States of America

10 9 8 7 6 5 4 3 2 1

ISBN 978-1-4391-3729-1
ISBN 978-1-4391-6655-0 (ebook)

DEDICATED TO JEN HEDDLE, JIM SPENCER, SEBASTIAN PHOENIX, AND DIANE (DT) STEINER

I can't thank each of you enough for seeing me through the medical consequences of my klutziness (Curb? What curb?) and for being so generous with your patience, support, and understanding as I healed.

Jen, working with you has always been a kick-ass pleasure, but your compassion and guidance and belief in me while I struggled to hit my deadline took off enormous pressure and allowed me to focus through the painkiller haze and write. It's truly an honor to have you as my editor.

Thanks from the bottom of my heart—Jim and DT—for all the rides home from work and to an endless parade of doctor appointments. I appreciate your generosity more than I can say, not to mention the time you both took out of every day to shepherd me around.

And last, but sure as hell not least, thanks so much, Sebastian, for leaving your family for three weeks to take care of me; and damned good care it was too. I love you, sweetie!

Without the four of you, this book might not have been finished.

Merci beaucoup!

ACKNOWLEDGMENTS

I want to express my deepest gratitude to everyone at AquaJogger for their continuing support and encouragement and for putting up with my absences whenever I'm off on a writing vacation: Jim Spencer, Bobby Criswell, Steve Bergstrom, Lew and Kathy Thorne, Mark Poorman—you've each made it possible for me to pursue my dream. Thank you!

Special writing thanks to: Sean and Rose Prescott, Karen Abrahamson, and Dean Smith for being my first readers and for helping me tell the best story possible; and to my editor, Jen Heddle, and my agent, Matt Bialer, for your passion, your humor, and your artistry—I'm honored to work with you both!

Big-ass thanks to: Mippy Carlson, Nate Gross, Sheila Dale, Louise Robson, Judi Szabo, and all the members of Club Hell and my street team for your support, enthusiasm, well wishes, and love for Dante and his world. Y'all ROCK!

Heartfelt thanks to: my sons, Matt Jensen and Sebastian Phoenix, and their partners, Sherri Lyons and Jen Phoenix, and my story-writing little Kylah Phoenix, for all their encouragement and love; and Kris Rusch, Lynn Adams, Sharon and Marty Embertson, and Jerry Robinson for your friendship and for your tireless efforts in spreading the word—I couldn't do it without you.

Special you-were-there-in-my-time-of-need thanks to: Jeri Smith-Ready and Patrice Michelle for running me around after my graceful plummet in Orlando; Sean Prescott for picking me up at the airport and for just being there; Kris Rusch, Dean Smith, Chris and Steve York, Rose Prescott, and all the talented and prolific members of OWN for showering me with welcome-home goodies; and everyone who visited me in the hospital and sent their well-wishes—thank you each so very much!

Thanks also to Abulia Paroxysm (Sebastian Phoenix) for creating music that is original and heartfelt and true. And to Queens of the Stone Age, Saul Williams, Saints of Ruin, Does It Offend You, Yeah?, and Rammstein for the music.

And last, but never least, Trent Reznor, whose music always provides an emotional soundscape for Dante and his world and is always a source of inspiration.

And, again, thanks to you, the reader, for picking up this book and plunging back into Dante, Heather, and Lucien's world. None of this could happen without you. If this is your first time, *bienvenue* and enjoy.

Please visit me at adrianphoenix.com, myspace.com/adriannikolasphoenix, and at facebook.com/pages/Adrian-Phoenix/.

GLOSSARY

To make things as simple as possible, I've listed not only words, but phrases used in the story. Please keep in mind that Cajun is different from Parisian French and the French generally spoken in Europe. Different grammatically and even, sometimes, in pronunciation and spelling.

The French that Guy Mauvais and Justine Aucoin use is traditional French as opposed to Dante's Cajun.

For the Irish and Welsh words—including the ones I've created—pronunciation is provided.

One final thing: **Prejean** is pronounced PRAY-zhawn.

Aingeal (AIN-gyahl), angel. Fallen/Elohim word.
Ami, (m) friend, (f) **amie. Mon ami,** my friend.
Anhrefncathl (ann-HREVN-cathl), chaos song; the song of a Maker. Fallen/Elohim word.
Apprentis, (pl) apprentices, (s) **apprenti**.
Arrivederci, (Italian) good-bye.
Assolutamente, (Italian) absolutely.
Beaucoup chaud tête-rouge, red-hot redhead.
Bien, well, very.

Bien compris, well understood.

Bon, good, nice, fine, kind.

Bon appétit, enjoy (as in eating), good eating, good appetite.

Bon chien, good dog.

Bonne nuit, good night.

Bonsoir, ma belle fille, good evening, my beautiful girl.

Buona sera, (Italian) good evening.

Buono, (Italian) good.

Calon-cyfaill, (KAW-lawn-CUHV-aisle) bondmate, heartmate.

Cara mia, (Italian) (f) my beloved, (m) **Caro mio**.

Catin, (f) doll, dear, sweetheart.

Ça va bien, I'm fine, I'm good, okay.

Ça y est, that's it.

Ça y revené, he had it coming.

Ce n'est pas possible, that is not possible.

Cercle de Druide, Circle of Druids, a sacred and select nightkind order.

C'est bon, that's good.

Chalkydri (chal-KOO-dree), winged serpentine demons of Sheol, subservient to the Elohim.

Cher, (m) dear, beloved, (f) **chère**. **Mon cher**, my dear or my beloved.

Cher ami, mon, (m) my dearest friend, my best friend; intimate, implying a special relationship.

Chéri, (m) dearest, darling, honey, (f) **chérie**.

Chien, (m) dog, (f) **chienne**.

Ciao, (Italian) hello or good-bye—generally used only among friends and family in this way.

Ciò è allineare, (Italian) this is true. **Sapere di c'è ne**, do you know of any?

Creawdwr (KRAY-OW-dooer), creator; Maker/Unmaker; an extremely rare branch of the Elohim believed to be extinct. Last known *creawdwr* was Yahweh.

Cydymaith (kuh-DUH-mith), companion.

D'accord, okay.

Elohim, (s and pl) the Fallen; the beings mythologized as fallen angels.

Enchanté, charmed.

Fallen, see Elohim.

Fi' de garce, son-of-a-bitch.

Fille de sang, (f) blood-daughter; "turned" female offspring of a vampire.

Fils, son.

Fils de sang, (m) blood-son; "turned" male offspring of a vampire.

Fola Fior, true blood, pure.

Forse sì, forse no, (Italian) perhaps yes, perhaps not.

Frère du coeur, brother of the heart.

Geis, A vow of obligation, and a taboo preventing certain actions. To break a geis results in dishonor and/or death.

Gêné toi pas, don't be bashful.

Grazie, (Italian) thank you.

J'ai faim, I'm hungry.

Je regrette, I'm sorry.

Je t'aime, mon fils. Toujours, I love you, my son. Always.

Joli, (m) pretty, cute, (f) **jolie. Mon joli**, my pretty boy.

J'su ici, I'm here.

Le Conseil du Sang, the Council of Blood, nightkind lawgivers.

Le coquin qui vole a un autre, le diable en ris, when one thief robs another, the devil laughs.

Lesbica, (Italian) lesbian. **Una lesbica**, a lesbian.

Llygad, (THLOO-gad) (s) eye; a watcher; keeper of immortal history; story-shaper, (pl). **Llygaid** (THLOO-guide).

Ma belle, my beauty. **Ma belle dame**, my beautiful lady.

Magnifico, (Italian) wonderful.

Mais ça vont jamais finir, but it'll never end.

Ma mère, my mother.

Marmot, (m) brat.

Ma 'tite-doux, (f) my little sweet one.

Menteuse, (f) liar, (m) **menteur**.

Merci, thank you. **Merci beaucoup,** thanks a lot. **Merci bien,** thanks very much.

Merde, shit.

Mère de sang, (f) blood-mother; female vampire who has turned another and become their parent.

Mia ballerina scura (Italian), my dark ballerina.

Minou, (m) endearing name for a cat.

Mio amico, (Italian) my friend.

Mio figlio, (Italian) my son.

Mio ragazzo bello, (Italian) my beautiful boy.

Moi aussi, me too.

M'selle, (f) abbreviated spoken form of **mademoiselle,** Miss, young lady.

M'sieu, (m) abbreviated spoken form of **monsieur,** Mr., sir, gentleman.

Naturellement, naturally, of course.

Nephilim, the offspring resulting from Fallen and mortal unions.

Nightbringer, a name/title given to Lucien De Noir.

Nightkind, (s and pl) vampire; Dante's term for vampires.

Nomad, name for the pagan, gypsy-style clans who ride across the land.

Oui, yes.

Où suis-je? where am I?

Pas de quoi, you're welcome.

Père de sang, (m) blood-father; male vampire who has turned another and become their "parent."

Peut-être que oui, peut-être que non, maybe yes, maybe no.

Piazza, (Italian) plaza.

Principe, (Italian) prince.

P'tit, mon, (m) my little one, (f) **p'tite, ma** (Generally affectionate.)

P'tite marmaille, (f) little brat.

Ragazzo pigro, (Italian) lazy boy.

Rappelle, remember. **Oui, je rappelle**, yes, I remember.

Rêves doux, sweet dreams.

Ritorna, bella (Italian), return, beautiful.

Sì, (Italian) yes.

Sì, esattamente, caro mio, (Italian) yes, exactly, my beloved.

Signor, (Italian) sir.

S'il te plaît, please (informal).

Sì, mia Signora, (Italian) yes, my lady.

Tais-toi, shut up.

T'a menti, you lied, you lie.

T'es sûr de sa? are you sure about that? **T'es sûr?** you sure?

Tout de suite, right away.

Très, very.

Très bien, very good, very well.

Très joli, (m) very pretty.

True Blood, born vampire, rare and powerful.

Una bella donna merita un uomo, non un ragazzo (Italian), A beautiful woman deserves a man, not a boy.

Vous êtes très aimable, you are very kind.

Wybrcathl (OOEEBR-cathl), sky-song. Fallen/Elohim word.

PROLOGUE

LIKE MOLTEN GLASS

"Are these the people who broke into your house, sweetie?"

Brisia Rodriguez didn't look up from her cup of hot cocoa. She studied the white swirls of whipped cream melting into the chocolate instead of the pictures Mr. Díon slid across the polished wood table.

Interview station, her dad would've called the small, pale green-painted room with its table and two chairs. But this wasn't a police station or the FBI field office. She knew because she and her fifth-grade class had visited both with her dad on a career-day field trip last month.

"Is my dad okay?" she asked.

"He's in the hospital," Mr. Díon said. "But your mom

and sisters are with him right now. As soon as we're done here, I'll drive you over there, okay?"

Brisia curled her fingers tighter around the warm mug. "Will he be . . . all right?" She prayed she wouldn't have to ask the other thing, the horrible thing she never, *ever* wanted to say aloud. She was scared if she did, it'd come true like a reverse wish.

Nononono. Don't even *think it!*

She drew in a shuddering breath laced with the thick scent of creamy, hot milk and dark chocolate. Her stomach knotted.

"Brisia." Mr. Díon's low, soothing voice felt like a hand to her chin, gently tugging her gaze up from the depths of her hot cocoa. "You're the only one who can help us find the people who hurt your dad."

She looked at Mr. Díon. His purple eyes reminded her of sunlit violets. "I told the police everything," she said. "They wrote it all down."

"Yes, but the police don't know who they're looking for. But I believe *we* do," Mr. Díon said, his voice as soft and warm as his eyes. "All you have to do is look at the pictures, okay?"

"Okay," Brisia said. She lowered her gaze to the trio of photographs lined up neatly on the table between her and Mr. Díon. The first one showed a man with curly blond hair, a smile curving his lips. Laugh crinkles V-ed out from beside each green eye. He reminded her of that actor, Matthew McConaughey.

Standing in the hall inside her house, Matthew McConaughey Guy smiles, all warm and friendly, almost slike he's supposed to be there, even with the gun in his hand. But when his gaze flicks over to Brisia, his eyes are like ice.

"He was there," Brisia said. "He had a gun too."

"Alexander Lyons. Good job, Brisia. What about the next photo?"

Brisia shifted her attention to the middle picture and recognized the pretty red-haired woman. Only a hint of a smile touched the woman's lips, but her blue-eyed gaze was open and direct. Brisia remembered the hushed urgency in the woman's voice as she'd hurried Brisia to the front door after Matthew McConaughey Guy had sauntered from the room.

I want you to run to a neighbor's house and have them call 911, okay?

Do you need help too?

Don't worry about me. Just go.

"Heather Wallace," Mr. Díon said. "Why did you think she needed help too?"

Brisia glanced at Mr. Díon. Had she spoken aloud? "Well . . . I could tell she didn't like this guy," she said, touching a fingertip against the first photo. "And she asked me to call 911. I don't think she would've done that if she was one of the bad guys."

Mr. Díon nodded. "Good observation. I'll bet your dad's proud of you," he said, his violet eyes full of light. "Are you planning to be an FBI agent like your dad?"

"Yeah," Brisia said, even though up until that moment all she'd ever wanted to be was a veterinarian. Helping and healing dogs and cats and guinea pigs. She wasn't sure if that was a new truth revealing itself to her or if she was just saying it as a bargain-promise to God. "Are you an FBI agent too? Do you work with my dad?"

"I'm FBI, yes. But I haven't had the pleasure of working with your dad."

Brisia wanted to believe Mr. Díon. She really did. Dad had told her the FBI was a part of their family—a family that stretched all across the country and around the world. You trusted family, went to them when trouble knocked on your door.

But he'd said he was *Mr.* Díon, not *Special Agent* Díon.

She lifted her mug and swallowed her doubt with a sip of cocoa and whipped cream, sweet and warm. She carefully set the mug back on the table, trying to slide it back inside the little ring of chocolate it'd made on the polished wood surface.

You trusted family.

"I've never been here before," Brisia said, looking around the room. It still smelled faintly of paint. "Is this a new office? I don't see a two-way mirror. There's not even a camera up in the corner."

Mr. Díon laughed, his voice as soothing as the cocoa in her mug. "You'll make a good agent, sweetie. This is a special room we use to interview FBI agents and their families when . . . tragedy . . . strikes, so we don't need to monitor anyone. It's a safe place from the bad guys." Leaning forward, he rested his clasped hands on the table. "One more photo, then you're done."

"Okay." Brisia looked at the last photo and she inhaled in sharp surprise at the man captured in the picture. He looked way young, for one thing, younger than she remembered. Black hair, dark chocolate-colored eyes, white skin, a tilted smile on his lips, a black collar strapped around his throat. He looked happy and sure of himself. And what surprised her was that without all the blood on his skin, he was cute, like pin-the-poster-to-your-wall-and-sigh-over-it cute.

He didn't look like a monster.

But she knew he was.

He appears in front of her in a gust of air smelling of autumn leaves and Halloween apples. Blood smears his white face. She backs up until she bumps into the sofa. She freezes, her heart drumming, frantic and wild. He kneels down on one knee in front of her, leather pants creaking. A smile tugs at his bloodstained lips. He reaches a trembling, blood-smeared hand for her hair and slides a lock between his fingers.

She catches a whiff of something pungent and coppery.

She sees blood on his pale fingers, glistening on his shirt, trickling from his nose. So much blood. But he's not acting like he's hurt. Maybe it isn't all his blood.

A thought loops through her mind, numbing her heart and stealing her voice.

Where's Daddy?

"Did he hurt you?"

Brisia shook her head. She tried to blink away the tears blurring her vision, but she couldn't blink fast enough. Tears spilled over her lashes and slid hot down her cheeks. No longer ten years old, but a bawling baby. And a baby couldn't help Dad.

"He was there," she said, her throat so tight, the words hurt. "He came outta my dad's office."

"Dante Prejean. Are you sure he didn't hurt you? Absolutely sure?"

"He didn't hurt me." She remembered the blood glistening on his shirt, smeared on his face, his hands. *He didn't hurt me, but he hurt Daddy.* She wiped at her eyes with the heels of her hands and another memory flashed into her mind.

The red-haired woman walks out of the hallway's darkness and stops beside the office door, a small black gun clenched in her hands. She looks at Brisia and her eyes widen.

"Help me," Brisia whispers.

The woman, face tight, lifts the gun and aims it at the blood-smeared man kneeling in front of Brisia, stroking her hair and speaking to her in a language she doesn't know.

But it isn't anger she sees on the woman's face, or even horror. It's sorrow.

Sniffing, Brisia wiped at her nose with the back of her hand.

"I don't see any Kleenex," Mr. Díon murmured, brushing a hand over his short caramel-brown hair as he glanced around the room.

"A lot of times it's kept under the interview table or in a drawer," Brisia said. Shoving her chair back over the low beige carpet, she peeked under the table. No box of Kleenex. Just Mr. Díon's polished black shoes and gray-trousered legs.

"I think we're about done, Brisia."

"So I get to go see my dad now?" she asked, sitting up and scooting her chair back to the table. She lifted her mug and took a swallow of the cooling cocoa.

Mr. Díon stood up and walked around the table. He crouched down beside her chair. Brisia's fingers clenched around the mug, and for a moment, she thought she smelled copper and Halloween apples, saw blood against white skin. Her stomach rolled, queasy. She set the mug back down on the table.

"Before I take you to the hospital to see your dad," Mr. Díon said, his voice low and smooth, "I want you to close your eyes and go back to the moment you walked into the house this evening."

Brisia looked into his eyes. His violet gaze was flecked with gold and burning bright—rimmed with fire like molten glass. She'd learned in art class last year that molten glass could be shaped into anything.

Offering Mr. Díon a smile, Brisia said, "Okay." She closed her eyes.

You trusted family.

"I'm going to touch your temples, but keep your eyes closed, sweetie."

Brisia nodded. Fingers brushed aside the hair at either side of Brisia's head, then settled against her skin. Their heat made her feel drowsy, all floaty, like a balloon.

"Go to the beginning," Mr. Díon whispered.

A wave of dizziness swirled through her and when she

tried to open her eyes, she couldn't. Fear rippled in, black and cold. "Mr. Díon? I don't feel good."

"Shhh. It'll pass. Just focus on what happened tonight."

The dizziness vanished, but an icy ball of dread lodged in her tummy. She gripped the sides of her chair to make sure she didn't fall out of it.

A thought breezed through her mind: *Everything's okay. You're safe and you'll be seeing Daddy soon.* She relaxed and let the thought curl through her like hot cocoa steam as she shifted her thoughts backward a few hours.

She opens the front door and walks into the empty living room. "Daddy?" she calls. "I forgot my iPod!"

And even as the memory and its sounds and images flowed through her mind, she felt each one being un-threaded and undone, like when her mom unhooked her knitting when she didn't like how the piece had turned out. Until it was just yarn, waiting to be knitted into something new. Or molten glass waiting to be shaped.

Then even those thoughts unraveled.

1

A NECESSARY EVIL

Emmett Thibodaux stood at the threshold of the victim's home office, light from the hallway casting his shadow across the body on the floor.

FBI SAC Alberto Rodriguez was stretched out on the carpet like a man seeking relief for an aching back. But the thick, coppery reek of blood and the crackling of police radios from the living room told a different story.

Emmett flipped on the light.

Rodriguez stared up at the glass-domed ceiling light with half-lidded, milky eyes. His throat looked shredded, savaged. Blood had soaked into the front of his pale blue sweater, staining it a dark maroon that matched the blood halo soaked into the carpet around his head.

"Christ, did his daughter see him like this?" Emmett asked.

"No," his partner, Merri Goodnight, murmured from just behind him. He heard the whisper of suede against his windbreaker as she leaned forward to look into the murder room. Caught a faint whiff of cloves. "Not according to what Abano told me. The kid only saw perps. She didn't know about her dad."

"Abano? The fed in charge of the scene?"

"You mean the fed that *was* in charge of the scene?" Merri replied dryly. "That'd be him."

"No doubt he's one unhappy camper at the moment."

"Given that the vic's one of their own, that's putting it mildly."

"Yeah, well, wonder how he'd feel to learn that some of his own might be involved in the killing," Emmett murmured. "The feds'll be even unhappier when they realize we're shutting this crime scene down altogether."

Controlling and sanitizing the situation. A clean wipe. Scraping clinkers into the furnace to watch them burn, as his granddad used to say. No matter how you put it, the result was the same. Events were being altered at best and erased at worst.

A necessary evil in his line of work.

From the front room, Emmett caught a low murmur of voices from the TV that no one had turned off, hoping to catch the result of the Garcia-Dowd middleweight championship bout and the latest sports scores while processing the scene. No more police radio static or low, irked mutters.

The Bureau's people had vacated along with the Seattle PD's people. Hell, maybe they had all gone to a local tavern to brew up a booze-fueled bitchfest about the Shadow Branch's glory-stealing theft of their case.

But nothing was ever what it seemed to be. Especially here.

Emmett stepped into the room, carefully avoiding the

spatters of blood marring the cream-colored carpet near the threshold. He caught a faint whiff of piss just under the blood reek.

"ETA for our cleanup crew is ten minutes," Merri said. "Gillespie's supposed to drop by with instructions from HQ."

"Wonder what's taking so long? Usually Gillespie's first on scene."

"HQ probably put the chief on hold while they were busy trying to figure out who to smear the sticky, gooey blame on. Once they have that figured out . . ."

"Heads are gonna roll," Emmett agreed. He allowed his gaze to rove around the room, ticking off each item he saw as normal or not, a mental what's-wrong-with-this-picture game that he played at each assignment. Hell, not just at assignments or crime scenes anymore. He found himself doing it everywhere he went—at Safeway, the mall, in a movie theater, picking up the kids from school.

Gun on the carpet against the north wall, a Smith & Wesson—not normal.

Desk with neatly parked chair—normal. Black, four-drawer file cabinet—normal.

Opened gun safe containing a single box of ammo—probably not normal.

And the late Alberto Rodriguez sprawled on the carpet in a drying pool of his own blood—well, hell, not even *close* to normal.

But normal had nothing to do with what had happened in this house.

"Abano and his people have no clue about vampires," Merri said, as though reading Emmett's mind. But he knew she hadn't; that was an issue they'd hashed out years ago. "They think Rodriguez was killed by multiple slash and stab wounds to the throat. And I sure as hell wasn't going to enlighten them."

Emmett chuckled. "They wouldn't've believed you anyway."

"Not at first," Merri said, a smile quirking at the corners of her mouth. "You didn't either, as I recall."

"Still don't," Emmett drawled.

Merri folded her arms across her chest, slung her weight onto one hip, and arched an eyebrow. "Uh-huh. Don't make me prove it to you, Thibodaux. Again."

Emmett shook his head, smiling. "Once was enough, thanks." He pinched up his trousers at the thighs, then crouched down beside Rodriguez's body. The man's ruined throat had been pierced and torn by sharp teeth.

"Not the neatest work I've ever seen," Merri said, her voice pitched low, and now right beside him. After five years of working together, her speed and stealth no longer startled him. Most times, he even forgot what she was.

"Looks to me like one outta control vamp." Emmett glanced up at his partner.

Merri tilted her head, her dark brown eyes studying all that remained of Special Agent in Charge Alberto Rodriguez, husband, father, Bureau man. "Young vamp, maybe. Or hungry as hell." She shifted and glanced back at the doorway and Emmett followed her gaze.

High-velocity blood spatter speckled the doorway's wood frame and the peach-colored wall beside it. "Looks like Rodriguez got one good shot off, though," she said.

"He did." Emmett agreed.

Merri nodded at the gun on the carpet. "For all it was worth."

"So what stopped the vamp from killing Rodriguez's daughter?" Emmett said. "Why didn't he snatch up that kid and drain her dry?"

"Good question." Merri crouched down beside Emmett and he smelled spice and cloves from the cigarettes she smoked. "And I think I have the answer."

"Yeah? Let's hear it, then, Goodnight," Emmett said, his voice a low drawl, a little bit of Louisiana creeping in underneath his words. "You gonna tell me this vamp's got a soft spot for kids?"

Merri shook her head and her straightened black hair, gathered and glossed into a high and neat ponytail, swung like a pendulum across her shoulder blades. "Nope. Someone else shot him again."

"Yeah? Who?"

A smug smile curved Merri's rosy full lips. She lifted her hand and displayed a small, slender dart pinched between two fingers. "One of the other perps dropped the vamp with a trank gun. I relieved Abano's techs of the one they'd bagged while processing the scene. But they missed finding the dart in the carpet."

Emmett grinned. "I knew there was a reason I kept you around."

"Because I'm a better field agent than you'll ever be?"

"That'd be it."

"Truth, brothah," Merri said, then chuckled, the sound warm and throaty. She slid the dart into an inside pocket of her black suede jacket. "Makes me wonder what else they missed."

"Truth, sistah. I'm guessing tons, but it doesn't matter. It's never going to court." Emmett rose to his feet, his knees creaking with the movement. An annoying new voice in the body-choir his joints, tendons, and bones had orchestrated ever since he'd turned forty. A body-choir that sang loud and strong when it rained. Given that he lived in Seattle, the singing was almost year-round and lusty as hell.

Looks like all those years of karate sparring are catching up with me.

"Do we know for certain that feds are involved in this?" Merri asked.

"HQ just said it was possible and to keep everything hush-hush until the perps were positively identified," Emmett said, offering a hand up to his partner.

Merri snorted. "When *isn't* something hush-hush?" She grasped his hand, her dark brown skin bleaching out his hard-won tan, and he pulled all five foot nothing of her up onto her booted feet. "It isn't called the Shadow Branch for nothing."

"Sing it, sistah. Wanna bet that even the director's dumps are classified?"

Merri shook her head. "Man, that's nasty. What's the matter with—" She straightened, her hand sliding free of his, her alert posture reminding Emmett of a hunting dog on point. She swiveled smoothly to face the doorway. "Our people are here."

Emmett heard the front door open, then click shut. A cold draft of air swept into the room and goosebumped his skin. He heard the squeak of wheels underneath the background noise of the TV, felt the thud of footsteps coming up the hall.

"Three," Merri murmured. "And Gillespie's reeking of Jōvan Musk as usual. Maybe that's why his wife left him."

"*Christ*, Merri."

"Just saying."

A white-uniformed medic with a neat 'fro and hipster black-framed rectangular glasses paused at the doorway. He nodded at Rodriguez's body. "He ready to go?"

"More than ready," Merri said.

The medic stepped aside as Merri and Emmett walked from the room. They passed the gurney parked in the hall waiting to receive Rodriguez's remains and the blonde female medic standing at its head. She nodded as they passed, a nod Emmett returned.

SB Section Chief Sam Gillespie stood in front of the

sofa, his hair buzz-cut to black stubble, the outline revealing a hairline in high retreat. At six one, he stood two inches shorter than Emmett, his skin just a shade lighter than Merri's. Beads of rain glistened on his wire-framed glasses and on the shoulders and collar of his deep blue Gore-Tex jacket. He held the handle of a black satchel in his right hand.

Gillespie's lips stretched into the taut line that he considered a smile. "Thibodaux," he greeted. "Goodnight."

"Chief," Emmett returned, stopping beside the sofa. His gaze fell upon a mug resting on the coffee table. The red letters etched upon its white surface read GROUCH, a mug Rodriguez was most likely sipping from just a few hours ago, unaware that death was climbing in through the laundry room window.

"Chief," Merri muttered as she strode past him to the front door. She flung it open, drawing in deep breaths of the moist air in noisy, drama-queen style. Rain pattered against the front steps and along the crime-scene-taped-off paving stones leading to the front door.

Gillespie *was* a little heavy-handed with the cologne, but at the moment, Emmett was grateful to smell something besides blood and piss and death.

"How's Rodriguez's daughter doing?" Emmett asked.

"Okay, I imagine," Gillespie said. "Her memory's been scrubbed by now."

"Christ," Merri muttered from the doorway. "She's just a kid."

"One who's still alive," Gillespie said, "*because* of the memory scrub. In the bad old days, she would've been turned into another victim of this official and tragic 'burglary gone wrong.'"

Emmett nodded, and shoved his hands into the pockets of his trousers. True enough. Lost time, missing memories, and a few misfiring synapses were a helluva lot better than the cold and permanent alternative.

But nothing said he had to like either option.

"Seems the Bureau has a few rotten apples in the proverbial barrel." Gillespie dropped the satchel onto the carpet. "The daughter positively IDed the suspects as FBI SAC Lyons, SA Wallace, and Dante Prejean—a vamp member of some top secret project."

Emmett whistled. "Wallace? Wasn't she just named as a hero by the Bureau a couple of weeks ago for taking down that serial killer?"

"The Cross-Country Killer—Elroy Jordan," Merri supplied from the doorway.

Gillespie nodded. "She was. But she ran into Prejean during the course of that investigation. It's now believed he corrupted her."

Merri snorted. "If he did, then he was only working what was already inside her."

Gillespie lanced a cold, icicle-sharp gaze her way. "Wallace just kicked her career into the gutter, Goodnight, and after she'd been offered the Seattle SAC position. Her service record was sparkling with intelligence, ability, and drive—full of promise. I think *corrupted by bloodsucker* is as good an explanation as any."

Emmett agreed, but he kept that opinion unvoiced. A rush of cold air smelling of cloves and rain swirled to a stop beside him.

"No offense," Gillespie said.

Merri held his gaze for a moment before asking in a crisp voice, "So what's the lowdown, Chief?"

"We're confiscating all evidence gathered by the SPD and the FBI," Gillespie said, his gaze traveling around the living room, as if envisioning how the scene would be officially reimagined and restaged. "We're making sure that statements already given to the SPD and the feds by the Rodriguez girl and her neighbors vanish."

"Any of the neighbors facing a wipe?" Merri asked.

Gillespie shrugged. "Could be. That's for someone else to decide."

"What kinda TSP was Prejean a part of?" Emmett asked.

"HQ's playing this one real close to the vest," Gillespie replied. "All I was told was that it was a joint project—us and the feds—devoted to the study of sociopaths."

The image of Rodriguez's ravaged throat and empty eyes popped into Emmett's mind. *The study of sociopaths.* A chill touched his spine.

"In other words, their monster slipped its leash and they want us to fetch it. Do I have that right, Chief?" Merri said.

Gillespie nodded. "Pretty much."

Emmett nudged the satchel with the brown toe of his Dingo boot. "What's that?"

A wry smile tugged up one corner of Gillespie's mouth. "It's your monster-catching kit. Cuffs, drugs, chains."

"We know how to handle vampires," Emmett said. "Monster or not."

"Not this vampire. He's enhanced."

"Enhanced?" Merri asked. "You fucking kidding me?" She dropped a hand to her hip, her dark brown gaze direct and challenging. "Why the hell would anyone enhance a vamp? It's not like we need it."

"I wasn't enlightened on that account," Gillespie said. He removed his glasses, held them up to the overhead light, and peered at the rain-spotted lenses. "But I *was* told that adrenaline implants to boost his speed, dexterity, and strength had been installed. So be prepared—he's going to be a helluva lot faster than you'll expect."

The chief had never been a good liar and his little oh-look-my-glasses-are-dirty routine gave away the lie. He knew a lot more than he'd just handed out about the *enhanced* vamp. Emmett tapped a *listen close* finger against the back of Merri's hand.

"Our assignment, Chief?" Emmett said.

Gillespie slid his glasses back on. "Intercept and detain our perps. Prejean is priority one, Wallace priority two, Lyons number three." He slipped a hand inside his Gore-Tex jacket and withdrew a plastic-encased flash drive that he handed to Emmett. "All pertinent data including files, photos, destination, and instructions. Study it on your way to Damascus."

The medics, the blonde in the lead, wheeled the gurney and its dark, plastic-body-bagged contents through the living room and out the open front door, wheels thumping down the steps. The male medic pulled the door shut behind him.

Even through the fog of Jōvan Musk, Emmett caught the nostril-pinching stench of blood and death.

"Our perps are in Damascus, Oregon?" Emmett asked, curling his fingers around the flash drive, tucking it tight against his palm.

Gillespie nodded. "We have reason to believe that Lyons might've taken Prejean home. Satellite scans of the area and of Lyons's home in particular revealed Wallace's Trans Am and Lyons's Dodge Ram parked in the driveway."

"A safe bet that Prejean's with them," Merri commented.

"HQ's thought too," Gillespie said as he walked around the sofa to the hallway. He stopped in front of the murder room. "And they've got a good five or six hours' head start, so move your asses. We've got a plane waiting for you at Sea-Tac. Rendezvous with Holmes and Miklowitz at the airport and bring them up to speed. You got stay-awake pills, Goodnight?"

Merri nodded. "I do."

"Good." Gillespie's jacket rustled as he folded his arms over his chest. He stared into the office.

Slipping the flash drive into his trouser pocket, Emmett bent and wrapped his fingers around the satchel's handle. "Chief," he said, straightening. "Is there anything else we should know about the project or Prejean's *enhancements*?"

Gillespie swiveled around to face them, the lenses of his glasses reflecting light, his arms still folded over his chest. "I wish I knew," he said quietly. "Be careful out there. Don't take any chances—especially with Prejean. Hell, not even with Wallace and Lyons. I know HQ wants them alive, but it's not worth your lives. Not to me."

"Might be better to take our time and wait for Prejean to Sleep," Merri said.

"Maybe so," Emmett said. "But then he could hole up someplace we won't find him. So I think moving our asses is our best option."

"Then let's hit the friendly skies and catch us some bad mofos."

"Truth, sistah."

"Be careful," Gillespie said again, voice low. His gaze once again fixed on the office's blood-spattered interior. "And *that's* a direct order."

"Roger that, Chief." Emmett exchanged a glance with Merri as he strode for the front door and the fresh air beyond. Doubt and a frown pinched the skin between her eyes. A dark realization glimmered in her eyes, the same realization rolling around in Emmett's skull.

He and Merri were being ordered into the forested hills of Damascus on a goddamned bureaucratic ass-covering operation without knowing the truth of what they were up against.

A monster waited for them in the forest's dark heart, a monster who savaged a man in his own home, but left his daughter untouched.

A monster named Dante Prejean.

2

THE PERSISTENCE
OF LOSS

Lafayette, LA
Eleven years ago

*C*hloe bounces out of the bedroom she shares with the other girls, wearing the purple Winnie the Pooh shirt he nabbed for her from Walgreens. Grinning, blue eyes bright, she throws her arms around him and hugs him. She smells like strawberries and soap and her red hair smells like baby shampoo.

"It fits, Dante-angel! It's perfect!"

He laughs and hugs her back. "It looks great on you."

"Do you want to practice reading?" she asks, releasing him and smoothing her hands down her new Pooh shirt. "I got some books from the library today. One is called The Scarecrow Walks at Midnight. It looks a little spooky."

"Spookier than Winnie the Pooh's adventures?" he teases.

"Winnie the Pooh isn't—oh!" Chloe giggles and smacks him on the shoulder with the plushie orca in her hand.

Dante grins. "Did you learn anything new in math that you could teach me?"

Chloe tucks Orem the Orca under her arm and considers. "Just more multiplication stuff."

"I like multiplication stuff."

Chloe's face screws up into her ick-gross expression. "Yuck."

"I see that you like it too."

Hands on her hips, Chloe sticks her tongue out at him.

"Wanna go to the park first? I'll push you on the swing."

Just as Chloe opens her mouth to answer, another voice carries in from the front room, the accompanying foot treads punctuating each word. "Boy, you got work tonight, you. Time to get yo' ass downstairs."

Those words scour the happiness clean from Chloe's face. Her blue-eyed gaze seems to age while Dante watches—no longer eight, but a wary forty. She hugs Orem against her chest.

It's okay, Dante mouths to her. A smile ghosts across her lips. He turns around.

Papa Prejean stands in the hallway in white T-shirt and khakis, his belt loops empty, an amused gleam in his hazel eyes. "Now why ain't I surprised to find you with Little Ms. Feisty, huh, boy?"

Dante's gaze tracks down to the belt folded in Papa's hand. He steps in front of Chloe. "I'm going. Ain't gonna need that."

Papa looks down at the belt in his hand. "Oh, this ain't for you, p'tit." His gaze slants past Dante. A chill ripples the length of Dante's spine. "Seems someone didn't vacuum the parlor like Mama asked."

"I was gonna," Chloe says.

"*I was talking to her and held her up, so punish me,*" Dante says.

Papa laughs, his voice cigarette-smoke rough, then coughs. "How'd I know that too? I ain't gonna let you do it this time, boy. How's she ever gonna learn to obey if you always take the belt for her, you?" Papa shakes his head. "Ain't gonna mark you up before your clients get here, anyhow. Get in the basement, p'tit. After you're done, I think I'll give you the belt anyway since you're so hellfire eager for it."

"No!" Chloe shouts. "It's not his fault!"

"Shhh, princess. It's okay."

Amusement gleams in Papa's eyes again. "Aw . . . ain't this sweet? Y'all wanting to protect each other from what y'all got coming."

"Get that *p'tite marmaille* in here, Papa!" Mama Prejean shouts from the front room. "I want this parlor vacuumed *tout de suite*. You can beat her lazy ass later."

"Looks like you get a reprieve, you," Papa says, nodding his chin at Chloe. "Go do what Mama wants. I'll deal with you later, me." His gaze flicks over to Dante. "You too."

Ice rims Dante's heart. He has an uneasy feeling that as soon as Papa cuffs him to the bed in the basement, Papa's gonna march upstairs and beat Chloe. Beat her while he's cuffed and unable to do anything but listen. That's gonna be his part of the punishment.

Dante whirls, hooks a hand around Chloe's biceps, and moves. She squeaks in surprise. Papa shouts and yells as he and Chloe blur down the hallway, into the brightly lit kitchen, blowing past a startled Mama, then out the back door into the night, screen door slamming behind them.

"We're flying!" Chloe breathes. "You really *are* an angel!"

"Ain't no angel. Ain't flying." But the houses blur past Dante as he zips down narrow Catherine Street, surprised by his own speed.

"Where we going, Dante-angel?"

"Dunno," Dante says. The cool night feels good against his face and smells of wet pavement, boiling crawfish, and rain-heavy roses. He swings onto Johnston, then blurs down to Lewis, heart pounding, a wild hunger knotting his belly. He tightens his grip on Chloe's arm.

"Are we running away?"

"Maybe we are, yeah." Only wanting to get Chloe out of Papa's reach, he hasn't even thought about where they are going.

As cars shush past them on rain-wet streets, headlights starring the night, Dante moves across the street to Girard Park. He slows to a walk, but slides his hand down from Chloe's arm to her hand and clasps his fingers through hers.

She looks up at him, her long red hair wind-blown and tangled. She smiles, and the sight of it buoys his heart. It rises within him as though on wings.

"Where will we live?" Chloe asks.

"Dunno. Maybe we can find an empty house and move in," he says, angling a path past the swings and into the evergreens and leafless elms. Leaves crunch underneath their shoes. "But we can't stay here. Papa'd find us."

Chloe's fingers squeeze Dante's hand hard. She stops walking, forcing Dante to a halt. She looks at him, and her eyes glisten with more than just starlight. "Papa'll kill you," she whispers.

Dante pulls her into him, wraps her up tight in a hug. He hears the frantic beat of her heart intertwined with the steady pulse of his own. Smells strawberries and soap and the sharp tang of fear.

"Shhh," he murmurs, pressing his face into her hair. "He ain't gonna catch us. I'll make sure of that. We'll leave here, go to New Orleans. Go anywhere."

"Promise?" Chloe's voice is muffled against his shirt, a tight-throated sob.

Dante drops down to one knee in the wet grass. He gently wipes away Chloe's tears with his thumbs. "Promise. Just you and me, princess. Forever and ever."

"Forever and ever," Chloe repeats, her blue-eyed gaze holding his, her face solemn. "Orem too?" She glances at the orca plushie squashed up against Winnie.

And just like that, she's eight years old again.

Dante smiles. "Oui, naturellement."

"Okay." Chloe hesitates, then says, "But what about Mark and Tami and Perry and Jeanette? Mama and Papa are mean to them too and . . ."

Dante touches his finger against Chloe's lips and her words stop. "I'll think of something, I promise. Once we find us a safe place, I'll come back and fetch them, one by one, d'accord?"

A smile curves the corners of Chloe's mouth and her eyes cross in an attempt to focus on the finger against her lips. Laughing, Dante removes it. "Oops. Now you can talk. Sound like a plan, p'tite?"

"Yup, Dante-angel. Sounds like a plan."

"C'est bon." He finger-combs the tangles from her tresses, his skin pale as moonlight in the red sea of her hair. "You ready to go?"

"Yup."

From the sidewalk circling the park, sharp, excited yaps pierce the air as someone walks their dog along the path. Looking over Chloe's shoulder, Dante sees a chubby woman in a yellow rain bonnet and rubber boots scolding a small white-and-brown-patched dog—maybe a terrier—straining on its leash.

"Behave, Jasper! Bad dog, bad!"

"Let's go." Dante stands and holds his hand out for Chloe's. Her cold fingers wrap around his and he pauses to switch their grips so he can warm her fingers against the heat

of his palm. He walks them deeper into the woods and away from the park proper.

Excited yaps, sharp with let's play! *insistence, chase after them, the rapid* tapa-tapa-tapa-tap *of four small paws hot on the heels of its barked invitation racing through wet grass and withered leaves.*

As Dante's putting distance between them with each quick step, the woman in the yellow rain bonnet yells, "Jasper! No! Bad dog! Come back to Mommy!"

Tugging her hand free of Dante's, Chloe stops and spins around just as Jasper reaches her. The dog leaps up, yapping, brown eyes glistening with joy, and dances around Chloe and Dante—a twirling, bowing, doggie whirlwind trailing a leash.

"Look!" Chloe says, her voice almost as excited as Jasper's. "He wants to come with us." Kneeling in the grass, she giggles as Jasper plants his muddy little paws on her shoulders and licks her face.

Rain Bonnet runs across the grass, huffing with each heavy step, her face flushed. "Please stop him!" she yells breathlessly.

Dante bends and nabs Jasper's leash. The dog's whole butt wags along with its stubby tail. He yaps, then sits, tongue lolling between his teeth. "Bon chien," Dante says, straightening. His gaze lifts to Jasper's red-faced mommy half running, half walking toward them. "Get behind me, Chloe," Dante murmurs. "Hold onto my belt."

Just in case I gotta move.

"'Kay." Chloe rises to her feet and Dante feels a tug at the back of his belt as her fingers slide underneath and wrap around it.

Rain Bonnet stumbles to a stop in front of Dante. She fans her flushed face with her hand. "Jasper," she pants. "Bad dog." She smiles at Dante. "Oh, thank you so much, sweetie."

Jasper leaps up, yapping and dancing around her jeans and rubber-boot-clad legs. Dante extends the leash to her. "Pas de quoi."

"He's still a puppy and he hasn't learned his manners yet," Rain Bonnet says, accepting the leash and slipping her gloved hand through its looped handle. She shifts her gaze to Chloe. "Hi, cutie. Why you hiding behind your brother?"

"I told her to," Dante says. He backs up a few steps, Chloe moving with him, her fingers still locked around his belt. "You're a stranger."

A wide smile parts Rain Bonnet's lips, warms her bonnet-shadowed eyes. "Smart boy," she says, nodding in approval. "I hope you listen to him, cutie. He's one smart boy." Her hand dips into her coat pocket. "I want to thank you kids for your help. Who knows where Jasper woulda ended up if you hadn't been here to stop him?"

"Ain't necessary," Dante says. "We gotta go."

"I've got some change here I'm happy to give you."

"We can use it to buy something to eat," Chloe whispers.

Dante turns and swings an arm around her shoulders, hugs her close. "You hungry, princess?"

She nods, then she looks past him. Her blue eyes widen. Something whirs through the air and bites into Dante's throat in several spots—like an angry wasp stinging and stinging and stinging.

Chloe sucks in a breath and she grabs his arm, her fingers digging into him.

Dante slaps a hand against the spot and feels a small, wheeled thing protruding from his throat. He plucks it free. A small ninja-type metal star, its points blood-slicked. It tumbles from his fingers into the night-shadowed grass.

"Run, run, run!" Chloe cries, tugging on Dante's arm.

Dante tries to run, but his feet refuse to move. Ice water spills inside of him, cascading from his punctured throat, *freezing his arms, legs, frosting his heart. His thoughts ice over as well, and he feels like he's skating and spinning on a glacial lake.*

The night whirls around Dante, a streak of pale clouds and glimmering stars and skeletal branches. He no longer feels Chloe's hand. He tries to shove her away, tries to tell her to run, but his voice and lips don't work either—numb and far away. He falls, the rain-beaded grass rushing up to meet him.

Rain Bonnet whispers into Dante's ear as darkness sweeps over him. "No escape for you, sweetie."

3

FRESH OUT OF TIME

Heather Wallace held the motel room door open as Von carried Dante inside, Caterina Cortini on his heels. Annie stood in front of the muddy Trans Am, hugging herself against the predawn chill despite her wet clothing and stocking feet, her gaze on the sidewalk. Her travel-frayed gym bag rested on the rain-puddled blacktop beside her.

"Annie, c'mon," Heather said. She scanned the dying night for any sign of black bird-*V*'s; for any sign that more of the Fallen hunted for Dante. She listened for the rush of wings.

Annie looked up, her gaze slipping past Heather into the room's dark interior. Her face, dirt-smudged and stark in the motel's buzzing outside lights, wore a troubled expression. "No," she said, her voice one twist of the knob past a whisper. "Let's just get back in the car and leave them here. They don't need us. Let's go home. C'mon."

"We can't go home," Heather said, stepping outside. She pulled the door shut behind her. "We're being hunted. We need to stick together."

"Stick together? Are you fucking *nuts*?" Annie laughed, the sound tight and incredulous. "You saw what Dante did, right? You saw what he *made* . . . saw him knock those fucking . . . angels from the sky, right? And turn them to stone?"

"I saw," Heather said quietly. She'd felt it too, as his furious song had pulsed between them, heart to heart, wild and dark and powerful, rippling into her core.

"Then why aren't we running the hell *away* from him?"

"He sacrificed himself for you," Heather said, holding up one hand and extending her index finger. "He saved my life." Extended a second finger. "Now he needs us." A third finger. "Reasons enough?"

Annie's mouth opened, then closed. She looked away, the line of her jaw tight. Her hands knotted into fists. "He's a fucking vampire," she grated. "So's Von. And that Caterina chick is a freaking assassin—one who said she was sent to kill *you*, by the way. They don't *need* us."

"Dante does." Heather's thoughts flipped back to what she'd been forced to witness, wrists flex-cuffed together, not even an hour ago, as Lyons and his demented twin had tried to pry open Dante's fragmented and hidden memories.

Dante falls silent when the seizure ripples the length of his body. His muscles lock, his back arches, and his limbs twist. His head whips back and forth, a blur. Blood flings into the air from his nose, his mouth, his pierced eyelids. The twins push Dante onto the floor and allow the seizure to have its way with him.

Athena kneels on the blood-flecked carpet beside Dante's

convulsing body and whispers to him: Rememberandremem-
berandrememberandremember . . .

*The seizure ends and Dante curls up on the floor, dazed
and trembling, sweat-damp black hair clinging to his forehead and cheek.*

*Lyons floats Dante up into the air and back onto the sofa.
He bends over Dante with a washrag and wipes the blood
from his face. And the process starts all over again.*

And each seizure is worse than the one before.

Heather shoved the memory away, throat tight. "Lyons
and his sister just tortured Dante for hours, Annie. You
heard his screams."

Annie swallowed hard and looked up into the dawn-
edged sky, the deep rose line streaking from behind the hills
lighting her face. "Aren't you scared of him?"

"No, I trust him," Heather said, joining her sister in
front of the Trans Am. "But his power—his magic, his gifts,
whatever you want to call it—*that* scares me."

"How can he do those things? What the fuck is he?"

"I'll tell you what I know, I promise," Heather said. "But
right now, I need you to get your butt inside."

Annie finally looked at Heather. Exhaustion shadowed
her face, pooled dark in her eyes. She bit her lower lip and
looked for a second so much like she had when she was
little that Heather's heart went out to her. *Annie-Bunny.*

Pushing her hands through her wet blue/purple/black-
dyed hair, Annie released her breath in a long sigh. "Fuck,"
she said. "Okay." She bent and looped a hand through the
gym bag's strap, then straightened. Snatching the keycard
from Heather's hand, she opened the door and stalked into
the room. She headed straight for the bathroom.

Heather closed the motel room door, latched the lock,
and hooked the little golden door chain in place. The bathroom door slammed shut, then the bathroom fan whirred

into muffled action. Heather's muscles knotted even tighter. She rested her forehead against the door.

Keep it together. Just one thing at a time.

She drew in a deep breath and immediately regretted it. The room stank of cherry blossom room freshener and, just underneath, the sour-milk odor of mildew.

"She going to be a problem?" Cortini's voice, laced with Old World charm, turned Heather around. The Shadow Branch assassin sat perched on the plump arm of the room's only easy chair, one arm slung casually along its vinyl top.

"No. And even if she *was* a problem, she'd be mine to deal with. Not yours. Are we clear?"

The gloom made it difficult to read Cortini's expression. Early thirties, Heather estimated, possibly older, but very well-kept if so. Her slim, boyish body was relaxed, but coiled, ready to run, fight, or kill. Even in her wet black sweater and black jeans, her shoulder-length dark hair rain-plastered to her skull, she managed to look unruffled. Deadly.

"We're clear," Cortini murmured.

"Glad to hear it."

"Me too," Von tossed in. "Annie ain't your concern, Cortini."

Cortini's gaze cut to the nomad. *"Llygad,"* she murmured, nodding in acknowledgment.

Von had eased Dante onto the double bed farthest from the curtained window. He finished pulling Dante's boots off and stood them together on the floor at the foot of the bed. A blur of movement, then Dante's bloodied and ripped hoodie and PVC shirt ended up on the floor beside his boots.

Cold fingers wrapped around Heather's heart when she saw the healing bullet wound in Dante's chest and thought of Rodriguez—the man who'd shot him in a desperate struggle to save his own life—sprawled on the floor, his throat bloodied and ruined. Thought of Rodriguez's daughter, Brisia, who would mourn him.

Where's my dad?

Von's fingers skipped over the purple and blue bruise stretched across the left side of Dante's rib cage. "Musta happened when the goddamned house exploded."

"Or during a seizure," Heather said, joining the nomad at the bed.

"Yeah, maybe." Von gently rolled Dante onto his side, his fingers sliding along the pale skin, flakes of dried blood falling onto the sheets from the healing spear puncture in his back. "Were they using him for target practice or something?" the nomad growled.

"The *or something* option," Heather replied. "Lyons's sister stabbed Dante when he was helping Annie escape."

"The sister Lyons wanted Dante to heal?"

Heather nodded. "Yeah, well, apparently she didn't feel the same way."

Von shook his head, his face grim. He eased Dante onto his back again, then unbuckled his belt. He glanced at Heather. Nodded at Dante's leather pants. "He got anything on under these, doll?"

"No."

Von snorted. "Why ain't I surprised? Well then, let's leave 'em on in case he has another seizure. The leather ain't all that wet and, hell, if it was me, I'd hope someone would safeguard my modesty if I was too unconscious to do it myself. If I had any modesty to safeguard, that is." He brushed damp tendrils of black hair from Dante's pale face. "Sleep tight, little brother," he said. He straightened, then swayed. "Whoa."

"You okay?" Heather asked.

"Yeah, doll. Just Sleep coming." Von looked her up and

down, his green eyes Sleep-dilated. "What 'bout you? Boy was drumming you hard during that last seizure in the car. You should get your pants off," he said, yawning.

As Heather opened her mouth to protest, he held up a placating hand, palm out, while he finished his yawn—a jaw-stretching one that revealed his fangs, his molars, and even his tonsils. "That didn't come out quite right, doll. I meant so I could see how much damage Dante did to you."

Heather pushed her wet hair back from her face, struggling not to smile. "Just bruises, doofus, and I think I'll keep my pants on, thanks."

"Just what every man wants to hear."

The chains on Von's leather jacket jingled as he shrugged the jacket off, revealing the double shoulder holster strapped on over his black, button-down shirt and the butts of his Brownings tucked into them. He undressed quickly, stripping down to damp royal blue boxers.

Tattoos inked in blue Celtic designs—dragons, antlered hunters, and ravens among them—swirled up from beneath his shorts to just under his pecs, and flowed around his sides, twining up around his spine to his shoulders.

"Are those clan markings?" Heather asked, too tired to truly appreciate the tall, lean-muscled view the nomad presented.

"Yup, rites of passage—from when I was mortal." A smile flickered across his lips as he traced a finger along an intricate Celtic knot near his right hip. "My first ride as a clan scout."

The tight, defined muscles in Von's chest and shoulders rippled as he gathered up his wet clothing and draped it piece by piece over the foot of the bed to dry. He hung his jacket on the back of the desk chair.

Leaning against the waist-high dresser, his gaze skipped from Cortini to Heather. He smoothed his mustache with thumb and forefinger. "Since I figure y'all would come to blows over who'll get to sleep beside me, I'll make it easy on everyone and share the bed with Dante. I know you're disappointed, but, hey, I'm trying to be fair here."

"It's kind of you to spare the loser like that," Heather said, keeping a straight face. Kicking off her mud-caked Skechers, she sat on the bed beside Dante.

"Ouch, woman. I said 'get to' not 'hafta.' Just for that, I ain't gonna leave room for you to snuggle up and snooze beside your man."

"That's okay," Heather said. "Given my sister's concerns, I think having one bed for nightkind and one for mortals might be best." Best, maybe, but she yearned to curl up beside Dante, to hold him close while he Slept, fevered and lost to darkness, to whisper into his ear, *You're not alone. I'm here, waiting for you.*

Von glanced at the closed bathroom door, the humor fading from his face. The sound of shower spray drumming against glass drowned out the whir of the fan. "Anything I should know?" he asked.

"No," Heather replied. "She was tossed into the deep end of the pool, but I've got ahold of her. She'll be fine."

Von searched her eyes and she knew what he was thinking: in which direction was the bipolar carousel horse Annie rode headed? Up or down?

Heather sighed and shook her head.

"I hear ya, doll."

Von tugged the elastic tie free from his wet hair, then slipped it around his wrist for safekeeping. He finger-combed his wet shoulder-length hair—hair that would be a deep, glossy brown when dry—smoothing it back from his face. A vertical line creased his forehead between his eyebrows, his *thinking-deep* line.

"Got a question for you, Cortini," he said, gripping the

edge of the dresser behind him. The muscles in his arms corded.

Cortini slid from her perch on the easy chair and stood beside it. She met Heather's gaze for a moment before settling her attention on Von.

"A sniper outside the house shot the shades right off my face." Von touched one of the small, rapidly healing cuts peppering his face. "Whatcha know about that? One-a your guys?"

Surprise flickered across Cortini's face. "No. My handlers only sent me."

"Great." Von sighed. "So we've got other players on the field."

"The shooter must've set up after I arrived," Heather said. "Or maybe he was just waiting to take down whoever came out of the house."

"He was hell-bent on keeping me from going in," Von said, "so I'm betting he didn't set up until after you arrived, doll. I'm also betting he followed you."

"I agree," Cortini said. "The SB instructed the Bureau to drop their surveillance on you and Dante Baptiste. Someone disobeyed orders," she said. "And I think I know who."

"Do you think it was ADIC Rutgers?" Heather asked. FBI Assistant Director in Charge Monica Rutgers had offered her a choice just a few days ago: accept a promotion and become a marionette for the FBI or have her career and reputation shredded.

Words whispered through Heather's memory, a warning from Stearns, her late supervisor and mentor, just a few weeks before in New Orleans, a day before he died:

You've been marked for termination. Me too.

How high up does this go?

I think it's best to behave as though it goes to the top.

"Yes," Cortini confirmed.

Well, she couldn't claim to be surprised. Heather closed her eyes and rubbed the bridge of her nose. Weariness siphoned her strength; she was running on empty.

"I can understand Rutgers disobeying orders by keeping the surveillance going," Cortini said, her brow furrowed. "But why would she jump from surveillance to murder? What am I missing here?"

An image flashed into Heather's mind of Dante standing in Rodriguez's living room, Brisia Rodriguez tucked behind him as he guarded her. Remembered her own words just hours earlier: *"That's not Chloe. She's long gone."*

Dante sucks in a breath. Touches trembling fingers to his temple. More blood trickles from his nose. Heather takes a step closer. Lifts the trank gun and aims.

He lifts his burning gaze to Heather's and the desolation she glimpses in the dark depths of his eyes breaks her heart. His muscles flex. "Run," he whispers.

"Dante's programming was triggered," Heather said quietly. She lowered her hand to her side and opened her eyes. "Lyons used him to kill an FBI agent."

Move away from me, chérie. *Get outta reach.*

"Holy fucking hell," Von breathed. His gaze lit on Dante's pale face. "Mother*fuckers.*"

"He gave himself for Annie," Heather said, voice low, "knowing they were going to use him. He didn't even hesitate."

A smile ghosted across Von's lips. "He wouldn't."

"What happened to the sniper outside the house?" Cortini asked. "Did you kill him?"

Von shook his head. "Nah. I put a bullet in his leg to keep him from going anywhere so we could question him later, but between the house exploding and the frickin' Fallen popping out of the sky, I lost track of him."

"Probably long gone," Cortini agreed.

"Hell," Von muttered. "I suppose it's too much to hope

the fucker bled to death. We're gonna hafta continue this later." He glanced at Heather, then nodded at Cortini. "Think you can work with her while I Sleep?"

"You tell me," Heather said.

Von crooked a finger. "C'mere, Cortini. Time for a little heart-to-heart."

Cortini padded across the carpet to where Von stood in front of the dresser, her footsteps almost nightkind-silent. And no wonder—she'd been raised by nightkind, a mortal in a household of vampires.

Von's words, spoken not even an hour ago in the pouring rain, curled through Heather's memory: *a child of the heart.* She couldn't help but wonder what that meant exactly, what it entailed, and what had happened to Cortini's mortal parents.

Cortini knelt on one knee in front of Von. *"Llygad,"* she said, bowing her head, her shoulder-length hair swinging forward to frame her elfin face in dark, rain-damp strands.

The fact that Von was wearing only his boxers made the scene a little surreal, but didn't lessen his rough dignity one bit. The crescent moon tattoo beneath his right eye glittered like moonlit frost. *Llygad.* Keeper of history. Poet warrior bard. Nomad. Nightkind.

Von was all of these things and much more. Heather remembered what he'd told her the night before . . . the long, heartbreaking, furious night that had just ended.

We're the keepers of nightkind history, the impartial Eyes of truth.

"I need to take a look inside," Von said, tapping a finger against his own temple. "Wanna know if I need to shoot you or not so I can Sleep."

Heather stared at him, hoping he was kidding, but his face remained deadly serious. No hint of a smile tugged at his mustache-framed mouth.

"I understand, *llygad*." Cortini lifted her face, shook back her hair. Her gaze, steady and open, held Von's. "All my life, I've walked the tightrope between the mortal and vampire worlds," she said. "But that changed yesterday when I learned that a True Blood prince and Fallen Maker had been born. Then hidden and abused. Programmed." Cortini's body remained still, but Heather heard the edge in her voice, each hard word stropping that edge razor-sharp. "I'll guard Dante Baptiste, and all those he cares for, with my life."

Fire sparked in the green depths of Von's eyes. "We'll see, darlin'."

He leaned over and tipped Cortini's chin up with a finger. She drew in a deep breath, then closed her eyes. Von's gaze unfocused as he dipped into the assassin's mind.

Cortini's breath caught in her throat. She swayed as though dizzy. Shivered. After a few moments, she touched fingertips to her temple, and opened her eyes.

Von's gaze refocused and then he nodded. "C'mere," he said to Cortini. She rose to her feet in a single, graceful motion and followed him to the bed Heather sat on beside Dante's Sleeping form. Von pulled one of the Brownings free of the double holster slung over the bedpost.

Heather's heart kicked hard against her ribs. She couldn't just let him execute Cortini. "Wait, she's got info on—"

Von handed the gun to Cortini. He glanced at Heather, amusement dancing in his eyes. "Ain't gonna shoot her." His gaze flicked back to Cortini. "Not yet, anyway," he drawled.

He pulled the Browning's twin from the holster and handed it to Heather. "Extra ammo's in my jacket pocket. But I'm hoping to hell you ain't gonna need it."

"Me too." The pistol's weight felt good in Heather's

hand and a bit more of the tension uncoiled from her muscles. She checked to make sure the safety was on. She missed her Colt, and mourned its loss along with the purse and cell phone Lyons had stripped from her.

Cortini tucked the pistol into the back of her black jeans, snugged it against the small of her back. "An honor, *llygad*."

"Name's Von, darlin'."

Von's gaze shifted to Dante's Sleeping form. His brows slanted together. "I sure as hell wasn't expecting him to have another seizure after we spiked him fulla morphine. That worries me, doll."

Heather shivered, her wet clothes clinging to her skin, cooling the hot ache in her battered thighs. But more than wet clothes chilled her. She remembered what Dante had said, words whispered and broken, just as the morphine took him the first time.

Her name was Chloe. She was my princess. And I killed her.

"He's remembering things," Heather said, fighting to keep her voice level. "Lyons and his sister kept showing him images from Bad Seed, kept trying to shove his past down his throat and he was having seizures over and—"

A creak of bedsprings, a whiff of motor oil and frost, then warm hands cupped her face. Callused thumbs wiped away the tears from her cheeks, tears she hadn't even known were there. "Hey, hey, hey," Von murmured.

Heather bit down on the underside of her lip to keep from bawling like a baby. She was too drained, too exhausted, to feel embarrassed.

"We'll get him through this, doll, whatever it takes." Von's voice, low and rough with emotion and thick with coming Sleep, brushed against her aching heart like fingers against her cheek. "We ain't gonna lose him to those fuckers."

"He never stopped fighting," Heather said.

"And he ain't gonna quit now." Von released her face to wrap her hands up in his. "You know why?"

"Because he's pigheaded?"

"Like a goddamned mule."

Heather felt a smile tug at her lips. "A pig-headed mule?"

"Thanks for that mental image, doll." Von smiled, squeezed her hands once, then released them.

"How is Lucien's death going to affect him?" Heather asked. "To have that dumped on top of everything else . . ."

"Not good." Von rubbed his face with his hands. "I still can't believe Lucien's dead. I don't know how the severed bond's gonna affect Dante. If it was gonna kill him, I think it woulda done so the moment it was cut."

"Not always, *llygad.*"

Heather twisted around to look at Cortini. She leaned one shoulder against the wall, her gaze on Dante, her dark hair framing her face. "Sometimes the damage is subtle," she said, "and takes hours to reveal the extent—a hemorrhaging brain or one seared from the inside out."

"Thanks," Von growled. "Just the note I wanna Sleep on."

"I can hang towels over the curtains if it needs to be darker in here," Heather said, scooting off the bed.

"Nah, we'll be just fine. Keep the curtains closed and the blankets up." Turning around, he yanked down the comforter and blankets on his side of the bed and tucked himself underneath. "*Bonne nuit,* y'all," he slurred. "Don't let the bedbugs . . ."

The nomad's eyes closed and he was gone, lost to Sleep's narcotic embrace before he'd even pulled up the blankets. His breathing slowed. All the tension eased from his handsome face, smoothing worry lines and creases from his skin. He looked peaceful.

Heather pulled the blankets up over his head, making

certain he and Dante were 100 percent covered. "Sleep well," she wished them both.

She sat down on the unoccupied bed and slid the Browning underneath the pillow. Despite Von's words, she was worried, deep and down to the bone. What had been unleashed inside of Dante?

Weariness burned through Heather, fogged her mind. Her thoughts kept circling, taking on a looping *Wizard of Oz* singsong rhythm: *the Bureau, the Shadow Branch, the Fallen. Oh, my.* She'd bet anything an APB was out on them—Dante, because of Rodriguez's murder, herself as an accomplice.

But Dante had been no more responsible for the death than a fired gun. He'd had no choice, his programming triggered by the man who'd implanted it. Dr. Robert Wells and his twisted son, Alexander Lyons, had used Dante like a weapon.

How could she keep Dante hidden and safe—and, most importantly, unused? The walls barricading his hidden past had been breached; how much of it had slipped through? The memory of Chloe's loss alone and his role in it would be enough to break his heart. And coupled with Lucien's death . . .

Heather's fingers felt along the outline of the plastic-case protected flash drive in her pocket. The drive contained all of Dante's documented life in Bad Seed from the moment he'd been born and his nightkind mother, Genevieve, slaughtered.

Heather had hoped to help him regain his past bit by bit, together, so he wouldn't have to face the nightmare hell of his childhood alone.

Dante needed time to come to terms with his past. To come to terms with himself. Time to grieve. To heal.

But they were fresh out of time.

The Bureau, the Shadow Branch, the Fallen. Oh, my.

"You should catch some sleep while you can."

Heather blinked, then looked up. Cortini still leaned against the wall, her body language relaxed, her gaze sharp. Heather forced her hands open. She shook her head. "I'll take first watch."

"Second would be better," Cortini said. "You're dead on your feet." Her gaze slipped over to Dante's blanketed form. "I won't let anyone near him or you."

"How did—" Heather's question died unasked when the bathroom fan fell silent and the bathroom door was yanked open.

Annie stepped out in too-big blue plaid pajama bottoms and a faded black Danzig skull tee, a white bath towel wrapped around her hair.

"We need to get more clothes and stuff," she said, beelining for the easy chair. "And I need shoes since I left my Docs at . . ." She waved a hand toward the window to indicate *out there*. She flopped into the chair, the vinyl squeaking beneath her.

"She's right," Cortini said. "When everyone's awake, that should be one of the first things you do. You also need to dump your car and get another."

Heather studied Cortini for a long moment, mulling over her choice of the word *you* instead of *we*. The assassin held her gaze, her face unreadable.

Even though she hated the thought of abandoning her Trans Am, she knew Cortini was right. Heather sighed, then nodded. "We can't risk renting a car. My bank and credit accounts are probably being monitored. What about you?"

"I doubt I'm being monitored," Cortini said. "Not yet. But if my handlers don't hear from me by the end of the day, that'll change."

"So what's your plan?" Heather asked. She slid her hand

underneath the pillow, the sheets cool against her fingertips. "I'm getting the distinct feeling that you won't be traveling with us."

A faint smile curved Cortini's lips. "I plan to return to the SB."

Heather's fingers wrapped around the Browning's grip. Her pulse picked up speed. Von had looked into Cortini's mind. Was it possible for her to fool him? "Part of your plan to guard Dante?" she asked, keeping her voice light.

"I'll be more use to him—and you—*inside* the SB."

"How do you plan to explain your absence?"

"I don't exactly punch a time clock," Cortini said. "I'm allowed downtime between assignments. I'll simply tell them I decided to sightsee."

Heather searched for deception in the assassin's face, her posture, her hands. Everything about her—from the top of her head to the toes of her sneakered feet—suggested sincerity. Steady gaze, open hands, relaxed posture.

If Cortini was planning to betray them, she never would've said she was returning to the SB. All she would've had to do was simply wait for all of them to fall asleep.

And Cortini was right. A pair of eyes inside the SB would be more than a little useful. "Christ," Heather muttered, sliding her empty hand out from under the pillow.

Cortini nodded her head at the pillow. "I would've done the same in your place," she said. "Except I probably would've pulled the trigger."

Heather met her gaze. "That's one of the differences between us."

A smile quirked up the corners of Cortini's mouth. "You should sleep. It's going to be a while before anyone knows what's happened or puts all the pieces together. We'll never be safer than we are right now."

Small comfort, but true. "I will. In a bit." Heather

looked at Annie slumped in the easy chair, fingering one of the small hoops piercing her eyebrow, pretending not to be interested in the conversation. "I owe my sister some answers first."

"The less she knows, the better," Cortini said.

"Too late for that," Heather replied. "She's involved now."

Annie flashed Cortini a triumphant look, then pulled her feet up into the chair and wrapped her arms around her legs. "So what's the SB?" she asked, returning her attention to Heather.

Cortini shook her head and folded her arms over her chest. Tension sharpened the planes of her face.

"The SB is the Shadow Branch," Heather replied. "A branch of the government that officially doesn't exist. Its members are composed of DOD, FBI, CIA, and Homeland Security agents. The SB and the FBI together initiated a black ops program called Bad Seed to create sociopaths."

"To *create*?" Annie said. "You fucking kidding me?"

"I wish I was," Heather said, pushing her fingers through her damp hair. "They wanted to see if certain criteria could create a sociopath. They studied their subjects' development and progress right up until they were either imprisoned or killed."

"And Dante? What's he?" Annie stabbed a finger in Dante's direction. "I just saw him create the Underworld and turn angels to fucking stone."

"Not angels, exactly," Heather said. "Well, they are, but they're the Fallen."

"Oh, *excuse* me," Annie muttered. "The Fallen, huh? First, vampires, now fallen angels. When will the unicorns and fairies prance on over for a visit, huh? What's next? The Flying Dutchman? Howling werewolves?"

"I know this is a lot to swallow—"

Annie laughed. "A nine-inch dick is a lot to swallow, this—this is just insane. I watched Dante twist the Psycho Twins and their unhinged Dr. Evil dad into . . . shit, I don't know *what* he twisted them into. And you want me to tag along with you and Gorgeous-But-Deadly? Nope. Nuh-uh. No way."

"I'm not leaving you behind," Heather said, rising to her feet and walking to the foot of the nightkind-only bed. She bent and scooped up Dante's wet clothes, intending to throw away his rain- and blood-soaked hoodie and PVC shirt. But as she straightened, breathing in the mingled scents of blood and anise-spiced absinthe and crisp autumn leaves, she hesitated, hugging the clothes to her chest instead.

"What if I went someplace else? Australia or China or Russia?"

"They'll *find* you," she said, holding Annie's gaze. "And they'll *hurt* you—because of me, because of Dante. I'm sorry I got you into this, I really am. But you can't stay behind."

"I got myself into this when I climbed into that asshole's pickup," Annie muttered, shifting in the chair and sitting cross-legged. "I could really use a smoke. Hey, hit woman, you got any cigarettes?"

A smile tugged up one corner of Cortini's mouth. "No."

"Fuck," Annie sighed. "Suppose there ain't any booze in this shithole either."

"No, and that's the last thing you need," Heather said. She dumped Dante's ruined clothes in the trash bin beside the desk, then sat down beside Dante, bedsprings creaking beneath her.

"So what the hell is he?" Annie asked. "I mean, besides a freaking vampire?"

"Dante Baptiste is a Maker and a True Blood prince," Cortini said.

Annie frowned. "What the hell does that mean?"

"True Blood means he was born nightkind," Heather said. She pulled the blankets from Dante's face. Even with blood trickling from his nose, the sight of him caught at her heart, his beauty lit from within, incandescent and riveting. She touched the backs of her fingers to his pale, fevered cheek.

"You can be *born* vampire?" Annie said. "Holy shit."

"Yes, but True Bloods are rare," Cortini said. "Very rare."

"So what's the Maker part?"

"Dante's father, Lucien De Noir, is . . . *was* . . . Fallen," Heather replied. "It has something to do with that. Do you know what?" she asked, glancing at Cortini.

The assassin's gaze lit on Dante, lingered. "A Maker is a Fallen creator. A *creawdwr*. According to vampire lore, the last known Maker was called Yahweh, though most knew him by his Old Testament name, Jehovah."

Cold fingers trailed down Heather's spine at Cortini's words. Her heart drummed hard and fast.

"The gods of this world—in all cultures and mythologies—have been the Fallen," Cortini said. "But the only Fallen who could create—places, beings, life itself—were *creawdwrs*, and only one *creawdwr* exists at a time."

"Wait, wait, hold on," Annie butted in. "You saying God was a fucking fallen angel? What kinda drugs you on? And you'd better've brought enough for everyone, dammit."

Cortini leveled her gaze on Annie. "I only know what my mother taught me," she said. "She told me that Yahweh died thousands of years ago. But only the Fallen know the details behind his death." She hesitated for a split second and Heather realized that Cortini knew *some* of those details at the very least. "All we know is that there's never been another Maker." Her gaze returned to Dante and her face softened. "Until now."

"Are you saying what I think you're saying?" Heather asked.

Cortini shrugged. Her gaze shifted to Von's blanketed form. "I think that's a question you should ask the *llygad* once he's awake again."

"You're fulla shit," Annie said. "That's all you are—a big old pile of walking, talking shit."

"Annie . . ."

"Well, she is!"

Cortini shoved away from the wall. "Think what you want," she said. "I really don't care." Stepping over to Heather, she said, "I'm going to move your car behind the motel, where it won't be seen from the highway." She held out her hand for the keys.

"Good idea," Heather murmured. Standing, she reached into her front jeans pocket and fished the keys free from its cold and wet interior. "Thanks," she said, handing over the keys.

Cortini nodded, closed her fingers around the keys, then went outside, closing the door quietly behind her. A moment later, Heather heard the low, powerful thrum of the Trans Am's engine.

"She's nuts," Annie declared. "You're all fucking loco, y'know that?"

"Maybe." Heather walked into the bathroom and flipped on the light. Moisture beaded on powder blue tile and chrome fixtures, remnants of Annie's shower. The smell of coconut oil shampoo lingered in the air. "But what if she's right?"

Heather wet a washcloth with cool water, then wrung out the excess. She returned to the bed and sat down beside Dante again. She wiped away the blood trickling from his nose. She hoped the wet cloth would cool the fevered heat spiking out from his pale skin and prickling against her. Dante's face wasn't peaceful like Von's, and blue shadows smudged the skin beneath his eyes.

"She can't be right. She *can't*. It's just . . ." Annie's voice trailed off. "I need a fucking smoke, dammit."

Heather placed her hand over Dante's heart, covering his little bat tattoo, and pressed her palm against his heated skin. After a moment, she felt the strong, reassuring thump of his heart.

Von's words from two nights ago—forever ago, another lifetime ago—whispered through her mind: *He is the never-ending Road.*

"So which is it?" Annie asked, her voice little more than a husky whisper. "Is he a sociopath or a fucking god? Hell"—she laughed—"maybe there ain't even a difference."

"I know he's not what Bad Seed tried to shape him into," Heather said, straightening up. "He's remained himself." But at great cost—damaged, maybe permanently.

"But you saw what he did—to those torturing assholes and to the . . . angels."

Heather doubted that the *thing* Dante had transformed the twins and their father into had been a deliberate decision. He'd been drug-dazed and pain-shattered, his power triggered by dark and desperate need. But still, the memory—only an hour or so old—left her queasy.

Athena's body twists like hot taffy into her brother's spiraling, stretching form. Wells entwines with his children, twirling around and into them, his flesh elastic.

They rise into the air, bathed in cool blue fire, a three-faced pillar of flesh. Arms and legs streamline into feathered tails. Eyes blink open in the triune creature's braided torso and back. Rotating mouths open in a chorus of song: Three-intoone . . .

"You *sure* he ain't a sociopath?" Annie asked.

"If Bad Seed had succeeded, Dante never would've saved my life, never would've offered himself up for you."

"How can you be sure? After all you've seen him do?"

"Because his heart's true."

"So you trust him?" Annie asked.

"With my life."

Annie sighed. She pulled the towel from her head and wadded it up in her lap. She combed her fingers through her blue/purple/black hair. "I'm not like you. I don't think I can do that. I liked him before"—she waved a hand toward the window again—"all that. And I know the only reason he was used and tortured was because of me, and I know he saved your life after you'd been shot in D.C., but he scares the shit outta me."

Rising to her feet, Heather walked around to the easy chair, perched on the arm, and wrapped her baby sister up in a hug. "It's okay. I don't blame you. Most people would've run away screaming a long time ago. You came back for us. Thanks."

"Jesus, you're welcome," Annie muttered, leaning into their hug, her breath warm against Heather's neck. She shivered. "Yuck! You're wet." She pulled free of Heather's embrace. "Aren't you freezing? There's extra pj's and stuff in my bag."

The door cracked open, slanting gray light into the room and across the floor. Cool air smelling of pine and wet concrete spilled into the room. Heather whirled, dived onto the far bed, across Von's body, and yanked up the blankets to shield Dante.

Cortini slipped inside and eased the door shut behind her. Locked it and rehooked the chain. Releasing her pent-up breath, Heather kissed Dante's heated lips. She gently covered his face with the blankets, tucking one errant and silky strand of hair back underneath. She scooted off the bed and stood.

"Car's out of sight," Cortini said. She tossed Heather the keys.

"Thanks," Heather said. She slid the keys into her pocket—her cold, wet pocket—then went into the bathroom to put on something dry.

Finding another pair of plaid pajama bottoms in Annie's duffel bag—red, this time—and a pink Emily the Strange tee, Heather stripped off her wet jeans, turtleneck sweater, and undies. Her skin goosebumped from the cold. The flannel jammies felt warm and comfortable.

When Heather stepped out of the bathroom, Cortini sat in the vinyl easy chair and her sister was a gloom-shadowed hump beneath the blankets in the mortals-only bed next to the curtained window.

"Does Dante know what he is?" Cortini asked.

"He found out a little over three weeks ago that he's True Blood." Heather sat down on the bed, the mattress creaking beneath her. "As for the other, I don't know if De Noir told him or not."

"A shame."

Heather nodded, then trailed a hand through her damp hair. With De Noir dead—a fact she had trouble grasping—and Von warned against trusting the Fallen, who could teach Dante what it meant to be a Maker when he was struggling just to survive?

Exhaustion blurred Heather's thoughts. She pulled back the sheet and blankets and climbed into bed. "Wake me up for the second watch in four hours. Okay?"

"Four hours. Got it."

Heather snuggled down into the pillow and mattress, grateful she'd rescued Annie's gym bag from the disintegrating house. The idea of leaping out of bed in her underwear,

Browning in hand, to defend herself didn't appeal in the slightest no matter how chic and sexy it looked in movies.

Heather closed her eyes. Everything whirled around her for a moment, like she was a knife spun on a table by a sure hand.

One thought chased another in a looping, closed circle: *The Bureau, the Shadow Branch, the Fallen. Oh, my. All we know for certain is that there's never been another Maker. Until now. The Bureau, the Shadow Branch, the Fallen. Oh, my.*

Wondering if she was too tired to sleep, Heather spun into darkness.

4

ANOTHER VERSION OF
THE TRUTH

Gillespie walked into his darkened living room, cell phone held tight against his ear. "Sounds like your coordinates are way off," he said, tossing his keys onto the mail-cluttered going-out table. He shut the front door and twisted both dead bolts into place. "Recheck your data. What you're saying's impossible." He switched on the lamp.

"I've triple-checked the coordinates, sir," the surveillance tech said, her words cool and precise.

"Check again. Run it until it's right. Then call me back."

"Yes, sir." A hint of frustration sharpened the tech's words.

Gillespie hit the END button, then tossed his cell onto

the coffee table. The phone smeared a clean spot amid all the dust layering the oak table's lacquered surface. He hadn't cleaned once in the six months since Lynda had split, leaving him a note and a half-empty closet and a strange sense of unbalance. And, though he kept nagging at himself, he still hadn't gotten around to doing chores.

Maybe this weekend. Could even run the vacuum over the carpet while he was at it. Air the place out. It stank of mildew, musty carpet, and of something ripening in the kitchen trash.

Unzipping his jacket, he pulled it off, the Gore-Tex rustling, and draped it across an arm of the pale green sofa. Gillespie stood in the middle of the silent room, thoughts racing, his muscles kinked up so tight he felt like one touch would catapult him through the wall.

He smoothed a hand over his head, scrubbing beads of rain into his scalp. Thibodaux and Goodnight hadn't bought the enhanced vamp line. His lie hadn't taken root and he was pretty damned sure they'd known he was lying. He sighed. Dropping his hand to his side, he walked into the kitchen, Special Ops Director Underwood's words kiting through his mind.

The truth will distract them and possibly get them killed.

With all due respect, ma'am, so will a lie.

You'd know, Sam. Still blaming yourself? After all these years?

Yes, until the end of time. But those had been words he'd kept to himself.

His muscles kinked one notch tighter.

The white refrigerator was a pale ghost in the predawn gloom veiling the kitchen. Gillespie yanked the door open and surveyed the contents—a package of American cheese slices, a quart of milk past the expiration date, a Jell-O dark chocolate pudding cup, and two six-packs of Pacifico beer.

Maybe he'd add grocery shopping to that mythical household task list for that mythical weekend.

Gillespie pulled a beer free, shouldered the refrigerator door shut, then pried off the beer cap. Flipping the cap into the stinky, garbage-bag-lined can—tally another chore for the weekend—beside the refrigerator, he walked back into the living room.

He plopped onto the sofa. Tipped the cold bottle against his lips and took a long swallow. Chilled and sharp, the beer tasted like amber liquid heaven, but did nothing to sluice away the dark thoughts rampaging through his mind like a grizzly through a tent full of steaks.

Goodnight and Thibodaux weren't the only ones lied to.

He was pretty damned fucking sure he'd been lied to also.

We have no idea what went wrong, Gillespie, but we have a situation that needs immediate cleanup.

Not true. They'd known *exactly* what had gone wrong. Maybe they hadn't been expecting it, but what had happened had been no mystery.

An FBI agent had been murdered and two other feds—both with stellar careers, one a hero—seemed to be involved in that death. Prejean had been in town with his band, Inferno. According to Underwood, he and his band had spent the night before Rodriguez's murder at SA Wallace's place.

Prejean—a True Blood.

In Gillespie's twenty-one years of law enforcement, the last ten with the SB, he'd never encountered a True Blood. Of course, he hadn't even been aware of the existence of vampires until the SB had recruited him from the FBI. Then he'd learned that not only did vamps exist, but they were an active part of the country's infrastructure.

That fact had never rested easy with him, not even when he worked with dedicated vamp agents like Goodnight.

Just what was project Bad Seed? And how the hell had a True Blood become part of a joint special ops program, anyway? From what Gillespie had heard, True Blood vamps were rare and elusive beings. If Prejean was a tagged and observed subject in a study devoted to sociopaths, why in God's name had he been allowed to remain loose?

Just how many things were wrong with this picture?

Underwood's words replayed through Gillespie's mind.

If Goodnight is told that Prejean is a True Blood, she might hesitate at a crucial moment and allow him to escape.

The SB is her life, ma'am. She's a dedicated agent.

So was Wallace. And Lyons. Until they met Prejean.

Since Prejean seems to have such a strong effect on humans, ma'am, it sounds like Thibodaux, not Goodnight, might be in more danger of letting Prejean slip away. If I warned them—

No. Prejean's status is classified. Your agents only need to know that they are to capture a dangerous killer—make him an enhanced one, given his speed—and two corrupted feds.

Ma'am, I'd prefer to tell my agents the truth—

Underwood laughs, the sound as warm as flannel on a cold day. Amused. When she speaks again, her voice remains warm: The last time you disregarded instructions, three agents died. I'm sure you don't want to add to that tally.

Tension ratcheted his muscles another turn tighter. Gillespie wasn't sure who he was angrier with—Underwood for rubbing his face in a big, steaming pile of shame, or himself for creating that big, steaming pile in the first place.

Gillespie downed his beer, then went to the kitchen and fetched two more. He paused by his desk long enough to scoop up his laptop. Time to do a little research on one Dante Prejean, SB classified subject, rock front man, and sociopath. He wondered what the feds and local Louisiana law had on the bloodsucking bastard.

Just as he slouched back down onto the sofa, one cold, moist bottle in hand, the other bottle on the coffee table creating a new ring in the dust, the laptop resting against his thighs, his cell phone trilled.

Snatching it up, Gillespie hit the TALK button and said, "Gillespie."

"Sam?"

Gillespie sat up straight, his heart kicking his ribs, pulse thundering in his ears. Even though her voice sounded sleep-fogged, he couldn't imagine her calling at this hour unless . . . "Is something wrong? The kids?"

"No, no, I had a dream, and . . . Are you okay?"

Gillespie closed his eyes and pressed the cold beer bottle against his forehead. "I'm fine." He wanted to ask her about the dream, wondered what it meant that she still dreamed about him and cared enough to risk waking him to make sure he was all right.

"Since you answered on the first ring, you must be up already," Lynda said with a soft sigh. "Or maybe you haven't been to bed yet. You drinking, Sam?"

"Nah, just up early. Busy day today."

"Well, if you're okay—"

"Hey, I made an appointment with that therapist your sister recommended," Gillespie said on reflex, looking for a way to keep her on the phone, a way to keep her sleepy, warm voice in his ear. He hoped she didn't hear the lie in his voice.

"Great, that's, uh, good news. I hope it works out. It wasn't your fault—"

Gillespie's phone clicked, interrupting Lynda's words. He opened his eyes and lowered the beer bottle to the cushion beside him. Call waiting. With a low groan, he said, "Babe, I gotta go. Got another call."

"That's fine. I gotta go too. Bye."

The relief in Lynda's voice curdled his thoughts, and for an instant he caught a flash of what he must look like to her: a man eaten so lean by guilt that guilt was all that held him together—sinew and tendons. A muscle in his jaw twitched. He switched to the incoming call.

"Sir?" The surveillance tech's voice curled into his ear. "I've run the coordinates two more times and the result was the same both times."

"Send me the images." Gillespie placed the beer bottle beside its mate on the coffee table.

"Downloading now, sir. The first image is from two hours ago. The second one is from five minutes ago."

Gillespie lowered the phone from his ear and watched the monitor. The first image showed two houses from above, the main building and a guest cottage, tucked into a clearing surrounded by pine and evergreens. Several vehicles were parked in the driveway: a Dodge Ram truck, Wallace's Trans Am, a Saturn sedan, and a tarp-covered vehicle.

The phone beeped as the next image was received. Gillespie stared at the screen, heart lurching into high gear. The guest cottage remained in place nestled into forest shadows, but now a huge hole in the earth yawned up at the sky where the main house had been. A black mouth ringed with what looked like statues—some capped like the standing stones at Stonehenge.

No main house. No vehicles.

Cold fear looped around Gillespie's guts, twisted.

"Sir?" The tech's voice sounded small and faraway. "Instructions?"

"Code 54," Gillespie managed to say, his mouth dry. "Seal it up."

"Code 54," the tech repeated. "Roger, sir."

Gillespie thumbed the END button. He picked up his condensation-slick bottle and drained it in several throat-stretching and painful gulps. Staring at the impossible image on the cell's screen, he set the empty bottle on the coffee table. It fell over with a muted *tunk*, then rolled back and forth for a few seconds in an ever-diminishing arc.

Gillespie stood and paced the floor, his cell clenched tight against his palm.

The house was gone.

Possibilities whirled through his mind. Earthquake. Sinkhole. Some unknown disaster. But none of those possibilities accounted for the figures—the statues—surrounding the hole.

The house was gone.

What had he sent Thibodaux, Goodnight, and the Portland agents into? It was bad enough he'd been ordered to keep the truth from them. He needed to pull his agents back until the danger level at the Wells/Lyons compound had been reassessed.

He needed to call Underwood. Gillespie stopped pacing, grabbed up the unopened beer from the table, and pried off the cap. He poured a long, frosty swallow down his throat, but his heart refused to ease off the throttle.

As though preparing to take a high dive into a pool, Gillespie took several deep breaths, then tapped Underwood's button on the speed dial.

She answered on the first ring. "Good morning, Chief Gillespie," she said. "I hope you have good news for me. Are the subjects in custody?"

"No ma'am, not yet. The agents should be arriving in Oregon any moment. But I'd like permission to recall them. We have an . . . unexpected . . . problem."

"I'm listening."

"The house is gone."

A long pause, then, "Are you drunk?"

"Not yet, ma'am," Gillespie said. "I'm sending you the satellite scans that the surveillance tech sent me. The first one is from 4 a.m. PST, the second is five, eight minutes old." He thumbed the SEND button. A moment later he heard a sharp intake of breath thousands of miles away in D.C. and knew the second image had arrived.

"Good God," Underwood breathed.

"I've already issued a containment code, ma'am. May I recall my agents?"

"No. They can ascertain what has taken place and whether or not the subjects are still there."

Gillespie resumed pacing, his fingers white-knuckling around the beer bottle. "The subjects may be *dead*, ma'am," he grated. "I'd rather call back my agents, or at least let them know what to expect."

"Those are statues circling the . . . pit. Someone had to place them there. So *someone's* alive. You may call your agents and warn them, but under no circumstances are you to recall them or tell them to wait. In fact, I want you on the next plane to Portland to join them."

Gillespie stopped pacing. "Understood, ma'am."

"Be sure to arrive sober, Sam. Call me when you've secured the scene."

The line went dead. Underwood's typical I'm-not-happy-with-you-and-you-are-on-thin-ice-asshole sign-off.

Gillespie studied the framed *Moulin Rouge* poster Lynda had hung on the wall several years ago. He tipped the Pacifico bottle against his lips and drained the rapidly warming beer. Then he tapped in Thibodaux's number and listened to it ring.

5

NOTHING IN HIS EYES

G LOCK IN HAND, MERRI edged up along the driver's side of the travel-grimed SUV parked on the shoulder of the road, just past the steep driveway marked PRIVATE. Washington plates. Bicycle rack on top. Condensation-fogged windows not yet warmed by the early morning light.

From inside, she heard the rapid patter of a mortal heart. One fluttering as fast as hummingbird wings, powered by fear, pain, or adrenaline, maybe all three.

Small twigs and needles crunched beneath her partner's boots, spiking the air with the sharp smell of pine and wet bark, as Emmett paralleled her path on the SUV's passenger side. Leather creaked as he pulled his Colt .45 from its shoulder holster.

From behind her, Merri heard shoes gritting against

gravel, followed by a pair of quiet clicks as Holmes and Miklowitz slipped out of the Saturn and eased the doors shut.

Holmes had called in a check on the license plate and they'd learned it was a Sea-Tac rental taken out by one Brian Sheridan. No criminal record, but a quick search on Miklowitz's iPhone revealed a D.C. address and an FBI occupation.

So what was SA Brian Sheridan from D.C. doing *here*? And what had his pulse racing through his veins at light speed?

From D.C. to Seattle to Damascus.

It didn't take a Magic 8 Ball to guess why. He was tailing Wallace or Prejean. *After* the FBI had been instructed by the SB to drop all surveillance on the pair days ago.

Merri edged alongside the rain-beaded SUV to the fogged-up driver's side window. She tapped against the glass with the muzzle of her Glock. The rapid heartbeat remained steady, no sudden spike or frantic thudding.

Merri frowned. Sheridan's lack of reaction bothered her. Wondering if the fed was sleeping or drugged, she *moved*, grabbed the door handle and yanked the door open. Stale air reeking of BO, urine, and greasy old burger wrappers poured out of the SUV. She shoved her gun against the temple of the man sitting in the driver's seat.

"Don't move, Sheridan," she said. "You're in deep shit. Who assigned you?"

He remained still. Never blinked. Never even flinched.

"Whoo!" Merri resisted the urge to fan the air. It smelled like Sheridan had been doing surveillance duty for a couple of days at least. Merri wanted to take a step back from the stink, but another odor, the thick, copper-edged tang of blood, held her, drew her gaze down to the mortal's thigh.

Blood seeped through the rain-drenched trousers despite the blood-soaked tie Sheridan had knotted above the wound. Hunger twisted through Merri like a lazy curl of smoke, but her pulse remained steady. No time for hunger. Not now. And like smoke caught in a breeze, her hunger dissipated.

The passenger side door jerked open and Merri looked up. Emmett aimed his Colt at Sheridan, his whisker-shadowed face Clint Eastwood–hard in the morning light. Morning light that Merri hoped remained barricaded behind the mist-trailing rain clouds. Her ugly-ass floppy-brimmed hat, thick sunblock, and brown leather gloves would protect her if the sun burned through the clouds, but sauntering around in daylight still made her nervous.

The last time she'd walked without fear beneath the sun had been over two hundred years ago when she'd been a slave on a tobacco farm in Virginia. And guess what? She didn't miss it. Not one damn bit. The stark and unforgiving light of day burned away illusions and revealed most things, no matter how beautiful or cherished, for what they truly were—ugly and heartless.

"Ripe," Emmett commented, fanning the air in front of his nose. "Is he alive?"

"Heart's beating. But it looks like he took a bullet to the thigh." Merri nudged the gun muzzle against the mortal's temple. "Hey, Sheridan." He didn't blink. His eyelashes didn't even quiver. "Maybe he's in shock," she said.

She patted him down for weapons and found none tucked into his cold, wet, and muddy clothing. But she *did* score a damp wallet from an inside pocket of his suit jacket. She flipped it open. "ID, badge, it's definitely Sheridan."

"What's the story?" Miklowitz asked, drawing up alongside Merri.

"Damned good question. But he isn't answering." Merri dropped the wallet into a pocket of her suede jacket. She holstered her Glock. "He's been shot. Let's see if he's been doped."

Cupping the fed's chin in her gloved hand, Merri turned his face toward her. He stared past her, hazel eyes gazing at something beyond what she could see. No dilated pupils, no shock or fever glassiness. But the slackness in his face made her flesh crawl. Made her want to slap at herself as if the *nothing* in his eyes could slither in through *her* eyes. Whisper against her skin from the inside out.

"Fuck," she whispered, jerking her hand away. His head returned to its previous position, his attention once more focused straight ahead on nothing. She wiped her palms against her jeans. "Not doped, I don't smell any chemicals," she managed to say. "No dilated pupils. No obvious sign of head trauma."

Merri looked past Sheridan to the SUV's rear seats. Crumpled fast-food wrappers and white sacks, empty Gatorade bottles, foil gum wrappers, an empty urinal littered the interior. But the thing that caught her eye was a small monitor screen resting on a folded flat backseat.

"He's got a camera rigged up somewhere," she said.

Emmett glanced up at the SUV's roof. "Now the bicycle rack makes sense."

"Why don't you and your partner head on up," Miklowitz said, tipping his head toward the driveway, a lock of honey-brown hair flipping into his eyes, "while we secure Sheridan and the vehicle." He absently pushed the errant lock back from his face, then pulled a pair of flex-cuffs from his jacket pocket.

Merri nodded. "Sounds good. We can search the vehicle and call medics afterward." She stepped back from the SUV so Miklowitz could take her place.

Holmes walked around the front of the SUV and joined his partner, gun still in hand. He was shorter than Miklowitz's six feet by a couple of inches and less thick through the middle, but probably close to the same age—mid-thirties—despite his full head of neatly trimmed white, gray-threaded hair.

Wonder what spooked the color outta him? Merri struggled to keep from smiling and managed—just.

"We'll catch up with you guys in a few," Holmes said, halting beside Miklowitz.

"Roger that," Emmett said. "We'll get the lay of the land and wait for y'all before we make any moves."

"Sounds good to me," Merri said. "I'm happy to let you deal with Zombie Boy."

"Man's probably in shock," Holmes said, his gaze locking with hers. "Have you had any experience with injured agents before? Mortal ones?" His voice was level, but his icy green eyes permafrosted his expression into one of arctic disdain.

"As a matter of fact, I have." Merri kept her voice low and level. *Keep talking if you wanna be counted among them.* "You got a problem with me?"

Holmes shook his head. "No, no problem," he muttered, then turned away to help Miklowitz cuff Sheridan.

Merri swiveled on the balls of her feet and stalked around the SUV to the driveway's tree-shadowed mouth. Her leather gloves creaked as she flexed her fingers.

No mystery behind what Holmes didn't have a problem with. Merri wondered what offended him most: Working with a woman? A black woman? A vampire? Or a black female vampire? Whichever it was, it'd made for a delightful forty-minute ride from the Portland airport.

She stopped beside the blue street sign reading PRIVATE, and studied the driveway leading up the mist-shrouded hill, lined with oak, pine, and fir trees. The mingled scents of wet, dark soil, pine, and moss, clean and thick with life, filled her lungs. Tatters of pale mist skirted the tree trunks and clung to undergrowth.

Gravel gritted beneath boot soles. She listened to the sound of her partner's approach. She caught Emmett's scent before he reached her—fresh ice and anise, cold and pure and licorice sharp.

"Time to catch some bad mofos," Emmett drawled.

"Truth, brothah." Merri pulled her Glock free of its holster. Chambered a round. "Bad and *beautiful* mofos."

An image of Dante Prejean from the file they'd studied on the flight down popped into her mind. One candid shot in particular stood out in her memory.

Sunglasses perched on top of his head, Prejean leaned against a stone wall, one leg braced behind him, thumbs in the pockets of his leather pants. He wore a long-sleeved mesh shirt underneath a black tee reading DOES IT OFFEND YOU, YEAH? and a steel-ringed collar buckled around his throat.

A Goth couple held his attention—a blond guy in an old-fashioned frock coat, white lace spilling from the throat of his shirt and over the coat's lapels, and a dark-haired beauty in a red velvet mini and thigh-high black stockings. The blond was speaking, his handsome face lit up, mouth open, hands lifted in the air.

A sexy smile tilted Prejean's lips—a warm and inviting smile—and his dark eyes gleamed with captured light and affection.

White skin, glossy black hair, Cupid's bow lips, Dante Prejean was beyond beautiful. Just the sight of him in a photo had made Merri's heart race, filled her mind with delicious and naughty thoughts. He'd also looked very young—twenty, twenty-two—and she was intrigued by the fact that nowhere in the file was his age listed or when he'd been turned or even by whom.

"Bad and beautiful," Emmett repeated. "Definitely. Prejean . . ." He shook his head. "If I was still single and if he wasn't a murderer, I'd-a tapped that in a heartbeat."

Merri snorted. "Assuming he'd want your sorry ass. I'm gonna tell Mark that you've been lusting in your heart."

"Tattletale. FYI? My heart isn't exactly the part of me that's lusting." A wicked grin parted Emmett's lips. He nodded at the driveway. "Ready, partner?"

"Let's do this thing." Merri swiveled around, then stumbled as dizziness whirled through her. She grabbed ahold of Emmett's arm for balance. She felt his muscles cording beneath his windbreaker sleeve.

"You okay?" he asked.

Merri sucked in a deep breath, then nodded. "Just the goddamned pills." Emmett's blue-eyed gaze remained on her face, studying her. She released his arm. "I'm fine. Enough with the penetrating gaze already."

"Roger that." A smile flickered across Emmett's lips.

She hated the stay-awake pills and used them only when duty required it. Designed for vampire metabolism, the pills effectively countered the narcotic embrace of Sleep. But with her natural rhythm disrupted, side effects were unavoidable.

Taking opposite sides of the driveway, she and Emmett walked up the hill at a slow pace, scanning the trees and undergrowth. Even though Emmett placed each foot carefully, she still heard the whisper of grass against his trousers, the crunch of pine needles, the soft thud of each footfall.

She heard Emmett's heartbeat pick up speed as they neared the crest of the hill, knew adrenaline was pumping into his veins, just like it was into hers. She slipped both hands around her Glock's grip, listening. Bird chirps and trills, the clicks of busy insects and small mammals doing their morning thang.

The rush of water, a river, echoed up from somewhere deep, and the chilly air clung to her skin, beading on her face. An odd scent lingered in the mist-laden air, the crackling smell of ozone. Merri drew in a breath, tasting the air, wondering if a thunderstorm had blown through Damascus a few hours earlier.

Merri held up a hand as she caught a glimpse of a house in between the trees. She tucked herself against the lichen-laced trunk of a pine. A flash of peripheral movement told her Emmett was doing the same.

She frowned. She should be able to see two houses. She only saw one. Maybe the satellite images had made the houses look closer than they actually were or maybe she was at a bad angle.

Motioning that she was moving forward, Merri slipped from one tree trunk to the next until she stood behind a rain-dripping oak at the driveway's beginning. What she saw slammed her heart against her ribs, trapped her breath in her throat.

A cave's dark mouth stretched across the ground, an opening into the earth's heart. An unseen river pulsed through its veins, its roar echoing into the air. But that wasn't even the most bizarre thing in view, wasn't the thing that dried her mouth, no.

"What . . . the . . . hell?" Emmett whispered.

Gleaming white statues of winged beings in various postures ringed the cave. Some stood, others crouched or knelt, while those captured in flight—wings slashing up or down—capped the standing statues like a celestial Stonehenge. Blue sparks flickered like fireflies over the white stone, skipped along the butter-smooth wings.

On the cave's east side, a small house squatted, its front door wide open, its interior dark, its windows shattered. The guest cottage looked like a bombed-out home on the edge of any war zone—minus the graffiti. Glass glittered in the dew-beaded grass like fire-sparked prisms.

No main house. No Dodge Ram, no Trans Am, no vehicles, period. Their perps had either driven them away or the cave had swallowed them all. Including their perps?

"What the hell happened here?"

Merri shook her head. "You got me, partner."

A low rumble, like distant thunder, rolled through her—the frantic drumming of dozens of hearts. She zeroed in on the guest house. She frowned. The pills were messing with her again. No *way* the cottage was filled to the rafters with panicked individuals.

Signaling for Emmett to hold, Merri *moved* past the statues, across the ravaged lawn and chewed-up asphalt to the guest cottage. Glock in both hands, she paused beside the empty front window. The rain-stained edge of a sage green curtain fluttered in the cool breeze. She listened.

No patter of hearts from inside. Just silence. The thunder seemed to be coming from . . . Merri's mouth dried. She turned to face the circle of statues, her own pulse pounding hard and fast through her veins. Not possible.

Emmett scrunched across what remained of the lawn to join her, Colt in both hands, his wary gaze on the cottage at her back.

"I didn't give you the all clear," Merri said.

"And you didn't wait for backup," Emmett drawled, coming to a halt beside her. "Anyone inside?"

A breath of fetid air wafted from a glassless window.

Merri shook her head. "No one alive, anyway."

She caught the sound of careful footfalls coming up from the highway below. Miklowitz and Holmes. When the two field agents hunched into view, guns in hand, rain jackets crinkling, she waved them to the guest cottage.

Both men stopped and stared, varying shades of alarm and confusion rippling across their faces. Miklowitz was the first to pull himself together and hurry across the remnants of the lawn and driveway to the guest house, Holmes following.

"Christ," Miklowitz breathed, stopping beside Merri. "What the hell happened?"

"Where's the freaking house?" Holmes added in a low voice as he joined them. "Any sign of Prejean, Wallace, or Lyons?"

"No," Emmett said. He nodded at the cottage's yawning doorway. "My partner says there's no one alive inside. Y'all check the house for bodies to ID. We'll check that." He pointed at the cave with his Colt.

Hearts hammered and pulsed through Merri's consciousness, a frenzied pounding. She found herself walking toward the circle of statues as if caught in a tractor beam, moving forward without thought, a single refrain drumming in her mind, over and over: Not statues. Not statues. Not statues.

She halted in front of a male figure. His hands were lifted in front of himself, his face averted, as though warding off a blow. She drank in all of the statue's details—the braided and twisted open-ended collar circling his throat, the nipples on the bare chest, the muscle definition, the fall of fabric in his kilt, the upper arch of his wings.

From within the white stone, a heart fluttered, the sound slowing as Merry listened. She touched a gloved and shaking finger to the figure's face. Tiny blue sparks crackled into the ozone-spiked air.

"This is unreal, Goodnight. What's going on?"

"I don't know," Merri replied. "But I *do* know these aren't statues."

"*Aren't* statues? Is that the stay-awake pills talking or are you actually saying these are real angels and that someone Medusaed them into stone?"

"Looks kinda like statues of the Fallen," Merri said, her

gaze lingering on the featherless wings. She drew in a deep breath of ozone-spiked air to calm her wild pulse.

"The Fallen? You mean as in fallen angels?"

"The Elohim, yeah." Merri stepped out from behind the oak, her palms sweating around the grip of her Glock.

"You shitting me?"

"Nope."

Merri moved to the next statue, a female, her gown clinging to voluptuous curves, her wings flaring behind her, her desperate gaze on the sky above, her hands at her mouth. Merri's gaze moved up as well, to the angel capping this statue and the previous one, an angel in flight, wind whipping through the length of her hair and rippling the fabric of her gown, wings cutting though the air, her expression one of joy.

"Merri?"

"I hear their hearts, Em. I hear their goddamned hearts."

Emmett whistled low and long. "Jesus Christ! Jesus fucking Christ. But who or what could turn fallen angels to stone?"

Merri sensed power in each stone figure, power that tingled against her gloved fingertips. She remembered tales of Fallen magic, whispers of angelic battles.

Back in the beginning—when the Elohim fought their wars for power over the mortal world—blue fire lashed through the air, girl, filling it with the smell of lightning just before it strikes.

Or so a wandering llygad *told me, back in the day, Merri-girl.*

Just fairy tales, or so she'd always believed. Even vampires had myths and legends. But as Merri paced her way around the circle of stone angels, each face was a masterpiece of shock, fear, disbelief, and horror. Except for the capping stone angels, who'd been captured in luminous white stone as they winged through the night sky—and it had to have been at night, right? Maybe even as she and Emmett had stood in Rodriguez's living room talking to Gillespie.

Maybe during their flight down to Portland.

She regarded the cave that the Fallen surrounded. Water roared in the darkness below. And she thought she heard something beneath that, a voice, no—*voices*. She held up her hand, motioning for Emmett to hold still and keep quiet, and listened.

Three different voices singing in unison: *Holy, holy, holy.*

The hair prickled on the back of Merri's neck. The voices sounded off, cold, inhuman. And not just vampire inhuman—something-out-of-deepest-darkest-nightmare inhuman. She shot Emmett a glance.

"I hear voices below." She pointed to the cave mouth. "Three voices, singing."

Emmett frowned. "Singing?"

Merri nodded. "But it's weird. The voices seem intertwined somehow."

Stepping past the stone-captured Fallen, she walked to the lip of the cave and knelt in the dirt. Holding her Glock down at her side, she leaned forward on her left hand and peered into the thick darkness below. Cold, moist air reeking of ozone and fresh-turned soil and rushing water wafted against her, chilling her to the bone.

She caught the faint gleam of the river far below. Moisture glistened on stones protruding from the cave's throat. Beneath the river's rush, voices drifted like mist, warbling a multiple-throated chorus, *Holy, holy, holy.*

Merri shivered. She had the strong and undeniable feeling that whoever—or *whatever*—was singing in the darkness below was about as far from holy as she was from mortal.

She felt Emmett kneel down beside her, caught his anise and ice scent and felt soothed. Her partner didn't believe in monsters or fairy tales, and that calmed her. He leaned forward to peer into the cave too.

Something moved down in the darkness beside the river, something pale and thick, humping along the stone like a gigantic slug.

Holy, holy, holy . . .

With a half-strangled gasp, Merri shoved away from the cave mouth, heart hammering, falling on her ass. "Something's down there," she choked out, refusing to take her eyes off the cave's black lip. "Something moving." Something that might climb out of the cave and hunch into the stark and unforgiving light of day.

"What?" Emmett asked, his voice tight, on alert. "What's down there?" A peripheral flash of movement told her he'd leaned over farther in his effort to see into depths mortal eyes couldn't fathom.

"No." Merri reached over and grabbed Emmett's arm, hauled him away from the cave. "I don't know what's down there, but I don't think it's—"

An abrupt bumblebee buzzing vibrated against Merri's taut nerves and she *moved* on pure instinct, locking her fingers around her partner's arm and hauling both their asses away from the cave and past the Fallen Stonehenge to the safety of the pines in a single blurring rush.

When she stopped, Emmett stumbled free of her grasp and up against the trunk of a pine tree. He dipped his hand into the pocket of his windbreaker, pulling out his cell phone. He held it up as it buzzed and bumbled in his hand, a huge grin on his face.

Cheeks burning, Merri glared at him, daring him to say anything.

Emmett glanced at the cell phone's screen. His grin

faded. *Gillespie,* he mouthed. Thumbing the TALK button, he said, "Chief."

Emmett raked a hand through his auburn hair as he listened, all mirth vanishing from his face. He nodded. "You got it, Chief. Just gone. No idea what happened. But we stumbled across a wounded fed, SA Brian Sheridan. Someone put a slug in his thigh." He listened for several more moments, then said, "Roger that." He ended the call and slipped the cell phone back into his pocket.

"What's the news?" Merri asked as his gaze lifted to meet hers.

"Gillespie wanted to let us know that the house was gone." A wry smile touched his lips. "Code 54. And he's on his way here."

"Great," Merri murmured. A secure-and-contain order meant that anyone who wandered onto the scene—a newspaper carrier, a hiker, a child chasing a ball—would be scooped up and tossed into an evidence van to be debriefed.

Looking past Emmett, Merri caught movement as Holmes and Miklowitz stepped out of the guest cottage, their faces grim. Spotting her, Miklowitz shook his head.

"Our perps don't seem to be here—alive or dead," she said. "Unless they were gobbled up by the cave."

Emmett sighed. "If they're alive, no telling where they are. Prejean's either Sleeping somewhere safe or buzzing on stay-awake pills."

Merri nodded. "Provided he's alive."

"What the fuck happened here?" Emmett asked quietly. Strain edged his voice. "I mean—fallen angels morphed into stone, a missing house, and a mysterious cave. How is this even possible?"

"Don't know, partner." Merri turned away and scanned the oaks and evergreens following the gentle slope of the land up to the stand of mist-garlanded pines at its crest.

A gleam of white from within the shadows beneath a fir's heavy branches caught her eye. Another of the Fallen or . . .

The image of pale, pale skin and deep, dark eyes flashed into Merri's mind and her pulse leapt into high gear. Her fingers tightened around the grip of her Glock.

Merri *moved*. She breezed through wet undergrowth, thorns catching at her slacks, her suede jacket, hooking, then tearing free. Even before she reached the figure, she realized it wasn't Prejean. Just more blue-sparked stone.

Halting in front of the kneeling fallen angel, Merri wondered why this one was so far from the others. Trapped within white stone, the angel's heart pulsed. Her waist-length stone locks rippled in chiseled waves from her bowed head, framing her face. A slender open-ended collar encircled her throat.

The fallen angel's wings were curved forward as if in an attempt to shelter herself, her eyes closed, her hands clenched into fists in her lap. She didn't look horrified or shocked or enraptured like the others ringing the cave.

Whatever had happened, they'd been caught off guard.

Not *her*. She'd knelt before the inevitable, a supplicant for mercy she'd known she wouldn't receive. Whoever she was, she would've had a prime view of what was happening to the house and her companions. Yet she hadn't attempted to escape.

Maybe she couldn't escape.

Merri crouched and touched the angel's knotted fists. Blue sparks snapped the smell of ozone into the pine-scented air. Cold iced Merri's spine.

Who or what had the power to transform the Fallen to stone?

And why had the Fallen come *here*?

6

KNIFE'S EDGE

CATERINA WAITED UNTIL HEATHER'S breathing had shifted into the easy rhythm of sleep, then she rose to her feet and padded to the desk. She plucked Von's leather jacket from the back of the chair and pulled it on, trying to keep the jingling to a minimum. She caught a faint whiff of motor oil and smoky incense from the jacket's lining.

The sleeves swallowed her hands and the shoulders hit her at the biceps. She had a feeling that she probably looked like a teen wearing her outlaw boyfriend's jacket. But at least the Browning snugged into her jeans at the small of her back was hidden from view.

Caterina's sneakers whispered across the carpet as she walked to the door. She unchained and unlocked it. Easing the door open, she slipped outside, pulling it shut behind her.

She scanned the motel parking lot. Barely visible white paint outlined the parking spaces in front of numbered doors. Only a handful of cars, windows fogged, occupied the slots. A crow hopped along the blacktop while, above, several white and gray seagulls wheeled in the gray morning sky, lamenting the lack of food.

Across the parking lot, between the cottage marked OF-FICE and the door numbered 1, several vending machines huddled behind a grilled cage. To the cage's left, a stainless-steel box full of ice hunkered beside a pay phone.

Caterina studied the mist-wrapped trees across the highway. An unusual shadow beneath a fir held her attention for a moment. Her muscles unknotted as she realized it was only that—a shadow cast by drooping branches. The cool, moist air smelled of pine and wet asphalt. Pale mist feathered the hills and floated ragged across the highway.

She touched her throat, remembered the heated touch of Dante's lips, the sharp pain as his fangs had pierced her skin, the pain vanishing as he drank her blood down—an offering from Alex Lyons.

She was still weak from blood loss and in poor shape to defend Dante as he Slept. She'd finally used up the adrenaline surge that had buoyed her on the hill at the Wells/Lyons compound, and she felt light-headed with fatigue.

Her hand slipped down to the front right pocket of her jeans, her fingers tracing the rounded shape of the quarters she'd taken from the console in Heather Wallace's car. Food first, then she had phone calls to place.

She wasn't sure what had happened to her cell phone. It had been tucked into a back pocket of her jeans when she'd dropped by the guest cottage to check on Athena Wells. Hours later, she'd regained consciousness bound and gagged inside the main house, surrounded by bits of the dead, and guarded by a demented woman. The cell? Long gone. She could only hope that it had disappeared along with the main house.

Caterina stopped in front of the vending machines, cold sweat beading her forehead. One held only drinks, the other candy and snack food. No orange juice, but Red Bull was offered. That'd have to do. Hands shaking, Caterina plugged in quarters, punched the appropriate button. A loud *clunk* into the vending machine's bottom tray announced the Red Bull's arrival.

Pulling it free and popping it open, Caterina poured half of it down her throat in one long swallow. She pressed the cold can against her face and sighed. The Red Bull hit her empty stomach like an iced brick. Stepping over to the snack machine, she studied its dubious offerings.

Hoping for a decent mix of protein and carbs, Caterina chose Reese's Peanut Butter Cups and a small bag of mixed nuts. She slotted in quarters, then gathered her purchases with shaking hands when they *clunk*ed into the tray. Finishing the Red Bull, she dropped the empty can into the blue recycle bin beside the trash can.

Caterina leaned against the black grille protecting the vending machines and reviewed her mental to-do list as she ate her snack food.

To-do number one: Call her hotel in Portland and let them know she wouldn't be checking out until later tonight.

To-do number two: Call the airline and book another flight. She'd already missed the one she was supposed to be on.

To-do number three: Check in with her handlers and see if Dante Baptiste's status had changed since Rodriguez's murder.

Dante's programming was triggered.

Heather Wallace's quiet words had created an avalanche of ice within Caterina. Who else knew how to activate Dante's programming? She not only needed to guard her

True Blood prince, she needed to protect him from himself as well.

The only thing was, she might not be able to do so alone.

She hadn't known yet that Dante was more than True Blood, that he was a Maker as well, when she'd last spoken to her mother, Renata Alessa Cortini. Von had said the Fallen couldn't be trusted. Not where Dante was concerned, anyway. Would Renata and the other Elders or the *llygaid* know how to guide Dante? How to teach him?

Creawdwrs had always been Fallen only. As far as she knew, Dante was the first vampire/Fallen Maker. What if the Elders, learning of Dante's programming, decided he was too dangerous? Decided that a monster lurked beneath his skin and behind his eyes?

If the damage is too great, then bring him to us so we may end his life with love and respect. He belongs to us. Alive or dead. Not in the hands of mortals, not even yours, my little love, child of my heart.

She'd felt his lips hot against her throat, felt him drinking in her blood, drinking in life, had seen the gold light glimmering in his dark eyes, the wonder on his gorgeous face when she'd told him that her mother was vampire.

Your mother's nightkind?

No monster this True Blood prince. Wounded and scarred, yes. But the future pumped within his heart and flowed through his veins.

The future for *all* of them: mortal, vampire, Fallen, and everything in between.

If he fell, the world would fall with him.

Calm and purpose unwound within her.

Caterina popped the last salted cashew into her mouth. She crumpled up the empty package and tossed it into the trash. Swiveling around, she bought another Reese's. She scooped it out of the bottom tray, then stepped over to the pay phone. She dropped quarters into the slot, then punched in the numbers and code for an international calling card issued in her mother's name.

If the SB ever felt compelled to go over her phone records, she didn't want a few calls from a pay phone in the Damascus area popping up like a screaming car alarm.

After she'd phoned the hotel and the airline, she made a third call. But not to the SB. *That* call would wait until she could call from her hotel room or via her laptop. As the phone trilled in her ear, Caterina tore open the Reese's package with her teeth.

The trilling stopped as, thousands of miles away in Rome, someone picked up the receiver and said in a low, musical voice, "*Si?*"

"*Ciao*, Mama," Caterina replied. "I found him."

THE MORNINGSTAR STOOD BEHIND a tall fir tree, one shoulder leaning into its rough-barked trunk. Rain dripped onto the fragrant green needles in the dirt beneath its branches. Mist undulated down the hill and across the highway, a ragged ghost.

A red neon sign flashed MOTEL VACANCY above the mist, bright as flame against the gray sky and shadowed hills. Brass numbers marked each motel room door. But he only watched number 9; the room with an empty parking slot in front of it now that the dark-haired woman had moved the sapphire blue Trans Am.

The door to room 9 opened and the dark-haired woman slipped out again, wearing the nomad's leather jacket this time. She eased the door shut. Walking with an easy grace, a predator's deliberate pace, she padded past the empty parking space, then stopped. She appeared to scan the parking lot, the highway, and the woods beyond.

Appeared to zero in on him.

The Morningstar drew in a breath. Held it. Shaped a hunting blind of tattered mist and rain and glistening, green leaves around himself; a seamless illusion.

Silence—except for the *pat-pat-pat* of the rain onto pine needles—filled the woods like cotton, absorbing and muffling all sound. Birdsong vanished. Insect clicking stopped. Nothing scurried or dug in the underbrush. Not with the Morningstar standing still and quiet, his radiance dimmed.

After one more long look at the spot where he stood, the mortal resumed walking, stopping at the vending machines.

The Morningstar released his breath and it feathered the air white. The blind vanished. He wondered about the lithe, dark-haired woman and the others who'd walked into room 9 with her. He needed to learn more about Dante's companions, needed to know who surrounded him and why.

Needed to learn more about Dante.

But the very fresh memory of how the others—including his *cydymaith*, his luscious Lilith of Lies—had been transformed into white power-sparked stone kept him on the safe side of the highway. Then, like now, the Morningstar had watched from deep within the pines as Dante had lost all control of his *creawdwr* magic.

"Did you kill him?" Dante says, fury lighting his face, seething in his husky voice. His gaze skips from face to face. "Did you? Or you?"

Blue light shines out from Dante, shafting into the aurora-glimmering air and into the Fallen, those on the ground and those still in the sky.

All are transformed into statues of exquisite detail, captured in gleaming white, blue-edged stone.

Wounded, exhausted, stumbling, only rage had kept

Dante on his booted feet. Since Dante believed his father—
Lucien—dead, the bond between them must have been
severed. Whether Lucien or Samael or whatever he wished
to call himself had severed it himself or Gabriel had killed
him, the result was the same: the lost bond had injured
Dante, and the Morningstar could only hope that it hadn't
damaged the young *creawdwr* beyond healing.

In any case, the Morningstar planned to keep the promise he'd given Lucien before leaving him in the pit, hanging
from hooks through his shoulders.

I find it amusing that the slayer of one creawdwr *fathers
the next. Dante, an intriguing name, but inappropriate,
don't you think? Once he's seated upon the Chaos Seat, he'll
finally be far away and safe from the hell politely referred to
as the mortal world.*

And he'll be mine.

The boy needed stability and guidance, a sure hand.
Before it was too late.

Before he lost his sanity. Before Gehenna ceased to
exist.

CATERINA EASED THE DOOR open and slipped into the
darkened room. She remained still as she waited for her vision to adjust. She heard a shift in someone's breathing—it
had to be Heather; Dante and the *llygad* wouldn't stir until
twilight. It pleased her that even as exhausted as the soon-
to-be former FBI agent was, her survival instincts were still
in high gear.

"It's me," Caterina said quietly. "Vending machines."

"Okay."

In just a few moments, Heather's breathing dropped
back into the low, easy rhythm of sleep. Eyes adjusted, Caterina turned, and locked and chained the door. Returning

to the desk chair, she stripped off Von's jacket. Draped it around the chair again, chains chiming.

The Red Bull winged jittery energy through her system and accelerated her heartbeat. Offered the illusion of wakefulness, an illusion she accepted and needed.

Caterina walked over to the bed shared by Dante and Von. Knelt one knee down on the carpet at Dante's side of the bed. She glanced at the window and gauged the amount of rainy-day light filtering in through the curtains. Not much. The gloom seemed thick enough even for a True Blood.

Winding her fingers tight around the warm, fleecy blankets, she slipped the covers down from Dante's face, ready to yank them back into place if she'd misgauged the amount of light in the room.

Dante's glossy black hair, smoothed away from his face by Heather's hands, trailed across the pillow. Kohl smudged his eyelids. Blood trickled from his nose and stained his lips and chin red.

His scent tugged at her, perfumed each breath—burning leaves and frost and deep, dark earth. She wondered what her mother would detect in his scent, wondered if his spell—cast unaware even as he dreamed—would also enrapture Renata Cortini.

Caterina touched the inside of her wrist against Dante's forehead and sucked in a breath as heat pulsed into her flesh at the contact.

He burned when he should be Sleep-cool.

Rising to her feet, Caterina padded into the bathroom and wet two washcloths with cold water. Wringing out the excess, she returned to the bed. Dante didn't stir as she placed the folded washcloth over his forehead. She used the other washcloth to clean the blood from his face.

Her mother's words whispered up from memory: *Earn*

his trust, cara mia, *then bring him to us. I'll tend to those hunting him.*

He'd be safer in Rome within the protective embrace of Renata Cortini, that was certain. If he remained in the States, the SB would eventually haul him in. Lock him up. Or worse—they'd use this True Blood child and Fallen Maker like a weapon against their enemies.

She wouldn't . . . *couldn't* . . . allow that.

But if Dante refused to travel to Rome? Refused the wishes of Renata?

Caterina wadded up the bloodied washcloth in her left hand and pulled the blankets back over his face with the other.

Given time, perhaps she could change his mind, persuade him to listen to her mother and the Elders composing the holy Cercle de Druide.

And if not? What then?

Caterina tossed the washcloth into the bathroom sink, then returned to the desk chair and sat down. She rubbed her face with her hands, trying to push away the exhaustion nibbling away at her awareness, despite the Red Bull and snacks.

She'd guard Dante with everything she had—heart, mind, and razor-sharp reflexes. And share with him everything she knew. From the interior of the Shadow Branch's labyrinthine heart to her mother's whispered bedtime tales about the Elohim.

But she didn't know if she could or should force him to do Renata's bidding.

Reaching behind, Caterina pulled the Browning free from the back of her jeans. She rested the gun on her thigh, her fingers curled around its grip.

What she'd seen up on the hill . . . Images of what Dante had done swooped like gulls through her mind.

Dante, curled up on the carpeted floor, shivering with fatigue and seizure-induced pain as spokes of blue light wheel from his hands, transforming everything they touch.

The carpet ripples, shifting into a forest floor of pine-needled dirt, thick underbrush, and tiny blue wildflowers. Thorned blue veins slither across the room.

Blue light stabs out from the house, from its shattered windows and yawning front door, as Heather and Von—Dante draped over his shoulder—run from the shuddering, quaking building.

Above, a massive rush of wings draws her gaze. Shapes dive and glide through the rain-cloud-paled night, outlined against a shimmering splash of vivid twilight colors—an aurora borealis—where none belongs. The night rustles, full of wings. Ethereal music rings through the wet air as the Fallen sing to Dante Baptiste.

Singing to guide their young creawdwr *home to Gehenna.*

But Dante had set the Fallen ablaze with blue fire, turned them to stone even as they sang to him. Even as they tried to flee from him, realizing too late that he blamed them for the death of his father.

Caterina recalled the words Von had spoken earlier: *Lucien asked me to guard Dante from the Fallen.*

And that was another marvel—a *llygad* who took action instead of remaining an impartial observer of events. From what Caterina had witnessed just a few hours earlier, Von had abandoned his essential impartiality and aligned himself with Dante Baptiste—against all precepts of *llygaid* law.

Caterina sighed, and leaned back in the chair. She had so many questions to ask Von and Dante both. But she realized Dante probably didn't have any answers for her—given how his mind had been ravaged by mortal monsters, his past fragmented and buried deep within him. She tried not to think about Dante's seizures or what they might mean.

And Von? Well, it depended on how much he trusted her. Or *if* he trusted her.

The less she knew, the better, in all honesty, since she planned to return to the SB. If something seemed hinky or off to her handlers when she spoke to them again, she could find herself facing an interrogator like Teodoro Díon who would destroy her mind as he stripped knowledge from it, piece by piece. And leave her a drooling idiot.

If she was unlucky.

Caterina shivered, goose bumps popping up on her arms. She tightened her grip on the Browning. Her cold, wet clothes would keep her awake. Another Red Bull wouldn't hurt either. In four hours, she'd catch some sleep.

She and Heather both needed to be on their toes, sharp and alert, balanced on a knife's edge for whatever would come next once twilight deepened the gloom.

The light seeping in beneath the door and at its edges vanished. Caterina bolted to her feet, snapped up the Browning. Adrenaline pumped into her system, kicking her heart into high gear. Her focus narrowed. She aimed the Browning head-height.

Blue sparks shot out of the lock's key-card slot, a miniature fireworks display. Caterina's heart kicked against her ribs. She kept her aim steady, though she now suspected a bullet wouldn't stop whoever stood on the other side of the door.

The door pushed in as far as the chain allowed, stopping with a *thunk*. Another shower of blue sparks. The chain fell from the door, links glowing, molten. Caterina caught peripheral motion and realized Heather had awakened and was swinging up her Browning too.

The door creaked open, but only mist and rain and green leaves swirled into the room on a strangely heated breeze. Caterina's finger flexed against the trigger, stopping just a hair short of firing the gun.

No one entered. But the hair rose on the back of her neck. She caught a whiff of ozone. The mist and rain and green leaves still spun in the air as though caught in a storm-fueled funnel cloud. A *man-sized* funnel cloud. A funnel cloud that glided into the room with a purpose.

"Shit," Heather breathed.

Caterina swiveled and shifted her aim, the Browning's muzzle now targeting the whirl of leaves and mist.

A voice rang out, chiming, scorching; a bell of fire. "Be still."

Those words rippled into Caterina's mind, searing away all thought. Just as her mind blanked and she plunged into darkness, she thought she saw a tall man with short white hair curling against his temples, thought she saw white wings folded at his back, thought she saw him smile — dazzling like diamonds caught in a waterfall spray.

She pulled the trigger.

7

DEEPER AND DEEPER

FBI ADIC Monica Rutgers strode down the beige-carpeted hallway to her office, stockings whisking, pulse pounding hard through her veins. Something had gone horribly awry at the Wells/Lyons compound.

Not only had Sheridan failed to kill Prejean and Lyons, he was in SB hands.

Worse? Now the SB knew she'd not only disregarded orders concerning Bad Seed, they knew she'd initiated retaliatory action of her own.

And risked the well-being and life of an agent, of a man, she trusted.

Based on Gillespie's phone call, Sheridan was in dubious condition.

We have your agent, ma'am. Sheridan.

He was only following my orders. I'm responsible, not him.

I understand that, ma'am. He was wounded—

I'll have the goddamned hide of whoever—

Ma'am, he took a bullet in the thigh and, no, it wasn't us. My people found him that way. He'll receive medical treatment before debriefing.

Debriefing. Yes. May I send a couple of my agents to accompany him? And to participate in his debriefing? Sheridan's a good agent, Chief Gillespie, a loyal agent, and he doesn't deserve—

No, ma'am, he doesn't. You should've considered that before you sent him to Damascus.

No arguing with the truth. But she'd sent Brian Sheridan out into the deep, dark woods. She'd guide him home again. What in God's name had gone wrong? With a down-and-dirty, under-the-radar plan to assassinate a sociopathic bloodsucker and a turncoat SAC? *Oh, let me count the ways.*

Sheridan was now a prisoner of war. A solider who'd followed his orders but hadn't completed his mission.

When did we become two opposing camps, the FBI and the SB?

But she knew the answer to that question—they'd never been anything else.

Her assistant, Ray Ellis, Bluetooth headset hooked around his ear, looked up from his monitor at her approach, fingers poised over the keyboard. Surprise flashed across his youthful face. Youthful, hell. He *was* young—only twenty-eight. A kid. But an efficient and competent kid—when she wasn't catching him off guard.

Ellis jumped to his feet from behind his tidy desk, smoothing a hand along his red diamond-patterned tie. Pausing to scoop up a pile of color-coded files, he hurried around to meet her.

"Did something go wrong at your luncheon, ma'am?" he asked. "I don't have—"

Rutgers held up a hand. Ellis stopped in his tracks. He held her gaze, his hazel eyes calm, face composed. "That doesn't matter right now. Clear my schedule and get me Underwood at the SB on the line."

"SOD Underwood?"

Government acronyms never failed to unintentionally amuse. Unintentional, hell. She was pretty damned sure unintentional had nothing to do with it. *SOD. ADIC. SAC.* "Yes, the SOD," Rutgers said dryly.

Ellis shifted his armful of folders to his hip, bright splashes of color against his dark gray trousers. He glanced at her closed office door. Nodded.

"Ma'am, SOD Underwood is waiting for you inside. She arrived about five minutes ago." Ellis hesitated, then added in a low voice, "She also requested that I clear your schedule."

Rutgers stiffened. "You refused, of course," she said, her voice cold enough to hang icicles from Ellis's well-formed nose.

"Of course, ma'am," he agreed. "I'll clear your schedule now."

"Good." As Rutgers stepped past her assistant, she paused to pat his shoulder. "Thank you, Ray," she murmured.

"Ma'am." A faint smile twitched at one corner of his mouth. "Give her hell."

"Count on it." Rutgers threw open the wood and frosted-glass door etched with her name, and stalked inside. Cold fury propelled her across the room.

Celeste Underwood, Special Ops Director for the SB, relaxed in one of two maroon leather chairs positioned in front of Rutgers's desk, her black trousered legs crossed. She shifted to glance over her shoulder at Rutgers.

"Monica," she greeted. "How are you?" A smile curved her glossed lips.

"How dare you give *my* assistant orders." Rutgers strode to her desk and, automatically smoothing her skirt beneath her, sat in the plush captain's chair, the leather creaking beneath her weight. She leaned forward, her forearms braced against the desk's polished surface, her hands clasped. "You have no authority here."

Smile still in place, Underwood rose to her feet and crossed to the door. She eased it shut, then turned around. Her smile had vanished. "Sure about that?"

"About you having no authority here? Absolutely."

Underwood shook her head. "Ah, Monica." She regarded Rutgers with almost maternal fondness, a neat trick for a woman the same age as Rutgers. "Still living in the good old days."

"Back when we actually upheld the Constitution?"

Underwood laughed, the sound warm, rich, and genuinely amused. "*That* we never did. Flawed instrument, the Constitution."

In her tailored black suit, rose button-down blouse, her modest and well-trimmed Afro sprinkled with strands of silver, gold jewelry glinting at her ears and left wrist, Underwood looked warm, accessible, every bit the boss with an open door policy.

Easy to imagine her as the grandmother she was, in jeans and gardening gloves, her round face shaded beneath a straw hat. Rutgers even caught a hint of cinnamon and apples, as though Underwood had baked pies just that morning.

Just an ordinary woman doing an extraordinary job.

But Rutgers knew better. Had learned long ago to look past the warm facade Underwood projected. Inside, the woman was empty, heartless, a golem of flesh manipulated by a keen and cold intelligence.

Underwood sauntered back to her chair, amusement lighting her face. Sitting down, she crossed her legs again, and leaned back. "Have you forgotten that when it comes to Bad Seed, I have authority over your every move?"

Rutgers's knuckles whitened and she unclasped her hands, dropping them to the arms of her chair. "I haven't forgotten. But the project's been terminated."

"Not completely." Underwood's eyes glittered, iced obsidian.

"Since when?" Rutgers said, trying to figure out what game the Special Ops director was playing. "I was instructed—"

"Exactly," Underwood cut in. "You were instructed." She tilted her head and studied Rutgers for a moment. She pointed at her ears. Arched her well-groomed eyebrows. "Unless you prefer to waltz around the bush . . . ?"

Rutgers sighed. Underwood was right, of course. Hidden electronic ears listened in each office and hallway within Bureau headquarters. Eavesdropping. Recording.

This particular conversation would be treacherous enough without misunderstanding greasing the cliff edge. She fetched the audio jammer out of her bottom drawer and set it up on her desk.

Small and slim, the jammer looked like an iPod. She switched it on and chirps and burbling bleeps filled the room instead of music, desensitizing any and all audio recording equipment in the room.

"I want my agent back." Rutgers's blunt words hooked Underwood's dark gaze.

"Impossible. He's being sent to one of our facilities for debriefing. And you're really in no position to make demands."

"Let's be honest, here. You intend to *interrogate* a wounded man," Rutgers said, voice flat and hard. "Not *debrief* him."

A smile skimmed across Underwood's lips, glittered in her eyes like sunlight on ice, dazzling and cold. "*You* sent him into the line of fire. These are the consequences of action *you* spun into play and your agent will pay the price."

A twinge of guilt tightened the muscles in Rutgers's chest. "There's no need to interrogate Sheridan. I take full responsibility for his actions. He was simply following my orders."

"And those orders were . . . ?"

"To kill Dante Prejean."

"Even after you were instructed to take your people off Prejean?"

"*Because* I was instructed to take my people off Prejean."

Underwood tsked and shook her head. "Defying instructions like a jilted ex slapped with a restraining order. That's not like you."

"How would you know?" Rutgers asked. "None of us are the people we were when we started this."

"True." Underwood's expression softened. "Very true," she murmured.

She glanced out the window and Rutgers wasn't sure if she was gathering her thoughts or simply taking in the view beyond the glass—pink cherry blossoms shivering on slender-branched trees, caught in a strengthening breeze as a late March storm rolled in, framing the delicate blossoms between green lawn and bruised sky.

"Prejean's not your concern," Underwood said, her gaze shifting back to Rutgers.

"He murdered one of my agents in cold blood."

"Seems to me Prejean was merely the means *your* agents used to commit murder." Underwood rose to her feet and smoothed the wrinkles from her slacks. "One SAC murdered. Another SAC and a much-lauded FBI hero implicated in that murder." She looked at Rutgers from under her lashes. "Seems to me you need to tend to your own house."

"Only because of Prejean."

"We'll deal with him," Underwood said. "You tend to your agents."

"Meaning Prejean will become just another shadow within the Shadow Branch? How appropriate." A muscle tightened in Rutgers's jaw. "I'd like Sheridan released ASAP and sent to the nearest hospital."

"He will be as soon as we've finished with him." Underwood strolled to the door.

Rutgers pushed back her chair and stood. "I've already told you what his mission was. There's absolutely no need—"

"Ah, but there is." Underwood paused at the door, swiveled around, her warm and matronly facade back in place. "He needs to corroborate your statement. Needs to let us know where Lyons, Wallace, and Prejean disappeared to."

Dread dropped cold pebbles into Rutgers's belly. "Disappeared?"

"Something else that's no longer your concern," Underwood replied. "I hope you don't plan to sacrifice more good agents in your quest for petty revenge."

"There's the pot calling the kettle black." Rutgers chuckled, the sound knotted and bitter. "How many people have died because of Bad Seed? Sacrificed in the name of curiosity?"

"Is that all you think the program was? A curiosity?" Underwood half turned as she grasped the doorknob. "By the way, I've informed your deputy director that we've severed all Bureau ties to Bad Seed. Bad Seed and its cleanup—and everything related to it—now belongs solely to the SB."

The skin along Rutgers's spine prickled. *And everything related to it.* "Sheridan had nothing to do with Bad Seed."

"Wrong. You involved him." Underwood opened the door and stepped over the threshold. "Now he's ours. I suggest you start doing damage control."

Rutgers stared at the Special Ops director, fury blurring her vision, scalding her cheeks. Just as she opened her mouth, Ellis's voice cut in from her desk intercom.

"The deputy director is on the line, ma'am."

Underwood offered a sympathetic smile. "Good luck, Monica." Turning, she strode down the hallway in brisk, efficient strides.

"Ma'am?" Ellis's intercom-tinny voice inquired.

"Yes," Rutgers said, closing the door and her eyes. She rested her forehead against the cool frosted glass. "Finalize the press release about SA Heather Wallace, then send it to me."

What was one more shitty lie in a whirling shit-blizzard of lies and half truths?

"Go ahead and put the deputy director through." With a sigh, Rutgers opened her eyes and turned around.

The large-screen monitor on the north wall flickered to life. Deputy Director Phil Beckett's angular face appeared, the deep blue, gold-edged FBI seal on the wall behind and just above him. Bannered beneath the emblem's red stripes: *Fidelity, Bravery,* and *Integrity.*

It represented the Bureau's idealistic heart, a dream bold and golden and brimming with hope for each agent, each division.

A dream long lost.

"Monica?" The DD's voice rumbled up from the com-con monitor. Far from pleased. It matched his tight-jawed expression.

"Here, sir."

RUTGERS SANK INTO HER chair and rubbed her temples. Her conversation with Beckett had lasted only five minutes, five *excruciating* minutes. In her favor was the fact that the DD was unaware that she'd sent Sheridan to kill Prejean.

Beckett believed that she'd provoked the SB by keeping a tail on Prejean. A tail who'd allowed himself to be caught.

Jesus, Monica, couldn't you have at least sent a competent agent?

He's one of my best. I suspect he was unlucky, not incompetent.

I'll see what I can do to get your man released or at least get one of us admitted into his debriefing.

I appreciate that, Phil.

As far as you're concerned, Bad Seed no longer exists. Stay the hell out of Underwood's business. In fact, keep as far from the Shadow Branch as possible.

Believe me, I'd like nothing more.

If you even feel the urge to pull another stunt like this, just tender your resignation and do it as a private citizen because you'll be done here.

Understood.

Rutgers's pulse pounded in her aching temples. Nothing had been accomplished. Sheridan was still wounded and in SB hands. And, despite Beckett's words, likely to remain that way. And she'd been assigned to do damage control. The old cover-your-ass tango.

Rising to her feet, Rutgers went to the beverage cart tucked in the corner, and brewed a cup of vanilla tea. When she returned to her desk, resting her plain lavender mug on a small cup warmer, she glanced at her monitor. The file she'd requested was waiting in her message queue.

Clicking it open, she reviewed the press release that would destroy SA Heather Wallace's career. And as collateral damage? The career of her father, the renowned and respected FBI forensic expert, SA James William Wallace.

Dammit, I warned her.

As Rutgers read the words she'd composed just a week earlier, she wished that Heather Wallace had never met

Dante Prejean or that she had failed to save Prejean from the psycho hunting him.

But most of all, she wished Heather Wallace had listened.

Wallace had been one of the Bureau's best, her desire to serve the cause of justice undimmed and untarnished, despite six years of working in the criminal investigative division; despite six years of studying the bodies of the brutally murdered.

I want to be a voice for the dead, Wallace had stated on her admissions application. And for six years, she'd been exactly that—a voice for those who'd had their own stolen. For six years, she'd spoken for them: *That's the person who killed me.*

Then she'd thrown everything away for a goddamned vampire.

Rutgers took a sip of tea, savoring the hint of vanilla creaminess flavoring the dark tea. *Time to quit stalling.*

As she punched the intercom, she realized it wasn't tension knotting the muscles in her chest; it was sorrow. The lovely, intelligent, dedicated agent she'd known as Heather Wallace was dead. Had died the moment she'd first set eyes on Dante Prejean.

Rutgers knew in that moment that she'd ignore Beckett's orders. That she'd never give up her quest to see beautiful, soul-stealing Dante Prejean dead.

"Ma'am?" Ellis asked.

"Send out the release. Everywhere—the usual drill. Then get me James Wallace at the West Coast lab on the line."

"Yes, ma'am."

Rutgers owed it to Wallace to let him know what was coming down the pike, courtesy of his daughter. And let him know who to call if Heather should happen to contact him.

Rutgers's gaze locked on the press release headline: TRAGIC MENTAL ILLNESS CLAIMS FBI STAR PROFILER.

8

IN THE SECOND BED

THE BULLET SLAMMED INTO the Morningstar's chest, the silence he'd woven around himself swallowing the gun's retort. He staggered back a step. Pain, hot and pulsing, spiked out from the wound beneath his collarbone.

The dark-haired woman crumpled to the floor, her fall silent, but the Morningstar felt the thudding vibration through the soles of his sandals. Her hair fanned over her face.

The other female, the lovely redhead who'd held the *creawdwr* in her arms on the hill as she'd drugged him, slumped over onto the bed, her pistol tumbling onto the blankets just beyond the reach of her fingers.

Blood trickled along the Morningstar's skin down to his belly. His body ejected the bullet fragments as the wound healed. The pain faded. His illusion no longer needed, he unthreaded it, then turned and closed the door.

Sound rushed in like water through a broken dam. Gulls cried outside. A toilet flushed in another room, water gurgling through the pipes. And in this room he heard the music of breathing and intertwined heart rhythms—the slow and steady drumbeats of vampire hearts and the mortals' dancing patter.

Mingled odors layered the air—lilac and wet clothes, wild mint and adrenaline, burning leaves and motor oil. But a faint, sour-milk odor lurked underneath—mildew, mortal taint.

The Morningstar swiveled around and scanned the room. In the first bed, the redhead and the female mortal with the blue/purple/black twilight-shaded hair, in the second bed . . .

The Morningstar stepped over the dark-haired woman's body, pausing long enough to kick her gun out of reach, then walked over to the second bed. Two figures slept, blankets covering their heads. He bent, grasped the comforter's edge, and pulled it down.

The Morningstar's breath caught in his throat.

Dante's beauty gleamed in the gloom like moonlight on a winter-iced lake.

Pale, pale skin. Thick, black lashes almost hiding the blue shadows smudged beneath his eyes. Luscious lips. Hair as black as a starless night. Five silver hoops rimmed each ear, glinting in the darkness as though fire-burnished. But blood trickled from Dante's nose and from one ear.

The severed bond *had* injured Dante.

The Morningstar stared, pulse pounding. The *creawdwr's* scent—crisp autumn leaves and frost, the smell of his blood—

A *mixed-blood* Maker. True Blood—*Fola Fior*—and Elohim.

The Morningstar's thoughts scattered at the impossibility.

"Freeze, motherfucker!"

The Morningstar blinked. Speaking of impossibilities . . . He lifted his head. The woman with the multicolored hair knelt on the bed in a T-shirt and flannel pants beside the unconscious redhead, gun clasped in both white-knuckled hands.

"Whatever you did to my sister and what's-her-name, fix it. Now!"

"You shouldn't be awake," the Morningstar said, tilting his head. Even if she'd been asleep when he'd uttered his command, the spell should've bound her and kept her still.

"Fix it," she repeated, voice strained. "Now!"

The Morningstar straightened, weaving another illusion around him. He drew in breath to craft another Word, but something hard *thwip*ped into his arm, near the shoulder. Pain burned along his nerves down to his fingers.

He glanced at the blood-oozing wound. He'd been shot. Again. He blew air out his nostrils, irritated. Simple reflex on the mortal's part? Or did she still see him? He shifted his gaze to the woman.

"Freeze means don't move, asshole," she said. The gun shook in her hands.

The Morningstar's wings snapped out behind him like a sail catching the wind, the tips nearly scraping the walls and ceiling of the small room.

"Fuck," the mortal whispered.

Ah. She *could* still see him. Blind to his illusions and deaf to his Word. Interesting. Who *was* this pretty little mortal with the twilight-colored hair?

Before the woman had time to blink, the Morningstar folded his wings behind him and vaulted the bed, landing in front of her. He wrenched the gun from her hands. She gasped in pain. He tossed the gun across the room and it hit the wall with a dull *thud.* Seizing her by the biceps, he yanked her off the bed.

The Morningstar allowed his illusion—useless, apparently, where she was concerned—to scatter like a pile of windblown leaves. The woman kicked and twisted and squirmed, and he found himself holding her at arm's length as if she were a hooded and spitting cobra.

She barbed the air with a string of prickly and creative invective. He tried to picture some of the combinations she suggested—*cocksucking motherfucker,* for one—and felt his imagination couldn't do her verbal creativity justice.

"Behave," he said, barely resisting the urge to shake her until her brain pulped inside her skull. "Or I'll never allow the others to awaken."

"Motherfucker," the woman spat, but she quit fighting. Her muscles quivered underneath his fingers, taut and ready to go again. Musky adrenaline and rancid fear seeped from her skin, mingling with the sweet scent of coconut in her hair.

The Morningstar lowered her to the floor, but kept his fingers locked around her arms. "I admire your devotion to the Maker," he said.

The woman's brow furrowed. "The Maker? What the hell's— Oh. You mean Gorgeous-But-Deadly, am I right? Dante?" She met his gaze, her sky blue eyes almost eclipsed by their pupils. "Take him," she whispered. "Just take him and go."

9

BENEATH ANCIENT SKIES

RENATA ALESSA CORTINI STEERED her Vespa along the narrow cobblestone streets, weaving almost without thought around pedestrians, tour buses festooned in bright colors and carnival lights, cars, scooter clusters, and compact delivery vans. Her black D&G sunglasses protected her eyes from headlight glare.

Giovanni's hands rested on her hips, a light touch, and warm. He still hadn't said anything. She wondered if he thought she was joking. In his place, she would've thought so, might've laughed, might've told him to stop wasting her time.

Might've asked for more stories and dreams and fancies.

He told such wonderful tales.

She did not.

In her heart of hearts, Renata loved fairy tales and mist-woven myths, had from the first night she'd curled warm and blood-fed in her blacksmith *père de sang*'s thick-muscled arms as he told her stories of magical True Bloods—the *Fola Fíor*—and of the mysterious Elohim.

Stories she'd passed on to her little Caterina as bedtime tales.

Ah, but now her little love, her strong and practical daughter, her graceful death-dealing ballerina, had returned the favor and gifted Renata with words magic-dusted and glimmering with endless possibilities, words wrapped in sharp, crisp truth.

The Bloodline still holds, Mama, and a myth from the ancient past now walks the world. I've seen him.

Fallen and True Blood, cara mia? How is it we never knew of his existence?

Because monsters seized him the moment he was born and hid him among even more twisted monsters who fed upon his beauty and tried to shatter his spirit.

And did the monsters succeed?

No, I think they failed. I was given to him as a meal. He could've drained me, let me die. He didn't—even though he was still hungry, still burning, still needing. He asked my name instead and left me to return to you. But he's hurt, Mama, and damaged. And he's being hunted.

Let me tend to that, cara mia. You tend to the things you do so well, mia ballerina scura. Serve Dante Baptiste heart and soul. Guide him true. Win his trust.

Renata glided the scooter between two white delivery vans with only inches to spare on either side. Their drivers, berating one another as incompetent, unworthy to even spit-shine the other's boots, paused in their mutual insultathon long enough to give Renata an appreciative once-over.

"*Ritorna, bella*," one of them called after her. "*Una bella donna merita un uomo, non un ragazzo.*"

"*Ciò è allineare!*" Giovanni shouted. "*Sapere di c'è ne?*"

Renata laughed. "You put yourself down too with that one."

"Worth it."

"Perhaps you *are* just a boy, and a silly boy at that."

"I haven't been a boy in centuries." Giovanni's fingers tightened on her hips.

"Perhaps."

<*Is Caterina certain?*> Giovanni sent.

<*Of the True Blood?* Assolutamente.>

Tourists in straw hats, fingering the cameras dangling around their necks like rosary beads, stared at her, shaded faces startled, whenever she buzzed past with a polite tap of her horn. Romans never even looked up, stepping aside instinctively.

The warm evening air fluttered her hair, chiming through her silver and amber earrings, and lacing the delicious smells of herbed fish, roasted tomatoes, and garlic through her curls.

<*I have difficulty believing this young True Blood is also a Maker.*>

<*Forse sì, forse no. But he* was *fathered by one of the Fallen. The things Caterina saw him do . . .*> Renata lifted her shoulder in a half shrug. <*I know of no other explanation. No other way that this child could turn one, let alone dozens, of the Fallen to stone.*>

Silence. Giovanni's finger tapped lightly against Renata's hip as he mulled over this latest bit of information. Careful, her *fils de sang*, each thought viewed from all sides and angles like a jeweler peering at an unpolished gem. She tamped down her impatience and let him think.

As she zipped her scooter into the tourist-thronged Piazza di Spagna, she eased off the throttle and guided it into a parking lot on the east end of the *piazza*. Parking between two smart cars, she switched off the engine.

"She *is* mortal, our Caterina," Giovanni said, his lips close to her ear, his breath warm. "Perhaps she was tricked, an illusion woven into her mind." His hands slid away from her hips. "If the boy really is True Blood, he might be capable of such a thing."

"Might be, *sì*, but why would he bother?" Renata stepped off her scooter, smoothing the gauzy violet bohemian-style smock she wore belted at the waist over her black leggings. Her gaze fixed on Giovanni. "He'd been drugged and tortured for hours by deluded mortals hoping to use him." Fury burned through her, hot and deadly, a summer sun at high noon. "He was exhausted."

"And you know what it takes to exhaust a True Blood, *sì*?"

Renata stretched her five-two frame erect and lifted her chin. "Perhaps I do."

Still lounging on her scooter, Giovanni regarded her with light-filled hazel eyes. His short, tousled, burgundy-dyed locks highlighted his handsome face with its long Roman nose. His lips curved into a wicked smile.

"Perhaps you do at that, *bella*."

Renata waved an elegant dismissal with one pale hand. "Sexy smiles and rote flattery, Vanni *mio*? How disappointing."

Giovanni swung off the scooter and stood in front of her. Tall, at least compared to her, just a shade under six feet. His jeans and midnight blue sweater fit him well, revealing a trim, athletic build.

Taking her hand, Giovanni raised it to his lips. *"Bella,"*

he murmured, his lips warm against her skin. He smelled of the sea, this eldest son, of brine and sand and deep, restless waters. He looked at her from beneath his dark lashes.

"Have I disappointed you?" he whispered, his lips caressing her captive hand.

"Many times," Renata said, her voice tender. She tugged her hand free. "But I love you still, *mio figlio*. That never changes."

But as for her trust, that was another matter entirely.

Giovanni glanced away, his gaze skimming over the crowds perched on the Spanish Steps and ringing the low, boat-shaped fountain in the *piazza*'s heart. Golden light gleamed on the Trinità dei Monti and its twin bell towers, glittered like jewels—ruby, sapphire, and emerald—upon the water in the gurgling fountain.

The sweet smell of azaleas and sugar pastries perfumed the night.

Soon, very soon, they would hunt and dine.

Giovanni slid his hands into his pockets. "When are you telling the Cercle?"

"Not yet," Renata said. "I'd like to keep this matter just between us and Caterina. Keep it in the family. For now."

A smile flickered across Giovanni's lips. "Ah, *sì*. You want to make sure that Caterina hasn't been deceived. So you admit the possibility."

"I admit no such thing."

"Say Caterina is right, that this Dante Baptiste is not only a True Blood—"

"Fathered by an Elohim high-blood," Renata tossed in.

"*Sì*—so not only a True Blood, but a Maker as well. Say that is all true." Giovanni's gaze came back to Renata, his eyes brimming with reflected color—gold from the church and ruby and emerald from the water, purple and deepest blue from the lingering twilight. "Whose hands do you most want to keep this True Blood out of? The Cercle de Druide? The Parliament of Ancients? Or Le Conseil du Sang?"

Renata felt a smile curve her lips. She always benefited by allowing Giovanni room and time to think. "Perhaps all three," she said.

"I have a feeling the Fallen might be a bigger concern," Giovanni said. "They will try to claim him."

"They tried once already and failed. Dante Baptiste seems quite content to turn the *aingeals* to stone," Renata said. "Perhaps his actions—if true—will buy us time. Dante belongs to *us*. He was born vampire."

"*Sì, mia signora*," Giovanni murmured. "Born vampire *and* born Fallen. We shall have a fight on our hands. A holy war."

"Are we ready to wage one?"

"With the Fallen? No. Not as divided as we are. The Cercle can call upon the mortal nomad clans and they would join our fight, *cara mia*, but we vampires . . ." He shrugged. "Both the Parliament and the Conseil will scheme to get ahold of Baptiste."

Renata agreed. Each vampire faction would slaughter the others for the opportunity to use and manipulate a True Blood, let alone what the youth truly was.

A *creawdwr*. Powerful and precious. Ready to be molded by whoever claimed him first—vampire or Fallen. And it would be vampire if Renata had her way.

"We shall keep him safe and secret for the time being, *sì*, Vanni *mio*? This True Blood *principe* needs time to heal, to recover from all the evil done to him." The fire burning within her heart flared to life. "And those responsible shall be dealt with."

"Has anyone asked *him* what *he'd* like to do?"

Renata considered for a moment for effect, then said, "No, I don't think so. But he's too young to know what he wants. He's a child in need of guidance. We will help him decide what is best for him."

Giovanni shook his head, a smile on his lips. "Of course."

Renata looped her arm through his. He looked at her, his face bright beneath the *piazza*'s lights, warm with humor.

"Shall we dine, *mio ragazzo bello*?" she asked.

"*Sì*, my beautiful Renata, we shall."

Arms linked, Renata and her eldest, her thoughtful Giovanni, strolled into the *piazza* proper and, mingling with the tourists crowding the steps, selected their dinner.

When she returned to her white stone and evening-cooled apartment later that night, she would place a few very important calls.

And those who refused to obey would soon find someone at their door bearing a final message, one delivered by a hungry and ruthless stranger. A message that would include all within the household—innocent or otherwise, family, friends, or lovers.

A message that wouldn't allow survivors.

Your time has come to an end. Arrivederci.

10

DEMON SEED

THE FALLEN ANGEL—AT LEAST that's what Annie assumed he was—tilted his head. The fiery glow in his eyes vanished. She looked into eyes colored the deep blue of a summer afternoon, framed with pale silver lashes.

A smile ticked up one corner of his mouth, but it wasn't a smile that made her feel all warm and fuzzy inside, oh, hell no. It iced her heart.

"Appears I'm wrong about your devotion," he said.

"Why the hell does that matter?" she said, lifting her chin. "Just take him."

His gaze, no longer summer, but frost-edged winter afternoon, swept her from head to bare toes. "I wish I could."

The goddamned bastard's white-taloned fingers—*Oh,*

look! Talons. Awesome! — locked even tighter around Annie's arms, the talon tips pricking through her T-shirt to the skin beneath. Her tingling fingers went numb.

"Let go, dammit," she said through her teeth.

"How is it you see me? That my Word doesn't bind you?"

"Huh?"

"Did the *creawdwr* — Dante — alter you in some way?"

"Fuck, no!" Fear spiked through Annie. "Am I *not* supposed to see you?"

"No, you shouldn't see me. My spoken Word is more than enough to bind mortals, but you . . ." He regarded her for a long, uncomfortable moment.

Annie didn't like the way he looked at her. Not one bit. She suddenly felt like a jumbled-up Rubik's Cube being contemplated by a puzzle master. "The main thing is," she said, her words tumbling over each other in their haste to get out of her mouth, "you want Dante, right?"

The fallen angel glanced over his shoulder at the nightkind-only bed and hunger sharpened the planes of his face. "Yes."

Annie couldn't see Dante and Von's bed since the fallen angel's body blocked her view. Fucker was huge. Tight muscles and flat abs. Short white hair, but not old lady white, no. Sleek and gleaming like polished ivory, like fresh snow, like the first star at twilight. A thick, open-ended twist of silver curled around his throat. And his skin seemed almost luminous, as if light flowed through his veins instead of blood.

But she'd plugged the bastard with a bullet and he'd bled like anyone else, so that axed the whole light-in-the-veins bit. And now, only a few moments later, just a pink spot on his skin remained of the wound.

He was gorgeous, in a weird, not-quite-human-but-still-an-asshole kind of way.

"Dante's right there, sound asleep," Annie said, voice low. "All you hafta do is scoop him up and go. I'll even hold the door for you."

The fallen angel laughed and the sound of it sheeted Annie's soul with ice. She shivered, arms aching and throbbing beneath his hands.

"And lo, *aingeals* learned the seductive art of temptation from mankind." He returned his attention to Annie, a sardonic smile sliding onto his lips. "Why are you so eager to get rid of the person the other females were guarding?" His wings flared behind him, fanning a smell like smoky incense into the room.

White, those freaking wings, and smooth as cream frosting, not a single feather. Huh. So much for that, or maybe feathered wings were a *good angel* perk, who knew? The tips arched over his head and, before he folded them shut again, she caught an opalescent mother-of-pearl sheen—swirling blue, purple, glimmering white—on the undersides.

"Dante turned a bunch of your kind into flipping statues," Annie said. "Reason enough?"

"I watched as it happened," the fallen bastard murmured. "Impetuous fools."

"Wow. I've never seen anyone so heartbroken. My sympathies."

"You have no idea what I feel," the fallen angel said quietly. "You aren't even capable of imagining."

"How the hell would you know what I'm capable of, you dick?"

The fallen angel tilted his head and Annie got that Rubik's Cube sensation again. Sweat trickled between her breasts even though she felt ice-cold.

"Who *were* you defending with that gun if it wasn't the Maker?"

"My sister," Annie replied.

The fallen angel glanced past her. One silver brow arched. "Ah."

"I mean it's weird enough that Dante's a fucking vampire, y'know?" Annie blurted. "But now he's this Maker thing too. He's having these seizures and shit and it's too much. Heather, she's so into him . . ."

"Seizures?"

Annie nodded. "They've been doping him up with morphine. I guess his mind's been messed with—bad, y'know? Maybe you can help him with that. Take him home— wherever the hell *that* is—and heal him."

Annie's chest tightened. Heather would never forgive her if she ever found out. And, in all fairness, she owed Dante much more than to sell him out. She liked him, hell, she'd craved a tumble with him big-time. But that was before.

Now, Dante scared the shit out of her. Anyone who could do the things he'd done to Dr. Whacked-Out Wells and his kids, the Amazing Demented Twins—

They rise into the air, bathed in cool blue fire, a three-faced pillar of flesh. Arms and legs streamline into feathered tails. Eyes blink open in the triune creature's braided torso and back. Rotating mouths open in a chorus of song: Three-intoone . . .

If it wasn't for Dante, Heather wouldn't be on the run. If it wasn't for Dante, this whole mess never would've happened. Yeah, but if it wasn't for Dante, Heather would be dead and in the ground.

The fallen angel's hands slid away from Annie's arms and she rubbed her bruised and talon-pricked flesh.

Her sister's words whispered through her mind: *He sacrificed himself for you. He saved my life. Now he needs us.*

Annie felt sick. She closed her eyes. "You're not gonna hurt him, right? 'Cuz he's a cool guy, don't get me wrong, and I usually love bad and dangerous boys with a capital L and Dante's *soooo* fucking beautiful and bad. He sang to me in Cajun, y'know? Even kissed me, but he's *too* goddamned dangerous and I'm scared he'll hurt Hea—"

"Enough."

Annie opened her eyes as a finger topped by a thick white talon pressed against her lips, stopping her stream-of-consciousness flow of words. She looked into the angel's blue eyes.

"He is the *creawdwr*," he said. "I would never harm him. I only want to take him home to Gehenna, where he belongs."

Annie pushed away the fallen angel's silencing finger. "Great," she breathed. "And Dante'd be happier there too, right? In his true home?"

"Of course. He's spent too much time in Hell as it is."

Annie frowned. "Hell?"

The fallen bastard waved a taloned hand around the room. "Here."

"You mean the motel? Yeah, it pretty much sucks. But the sun was rising and we needed to get Dante and Von inside so they wouldn't burn and—"

The fallen angel sighed. "I meant the mortal world."

"What the fuck's wrong with the mortal world, asshole?"

"Aside from the fact that it's filled with mortals?"

"Fuck you."

The fallen bastard smiled, but his holier-than-thou expression made a liar of his lips. "What's your name?"

"Annie. What do I call you besides asshole?"

"Star shall suffice."

Annie rolled her eyes. "Star, huh? Think it might've been the ego that got you kicked outta heaven, dude?"

The fallen angel—Star—regarded her with icy disdain. "Hardly—even if you choose to believe that particular fabrication." He crossed his arms over his bare chest. His knee-length cobalt blue kilt rippled like water whenever he moved, a braided black belt with a gleaming silver Celtic knot-work buckle holding it in place at his waist.

"You promise you won't hurt Dante?" Annie said. "Everyone's gonna be pissed as hell that he's gone and I'm gonna just pretend that I slept through everything like they did and—"

"I said I *wished* I could take him. I never said I *would* take him."

"Why the hell not?"

"Free will. Perhaps you've heard of it?" Star arched an eyebrow.

"You fucking kidding me?"

"Not when it comes to free will," Star replied. "I need to win Dante's confidence, his friendship, so I can bond with him. Then I'll return home, the *creawdwr* at my side. If I take Dante with me now, he might turn every living thing in Gehenna to stone. Or side with my enemies. No, given the seizures you mentioned, I need to bond with him and soon."

Star's face blazed and Annie squinted, wishing for sunglasses. "What if you don't become BFFs? What if he hates you on sight?"

"BFFs?"

Annie sighed. "Best friends forever. What then?"

"Of course we'll become friends. He'll choose me to be his first *calon-cyfaill.*"

"Kaw-lawn what the fuck?"

"Best friends forever. Heartmate and bondmate."

"But what if he doesn't?"

"I have you, Annie," Star said, another smile gracing his lips. But this one was warm and ripe with lusty possibilities.

"Me?" Annie shook her head, but stepped closer, surprising herself. *Great—his magic Word or whatever the fuck it is doesn't work on me, but sex does. Lovely. Just. Lovely.* She couldn't stop wondering if his lips tasted like Dante's, amaretto sweet and heady. "No. No way. Keep me outta this. I just wanna protect Heather."

"You'll be sowing the seeds that'll allow Dante to open himself to me." A seductive whisper, Star's voice reeled her in.

Annie kept shaking her head. "No. No. No."

The fallen angel chuckled and the sound of it, musical and fluid and warm, poured through her mind and down her spine like heated oil. "But you're already in it, Annie."

He tipped her chin up with a talon, the point pressing delicately into her skin. "You need to do this for your sister. The *creawdwr's* beauty has bound her heart. You can free her, keep her safe. Plant the seeds, little mortal. Make Dante yearn for the Elohim. For his place among us. Then I will take over and make him yearn for me."

Annie chewed her lower lip. "Okay," she whispered.

"Close your eyes," Star said. His fingers settled on her temples. Hot hands. Dizziness whirled through Annie. "I'm going to find out how you resist my spells and I'm going to learn who your companions are and then I'm going to make you forget all of this so Dante doesn't pluck it out of your pretty little mind. But the seeds—those will remain—in your subconscious, your dreaming mind."

Annie closed her eyes, her heart kicking hard against her ribs. Splinters of ice shivved her mind and she gasped. Then everything disappeared in a blaze of molten heat and honeyed light as Star's lips pressed against hers and his hands began to peel off her clothes.

11

A NIGHTMARE BEYOND IMAGINING

EMMETT STEPPED PAST THE headless body on the dirt-streaked bed, his gaze drawn to the photos thumbtacked to the walls. The same photo over and over. Dozens, maybe a hundred. Pictures of Dante Prejean in night-vision green/gray. Emmett studied the image, the vampire's rapt face, his closed eyes, the rays of pale light whipping around him. *From* him.

Emmett's skin prickled. What the hell was *that*?

What the hell. His new catchphrase, used ad nauseam throughout the day. A catchphrase he heard repeated every few minutes by the jumpsuited techs prowling the compound grounds.

Emmett caught another rank whiff of decaying flesh, of mud and clotted blood, and his stomach rolled. Pulling out a stick of Vicks VapoRub from his pocket, he smeared more underneath his nose. The sharp scent of menthol burned through the stench—for now. No matter how many bodies he'd dealt with throughout his years in the SB, the smell always got to him. Sometimes it lingered in his nostrils for days, effectively murdering his appetite until the stench no longer haunted him.

"Where's the head?"

Emmett turned around to face Gillespie. The chief stood beside the bed, his gaze on the headless body dolled up in a blue, dirt-streaked nightie. A small black beetle scuttled from beneath the nightgown's neck.

"Damned good question," Emmett replied.

Gillespie's jaw moved as he chewed a wad of gum. He studied the dirt clods leading to the mud-streaked bed and the headless body that rested on it. "Looks like she was in the ground first. Someone dug her up."

Emmett took in the body's withered arms, the wasted flesh, the bony fingers half-curled into claws. "Doesn't look like any of our perps."

"I heard that Lyons's mother had cancer," Gillespie said.

Emmett nodded. "Could be her body, yeah. But I get a feeling it wasn't the cancer that killed her."

Gillespie sighed, scrubbing a hand back and forth over his scalp. "I get the same feeling." His hand dropped to his side, balled into a fist.

The chief looked tired, his eyes bloodshot behind his glasses. He chewed his gum with grim determination. Emmett wondered how much booze Gillespie had downed before being ordered to Damascus. Not enough, judging by the chief's weary expression.

"Looks like a high tide of madness rolled in over this place," Gillespie said.

"More like a goddamned tsunami of crazy, Chief. A tsunami of monumental proportion."

Gillespie's gaze skipped past Emmett to the Dante Prejean pinup-fest on the wall behind him. He nodded. "Yeah, you can say that again." He waited a beat before adding, "Where's your partner?"

"Outside," Emmett said with a nod toward the door. He knew Merri was watching the crew load up the stone-trapped Fallen for transport—to Alexandria, most likely. The Virginia facility was the SB's largest and best, equipped with state-of-the-art labs and detention facilities.

Gillespie's attention shifted back to Emmett, his gaze sharp. *Might be tired, might even be a bit soused, but looks like his mind's working fine.* "Do either of you have any theories about what happened here?"

"Nope. Wish I did."

"Any thoughts about the statues?"

"The level of craftsmanship is amazing," Emmett said. "But I haven't a clue on where they came from or who played Stonehenge with them."

"What does Goodnight think?"

Emmett trailed a hand through his hair and ordered his thoughts. Kept his voice thoughtful. "She thinks the statues are supposed to represent fallen angels. Something about the wings. But other than that . . ." He shrugged.

Merri's words, spoken while standing in front of the white stone angel kneeling among the pines, sounded loud and clear in Emmett's mind.

Let's keep this just between us for right now. I'd like to talk to my mère de sang first, get her advice. This is huge, Em.

I know it's huge, but why keep it a secret from HQ?

Uncertainty flickers in Merri's eyes, her expression shadowed beneath the brim of her straw hat. She shakes her head, her words low, almost whispered: I don't know. I just feel it in my gut.

And that's all Emmett needs to know. He nods. Good enough.

Gillespie looked at Emmett for a long moment, his jaw working his gum fast and furious, then he said, "Walk with me. I've got an assignment for you and Goodnight."

"Sure, Chief."

Emmett followed Gillespie from the bedroom, through the cottage, and out into the gray morning drizzle. Gillespie paused on the front step, just underneath the roof overhang. Rain misted the air, fragrant with pine, and Emmett sucked in deep draughts, trying to clear the stench of death from his nostrils and the back of his throat.

A couple of techs walked the cave's perimeter, tapping in data on their handhelds. A semi with a WE MOVE U! slogan painted on the trailer was parked ass end toward the angelic Stonehenge, its doors wide open, a ramp extended from its interior like a metallic tongue.

A forklift loaded one of the stone angels into the trailer. Two yellow-jumpsuited men wrestled it into place inside the trailer.

Merri stood beside the ramp, her back to the cottage, her weight slung on one hip. Rain dripped from the brim of her hat, darkening the shoulders of her suede coat. She looked even smaller beside the semitrailer and the circle of stone angels, like a child. Smoke curled up into the air from the cigarette held between her fingers.

As though sensing his presence, Merri swiveled around in a graceful little twist of motion, her gleaming gaze catching his. Emmett tilted his head—*C'mere.*

Merri nodded, took one last drag from her cigarette, then flicked it onto the wet grass. Breathing pale smoke into the air from between her lips, she strode across the ruined lawn to the cottage.

"Chief," she murmured as she joined them. "What's up?"

"The two of you will be escorting Sheridan to Alexandria for debriefing," Gillespie said. "A plane's waiting at Portland International. The sooner you get going, the better. Things are starting to heat up around here. Reporters. Nosy neighbors."

Emmett studied the camouflage netting strung over the entire site. "What about Sheridan's injury?"

"A medic will be flying with you," Gillespie said.

"The statues going to Alexandria too?" Merri asked.

Gillespie nodded. "Why the interest?"

"Plain ol' curiosity, Chief," Merri offered with a half shrug. "Never seen anything like them before."

Gillespie grunted, crossing his arms over his chest, Gore-Tex jacket rustling.

From the cave mouth a now-familiar song swirled into the air: *Holy, holy, holy.* A chill breathed against Emmett's neck. The techs circling the cave's mouth stopped, their bodies still and straight as they listened.

"What the hell *is* that, anyway?" Gillespie asked, voice tight.

Merri hugged herself as if cold. "Whatever it is, my advice is to leave it alone."

Gillespie looked at her. "Leaving it alone isn't one of my options, unfortunately. So if you know anything I don't, I want to hear it."

Merri's arms dropped to her sides. Leather creaked as her gloved hands curled into fists, then relaxed. "I saw something move down there," she said quietly. Her gaze slipped over to the cave's ragged rim. "It . . . humped along like a slug or something. But large, y'know?" She looked at Gillespie. "It was just a glimpse."

"Duly noted," Gillespie said. He didn't look any happier now that he had additional info. He nodded toward the driveway. "Get going before more civilians stumble across the scene and Sheridan."

"We're on our way." Emmett glanced at Merri. "Ready, partner?"

"To get out of the rain and into a comfy jet with a wounded and whacked-out fed?" she murmured. "Bring it on, baby."

"Roger that," Emmett said, bumping his bare knuckles against Merri's gloved fist. A weary, buzzed-on-goddamned-stay-awake-pills smile brushed her lips.

He stepped out into the rain, Merri beside him, somehow managing—as always—to keep up with his long-legged stride. Cold rain trickled down the back of his neck as his windbreaker decided to prove it wasn't waterproof.

"Hey, let me have one of those clove cigarettes of yours," he said.

Merri snorted. "Man, it's gonna take more than that if you're hoping to go all hip and cool," she drawled. But understanding softened her expression and she handed him a slim, brown cigarette.

After it was lit, Emmett drew in a deep breath of spiced smoke. But beneath the smoky taste of cloves, tobacco, and caramel, he still smelled the greasy stink of death.

Even though he was glad to be getting out of the wet and the weird, his internal alarm system was still on a hair trigger, just a mispunched number away from an earsplitting siren wail.

Gut feeling: They weren't escaping. Not in time, anyway.

The weird's coming with us, and a nightmare beyond imagining is riding hard on its twisted heels.

* * *

GILLESPIE WATCHED THIBODAUX AND Goodnight walk down the driveway until they disappeared from view. He pulled his nearly empty jar of Vicks from his jacket pocket and smeared a dab beneath his nose. The pungent scents of camphor and menthol iced his nostrils. But his mind wasn't fooled.

Whenever he caught a whiff of Vicks, his thoughts automatically flipped to images of bloated bodies, mummified bodies, bodies in every stage of decay. He'd never allowed Lynda to use Vicks at home; if the kids were sick, she could use anything else as long as it didn't contain menthol.

Dropping the jar back into his pocket, Gillespie turned around and strode into the cottage. Clumps of dried and flaking mud led across the living room carpet and down the hall like a trail of bread crumbs in some dark fairy-tale forest.

Gillespie's gaze settled on the coffee table in front of the green vine-patterned sofa. A tray holding a bottle of alcohol, cotton balls, and sealed syringes cluttered its surface along with a spiral-bound notebook, two Bic pens, an empty glass, and a CD or DVD glinting beneath the overhead light like a sunstruck rock in a river.

Stepping to the table, Gillespie bent and picked up the disk. A red stripe banded its outer and inner edges; black letters edged the red stripes. His heart kicked hard against his chest as he read the disk.

MED UNIT 1 SECURITY CAM BUSH CTR

Gillespie's thoughts flickered back to a conversation a few weeks ago with Prues, an East Coast section chief:

Word on the grapevine is that Bureau ADIC Johanna Moore vanished from the center along with security-cam footage. Word is the powers that be are pissed as hell. They want both back and I wouldn't want to be Moore when they find her.

Gillespie unzipped his jacket to mid-chest, then slid the disk into an inner pocket close to his hammering heart.

On the other hand, I wouldn't mind being the one to stumble across her, know what I mean?

Gillespie rezipped his jacket. He'd known exactly what Prues had meant—finding Moore or the disk would be career gold, a way to heave Underwood off his back, a way to ease fingers between his throat and the stranglehold of the past so he could finally breathe without guilt.

Still blaming yourself? After all these years?

And maybe it wouldn't make a difference; nothing would change and Lynda wouldn't come back. But he'd be a fool—well, okay, a *bigger* fool—if he didn't try.

Someone walked into the cottage, jumpsuit crinkling with each step. "Chief, what's the scenario?"

Gillespie swiveled around, pulse racing.

FA Kaplan, wheat-blonde hair pulled away from her face into a ponytail, waited. Rain beaded her jumpsuit. Nothing in her expression or her gray eyes suggested she'd stood at the open door watching as he'd pilfered the disk; nothing suggested she'd just scooped up a lovely pile of dirt against her SC to store for a rainy day.

Relief cascaded through Gillespie.

"We're staging this as a natural disaster," he said. "Sinkhole, noxious and lethal underground fumes, tragic loss of life, including an FBI agent and his family."

Kaplan nodded. "How long will the fumes scenario be played?"

"Let's plan on a few days. Detained any looky-loos?"

Kaplan nodded again. "A curious civilian from up the highway, a local reporter checking up on calls about lights in the sky just before dawn."

"Lights in the sky?" Gillespie asked. "Like UFOs?"

"More like the aurora borealis," Kaplan said.

"Okay, that works—we can use it. We'll say that the lights were a result of noxious fumes as the sinkhole opened up—the initial release. Maybe an interaction with the rain or something. Have the science brains whip something up."

"Will do, Chief." Kaplan's gaze skipped past him and around the room. "Clean up everything in here?"

Gillespie pulled another stick of Juicy Fruit from his pocket, the foil crinkling as he unwrapped it. "Everything that contradicts the scenario."

As if to underscore his words, two techs rustled down the hall, carrying the headless body between them in a black body bag marked with a bright red biohazard symbol.

Kaplan's face tightened and her gaze shifted to the techs and the body bag they carried through the room and outside, a fetid odor trailing in their wake.

"Like that," Gillespie said dryly, then stuffed the stick of gum in his mouth to join the old wad. He shoved the balled-up piece of foil into his pocket. "Everyone you detain here will have to go through a medical exam—tell them it's necessary to make sure they haven't been exposed, work hard on the fear factor."

"Got it. Make them feel like they're lucky we detained them. Do we also hold them for observation?"

"Yeah, twenty-four hours sounds good. Keep them on edge by checking their vitals every hour. Oh, and put them in scrubs. Contaminated clothing, our apologies, it's for your own good, yada yada, the usual."

"When do we break the news to the media?" Kaplan asked.

"As soon as the truck is loaded and out of here," Gillespie said. "Keep the perimeter guard strong. If anyone actually sneaks onto the scene, they'll have to become another casualty of this tragic, but natural, disaster."

Kaplan blinked, sucked in a breath. "A . . . casualty, Chief?"

"Absolutely. To keep others from sneaking onto the site," Gillespie said. "It's one thing for a person to risk possibility of arrest for sneaking into a quarantined site, another thing altogether to risk the possibility of death."

Chewing her lower lip, Kaplan looked away.

Gillespie waited for her to reconcile her duty with her conscience. He wished the process was as easy as syncing an iPod with iTunes. Wished it wasn't necessary. "Keep the perimeter strong and it won't even be an issue," he said quietly.

Kaplan's attention returned to him and her gray-eyed gaze was steady. Grim, but steady. "Understood, sir." Turning around, she walked out of the cottage.

Gillespie smoothed a hand over his head, his buzz-cut hair soft beneath his palm. What if the techs and science brains couldn't figure out what had happened at the compound in between one satellite scan and the next?

House. No house.

And the reported lights in the sky? Was that even connected?

What if they never found Prejean, Wallace, or Lyons? What if they just faded away into law-enforcement myth like D. B. Cooper and all his money, and the mystery of the cave and the statues was never solved?

He could live with Wallace and Lyons wriggling away from justice. He wouldn't like it, but he could live with it. But Prejean? That was another matter.

The memory of Rodriguez dead on the floor of his blood-spattered office while the coffee cooled in his GROUCH mug prickled, a burr stuck in what remained of Gillespie's conscience.

This mystery *would* be solved, his perps—mortal and

vampire—found, and the dead avenged. But to do that, he needed more information about his perps than he'd been given. What was Underwood hiding?

He patted his jacket, imagining the disk tucked inside. Just might be the pry bar he needed to leverage enough truth from the Special Ops director to do his job.

Wishing for a frosty-cold Pacifico, a lime slice wedged into the neck of the bottle, Gillespie strolled out of the cottage and into the chilly March rain.

12

FOREVER AND EVER

"*Dante? Dante-angel? Wake up. Please wake up.*"
Chloe's voice pats against Dante's consciousness like the fingers against his face. Her words sound small and scared and hoarse, like she's been saying them over and over and over.

Papa Prejean's voice slithers through his memory: *Aw . . . ain't this sweet? Y'all wanting to protect each other from what y'all got coming.*

Dante's eyes fly open. Chloe's tearstained face meets his gaze. "Dante-angel," she hiccups, wiping away her tears with the heels of her hands.

"What's wrong, princess? You okay?" Dante's words feel fuzzy, his voice too thick. He doesn't feel like he's waking up at twilight, alert and hungry; he feels more like he does at dawn, when the need to sleep rushes over him like black water and he can't keep his eyes open no matter what.

Beyond Chloe, he sees a white ceiling instead of the shadows lurking in Papa Prejean's basement. And he doesn't feel the bite of metal around his wrists, doesn't smell dank stone or moldering cardboard boxes or the musky sweat of the pervs who visit him in the basement.

"Where are we?" Dante's eyes shutter closed again; he can't seem to keep them open. He knows something's wrong and he knows he and Chloe are in a strange place, but he's drifting like smoke. On the verge of dreams. "Did Papa take us someplace? Did that fucking asshole hurt you?"

"No," Chloe whispers. "Not Papa. The lady with the little dog. And she hurt you, Dante-angel, not me."

Chloe's words kick-start Dante's memory and a ton of images burn rubber through his mind. Running from Papa's house and darting across the rain-slick grass of the park; Jasper's leash-trailing dance, his little paws on the shoulder of Chloe's Winnie-the-Pooh shirt; the huffing rain bonnet lady in her rubber boots reaching into her pocket; the little wheel stinging his neck, cold icing him from the inside out, frosting his vision white.

Rain Bonnet's words snake through Dante's memory, loop diamond-sharp chains around his heart.

No escape for you, sweetie.

Dante sits up, eyes open, pulse racing. No handcuffs. No basement. No bed. Black specks pepper his vision and the room's white padded walls whirl around him. He tastes something familiar at the back of his throat—cool and dandelion-bitter.

A weird déjà vu feeling twists through him and his vision darkens. "Fuck," he whispers, closing his eyes again and drawing up his knees. Pain spikes his temples. He feels shaky, hungry in that new way he's been experiencing off and on the last *few months. Sweat springs up along his hairline. His gut knots.*

"You okay?" *Chloe strokes his hair back from his burning face, her cool fingers tucking a strand behind his ear.* "You want me to sing to you until you feel better?"

Dante nods. Swallows hard. He's never thrown up before, and isn't sure what nausea might feel like, but he figures this gut-churning, throat-burning, gonna-turn-inside-out feeling might be close enough.

Chloe sings one of his favorite songs by The Real Thing, "BTW," and Dante smiles as she jumbles the lyrics, changing "in my hair" to "anime bear." And as he focuses on her sweet and off-key voice, the weird, queasy feeling fades. He breathes in the mingled smells of strawberries and soap, grass and rain and wet sneakers, the sweetness disappearing beneath the sour tang of fear.

Dante opens his eyes and lifts his head. Offers Chloe a smile as he reaches out and pushes a long strand of red hair back from her face. "Merci beaucoup."

"You feel better?"

"Yeah, ça va bien. What happened? After I went down, I mean? Do you—?"

Dante stops speaking, his words dying in his throat. He stares past Chloe, his attention riveted on the steel hook bolted into the ceiling above the center of the room. The hook gleams in the light.

Ready for business.

Dante's heart kicks against his ribs. Ready for business? What the fuck? Where the hell did that come from?

He jumps to his feet and prowls the room in his battered and duct-taped Converse sneakers. He searches for a way out. Blind white walls surround them, no windows except for a small viewing window set high in the big, thick door.

A red light glows beside the door. LOCKEDLOCKED-LOCKEDLOCKED scrolls past on the LED screen.

Dante walks into the heart of the room, stopping beneath the hook. It stinks of old blood and musky adrenaline. A cold finger trails the length of his spine.

"What happened after I went down, princess?" Dante repeats, his gaze on the hook. "Do you know where we are?"

"After you fell into the grass, a man came up and joined the lady. He handcuffed you, then picked you up and carried you."

"What'd the man look like? Ever seen him before?"

"Nuh-uh. Never seen him before. He was tall and had short hair . . . and, um . . . he was wearing a trenchcoat. He kinda looked like one of the social services people Papa talks to. He wasn't mean-looking, but he didn't look nice either, especially when he picked you up."

"Yeah?" Dante questions softly. "So how'd he look when he picked me up?"

Fire flashes in Chloe's eyes. "Like he was picking up smelly garbage."

A smile tugs up one corner of Dante's mouth. "C'est bon, yeah? I'm glad I inconvenienced the fucker."

Chloe giggles, hand to her mouth. "Dante-angel!"

"So, what happened after that?"

"The lady grabbed my hand and we followed the man to the parking lot. Jasper came with us," Chloe said. "We got into a van and the lady put a hood over my head."

"You know how long we were in the van?"

"I'm not sure. Maybe an hour? We went through a bunch of stop-and-gos, then we drove faster and without any stops for a long time."

"Did they say anything during the drive?"

"No, not really. Just . . ." Her words trail away.

Dante looks at her. Fresh tears spill over Chloe's ginger-brown lashes. She wipes at them with the heels of her hands.

Dante's chest tightens. Spotting Orem abandoned on

the floor, he scoops up the plushie orca. He kneels in front of Chloe and hands her the plushie. "Look who's pining for you, chère. Did they hafta knock Orem out too?"

Chloe hugs the plushie against her chest. "Nope. He isn't real, Dante-angel."

"Don't tell Orem that."

Dante wraps his arms around Chloe, pulls her close and holds her tight. He wishes he could tell her everything is going to be okay, but that'd be a lie since he has no idea what will happen next.

"When they dumped you on the floor in here," Chloe says, voice breaking, "I thought you were dead. I thought maybe they'd killed you without even knowing it since that man really, really wished you were garbage he could just throw away."

"Shhh, ma 'tite-doux." Dante sits down on the concrete floor, crossing his legs under him, and settling Chloe in his lap. She leans her head against his shoulder and slips her arm around his neck. She snuggles close, sniffing and wiping at her nose with the back of her hand. He loops his arms around her.

"Is Papa punishing us for running away?" she asks, her voice muffled against his fading-to-gray Muse T-shirt.

"Nah, ain't Papa." Dante finger-combs the tangles from her hair, the clean scent of baby shampoo rising into the air with each pass of his fingers through her strawberry-red locks. "I think Papa'd chase us down himself and whip us with his belt until we were bloody, but I don't think he'd go to all the trouble of hiring someone else to do it for him. Besides, we were grabbed too soon for Papa to've called anyone even if he'd wanted to."

"Is this stranger danger, then? Like they taught about in school?"

"I ain't sure. What's stranger danger?"

Chloe tips up her face to look at him, her blue eyes solemn. "I forgot to tell you about it, huh? About the bad grownups who wanna steal kids or do bad things to them?"

"Someone stole us, so maybe it is stranger danger," Dante says.

"I'm scared, Dante-angel." Chloe's arm tightens around his neck. "But I'm glad I'm with you."

"Same here, Chloe-princess," he murmurs. "No one's gonna do bad things to you. I won't let 'em."

"Promise?" Chloe whispers.

"Promise. Cross my heart."

"'Kay."

Dante rubs Chloe's back. Her eyes close. Tears still glimmer in her brown lashes and her breathing's fast. Not asleep, but wishing for it.

He wants — needs — to protect Chloe from whatever's coming and he knows it's something bad, knows it heart-deep. The weird sense of déjà vu curls through him again. His thoughts whirl.

Have I been here before? *His pulse races, and a part of him whispers,* Oh, yeah.

Dante spots a camera tucked into the corner of the wall across from them, tiny green telltale lights glowing amongst all the white. He lifts a hand and flips off whoever's watching.

But the thing that scares him to the bone, scares him spit-dry, is the goddamned metal hook hanging in the center of the ceiling.

His gaze keeps returning to it like a fly to a sunlit window. And a sense of dread seeps in through his skin, soaking in down to his core, steeping in his mind like black and bitter tea.

Why is it here?

His arms lock even tighter around Chloe. His heart pounds hard, his body quivering with each sternum-kicking beat.

A tiny chirp draws his attention to the door. A green light reading OPEN scrolls across the little LED screen beside the door. A lock ka-chunks open. Dante moves, jumping to his feet and shoving Chloe behind him in one blurring moment.

"Stay back there," he whispers.

"'Kay."

The door pushes open and a woman walks into the room. A warm smile curves her lips and lights her almond-shaped blue eyes. Short blonde hair frames her pretty, pale face. Gold glints at her earlobes. Her scent curls through the room—cinnamon and cloves and freezer-frosted ice.

But she smells of something else too, something Dante can't name, something he's only smelled on his own skin— earthy and cool, like night-frosted ground.

This scent whispers: I'm like you.

The door slams shut behind her. The lock chirps, then red letters reading LOCKED scroll across the LED screen once more.

Pain snakes through Dante's mind and he lifts a hand to shade his eyes, the lights suddenly way too fucking bright. Déjà vu spirals through him again.

"Hello . . . Dante," the woman says, pausing as if she wants to call him by another name. She saunters to a stop beneath the hook. She wears a doctor's white coat over her deep blue skirt and pale rose blouse. "Do you remember me?"

Dante shakes his head. "Should I?"

Light sparkles in the woman's eyes like moonlight on restless water. And he has a feeling that even in the dark, her eyes would gleam like a cat's caught in a flashlight beam. Like his own. Uneasiness and curiosity twist through him.

"Probably best for you that you don't," she says. "Well, then. I'm Johanna."

At the back of Dante's mind, memory tickles. An image feather-floats behind his eyes: Johanna—her doctor's coat smeared and spattered with dark droplets of blood—bends over him, brushing his hair back from his face. Her eyes, bright and blue and hungry, hold his gaze. Her nostrils flare as though she smells something delicious.

My beautiful boy. It won't hurt as much if you'd just stop fighting.

Dante stares at Johanna, his heart thundering beneath his ribs.

"Ah," she says. "You do remember."

But the memory—more like a fleeting glimpse into a bad dream instead of something that actually happened, something he'd never forget if real—vanishes. Dante blinks. His head aches, pain a brass-knuckled fist pounding behind his left eye. He tries to think back to what was just going through his mind and finds nothing.

Something the woman—Johanna—said? Uneasiness prickles along his spine.

Johanna tilts her head to one side, trying to look behind Dante. "Hello, Chloe."

Chloe's breath catches, but she stays quiet, stays close to Dante, her fingers looped through his belt. Dante shifts so Johanna can't look at Chloe.

"Don't talk to her," he says. "Leave her outta this. Whattaya want?"

"Nothing. I'm here to help you," Johanna replies. "Papa Prejean thinks it's time Chloe starts earning her keep on a mattress down in the basement. Just like you do."

Dante moves.

Behind him, he hears Chloe's surprised gasp as he tears away from her tight-fingered grip on his belt, leaving her behind. He catches a glimpse of shocked blue eyes as he slams into Johanna, bulldozing her into the wall. Her head bounces against the padded wall. Fire rages in his veins, blazes in his heart.

"Tais-toi," he snarls. "Shut the fuck up! She doesn't need to hear that shit! She's just a kid!"

"So are you, Dante," Johanna whispers. "Just a kid." She cups a warm palm against his face. "My little night-bred beauty."

"Ain't a kid." Dante jerks away from her touch, her words echoing through his mind—my little night-bred beauty—but in another voice, a deeper male voice. A name memory-flickers—Dr. Wells—then vanishes. Dante holds her gaze, pain a jackhammer in his skull.

"Why ain't that fi' de garce Papa Prejean talking to me instead of you?"

Johanna straightens against the wall. She casually combs her fingers through her blonde hair and smoothes her white doctor's coat as though she gets slammed into walls every day.

"If you want to keep this between us, you need to come closer so I can whisper into your ear." She glances meaningfully behind Dante to Chloe.

Not wanting to look away from Johanna in case she has a pocketful of drugged little wheels too, Dante backs up to Chloe, a step at a time. "Hey, princess," he says, pausing beside her. Grasping her shoulders, he moves her in front of him so he can keep an eye on Johanna over Chloe's shoulder.

Chloe looks at him, her freckled face solemn. She clutches Orem tight against her chest. "Papa is punishing us."

Dante shakes his head. "I think she's fulla shit, chère. Forget everything she said, d'accord? And don't listen to nothing else she says either. I need you to keep Orem calm for me. He counts on you, y'know."

A smile whispers across Chloe's lips. "Orem's an orca, Dante-angel, he could eat anyone who comes into this room if he could just find the magic words."

"Maybe you can help him, princess," Dante says, voice

husky. "We could really use a people-eating orca right about now."

"'Kay." Her blue-eyed gaze searches his face. "I'm not just a kid, y'know."

Dante's chest constricts beneath her steady gaze. "I know. But this is stuff you shouldn't hafta know about yet, d'accord?" With a quick squeeze of her shoulders, he releases her and returns to Johanna's side of the room.

The woman's cinnamon and cloves and freezer ice scent intensifies and, like a shattered bottle of perfume, saturates the air. Each breath Dante takes draws a little more of her into his lungs, leaving him light-headed.

Dante stops beside her. "Talk."

Johanna sidesteps closer, bending to bring her lips close to his ear. "I'm offering you a chance to save Chloe from Papa's plans," Johanna whispers, her breath warm, her voice so low it's nearly inaudible. "Soon, you'll be drugged, bound, and hung from that hook so you can watch as men teach Chloe the ropes. Teach her all the things you've learned in Papa's basement."

Dante feels like his insides have just been scooped out. He feels hollow and cold. His hands knot into fists. "Who are you?" he whispers. "Why ain't you putting a stop to that fi' de garce if you know what he's doing?"

"Because this is a test."

Dante shoots her a sideways glance. "What kinda test?"

"A test for the sake of curiosity. A test just to see what you'll do. No one in this world cares about you, Dante. No one is looking for you or missing you. No one is going to save you. Ever. You can only save yourself."

"Bullshit. I'm gonna save Chloe even if it costs me everything."

"And if you don't?" Johanna smiles and Dante stares at the fangs her smile reveals. Fangs like his own.

"What are you?" he whispers again and, unspoken: What am I?

Johanna sidles closer and Dante gets another whiff of the earthy, cool undertone in her scent, the undertone he shares. "I'll keep the drugs, straitjacket, and chains away," she whispers. "All you have to do is defend Chloe from the men who will come for her. You do that, and you and Chloe can walk away."

"Yeah? Why should I believe you?"

"Because if you can do that, then there's nothing I can do to stop you from walking away with Chloe."

"Again, why should I believe you? People always lie. Most of 'em, anyway." Dante glances over his shoulder at Chloe. She sits against the wall, her knees up, Orem cradled in her arms, her attention on the plushie.

Johanna laughs, the sound low and throaty and pleased. "That's my boy." Her fingers curl around Dante's biceps. He feels the heat from her palm even through his T-shirt. He looks at her.

"The medicine that Mama Prejean gives you every day isn't enough anymore."

"The stuff that looks and tastes like blood, yeah?"

Johanna nods. "You've been restless at night. Hungry in ways you don't understand, drawn to the sounds of hearts and the blood pulsing just beneath the skin. You want, you need, to bite. To feed."

Dante's muscles tense and knot. He holds her knowing gaze. Refuses to acknowledge that she's right. Questions pile up in his mind. Questions he yearns to ask.

"S . . . Dante . . . I've seen what you've been doing with Jeanette at night, and with Mark, while everyone else is busy. Before you get handcuffed to your bed. I've seen how much you've enjoyed their blood, their hands and mouths."

Johanna reaches for his hair like she plans to curl her finger around a lock or maybe tuck it behind his ear, but Dante jerks his head out of reach.

A rueful expression flickers across her face. Her hand drops to her side. "I've seen how they've enjoyed you, too."

"How'd you see?"

Johanna touches a finger to her lips, then says, "My secret." She walks to the door, stopping in front of its little window and nods at someone on the other side. She returns her attention to Dante. "You're entering adolescence and I don't know what the process is like for someone like you. Should be fascinating to observe."

For someone like you.

Dante holds her gaze, but keeps his sky-high pile of questions close to his heart and unasked. "Yeah? Then observe this." He lifts a hand and flips her off. "Oh look, even more fascinating stuff to observe," he adds, extending the middle finger of his other hand.

An amused smile twitches across Johanna's peach-glossed lips. She pauses, her hand on the door's latch, a thoughtful expression on her pale face. "You won't save her, you know." She glances over her shoulder at Chloe. "You'll fail."

Her words, so casual and certain, ice Dante's heart. She might as well be saying, It's a full moon tonight. You won't save her, you know. The sky is clear. You'll fail.

He expects his breath to plume the air when he says, "I won't fail," but it doesn't. The room temperature hasn't changed. The cold and ice are inside of him. He meets her gaze. "I. Won't. Fail," he repeats.

Another amused smile curves Johanna's lips. Then the door clicks open and she slips through without another word. The door ka-chunks shut again. LOCKED scrolls in red across the LED screen.

Dante joins Chloe against the wall, sits down beside her, and wraps an arm around her shoulder. Hugs her close. He listens to the fast flutter of her heart, smells strawberries and soap and baby shampoo.

The need to protect her stokes the fire burning at his core. Inside, the ice melts, but one sliver pierces Dante to the heart. In trying to save Chloe from Papa's belt, he's managed to fuck things up instead and land her into even hotter water. He doesn't care what it takes, he'll do everything he can—fight, kill, die—to get her out again, and free.

"You and me, princess," Dante says. "Forever and ever."

"You okay, Dante-angel?"

"Oui, sorta. Orem found that magic word yet?"

"No, but we're trying."

"C'est bon, princess. Keep trying. I'll try too."

You'll fail.

Johanna's promise locks up Dante's heart in chains even colder and harder than Rain Bonnet's diamond-bright links: No escape for you, sweetie. He doesn't care if Rain Bonnet's words prove true as long as Johanna's prove false.

"Let's work on multiplication tables," Dante says. "You got any new ones to teach me?"

"Yup. The eights. We learned that one today," Chloe says, her fingers stroking Orem's plushie head over and over. "But first you need to practice what you've already learned, Dante-angel. Orem too."

"Sounds good to me and Orem both."

"What's six times two?"

"Twelve."

"Six times three?"

"Eighteen."

Just as Chloe reaches eight times eight, an electronic chirp sounds from the door. A green light reading OPEN scrolls across the little LED screen.

Dante's heart skips a beat. So soon? He stands, pulling Chloe up with him. He backs her into a corner. "Get down," *he whispers.* "I won't let them have you."

"'Kay." *Fear peppers her scent.*

As Chloe crouches, Orem clutched to her chest, Dante stands in front of her. The door swings open and Dante hisses. Three men in black suits—bad fucking men like Wells, like Papa Prejean, like all the groping assholes who walk down the basement steps—spread out in the white padded room.

Hunger/want/need burns through Dante and their pounding hearts draw him. Their sweaty, hopped-up smell dizzies him. All three rush him and Dante drops low, spinning, slashing with his nails. Blood spurts hot across his face. Someone gurgles. Someone else gets behind him. Dante moves. Punching, kicking, biting. Whirls.

The blood smell coils through him; he's lost to it. He drops to his knees and sinks his teeth into warm flesh. Blood pumps into his mouth, sweeter than licorice, headier than sneaked whiskey, and he can't get enough. He drinks until nothing's left.

On his knees, Dante looks around. All three badass men sprawl on the bloodied floor. He swivels, wiping his mouth and reaching for Chloe. But she's no longer in the corner. His hand freezes at his mouth.

Chloe lies on the concrete floor, snow-angeled in a pool of blood. So pale even her freckles look faded, rubbed-away. Blue eyes wide and as empty as a doll's. Her hair halos her head on the concrete in tendrils wet with blood from her slashed throat.

Orem rests on the concrete just beyond the reach of her fingers and Chloe's blood stains the plushie orca's white-furred patches maroon.

Dante looks down at his blood-sticky hands, his fingers. The blood caked beneath his sharp, sharp nails doesn't belong to the badass men alone. And the blood he sucked down, so hungry and fucking delirious? His heart thumps hard and fast; breaking. He can't finish the thought. The gut-churning, *throat-burning, gonna-turn-inside-out feeling knots him up again.*

Dante crawls to Chloe, her warm blood soaking in through the knees of his jeans and mingling with the blood already smeared on his hands.

Gathering her into his arms, Dante hugs Chloe tight against him, buries his face in her hair. But he only smells blood, rich and coppery. He's lost her strawberry and soap scent. He closes his burning eyes, struggles to breathe through a throat so tight it hurts.

Chloe, his princess, his little sister, his heart.

Forever and ever.

On his knees, Dante rocks back and forth, Chloe in his arms. He whispers nonsense words into her hair, seeking the right one, the magic one, that'll drum life and rhythm back into her silent heart or turn back time.

He's still rocking and whispering when they finally come for him.

13

NOTHING CONVENIENT

WASHINGTON, D.C.
March 25

"YOU'RE LATE," CELESTE UNDERWOOD said as her assistant slid into the seat across from her at her booth in Applebee's. "I hope you have a good excuse."

"Sorry, ma'am," SB Field Agent Richard Purcell said. Rain beaded the shoulders of his black trenchcoat and glistened in his honey-blond hair. "Traffic sucked." He set his sleek, black briefcase beside him on the orange vinyl seat.

"So does that excuse," Celeste said, dipping a chunk of grilled chicken into the small bowl of cayenne-spiced lime juice beside her plate.

Purcell met her gaze, sympathy in his eyes. "I heard the news," he said quietly. Almost too quietly, given the noise level in the restaurant—clattering plates, the high-decibel buzz of dozens of conversations accented with short bursts of laughter and children's shrieks—and the precise reason Celeste had chosen the restaurant for their discussion. No need for audio jammers. "My sympathies."

"The bitch got off. Self-defense. The jury actually bought her story." Celeste pushed her folded-up newspaper across the table to Purcell. He flipped it open and scanned the headline that had burned itself into her retinas:

VALERIE UNDERWOOD ACQUITTED IN MURDER-FOR-HIRE CASE; MOTHER OF TWO WEEPS AS VERDICT READ, THANKS JURY.

Celeste chewed her bite of lime-and-chili grilled chicken, but she didn't enjoy it. She swallowed hard, forcing the chicken down.

"Convenient that the man Valerie hired to kill your son hanged himself in his cell," Purcell said. "With shoelaces he wasn't even supposed to have."

Celeste laid her fork carefully on her plate. "Also handy that he left a note stating that he'd implicated Valerie in Stephen's murder as payback for rebuffing his advances. Painted her as the virtuous wife."

"Very handy," Purcell agreed. "And your custody suit?"

"Quashed. Null and void." She pushed her plate away, no longer hungry. She picked up her wineglass. "Valerie sent me an e-mail this morning saying I'd never see the girls again. Those girls are all I have left of Stephen. And she knows that."

"I'm truly sorry, ma'am. What can I do to help?"

A waitress stopped at the table and took Purcell's order for a grilled cheese sandwich and an iced tea with lemon.

Celeste took a sip of wine, a house zinfandel, good, but not too sweet. "You were there when Wells and Moore were programming Prejean. Fragmenting his memories."

"Yes, ma'am. For most of it, anyway."

"So you know how Prejean's programming works? How to activate it?"

A knowing light sparked in Purcell's eyes. "Yes, ma'am, I do. Once you have the little fucking psycho in hand, we can flip the switch and put him to work."

"And switch him off again? Permanently?"

"Yes, ma'am."

Celeste nodded, then took another sip of wine. "Good. I've never been fond of vampires." She doubted that her so-called daughter-in-law would find anything convenient or handy about Prejean when he showed up on her doorstep or climbed in through her window.

No, not at all.

14

WHITE SILENCE

THE SMELL OF BLOOD haunting his nostrils, and loss haunting his heart, Dante opened his eyes. Darkness, warm and close. Blankets, maybe a fucking hood. Voices, low and urgent. He had to move before they tried to wrestle him into a straitjacket and hang him from that gleaming hook.

Before they tried to take Chloe from him.

Dante rolled out from under the blankets and off the bed, tumbling across the carpet on one bare shoulder before jumping to his feet. Bare feet. Rough carpet, not blood-slick concrete.

"What the fuck?" A female voice. Not that *chienne* Johanna's, but familiar.

Light dazzled his vision. Hammered the spike piercing

his skull and left eye a notch deeper. His vision bisected, a mirror cracked in two, the halves no longer quite matching up.

Padded, blood-sprayed walls, the word OPEN scrolling in green across the door's security panel./A strange room, warm light spilling from a lamp on top of a bureau beside a vinyl easy chair, a wide-eyed chick with blue/black/purple hair staring at him, her hands clutching the chair's arms.

A chill touched Dante's spine. *Who's she?*

In both halves, he smelled blood, pungent and coppery—Chloe's blood.

Diamond-edged chains twisted tighter and tighter around Dante's heart. He shaded his eyes with one trembling hand as he backed up against a wall. His muscles coiled, ready to fight, to take every single one of the motherfuckers down.

They'd hafta kill him before he'd let them anywhere near his princess.

Wasps buzzed and vibrated beneath his skin. Stingered venom into his muscles and veins. Slicked poison along the sharp-edged wheel of his thoughts.

But Dante-angel, I'm already dead.

"They ain't taking you," Dante whispered back.

Promise?

Promise. Cross my heart.

Blood trickled hot from his nose. He tasted it, ripe red grapes and copper, at the back of his throat, on his lips.

The door swings open and three wary-eyed men in black suits step into the blood-spattered room, guns in hand. One carries a white straitjacket. /A guy—no, a nomad—wearing only blue boxers stepped around a bed and faced Dante, his hands raised palm out, a gentling motion. The crescent moon tattoo beneath the nomad's right eye glittered silver in the light like ice beneath a new moon.

Pain pulsed at Dante's temples. He had a feeling he should know what the tattoo meant, should also know the nightkind nomad wearing it inked into his skin.

"You can do this hard or easy, kid." / *"Hey, little brother."*

Dante's heart drummed hard and fast, thundered in his ears. His thoughts scattered in all directions like a hurled deck of cards, slippery with pain.

He struggled for balance in the fractured, tilting world he straddled as his reality flipped between blood-wet concrete and hushed carpet. Dizziness pirouetted the room around him. Wasps buzzed. He closed his eyes and touched a hand to the wall at his back. Steadied himself.

Focus, dammit. Send the pain below. Or they're gonna take her away and you'll never, ever, see her again.

And in that split second Dante no longer knew if he was thinking about Chloe or someone else, someone—

Dante heard a single footstep, a slow slide of bare foot over carpet or maybe—with all the noise in his head, it was hard to be sure—the sole of a shoe treading across blood-smeared concrete.

"You ain't taking her," Dante said.

"Looks like the kid's selected the hard option, gentlemen. Fire at will." / *"Dante, man, it's okay. You're in a motel and you're safe. Everyone's safe."*

Dante opened his eyes.

The douche bags in suits lift and aim their goddamned guns.

Dante *moved.*

He tackled the closest douche bag, rode him down to the floor. The fucker's breath exploded from his lungs in a startled *whoof* when they slammed onto the concrete, Dante on top. Someone screamed and the shrill sound, like long nails lacquered and sharp, scraped furrows through his mind. He sucked in a pained breath.

"Someone shut her the hell up," Douche Bag yelled, his voice strained through his clenched teeth. "It ain't helping!"

The screaming cut off abruptly. A door clicked open, then slammed shut.

Dante pounded Douche Bag's gun hand against the concrete until the gun finally tumbled from his fingers and skittered out of reach.

Dante dipped his head for the jugular pulsing in the taut-muscled neck beneath him. Douche Bag's fingers locked around Dante's biceps, bracing him up and away from his vulnerable throat. Dante's muscles quivered as he struggled against Douche Bag's white-knuckled hold.

Voices—some from within, some from without—crashed against Dante's mind like foaming storm-tossed waves against rugged cliffs.

She trusted you. Guess she got what she deserved.

"Little brother, look at me. Dammit, Dante, *look!*"

Little fucking psycho.

"Baptiste."

Her voice cupped his mind, cool and soothing and familiar, just like the hands now cupping his face. Dante looked up into blue eyes, the last glimmer of twilight as the first stars lit. White silence enveloped him. The voices hushed. The wasps stilled.

Her scent—desert sage sweetened with lilac, clean and fresh like evening rain—cut through the stench of blood.

Creamy skin, lovely heart-shaped face framed with red hair tumbling past her shoulders, lips soft as wild rose petals, a woman of heart and steel.

Heather.

She was kneeling on the floor beside him, her hands holding his face, her expression worried, a little scared. "Listen to me, Baptiste," she said. "You're in a motel with me, Von, Annie, and Caterina. We spent the day here while you and Von Slept. We're safe for the moment. What's the last thing you remember?"

Dante blinked.

Chloe lies on the concrete floor, snow-angeled in a pool of blood.

No escape for you, sweetie.

Something pricks the skin on Dante's throat. Cold threads into his veins, chills his blood. Heather's face lowers over his. "Can you hear me, Baptiste?"

Blue rays spiked into the fleeing Fallen, one by one. And turned them to stone.

Pain throbbed at Dante's temples, skewered his left eye with a red-hot ice pick. He squeezed his eyes shut. He felt like he'd been tossed headfirst into a blender set on puree. His memories whirled and meshed—then and now, then and now, then and—

"I remember being in your car," he said. Heather's thumbs gently stroked his cheekbones, trailing ice over the fire raging beneath his skin. "I remember you dosing me with morphine." He opened his eyes and looked into the evening-star steadiness of Heather's gaze.

Some of the worry eased from her expression, but only some. She nodded. "You were having another seizure. Are you with me—with us—now?"

"Hey, little brother." The voice, low and calm and full of smoky, familiar undertones, drew Dante's gaze down.

His fractured vision shifted, slid together, and Douche Bag's sweaty, straining face morphed into the nomad's rugged and handsome features. A mustache framed his mouth and a crescent moon tattoo glimmered beneath his green eyes.

Llygad.

A frost-edged scent, smoke and motor oil, adrenaline spiced.

"Von," Dante breathed. *"Mon ami."*

A relieved smile quirked up the corners of Von's mouth. "Damn straight."

Heather's thumbs caressed Dante's cheekbones one more time, then vanished from his face as she stood up. "Be right back," she murmured.

"Don't mean to complain and shit, but think you could do me a solid and get your knees outta my ribs?" Von said, releasing his steel-fingered death grip on Dante's arms. "Annoying habit, breathing, y'know? But it's one I just ain't ready to give up yet."

"Fuck." Dante jumped up, then offered a hand to Von and pulled the nomad to his feet. "You okay?"

Von pressed a palm against his ribs, winced, then said, "I'm good, man." His gaze met Dante's. "How 'bout you?" He tapped a finger against his own temple. "Your nose is bleeding," he added softly.

"Merde," Dante muttered, wiping his nose with the back of one shaking hand, smearing blood on his wrist and face. The room did a slow pirouette and broken, jagged things shifted in his head. So did his balance. He stumbled.

Hands, warm and callused, grasped Dante's shoulders and steadied him.

<Gotcha, little brother,> Von sent.

The room decided to play possum and stopped moving. Dante exhaled in relief. <Merci—> But the sending died unfinished as pain—white-hot and barbed—shafted through his mind, pain he saw reflected in Von's eyes. The nomad sucked in a sharp breath, wincing.

Dante smelled strawberries and baby shampoo and blood. The scent shivved his heart. His breath caught, rough in his throat.

Chloe.

The blood-soaked knees of his jeans clung to his skin,

wet and cold. Dante turned around, but Chloe was gone and beige carpet had replaced the concrete floor.

He'd just been holding her. How had they slipped past and . . .

Dante squeezed his eyes shut. Clenched his fists. In a motel, not the white, padded room. Grown-up, no longer a kid. In leather, not jeans. *Focus, dammit.* Sweat trickled along his temples. He eased his eyes open.

Von stared at him, expression stricken. "Holy hell," he whispered. "Jesus fucking Christ. Dante . . ." He grabbed Dante in a hard-muscled hug, held him tight, the fingers of one hand caught up in Dante's hair.

Dante wrapped his arms around Von. Face against the nomad's neck, he breathed in Von's frost-and-gun-oil scent; felt the scratch of his whiskers against his cheek. Felt/heard Von's heart thudding hard and fast almost in perfect time with his own, chest to chest and skin to skin, a comforting, musical rhythm.

"You ain't there anymore, little brother," Von murmured, voice rough, his lips against Dante's hair. "And you ain't never going back. What those fuckers put you through . . ." His arms squeezed tighter. "What happened to her wasn't your fault."

"I killed her, so, yeah, it is."

"*Was*, not *is*. It's long over and it ain't and never was your fault."

Dante pulled away from their embrace, slipped free of Von's strong arms. Cupping his friend's face, Dante kissed him, savored his juniper-sharp taste. "*Merci beaucoup, mon cher,*" he whispered against Von's lips. "*Mais ça vont jamais finir.*"

"It *will* end, little brother," Von whispered back. "It *has* ended."

"*T'es sûr?*" Releasing him, Dante took a step back. Pain throbbed at his temples.

"Sit down before you fall down," Von said.

Dante shook his head. "I'm okay, *mon ami*."

Von arched an eyebrow. Gave him a gentle shove. Dante stumbled, the back of his legs hitting the mattress behind him. He half fell, half sat on the bed, landing on his ass and elbows.

"Yeah, you look okay," Von drawled.

"Blow me." Dante flipped him off with both middle fingers, then pushed himself back onto his feet.

A smile whispered across Von's lips. "Ah, there he is, my stubborn sonuvabitch."

Heather returned and handed Dante a wet washcloth. "You're a mess," she said.

"That ain't nothing new, *chère*," Dante said, offering her a smile. His smile deepened when Von snorted.

Heather glanced at the nomad and her lips curved into a mock-innocent smile. "You okay?" she asked him. "It sounds like you're choking."

"Nah, I'm peachy, doll. Just peachy. Now, if y'all will excuse me, I'll get dressed. Try to contain your disappointment."

Heather lifted her hand, her thumb and forefinger not even an inch apart. "All contained."

"Ouch, woman."

Dante wiped his face with the washcloth, scrubbed at the blood on his face. Heather had wet it with cold water and his fevered skin drank in the moist chill. Baked the cloth nearly dry. He shivered.

"What do you remember from yesterday?" Heather asked.

Dante wadded up the bloodstained washcloth in his hand as his thoughts reeled backward. His muscles kinked into hard knots. Images sparked through his mind like broken flame from a dying lighter.

Spark: *Lyin' Lyons shoves the muzzle of a gun against Heather's temple.*

Spark: *Gone-gone-gone Athena throws herself on her spear.*

Spark: *The man whose name he can't remember entwines with his children, twirling around and into them, his flesh stretching as though elastic.*

Spark: *Your father's dead, little one.*

"Lucien," Dante whispered.

"Shit. I was hoping you wouldn't remember his loss right away," Heather said. She grasped his hand, folded her fingers through his. "I'm so sorry."

Pain needled Dante's mind. Grief twisted the diamond-thorned chains around his heart another turn tighter. Emptiness stretched dark and endless in the place Lucien had once lit with his warm, steady presence.

"Ain't gonna believe Lucien's dead," Dante said, throat tight. "Not until I see his body for myself."

Von paused, jeans in hand. "Did you feel Lucien die?" he asked, voice soft. "Or did you just feel the loss of your bond?"

Je t'aime, mon fils. Toujours.

"He told me good-bye. Then . . ." The words stuck in Dante's throat. He looked away, muscles taut and twitching.

"Did that Fallen chick tell you anything about Lucien? About what happened to him? Or how he died?" Von asked.

Frowning, Dante looked up. Fallen chick? Memory flickered.

Wing-musk. A woman's rain-beaded face—golden eyes, midnight hair, a slender sapphire blue torc around her throat.

You may call me Lilith.

Dante met Von's gaze. "She gave me some bullshit about Lucien sending her to protect me from the Fallen and about him being nothing but ash."

"Lucien wouldn't've sent her," Von said. "He warned me against the Fallen."

Dante's muscles tightened and a shadow fell over his heart as his thoughts flipped back to his last conversation with Lucien and the warning he'd given: *The Fallen will find you one night and bind you.*

"Do you know where to look for Lucien?" Heather asked. Even though the words remained unspoken, Dante saw them in her searching gaze: *If Lucien's still alive.*

"No, not yet," Dante said, voice low and rough. "But I'm gonna find him."

Dante watched as Von and Heather exchanged a quick, worried glance. "I know we need to get home first," he said. Angling back slightly, he lobbed the bloodstained washcloth into the bathroom. "And those hunting us? Gonna take care of them."

Promise?

Promise. Cross my heart.

The room flipped between beige carpet and blood-slick concrete.

Focus. You gotta stay here.

Dante straightened, moving slowly to make sure he remained in the motel room, remained a man, not a kid hanging from a hook. He squeezed Heather's hand, palm to palm. "Gonna make sure you and Annie and Eerie are safe, *catin*."

"Not alone, Baptiste," Heather said. "It's our fight—all of us."

"Yeah, *chérie*. Not alone." Dante lowered his head and touched his forehead to hers. Looked into her eyes. Concern flickered in their blue depths. He felt the heat of her body through her pink T-shirt and red plaid pajama bottoms. Her lilac, sage, and evening rain scent perfumed his senses. Awakened more than one kind of hunger.

"Damn straight, not alone," Von said. "We're all in on this."

Dante lifted his head, a smile tilting his lips. "Hey, how'd you end up here, anyway? I thought you flew home."

Von shrugged. "Felt a few things. I was already on my way here when Annie contacted Silver for help. But don't worry, the guys and Silver all made it home safe and sound."

"I'm glad you're here," Dante said.

"Naturally," the nomad drawled. He buffed his nails against the waistband of his blue boxers.

Cupping his face between her hands, Heather kissed Dante, soft and lingering. "You're burning up," she murmured. "How are you feeling?"

"Still on my feet and *j'su ici*. But where's here?"

"In a motel outside Damascus," she said. "We didn't have time to get far. And we've got to get moving as soon as possible. We've got the Bureau and the SB on our tails and—"

The door cracked open, and Heather stopped talking. She tensed and broke their embrace, her hand reaching for her waistband, then balling into a fist. "Shit. Gun's on the nightstand," she muttered.

A mortal's rapid heartbeat, alternating rhythms—two.

"Just us," an unfamiliar female voice said.

But Dante was already *moving*. He grabbed the chick's wrist and yanked her inside. Her shoulder slammed into the door, knocking it against the wall. Plaster crunched. Dante caught a whiff of mint and wild roses—a familiar scent. He whirled her by the wrist up against the bureau. Things clattered and thudded to the carpet.

She regarded him with calm hazel eyes, this chick with shoulder-length dark brown hair and dressed all in black. No, not calm. Her pulse pounded through her veins, her breathing fast and shallow. Something else flickered behind her calm facade. Her cheeks flushed a deep rose.

Dante suddenly remembered the berry-sweet taste of her blood. Hunger coiled through him. Tightened his muscles.

Memory clicked into place with a minimum of fuss and pain.

Your name. You know mine.

"Caterina," Dante said, releasing his hold on her wrist. "I remember you." He stepped back, studying her, trying to figure out the emotion he'd glimpsed hiding behind her mask. Not disappointment, but something close to that.

"Dante Baptiste," she murmured, straightening. "I remember you too." She rubbed her wrist. Her gaze slid past him and her mouth tightened. She drew in a deep breath, squared back her shoulders. *"Llygad."*

Dante felt Von's warm, strong presence behind him.

<She's an assassin for the SB,> the nomad sent, his mental touch cautious. *<But she changed sides when she learned more about you.>*

Dante shoved both pain and capering stray thoughts— *Put him in the trunk with the other, you; What's the little psycho screamin'?*—down below and away from Von's mind. *<Yeah? She still alive because you trust her, llygad?>*

<For now.>

<Anything else I should know?>

<She's the daughter of one of the core members of the Cercle de Druide.>

<That'd be Renata Alessa Cortini, yeah?>

<You got it.>

"Next time, I'd suggest knocking on the door first, Cortini," the nomad said. "Dunno, Dante, should we work up secret codes in the form of knock-knock jokes?"

"You mean like 'knock-knock, who's there?'"

"Yup. As in 'Ewe Butter.' 'Ewe Butter who?' 'Ewe Butter run like hell.'"

Dante felt a smile tilt his lips. "Nice."

With a groan, Heather crossed to the open door and pulled her sister inside. "It's okay now," she said.

"Easy for you to say." Annie, in a black Danzig tee and blue plaid pajama bottoms and bare feet, shrugged free of Heather's hand and slouched into the easy chair, the vinyl squeaking beneath her. She folded her arms across her chest and stared at the carpet as if it were the most fascinating and fucking awesome thing *ever*.

The mingled odors of coconut and wet pavement trailed into the room with Annie, layered over a faint undertone of sweet, smoky incense and deep, dark earth. Something in that undertone fluttered mothlike about in Dante's memory, seeking a light, and left him uneasy.

A muscle in Heather's jaw jumped. She carefully closed the door, then turned around and put her back against the door. She pushed her sleep-wild tangle of red-hair back from her face. Her gaze skipped from Dante to Caterina.

"I was about to tell them what happened," she said to Caterina.

Caterina nodded. "Let me do something first," she murmured. Reaching behind her, she pulled a gun from the back of her black jeans.

It looked like one of Von's Brownings, so Dante was mystified when Caterina knelt on the floor in front of him and laid the gun at his bare feet. She looked up at him, and then he recognized what he'd seen in her eyes before: shame.

"I vowed to guard and defend you, my True Blood prince, and all those you care for," she said. She swallowed hard. Drew a deep breath in the now-silent room. "But I failed."

"Jesus Christ," Von muttered.

Dante stared at her, not sure he'd heard right. He'd

heard some pretty bizarre things from Inferno fans during show meet-and-greets, things ranging from secret cousins hidden from one another in a conspiracy to keep them apart to claims of "you stole my life and put it in your songs now you owe me royalties or a new life," but Caterina's statement left him off balance.

"You kidding me? Stand the fuck up and drop the 'True Blood prince' bullshit."

Caterina blinked. "But you're a—"

"So? Knock it off. Christ! I never asked . . . Fuck, I don't even want . . ."

"No, course you didn't ask," Von tossed in, stepping up beside him, his jeans slung over his shoulder. "She promised all on her own. So, spill, Cortini. How'd you fail?"

"I think I fell asleep while on watch and I believe someone broke into the room."

"You *think*? You *believe*?" Von's brows slanted down, a deep vertical line creasing his forehead. "Mind explaining to me how that could happen? You promised to guard Dante with your life."

"Ain't no one risking their life for me. Ain't no one responsible for me, but me."

"Yeah, yeah, says you," Von growled. He folded his arms over his chest. "So answer the question, Cortini. How'd this happen? And stand up, woman."

Caterina picked up the Browning and stood, rising easily to her feet. She glanced at Dante, her eyes a warm hazel—pale green and golden brown—her cheeks still flushed, before returning her attention to Von.

"I don't think she fell asleep," Heather said. "I think someone put her out and possibly me too."

"Keep it coming. I'm listening," Von said, but his attention remained fixed on Caterina.

"We were messed with," Heather said. She nodded her

head at the nightstand between the beds. "I tucked the Browning under my pillow when I went to sleep. When I woke up, the gun was on the nightstand, safety off."

"And my Browning was in my lap," Caterina said. "Not only was the safety off, a round'd been fired." She slid a hand into her jeans pocket, pulled it out again and uncurled her fingers. A bullet casing rested in her palm.

Dante glanced at Von. Frowning, the nomad plucked the shell from Caterina's palm and held it between his thumb and forefinger.

"That's not all," Heather said. She bent and picked something up from the carpet. Straightening and automatically pushing her hair back from her face, she dangled a small golden-linked chain between her fingers.

Von whistled. "Hell. The door chain. Was it broken off?"

"Top link looks melted," Heather replied. "And the door lock doesn't work anymore. Like maybe the mechanism was disabled or fried somehow."

Dante joined Heather at the door. Without a word, she dropped the chain into his palm. Magic sparked and prickled against his skin. His song kindled, strummed a single burning chord through his heart.

Smoky incense and deep, dark earth.

His moth-flitting memory finally landed. Now he knew why the smells that had traveled into the room with Annie had left him uneasy.

Wing-musk. It'd reminded him of Lilith's scent as she'd held him, and of Lucien's earthy green leaves and dark earth aroma. But just different enough to unsettle instead of comfort.

"Fallen power," Dante said. He rubbed the chain between his fingers. His muscles coiled tighter yet. Lucien's words sounded through his mind, clear and deep.

I hid you from others. Powerful others who would use you without mercy.

Dante's throat tightened. *Shoulda listened. Shoulda never shoved him away.*

"Holy fucking hell," Von muttered. He looked at Dante. "Not that I ain't glad, but why the fuck would they leave you behind?"

Dante shook his head and instantly regretted it as the room dipped. Heather braced herself against him, slipped a steadying arm around his waist, offering balance. "I don't think they woulda," he said. "We're missing something."

"Maybe whoever it was saw what you'd done to the others," Heather said, "and was worried that you'd do the same to them."

"Or maybe this Fallen guy was just checking to make sure Dante was okay," Annie suddenly tossed into the conversation.

"Guy?" Caterina questioned.

Annie rolled her eyes. "Just a figure of speech."

"Then why not just knock on the fucking door?" Von said. "Nah, something else is going on here."

"Time to get our asses on the road," Dante said. "We can puzzle this out later."

"We need to get another car," Heather said. "Clothes and supplies too."

"I'm gonna need my guns back, ladies," Von said, sliding his jeans from his shoulder. "Still wet," he muttered.

"Nice boxers by the way," Dante said.

"I'd be telling you the same," Von replied, pulling on his jeans. "If you'd bothered to wear anything under those pants."

"Wait. Hold on. Let me check," Dante said. He glanced at the ceiling and tapped his chin, then returned his gaze to Von. "Nope. Still don't need a nanny."

Von snorted. He extended a middle finger. "Sounds like you need more of this."

"Always. Can't get enough." Dante felt a smile tugging at his lips. For a moment, everything felt normal. No one hunting them and the memory of killing his Winnie-the-Pooh princess, her blood sticky on his hands, her body cradled tight against him, just a nightmare.

For a moment.

Then he slipped free of Heather's warm half-embrace and walked into the bathroom. Flipping on the light and closing the door, he stopped in front of the sink. Turned on the cold water.

I'm scared, Dante-angel. But I'm glad I'm with you.

Same here, Chloe-princess. No one's gonna do bad things to you. I won't let 'em.

Dante bent over the sink and splashed cold water on his face. His pulse pounded at his temples. He felt cold inside, ice-scraped raw, his heart honeycombed with frost. Clutching the sink, the porcelain slick beneath his fingers, he closed his burning eyes.

Promise?

Promise. Cross my heart.

He'd kept that promise. No one else had done bad things to Chloe.

He'd done worse instead.

15

SLIPPING AWAY

GILLESPIE SLID THE KEY card into the lock. A bar of green flashed. He unlocked the door to room 5 and stepped inside, switching on the light as he did. Dropping his suitcase on the carpet, he placed his laptop and the 7-Eleven branded plastic bag containing the beer he'd bought on the desk. Then he turned, relocked the door, and slid the chain into place.

He glanced around the room. Queen bed. Desk. Bureau. Small TV. A door on the left led to the bathroom. The room stank of stale smoke and a yellowish patina stained the '70s-style paisley wallpaper. No doubt the smoke reek permeated the beige carpet too, and the bedding, including the pillows. And lurking beneath that? A deep sniff—yup, he smelled damp and mold.

Gillespie sighed, scrubbing a hand over his scalp. Probably a smokers-only room before cigarettes had been outlawed in public places. He reconsidered his impulsive decision to grab a room at the Happy Beaver instead of driving into Portland and getting a room at a decent hotel. His reasons ticked through his mind as if projected on a whiteboard.

A. *Closer to site. Quicker response time if needed.*
B. *Too tired to drive into Portland.*
C. *Time saved on drives to and from the site.*
D. *See B above.*

Gillespie yawned. Fuck it. He'd stay here tonight. This was the first motel he'd spotted on his drive from the Wells compound to the highway. He could always grab a better room closer to Portland tomorrow. The room was for sleeping only, after all.

He shrugged off his Gore-Tex jacket and dropped it over the desk chair. Reaching into the 7-Eleven bag, he pulled out a chilled and frosty bottle of Pacifico. He plopped down onto the edge of the bed, the mattress creaking as it gave beneath his weight.

Great. Soft and smelly mattress to boot.

Gillespie toed off his mud-caked Sperry Top-Siders, then popped off the Pacifico's cap with the opener on his key chain. He poured a long, cooling swallow of beer down his parched throat. It tasted so golden and good, he didn't even miss the fresh lime he usually enjoyed wedged into the bottle's long neck. His muscles unkinked a little.

Taking another long, cold draught, Gillespie closed his eyes. Something niggled at his mind. Scratched at the inside of his skull, begging attention. He allowed his thoughts to roll back over what he'd just been thinking about. Smoke reek. Too tired to drive into Portland. First place he'd seen . . .

Gillespie's eyes flipped open. He lowered the half-empty bottle of Pacifico to his lap. His pulse picked up speed. Wait. Wait. In one satellite scan, the house and cars are still on the hill at the compound. In the next scan, just before dawn, house and cars have vanished.

What if Prejean and the others escaped whatever the hell happened on the hill and what if, in this little scenario, they needed a place for Prejean to Sleep? And let's pretend he didn't have any stay-awake pills or heavy-duty sunscreen, so they would've had to race the dawn.

This was the first motel he'd spotted on his drive from the Wells compound.

Gillespie lifted the beer bottle and drained it. The sun had disappeared behind the forest-thick hills a half hour ago, twilight still smudging the sky with brooding blue and purple. Prejean should be awake by now. Hell, he probably split the moment he opened his eyes.

Wherever he'd holed up. Provided he'd survived.

Gillespie rose to his feet, wincing at the pain in his lower back, stiffening up after only sitting still for a few minutes, *kee-rist!* He walked to the desk, intending to grab a second beer, but instead he found himself setting the empty bottle beside the plastic bag, then sliding his feet into his shoes. Found himself grabbing up his key card, unchaining the door, and walking outside.

Light spilled from occupied rooms, just a soft glow behind rooms with closed curtains. Fog curled white down from the trees and hung in the moist air.

Gillespie walked in long strides to the motel office. As he passed the ice and vending machines, he noticed a brunette in black opening the rear passenger door of an idling yellow cab. She glanced at Gillespie as he approached. Attractive, young. She offered him a quick smile, an intriguing impish curve of her lips.

Gillespie found himself sucking in his gut and pulling himself up as tall as possible. But the brunette didn't give him a second look. Instead, she ducked into the back of the cab, shutting the door behind her. The cab motored out of the parking lot, exhaust puffing white behind it like dragon's breath.

Gillespie released the breath he'd been holding in a low sigh, disgusted with himself. Yes, that would be the way to win back his wife—strutting in front of younger women, especially white ones. Good God.

A bell chimed when Gillespie pulled the glass door open and held it as a young Asian woman with bobbed black hair exited, nodding her thanks, a cute little girl with startling jade-green eyes following in her wake like a baby duck.

Gillespie stepped into the office, the door swinging shut behind him. The heavyset woman managing the motel muted the small TV she watched behind the check-in counter, then stood up.

A welcoming smile curved her lips. She nodded a greeting, her blue-tinted curls bobbing with the movement. "Mr. Gillespie," she said. "Is everything all right with your room?"

"Everything's fine," Gillespie said, returning her smile. Pulling his badge/ID wallet from his back pocket, he flipped it open on the age-scarred counter between racks of Oregon picture postcards. "It's actually Chief Gillespie. I work for Homeland Security," he lied.

The manager's smile vanished and her brow crinkled into furrows. She picked up the wallet, peered at the badge and the photo for several moments before carefully resting it back on the counter, almost as if she feared that it'd snap shut on her hand like a mousetrap.

"I don't understand. . . ." She paused, then said, "I mean, how can I help you?"

"Did you have any guests check in today, close to dawn?"

"Yes, I did." The manager nodded at a computer monitor behind the counter. "Do you need to know who?"

"Names, please. And let me know if they've checked out yet."

She tapped away on the keyboard. "Two different check-ins this morning. The first was Tyree Williams and family, and the other was Annie Wallace and family."

Gillespie's heart skipped a beat. "Annie Wallace? Not Heather Wallace?"

The manager nodded. "Annie it is. And they haven't checked out yet."

Gillespie rolled that juicy little nugget of information around in his mind. Had Wallace brought her sister along with her? That seemed more than a little unlikely unless . . .

Unless Annie was the reason Wallace had participated in this whole mess. Maybe Wallace had never been an active participant.

His thoughts flipped back to Brisia Rodriguez's statement.

> FI Díon: *Heather Wallace. Why did you think she needed help too?*
> B. Rodriguez: *Well . . . I could tell she didn't like this guy (witness pointed to photograph of SAC Alexander Lyons), and she asked me to call 911. I don't think she would've done that if she was one of the bad guys.*

Possible, yeah, but Gillespie would lay serious odds that Wallace was simply being clever and using her sister's identity instead of her own, keeping a low profile. Only one way to find out.

"What room is Annie Wallace in?"

"Number 9."

"Thank you," Gillespie said, grabbing up his ID wallet from the counter and sliding it back into his pocket. He hurried outside, the door *ding*ing behind him. Gillespie pulled his cell phone from his pants pocket and called FA Miklowitz at the Wells site.

"I think I've located Wallace," Gillespie said. "Grab your partner and two or three more agents just in case she isn't alone and get your asses to the Happy Beaver Motel pronto." After giving directions to the motel, he signed off.

A faint glimmer of light behind the closed curtains of room 9 suggested it was still occupied, despite the empty parking slot. Pulse racing, Gillespie ran for his room and for the Glock he'd locked inside along with his beer.

He wished he'd thought to reclaim the goddamned monster-catching kit designed for Prejean from Thibodaux and Goodnight before they'd left for the airport. Hoping backup would arrive fast-fast-fast, a mantra zipped through Gillespie's mind over and over: *Aim for the head or the heart. And. Don't. Fucking. Miss.*

HEATHER LOOKED UP WHEN she heard the bathroom door open and Dante walked out wearing a Saints of Ruin T-shirt with fishnet sleeves ending in a wide PVC strap buckled at each wrist. She drank in the sight of him, her blood pulsing a little faster.

He held a black-and-white composition notebook in his left hand. A smile tilted his lips and lit his pale, beautiful face. He'd found his stolen song journal in Annie's bag and, given how well the shirt fit him, he must've discovered one of his stolen shirts also.

At least Dante'd fared better in the fashion department

than Heather had. Her sweater still damp, she'd added her bra beneath the pink Emily the Strange T-shirt she'd borrowed from Annie, but opted to wear her damp jeans instead of the red plaid pj bottoms—no matter how warm and comfy.

Sitting cross-legged in the easy chair, Annie watched Dante, her expression a blend of parted-lips lust, wariness, and defiance. "Hey," she protested. "What the hell, dude! I didn't give you permission to go through my stuff."

"Le coquin qui vole a un autre, le diable en ris, p'tite." Dante raised the notebook to his forehead and saluted her with it. He flipped her off with his other hand.

Annie returned the favor, pointing her middle finger up, then down, then all around. "Yeah? Right back atcha."

"Sucks getting caught with stolen goods, huh?" Heather said, leveling her gaze at her sister.

Fire blazed to life in Annie's eyes. "You always take his side! I got no idea how that stuff wound up in my bag."

"Menteuse," Dante said. "That tee you're wearing? Go ahead and keep it."

"I'd planned on it."

Frustration grated like sandpaper across Heather's nerves. "Dammit, Annie, we don't have time for your—"

Annie jumped to her feet, grabbed the hem of the Mad Edgar T-shirt with its purple illustration of Edgar Allan Poe, and yanked it off. No bra. Just bare breasts, her skin flushed pink with fury.

"Nice tits, *p'tite.*"

Wadding the tee into a ball, Annie hurled it at Dante. The T-shirt fluttered to the carpet in front of his bare feet.

"Take your precious shirt," Annie snarled, "and fuck you both!" Whirling, she stormed into the bathroom, slamming the door behind her.

"Christ." Heather rubbed the bridge of her nose, a

headache forming behind her eyes. "Sorry about that," she murmured.

"Ain't your fault," Dante said, scooping up the tee. Turning, he tossed it onto the nightkind-only bed. "Me and Annie are gonna have a heart-to-heart later."

"She's off her meds and—"

"Don't make excuses for her," Dante said, swiveling around to face Heather. "I know she's bipolar, I know she needs meds, but she also needs to take responsibility for her actions, yeah?"

"Yeah, I guess," Heather said. "I've always felt that I needed to make up for all the absences in her life—Mom, Dad, stability."

Dante brushed the backs of his fingers against Heather's temple, trailing heat across her skin. "I know you did, *chérie*," he said, voice soft. "But it wasn't your burden."

"Maybe not," Heather said, admitting the possibility to herself for the first time, "but I couldn't count on our father to take it up."

"Your old man sounds like a prick."

A smile tugged at Heather's lips and she hoped it didn't look as bitter as it felt. "Accurate assessment." Drawing in a deep breath, she changed the subject. "Caterina's on her way back to the SB so she can be our eyes on the inside. I gave her your home number."

"You must trust her, yeah?"

Heather nodded. "As much as I can—all things considered. She could've killed us as we slept or turned us in." She paused, held Dante's dark gaze. "You're the reason she didn't. And won't."

Dante sighed. "I kinda got that," he said, trailing a pale hand through his hair.

"We can use her help."

Dante's eyes unfocused for a moment and Heather

figured he was listening to Von, an intimacy she wished she was capable of sharing with Dante beyond the temporary blood-forged links created between them whenever they had sex—well, whenever he drank a bit of her blood, which, so far, had happened only during sex.

And she planned to keep it that way. The thought of Dante feeding on her out of hunger instead of passion left her cold. But what if his need was desperate?

One thing at a time, Wallace.

When Dante focused on her again, she noticed his dark eyes were dilated, rimmed with darkest brown. Gold light seemed to shimmer in their depths.

So did pain and heart-deep loss. She saw it in his taut muscles, in the tight line of his jaw, in the blue shadows smudged beneath his eyes, even though she knew he was trying to hide it. The conversation she'd had with Von while Dante'd showered rolled through her mind.

I'm really worried about him, doll. The images I got from him . . . his reality keeps shifting between now and then. He's fighting damned hard to keep himself here and now and with us. But . . .

But what?

Von looks away. He trails a hand through his hair. When he meets her gaze again, his words are as grim and sorrowful as his green eyes.

I think he's had all he can take, doll. Heart and mind. If I knew a way to hide him from the world until he could regain his balance, until he had the chance to face his past on his own terms and reconcile himself to it, had time to grieve . . .

He needs a safe place. And time to heal. Just being home will help—

You're a safe place, Heather. Whenever you're near him, things quiet down inside-a him. Keep close, doll. Keep close to your man until we can get him home.

"Von said he's picked up the rental car Trey arranged for him," he said.

"And my car?" Heather asked, already missing her Trans Am. Just a vehicle, just a form of transportation, one that can be tracked, she reminded herself. It helped a little, but she loved that car.

"Ditched, but in one piece, as safe as it can be," Dante said, voice soft. He lowered his pale face and kissed her with soft, heated lips. She tasted amaretto, sweet and heady, as his autumn-harvest scent of frost and burning leaves enveloped her.

He burned against her, hot as a star.

Heather wished they had time to be alone together, to lose themselves in each other. Later, she promised herself. But something dark and knotted and cold in the pit of her stomach seemed to whisper, *Fresh outta time*. Seemed to whisper, *You're going to lose him. He's already slipping, falling, tumbling past your reach*.

No. She refused to accept that. She'd fight for him with everything she had.

When the kiss ended, Dante tucked a lock of Heather's hair behind her ear. His eyes searched hers, his dark gaze looking deep, stoking fire white-hot at her core. "It's quiet, *chérie*," he said.

"I'm glad," she said. "Maybe we can keep it that way."

"Maybe, yeah." A smile ghosted across Dante's lips, then vanished. He stepped past her and sat on the nightkind-only bed. Setting the notebook on the rumpled blankets, he pulled on his socks. Grabbed his boots and strapped them on.

"What's Von's ETA?" Heather asked.

"Five minutes or so."

"I'll get Annie." Heather swiveled around, steeling herself to talk her sister out of the bathroom and to coax her into cooperation, but before she could even open her mouth, Annie opened the door and walked out of the bathroom, gym bag at her side, its strap looped around her shoulder.

Annie wore the Danzig skull tee that she'd slept in, and on her feet, fuzzy purple slippers. "I'm ready," she said, voice level. She pushed a strand of blue hair out of guarded eyes.

"Great," Heather said, wondering at the sudden change in Annie's demeanor. Wondered if she could trust it.

What game is she playing now?

Heather heard the creak of leather behind her as Dante rose to his feet. Annie's blue-eyed gaze shifted past Heather, followed Dante's movement. Then she swallowed hard and looked away.

Still afraid of Dante after what she saw him do. Heather didn't blame Annie for that—she understood and sympathized.

"You should just let me go," Annie said, her voice little more than a whisper. "You don't want me with you. You really, really don't."

Heather's muscles knotted even tighter. "We've gone over this already," she said. "We need to stick together."

"I'm willing to take my chances. Send me away." Annie flicked another glance past Heather to Dante. "You'll be safer."

"No," Heather said, voice flat. "That's the end of it."

"We ain't leaving you behind, *p'tite.*" Dante scooped his song journal up from the rumpled bed and snugged it into the back of his leather pants. "Got everything?" he asked, his gaze meeting Heather's.

She looked around the room, nodded. "Pretty much." She freed the Browning Von had given her from the back of her jeans. She flicked off the safety and chambered a round, the *ka-chunk* echoing in the silent room, then switched the safety back on. "Did Von see anyone suspicious at the car rental office?" she asked, tucking the Browning into the back of her jeans again.

Dante shook his head. "All clear so far." His gaze turned inward for a moment, then a smile tilted his lips. "In fact, he's here now."

Heather cracked the door open in time to see a forest-green SUV pull into the parking lot, the headlights dipping for a second as it negotiated the lot entry. Von steered the SUV into the parking stall in front of the room, then switched off the headlights, but kept the engine running. The heady smell of gasoline and exhaust wafted into the room.

"Time to go," Heather said, glancing at her sister. Annie stood beside the easy chair, her gaze on the floor, her eyes hidden beneath mascara-lengthened lashes.

"Leave me." Annie looked up. "Please."

Heather stared at her sister, caught off guard by the vulnerability in her voice and in her eyes. Eyes brimming with unshed tears. *Annie-Bunny.* "Sweetie, no," she said. "No matter what, I'll never leave you behind."

Annie nodded, blinking away her tears. A familiar sardonic glint sparked in her eyes, armored her face. "Yeah? We'll see." Hoisting the gym bag's strap up higher on her shoulder, she stalked from the room and outside.

"Shit," Heather muttered.

Warm hands cupped her face. Heather looked up into Dante's dark eyes. "Ain't your fault, *chérie*, you know that, yeah?" He planted a quick smooch on her lips. "Ready to go?"

She nodded, offered him a smile. "Thanks, Baptiste."

Dante winked, his hands sliding away from her face. Wrapping his left hand around her right, he folded his fingers through hers. But, as he turned away, leading her to the partially open door, Heather noticed the gleam of sweat at his hairline, the taut line of his jaw and Von's words rolled through her mind.

He's fighting damned hard to keep himself here and now and with us.

I'll stay close, help him fight.

As Heather stepped out into the parking lot and the pine-fragrant night just a pace behind Dante, a harsh, authoritative voice yelled, "Halt! Drop your weapons and get down on the ground!"

16

NEVER PRESUME

Emmett sipped at his coffee, pretending not to notice that it tasted burnt and bitter, even with three single-serving creamers muddying its color from black-as-hell to black-as-purgatory.

"You're certain Sheridan never said a word at the site or during the flight?" Purcell asked. His leather chair creaked as he relaxed into it. His eyes, deep set and olive green, slid from Merri to Emmett, then back.

"Positive," Merri replied. She looked weary and unfocused, strung-out on stay-awakes, her natural rhythms disrupted. "He never answered a single question."

She'd complied earlier with Purcell's order to put out her cigarette by dropping it into her untouched cup of coffee. The cool, recycled air in his office still smelled of cloves and tobacco.

"Ah." Purcell tapped his keyboard and studied whatever appeared on his monitor. "Did you ask him about . . . Prejean?"

Merri considered for a moment, then shook her head. "I don't believe so."

Emmett found Purcell's pause before saying Prejean's name interesting. He doubted Purcell had forgotten the vampire's name, and wondered what name he'd almost used instead of Prejean.

"You don't believe so? The answer is either yes or no, Goodnight," Purcell said.

"Make that a no then."

Despite the long flight, Emmett felt wide-awake, alert—a good thing during a debriefing with SOD Underwood's assistant, FA Richard Purcell, at least according to all the whispered wisdom via the field-grunt grapevine. Emmett had never met Purcell before today, knew of him only through reputation. Another first? This visit to HQ's underground facility.

"Sheridan seemed to be in shock," Emmett volunteered. "He never made eye contact with anyone during the flight or at the site. Not deliberately, anyway."

"He isn't there," Merri said. "I looked into his eyes at the site and he was empty."

Purcell looked up from the monitor and fixed his gaze on Merri. "Empty?"

Merri twirled a finger in the air beside her head. "As in Sheridan has left the building."

Purcell leaned forward in his seat. "Do you have any thoughts on how or why?"

Merri shrugged. "I'm no psychic and definitely not a shrink, so your guess is as good as mine."

A smile played across Purcell's lips and humor lit his eyes. Emmett tensed. He saw nothing pleasant or warm in that smile. His fingers curled tighter around his cooling Styrofoam cup.

"But you *are* a vampire," Purcell said. "You have senses we mere mortals don't possess, not to mention centuries of experience we, as individuals, will never achieve, and you can't even give me an educated guess?"

Merri stiffened in her chair. "Of course I can," she said, each word clipped and tight. "But you just want me to tell you what you already suspect."

Purcell's smile deepened. "And that would be?"

"That witnessing the events at the Wells compound fried Sheridan's sanity."

Purcell nodded. "A possibility, yes. It's also possible Prejean got to him, fucked with his mind."

"Judging by what I've seen of Prejean's handiwork, I think he would've just killed Sheridan," Emmett said, placing his cup on the edge of Purcell's polished rosewood desk.

Purcell's expression frosted over and he fixed his attention on Emmett. "Never presume to know what Prejean would or wouldn't do. I've seen that little psycho in action. I've seen him tear people apart just for the pleasure of it—including a little girl. I've watched him for years, Thibodaux, so I know more about that bloodsucker and what makes him tick than you ever will."

Emmett lifted his hands, palms out. "Just offering an opinion, Purcell, that's all."

"Fine. Just so we're clear." Brushing a hand through his gray-flecked sandy hair, Purcell pushed back his chair and rose to his feet. "SOD Underwood plans an additional debriefing for both of you tomorrow." His gaze flicked to Merri. "Tomorrow evening, that is."

"Lovely," Emmett said. "Can you recommend a good hotel?"

"I could," Purcell replied, "but the SOD wants you to

remain on premises until after your meeting with her." He tapped a button set into the surface of his desk. "We have rooms here for agents working long shifts. You'll be comfortable. There's a cafeteria if you're hungry, Thibodaux."

Emmett glanced at Merri as they both stood. He arched an eyebrow and she answered with a quick, one-shouldered shrug. *No understanding the upper echelons.*

"Sounds good," Emmett said.

The door clicked open and a young agent with short auburn hair, a pin-striped skirt suit, and a bright smile gestured for them to follow her.

"At least we'll save money," Merri murmured as she passed him.

"Roger that," Emmett murmured. But his muscles remained wound-up and his inner alarm system seemed stuck on Imminent Disaster.

Purcell's comment about having watched Prejean for years troubled Emmett. Not *tried to apprehend*, not *tried to stop*, but *watched*. The wrong word choice, maybe? Had to be. Who the hell would just watch a killer work his slaughtering mojo—for years—and do nothing about it?

Emmett scrubbed his face with one hand, felt the rasp of whiskers against his palm. He needed a shower and a shave, some hot chow, and a few hours of sleep. Then maybe things might make a little more sense.

I've watched him for years, Thibodaux.

More sense later, yeah. Maybe. But a chill slid down Emmett's spine.

PURCELL WATCHED THIBODAUX AND Goodnight follow FA Cooper out of his office and into the corridor. Purcell listened as the *tap-tappity-tap* of Cooper's heels against the linoleum gradually faded. When the sound vanished completely, he slipped his iPhone from his pocket, thumbed in a brief text message, touched SEND, then returned it to his pocket.

While waiting for a reply, he picked up the Styrofoam cups of coffee that the pair of field agents had so fucking thoughtfully left on his desk. A drowned clove cigarette floated in one. A trace of its perfumed, smoky stink still lingered in the air.

Damned Goodnight. She knew better, but like most vampires couldn't give a rat's ass. It wasn't like they needed to worry about the health effects of first or secondhand smoke.

Dumping the coffee down the sink in his attached bathroom, Purcell tossed the cups and the wet cigarette into the trash can. He paused in front of the mirror above the sink and finger-combed his hair. Straightened his gold-checked blue tie. A beep from his iPhone alerted him to an incoming message.

Pulling the iPhone free again, he glanced at the screen—*on my way*—before slipping it back into its silk-lined home again. Purcell returned to his desk, his gaze drawn once more to his monitor and the picture it displayed of the Stonehenge of angels guarding the mysterious cave in Damascus, Oregon.

Such a intriguing puzzle. And unsettling.

The statues would soon be on their way to Alexandria. And the cave? To be explored once the site was secured.

One question burned in his mind, searing the edge of each thought: What did any of this have to do with Prejean—with S? And Purcell was sure the bloodsucker was, indeed, involved in some way, shape, or form. Had to be.

Look at what had happened at the Bush Center for Psychological Research in D.C. when S had dropped in for a visit earlier in the month. Purcell presumed that the Bureau's missing ADIC—Dr. Johanna Moore—was actually dead.

He'd warned everyone in the know about S, warned them to put him down before he slipped free of their leash. Had warned Wells more than once.

He's a little fucking psycho.

Say that again, Purcell, and I'll give you to that little fucking psycho.

Purcell mulled over his conversation with Thibodaux and Goodnight and felt reasonably sure that neither agent knew much about Prejean beyond Rodriguez's murder and what little info they'd been given. He also felt reasonably sure that both agents had answered his questions truthfully.

From what Purcell had observed, Thibodaux and Goodnight seemed to work well together. But, to be honest, he couldn't imagine how Thibodaux—or any mortal—could stomach working with a vampire.

In any case, their partnership would need to be dissolved, and each agent reassigned to different branches. In fact, all field agents and techs at the Wells compound would be subjected to the same process that Thibodaux and Goodnight would undergo during their debriefing tomorrow with SOD Underwood and Field Interrogator Teodoro Díon—memory wipe and reassignment.

They knew too much.

With one last glance at the photo, Purcell strode from his office to his appointment in the medical wing.

PURCELL STOOD BESIDE THE railed hospital bed and studied the man sleeping in it, one wrist handcuffed to the rail. Sheridan had come through surgery just fine, the bullet—a .40 caliber slug—removed from his thigh. It was a miracle he hadn't bled to death.

Medical monitors on stands beside the bed tracked Sheridan's vitals, green lights sketching his heartbeat and respiration, beeping at regular intervals. Clear plastic nozzles carried oxygen into his nostrils. The room smelled of pungent antiseptics and, laced underneath, a hint of vanilla spice and yellow dandelions—Díon's cologne.

"Needs a shave," Díon commented.

Purcell looked away from Sheridan and up—six three, shoulders as wide as a linebacker's, hair the color of butterscotch, late thirties or early forties—to meet the interrogator's violet-eyed gaze. "So?"

"Just an observation." Díon returned his attention to Sheridan. "What do you need from me?"

Purcell held up a finger, then bent over Sheridan, leaning down to whisper one word in his ear. "Prejean."

Sheridan's heart rate and respiration picked up speed on the monitors. His eyelids fluttered. Purcell felt a smile curve his lips. Goodnight was wrong. Sheridan hadn't left the building, his body empty—he was still inside.

Terrified.

Lowering his finger, Purcell straightened and looked at Díon. "He's intact enough to recognize a name and react to it," he said. "Go in and find out why. Ferret out everything he knows, then report to me."

The interrogator nodded, then pulled a blue molded-plastic chair up beside the bed. "Hard or easy?" he asked, settling himself into the chair.

"Whatever it takes."

17

AND NEVER WOULD

Prejean and Wallace stopped. Their hands unlinked, but Wallace didn't reach for the gun snugged into the back of her jeans. The man behind the wheel of the idling SUV twisted his head around and fixed his shaded gaze on Gillespie.

Gillespie flipped through a mental lineup of Prejean's known associates and identified the driver: a vamp nomad known as Von McGuinn aka Von Two-Guns. Handy thing, nicknames.

"Gun on the pavement, Wallace!" Gillespie stepped out of his doorway, Glock in both hands and aimed at Prejean's head.

The vampire swiveled around to face Gillespie, a smooth and simple action so fast, Gillespie never saw him move. Heart thundering in his chest, he kept his Glock aimed at the bloodsucker's pale forehead.

Gillespie had seen plenty of photos of Prejean, knew the bloodsucker had shattered the vampire drop-dead-gorgeous meter. But neither the photos nor Gillespie's dispassionate knowledge prepared him for the black-haired beauty now watching him with gleaming eyes; did nothing to prepare him for Prejean's preternatural grace and deadly allure.

A smile tilted Prejean's lips for a moment, then vanished.

Captivating—this lean and, most likely, *hungry* predator.

An image of Rodriguez's empty eyes and ravaged throat, blood glistening in light reflected from the hall, filled Gillespie's mind, chilling him like a blast of ice water.

Dry-mouthed, palms sweaty, Gillespie locked his fingers even tighter around the Glock's grip and kept his focus sharp. His finger flexed against the trigger.

Bloodsucker murdered a man in his own home—an FBI agent to boot.

"Gun on the pavement, Wallace," Gillespie shouted. "Last warning!"

"Hold your fire," she called. "I'm complying." Wallace reached back for her gun, her other hand up and open. A breeze blew strands of red hair across her composed and lovely face.

"Slow and easy, Wallace. Prejean, stay right where you are. Don't move," Gillespie barked. "McGuinn, show me your hands!"

As soon as the commands left Gillespie's lips, headlights lit up the parking lot as a car peeled in from the highway— Miklowitz's rented Saturn—followed by another vehicle, a Crown Victoria.

Gillespie breathed a sigh of relief. *At fucking last.* And with that thought, everything went to hell in a handbasket.

The Saturn and Crown Victoria screeched to angled halts, blocking the idling SUV. Miklowitz, Holmes, Kaplan, and others slid low out of the vehicles, ducking behind the open doors, guns lifted. Tight-throated shouts peppered the air.

Prejean lifted a hand to shade his eyes. Winced.

Wallace brought her gun around, swiveling toward the parking lot, and locked both hands around the grip.

The nomad appeared like magic outside the SUV, its driver-side door wide open and *ding-ding-dinging*. Mustached face grim, he raised the pistol in his hand and fired at the agents taking cover behind the Saturn's doors.

Muzzle flash, multiple gun cracks, dull thunks as bullets hit metal. Blood sprayed into air thick with the stink of cordite and hot rubber as bullets zipped into flesh. Holmes grunted and sprawled onto the pavement and the nomad staggered back a step.

Prejean lowered his hand and knotted both into fists. His gaze locked with Gillespie's. The bloodsucker's coiled muscles unwound. Gillespie pulled the trigger and kept pulling, but Prejean was gone.

A semi hauling steel and cruising at the speed of light slammed into Gillespie, bulldozed him down to the pavement. Blue light swallowed his vision as the back of his skull bounced against the blacktop. The air exploded from his lungs and his Glock flew from his grasp.

Pain and dizziness ricocheted from one side of his skull to the other, banging back and forth, back and forth, in an ever-diminishing cycle.

Weight pressed down on his abdomen, something— knees?—jabbed into his ribs on both sides. Gillespie gasped for air, sucking in the smells of burning leaves and early morning frost. Heat radiated against him, and his survival instincts jerked his arms up and over his throat as his stunned mind belatedly realized that a bloodsucker had flattened him, not a steel-hauling semi.

And not just any bloodsucker, but a designer monster called Dante Prejean.

Hot hands seized Gillespie's forearms and wrenched them away from his throat. His vision cleared in time to look up into Prejean's eyes—only a sliver of red-slashed dark brown circled the dilated pupils. Gold light flared in their hungry depths.

What the . . . ?

Gillespie squirmed and twitched, struggling to bring his knee up in the hope he could jerk free of the vamp's iron grip and yank his backup weapon free from his ankle holster.

But a very quiet, calm, and resigned part of him knew it didn't matter. It was too late. Had been too late from the moment he'd locked gazes with Prejean.

He was going to die and not in a good way.

"Hey, Papa, my turn, yeah?" Prejean said. Blood trickled from one nostril. "*J'ai faim*, motherfucker." His pale, beautiful face dipped for Gillespie's throat, lips parting and revealing his sharp, white fangs.

Papa? Was the bloodsucker confused or just toying with him?

Heated lips touched Gillespie's throat. Twin stabs of pain followed. He renewed his struggle, but couldn't yank his arms free of Prejean's steel-fingered hold or roll free of his pinning knees. And his jackhammering, frantic heart would only feed his life away faster.

Gillespie went still.

PAIN JABBED DANTE'S TEMPLES, white-hot and ragged. His vision fractured. Pain chiseled away at the boundary between *then* and *now*. Wasps droned. Burrowed under his skin.

Don't put nuthin' in his mouth. Boy bites.

No escape for you, sweetie.

Prejean, stay right where you are. Don't move.

The black detective or cop or secret fucking agent twisted underneath Dante, struggling to roll free, sweat beading his face. Behind his gold-rimmed glasses, his eyes narrowed with effort. Probably the hardest workout the fucker'd had in years./*Papa squirms under Dante like a huge fucking worm. The bastard's heartbeat thunders in Dante's ears, a primal and compelling sound, drumming up his hunger, his rage from deep within.*

"Hey, Papa, my turn, yeah? *J'ai faim*, motherfucker."

The cop kicked and pounded and panted./*Papa's heels drum against the dining room floor as blood spurts from his slashed throat. Disbelief widens his eyes.*

Just as Dante's lips touched Papa's whiskery throat, his fangs piercing the skin, a woman's scream—raw and anguished—scraped away all other sound. "My baby!"

Dante's heart skipped a beat. He lifted his head from Papa's bleeding throat, tore himself away from its hot, intoxicating smell—sweet berries spiced with the juniper-bitter taste of adrenaline—and twisted around.

An Asian woman knelt on the sidewalk in front of room 10's open door, glass from a bullet-shattered window surrounding her. She clutched a little girl in jeans and a purple sweater against her chest. Rivulets of blood streamed from the back of the girl's head, glistening in her long, black hair. Her mother wailed, blood smeared on her hands, and soaking into her khaki slacks.

Time paused, a caught breath, as the woman's cry froze everyone in the parking lot in place. Gunfire stopped. Shouts and yelled orders ceased—except one, issued by an unfamiliar male voice: "Call 911!"

Dante jumped to his feet and *moved* across the parking lot, past the SUV, and the redhead crouched in front of it, gun in her hands. Dropping to his knees in front of the sobbing woman, he said, "Give her to me."

"She's not breathing," the woman choked out. "Can you help her?"

No one is going to save you. Ever. You can only save yourself.

Liar, liar, goddamned fucking liar.

"Give her to me," Dante repeated, voice soft. "I'll do everything I can." Pain pulsed at his temples. "Ain't gonna let 'em have her."

The thick smell of blood filled his nostrils, hitting him like an open-handed slap to the face. Hunger scraped through him. Shivering, he denied it. Pushed it down into the wasp-crawling depths below.

The woman stared at him for a moment, desperation brimming in her tear-reddened eyes, then glanced down at her daughter. She whispered, "Dear God, if you can do anything, anything at all, help her, please."

Dante scooped the girl's limp body into his arms. Glass crunched underneath him as he sat cross-legged on the sidewalk, cradling the girl in his lap. Her almond-shaped jade-green eyes stared up at the stars, empty, unseeing. Blood trickled from a hole in her forehead.

She was silent, still. No heartbeat. No breath. All rhythm gone.

Chloe lies on the concrete floor, snow-angeled in a pool of blood.

It's too late, Dante-angel.

"Nah, it ain't. I won't let it be," Dante said, stroking a finger along one blood-soaked lock of hair. "*J'su ici*, shhh." He caught a whiff of cinnamon, cloves, and freezer-frosted ice, a phantom scent.

You won't save her, you know. You'll fail.

Yeah, you know what? Fuck you.

Electricity prickled through Dante. Crackled along his fingers. His song swept up from his heart, a dark and intricate aria, dancing in time to the blue flames flickering around his hands—one of which he rested on the girl's chest, above her ash-filled heart. Blue sparks skipped along her Hannah Montana Comeback Tour sweater.

Closing his eyes, he plucked at the dying DNA refrain within her; strummed the fretted fingerboard of her escaping essence, and reeled it back inside with a burning glissando—rearranging, shaping, composing.

Bowing his head, Dante touched his lips to the girl's, breathed blue fire into her lungs. Molten music flowed into and illuminated the dark chambers of her heart and swirled among the ashes, a fiery and pulsating rhythm.

He imagined her eyes bright and warm, imagined her hair moonlit and clean, imagined her giggling, a plushie orca tucked under her arm.

Let me go, Dante-angel.

The past uncoiled, then played back in reverse.

Dante crawls away from Chloe, the knees of his jeans dry. The blood that's smeared and sticky on his hands, his fingers, and beneath his sharp, sharp nails belongs only to the assholes sprawled dead on the concrete floor.

Orem floats up from the concrete, the plushie orca's fur no longer stained with blood but clean-clean-clean, and snuggles into Chloe's hand again.

The pool of blood surrounding Chloe glides up from the cold floor, beads up and rolls along her skin, trickles away from her hair, all of it pouring back into her slashed throat. The wound zips shut, never was.

Dante's sharp, sharp fingernails never touch Chloe's soft throat. Color blossoms in her cheeks, brightens the freckles spilled across her nose. She sits up, her blue eyes wide and scared, but no longer empty.

Dante grabs her and hugs her tight against him. She's in his arms, warm and alive. It doesn't happen; he doesn't kill her. It never happens and never would.

Pain brass-knuckled against Dante's mind. His breath caught in his throat, rough. His song splintered, then scattered, the complex arrangement not quite complete.

You'll fail.

Heart hammering against his ribs, Dante kissed Chloe's forehead. He tasted blood, felt it sticky against his lips. Hunger stirred, hunger once again denied. He breathed in the sweet scent of strawberries and soap.

"Wake up, princess," he whispered.

A CHILL RIPPLED ALONG Heather's spine and iced her from the inside out as music, jagged and discordant, prickled against her healed heart for a pulse-pounding moment, then vanished. She stared at the child in Dante's arms.

Dear God . . .

The girl's eyes focused on Dante, no longer empty or unseeing, and no longer jade green, but blue. Long red hair fluttered beside her now-freckled face. Drying blood streaked her new fair skin, but Heather had no doubts that the wounds in the girl's forehead and the back of her skull had healed.

"My name's Violet, not Princess," the little girl said.

Dante lifted his head and shook his hair back from his face. A smile tilted his lips. "Violet? Yeah? *T'es sûr de sa?* That don't sound right, *chère.*"

"It's right, just ask my mama. Are you an angel?" She touched a finger to Dante's pale face. Awe lit her sleepy blue gaze. "Your eyes are like gold stars."

"Ain't no angel, *p'tite*."

"Uh-*huh*, you are too. Why're your wings black? You a nighttime angel?"

"Ain't got wings, princess." Dante paused, his dark brows slanting down, his expression perplexed. "I'm . . . nightkind."

"Nuh-uh, you're an angel," Violet declared. She yawned. Her eyes shuttered closed. "Pretty angel . . ."

Dread settled in Heather's belly like a bucket of bricks. She doubted Dante was even aware of what he'd done. The taut lines of his body, of his jaw, the sweat beading his forehead, all shouted pain. His words and voice and actions said something else altogether: he was lost in the past.

He's fighting damned hard to keep himself here and now and with us. But . . .

Not even twenty-four hours had passed since Lyons and his sister had tried to torture their way past the programming their father had implanted in Dante's mind, had tried to shove together the fragments of his broken and buried memories.

Not even twenty-four hours since he'd lost Lucien.

I think he's had all he can take, doll. Heart and mind.

He needs a safe place. And time to heal.

But we're fresh outta time.

Violet's mother, still kneeling on the sidewalk and surrounded by blood spatter and glass shards, stared at Dante, her dark eyes wide with horror and shock, both hands pressed against her mouth.

Heather glanced up and saw the same look of stunned disbelief on most of the faces of the people—agents in grimy yellow jumpsuits, staring motel guests—scattered across the motel parking lot and sidewalk. Silence curled through the cordite-smoked air.

Snugging her Browning into the back of her jeans, the

barrel hot against her skin, Heather knelt beside Dante, just out of arm's reach. Blue flames still flickered and snapped around his hands.

"Baptiste," she said softly. "You hear me?"

He shuddered, blood trickling from his nose, then nodded. *"Oui, chérie,* I hear you." He kept his gaze on Violet.

"She's alive and breathing now, Baptiste. You need to turn off the magic."

Dante squeezed his eyes shut. "Focus," he muttered. "Fucking *focus.*"

Dropping her hands from her mouth, Violet's mother whispered, "Oh my God. Oh dear God," her voice rising in volume with each word. "What have you *done* to her? You changed her! You *changed* her! *Give her to me!*"

Panic burned through Heather when she saw the woman lean forward and realized she intended to snatch her daughter away from Dante—from his glowing blue grasp.

"Stop!" she shouted. The woman instinctively froze, her hands still lifted. Her gaze flicked over to Heather. "If you touch him, he might change you too."

Fear flashed across the woman's face and she pulled her hands back, knotting them together on her thighs. "I want my daughter back," she said, her voice quavering. "I want her back right now."

"I'm working on that," Heather said, shifting her attention back to Dante and the little girl curled up in his lap.

She wished she could move closer to him, touch him, connect with him in a deeper, more immediate way than just speaking. She worried that words alone wouldn't be enough. But as long as blue fire flared around his hands, she couldn't risk it.

"You still listening, Baptiste? We're at a motel in Damascus—"

"Put the child down now!"

The agent that Dante had knocked down stood a couple of yards away, his face ashen and his glasses askew. Blood trickled along one side of his throat. He held his gun in both hands—*shaking* hands—the barrel aimed at Dante's head.

"Back the fuck off, asshole," Von growled. "You ain't helping the situation. Let the lady do her thing."

A muscle ticked in the agent's jaw, but he didn't say anything else. His gun, however, remained aimed at Dante's head.

"Keep talking, doll."

Heather drew in a steadying breath. "We're in Damascus, Oregon, Dante. You, me, Von, and Annie, and we're headed home. The girl you're holding is *not* Chloe. Your princess died eleven years ago."

"Eleven . . . ? No, it just happened," Dante said, his eyes still closed. Blood from his nose streaked a dark and glistening trail down his lips and chin. "But I rewound everything, took it all back. Chloe's safe. Orem too."

Heather stared at Dante, another bucketful of bricks dropping into her belly. Dante wasn't just *remembering* horrific bits of his past, he was *reliving* them. Tears stung her eyes and she blinked them away.

"You can't rewind the past," she said, hating each word as it slipped past her lips. "Chloe's dead and you can never take that back. It happened."

Dante's muscles coiled and flexed as if each word pounded into him like a steel-knuckled fist. His arms tightened around sleeping Violet.

Heather was fairly certain that Violet had died the moment the bullet had slammed into her forehead. Her eyes had been empty. Dante had done more than save her life, he'd brought her back.

Maybe Violet could've been resuscitated with CPR, a

defibrillator, and drugs and returned to her body; a near-death experience. Not out of the realm of possibilities.

But Dante had rested a hand on Violet's chest and breathed into her.

He is the never-ending Road.

"You saved Violet, Baptiste. She's alive—here, now—because of you. Give her back to her mother. Let her go."

Dante sucked in a breath, then opened his eyes. He looked at Heather. The gold light had vanished. The blue flames engulfing his hands winked out. "*J'su ici*," he said, voice a husky whisper.

"*Monster!* Give me my daughter!"

Fury scorched all other emotion from the woman's face as she leaned forward and grabbed Violet. Dante opened his arms and the woman jerked her changeling daughter free.

Violet awakened, rubbed at her eyes. "Mama?"

Heather rose to her feet and held up a wait-and-listen hand, palm out. "He can change your daughter back," she said, hoping to hell it was true. "All we need is a little quiet and—"

"He can change her back?" A ribbon of hope curled through the woman's voice. "Just like the way she was before . . . before—"

"I believe so," Heather said. "As soon as things quiet down."

"Ma'am," the man Heather figured for SB, not FBI, interrupted. "I need you and your child to go to the office until the situation here is contained."

"But he can change her back," Violet's mother protested.

"You're in danger here," the SB agent said, voice strained. "You're in the middle of a firefight. You and your daughter risk being shot—again—or becoming hostages. Get the hell out of here."

"Wait," Heather said, "how about a time-out until Dante's restored Violet back to herself? Then—"

"Then nothing," he replied. His gaze remaining on Heather, though he directed his words to Violet's mother. "You're asking to give your daughter *back* to a bloodsucking vampire who's just angling to find a way outta the mess he landed himself in. Get your daughter out of here before I have you arrested for endangering a child. Now!"

Bewilderment flashed across the woman's face and Heather could just imagine her thoughts: *Did he just say bloodsucking vampire?*

With a teary glance at Heather, the woman stood, then hurried across the parking lot, Violet clutched against her. Heather watched as Violet and her mother disappeared inside the motel office. She hoped Dante would have a chance to undo her daughter's physical transformation into Chloe.

A peripheral flash of movement followed by the crackle of glass under boot soles told Heather that Dante had risen to his feet. She looked at him, and the pain and raw grief she saw pooled in his dark eyes tore at her.

Chloe's death just happened for him.

"You and Chloe never stood a chance against them. You were just kids," Heather whispered, stepping up beside him. His fevered heat baked against her.

He looked away, blinking, his hands clenching into fists. "I fucked up."

"Hold it right there, Prejean. Move again and I'll put a bullet in your head."

And with those words, the détente created by a dying or dead little girl ended.

Adrenaline surged electric through Heather's veins, sparked clear and cool in her mind. She reached for the Browning tucked into the back of her jeans.

Fresh outta time.

* * *

GILLESPIE TIGHTENED HIS DOUBLE-HANDED grip on his Glock, his palms sweating despite the cool, moist air chilling his face and hands. Clicks and *ka-chunks* echoed all around him as guns swung up and fresh rounds were chambered.

"Name ain't Prejean," the vampire said. He wiped at the blood trickling from his nose with the back of one pale hand.

"I don't give a shit what your name is," Gillespie said. "On the ground. Hands behind your head and interlace your fingers."

"Blow me."

"We don't have to do this," Wallace said, her gun aimed at the center of Gillespie's forehead. "More innocent people might get hurt or killed. Two of your agents are already down."

"That's rich coming from a woman who stood by while her bloodsucking squeeze murdered an FBI agent in his own home," Gillespie said.

"She had nothing to do with that," Prejean said, voice taut. "That was all me."

"Good to know. If you wanna save lives, Wallace, surrender."

Wallace's attractive face was calm, resolute. "We can't—"

Her words were cut off as Prejean staggered against her. Concern flashed across her face. She unwrapped a hand from the grip of her gun to help brace the vampire upright, but he slipped from her grasp. Fell to his knees.

Gillespie adjusted his aim at Prejean's head, his heart jackhammering against his ribs. Sweat dampened his shirt at the small of his back. And at this very moment, he'd sell his soul without an ounce of regret for just one shot of Jack Daniel's.

Prejean's golden eyes. The blue flames from his hands engulfing the little girl.

What the hell had Prejean done to that kid? *How* had he done it? How was such a thing—turning a little girl into someone else—even possible?

Not just a bloodsucker and murderer, Dante Prejean. But whatever the hell he was, he definitely wasn't what the kid claimed him to be.

Are you an angel?

Images of the white stone angels at the Wells site scrolled through Gillespie's mind. The hair on the back of his neck prickled. His finger twitched against the Glock's trigger. *Take the goddamned shot.*

But before Gillespie could decide whether or not to shoot an unarmed man—*he's got fangs, speed, and strength, he's NOT unarmed*—the vampire keeled over onto the glass-strewn sidewalk, his body spasming with mind-numbing speed and violence, his black hair whipping across the pavement.

"Shit!" Wallace dropped to her knees beside Prejean. "Von!"

Gillespie stared, amazed. A seizure? He'd had no idea vampires were subject to physical ills or mental short-circuits. He relaxed his finger against the Glock's trigger.

In a blur of motion, the nomad vamp, Nightwolf colors on the back of his worn leather jacket, appeared on the sidewalk beside Wallace and Prejean, a zippered black bag in his hand.

A gunshot cracked through the night as one of Gillespie's men fired in a belated response to the nomad's unexpected movement.

Back turned, McGuinn flipped off whoever had fired, then knelt. He unzipped the bag, pulling out a syringe and vial.

Crisscrossed headlights shafted light across the trio on the sidewalk, spotlighted Prejean's limb-twisting spasms.

Fresh blood from the vampire's nose and mouth sprinkled the pavement.

"Chief, what the hell is he? How did he change that little girl?" Kaplan asked.

"Your guess is as good as mine."

"Kid took a bullet square in the forehead, Chief. She should be dead."

"Doesn't mean she *was* dead," Gillespie murmured. "I've seen people chat about baseball statistics with a crowbar planted in their skulls."

"But how do you explain that the kid's no longer Asian?"

Gillespie pulled his gaze from Prejean and looked at the field agent. She'd trotted from the dubious safety of the bullet-pocked car door she'd crouched behind to join Gillespie on the sidewalk, her Sig Sauer down at her side. Several strands of blonde hair had worked free of her ponytail and now curved along her jawline.

"I can't," Gillespie said, meeting her troubled gaze. "I haven't a clue how he changed her."

"She called Prejean an angel. Do you think . . . I mean, could he be—"

Gillespie's phone *beedle-beedled* and his heart launched itself into his throat. *Christ! I'm wound up tighter than a pig's tail.* Pulling his cell from his pants pocket, he glanced at the incoming number. Underwood. A grim satisfaction curled through him. For once, he had good news to report.

"For now, Prejean's a murderer. Initiate the arrest," he said to Kaplan, nodding at the trio on the sidewalk. "But not alone. Shoot if they resist."

Kaplan nodded, her expression unhappy. She jogged back to the Saturn and the surviving agents.

Gillespie answered the SOD's call. "Ma'am, good news. We have them—Prejean and Wallace. No sign of Lyons, though."

"Release them," Underwood said, her voice flat.

Underwood wasn't given to jokes or pranks, so Gillespie could only assume he'd misheard. "Ma'am?"

"I told you to release them."

Or maybe *she'd* misheard. "We located Prejean and Wallace. We have them."

"Perhaps the third time will be the charm. Release. Them. The official search for them has been terminated. That order comes from the director himself."

"Ma'am, no disrespect, but have you been drinking?"

Underwood laughed, a soft and humorless sound. "No, Sam, *I've* never needed booze to bolster me when things unhinge. Release Prejean and Wallace."

Gillespie heard a click as Underwood broke the connection—hanging up on him as per the norm. And just like that, his good news had turned into a pile of stinky shit. Acid churned in his stomach, burning its way up his throat.

Gillespie thumbed END, then tucked the cell back into his pocket. He rubbed a hand over his scalp. What the hell had happened at HQ? Why would Director Britto call off the hunt for Prejean, Wallace, and Lyons?

He pondered disobeying the order, pondered telling his agents to open fire—shoot to kill—and end his career. He sighed. Pulling a half-empty roll of Tums from his shirt pocket, he popped the remaining tablets into his mouth, then crumpled up and tossed the empty wrapper. The chalky, mock-fruit flavored Tums masked the sour taste of acid on his tongue.

"We've been ordered to release them," Gillespie called. "Back off."

His agents, semicircled around the trio on the sidewalk, froze. Relief washed over Kaplan's face—and not just hers, Gillespie noted. Several other field agents seemed to regard Prejean with something dangerously close to awe.

"What the fuck? Chief, that can't be right," Miklowitz protested, turning around to face Gillespie. "They shot Holmes and Cantnor and—"

"And that's who we need to take care of right now. Have medics been called?"

"Yeah, but . . ."

"Trust me, I don't like this any more than you do, but this comes from the top—release them."

A scowl darkened Miklowitz's face. Jamming his gun back into his shoulder holster, he jogged back to his partner's sprawled body and hunkered down beside him.

Prejean's seizure had ended or maybe he'd been pumped full of vamp meds, Gillespie didn't know and really didn't care. His stomach tossed more acid up his throat and he thought of the beer in his room growing warmer with each passing moment.

The nomad gathered Prejean into his arms and rose to his feet in a smooth, graceful movement. He carried Prejean to the SUV. Eased him into the back, then climbed into the driver's seat.

Wallace stood also, her gun at her side, barrel pointed at the pavement. She turned around to face Gillespie. She studied him for a long moment, her eyes shadowed and unreadable. A breeze fluttered through her red hair.

"You're SB, not Bureau, right?"

"That's right."

"They're lying to you," she said. "Ask about Bad Seed."

"I know about Bad Seed," Gillespie replied. "I know what Prejean is."

Wallace shook her head. "I doubt that." Gun still in hand, she trotted to the SUV and jumped into the backseat beside Prejean's prone body, closing the door after her.

Wallace's sister, the girl with triple-colored hair, poked her head up from the back, then slithered over into the front passenger seat. Gillespie guessed that she'd played it smart and had huddled on the floorboards during the firefight.

Gillespie watched the SUV pull out of the bullet casing–littered parking lot and peel onto the dark highway. His stomach knotted as he remembered the feel of Prejean's fangs piercing his throat.

I know what Prejean is.

I doubt that.

Thinking of the little Asian girl with jade-green eyes and black hair and how Prejean, with blue light dancing around his hands, had transformed her into a girl with red hair and freckles left him cold.

Gillespie had a feeling Wallace was right.

And that scared the living daylights out of him.

18

UNTIL YOU FADE INTO NOTHINGNESS

SOMETHING COOL AND WET trailed across Lucien's forehead, dampening the fire raging inside his skull. The pungent aromas of lavender, peppermint, and eucalyptus curled into his nostrils and prickled against his consciousness.

A hand slipped behind his aching head, eased it up. A cup pressed against his mouth. Lucien allowed his lips to part. He swallowed a sip of ginger and hyssop tea, hot and minty-sweet.

"That's good," a woman murmured, her voice soft and rimed with music—a delicate bell. "Drink more. It'll help ease the pain."

Lucien did as she suggested and swallowed more of the soothing and fragrant tea. The cup vanished from his lips and the hand lowered his head back onto a pillow. The fire and pain inside his skull diminished into glowing embers, as did the throbbing ache in his shoulders.

He listened to the sounds around him: a skirt rustling, perhaps; the clinking of a cup, spoon, and teapot; and the fleshy padding of bare feet upon stone. But underneath, a river of voices, thoughts, feelings, and pealing *wybrcathl* rushed through his mind like foaming white water over rocks—a swirling and dangerous current.

Shields must be down.

Lucien tried to strengthen his shields, but failed. Pain exploded in a white burst behind his eyes. His strength continued to ebb, leaving his shields as flimsy as gauze. The reason why flickered through his memory.

Gabriel speaks Lucien's true name. "I bind you, Sar ha-Olam of the Elohim to the soil of Gehenna and bind your power within you, unused and unvoiced, until I set you free again." As Gabriel paints a blood-glyph on Lucien's forehead, translucent light streams from his palms and coils around Lucien, binding him with an ethereal rope. "As Gehenna fades, so shall you."

Gabriel's smug voice roiled through Lucien's mind, awakening other memories.

Dante's anhrefncathl, dark and burning and razor-edged, stabs into Gehenna's fading night sky, madness glimmering in each exquisite and haunting note.

Closing his eyes, Lucien sends one last thought to Dante then, in a final, desperate act to keep his ties to Dante from revealing his location to the Elohim, he severs their bond.

Je t'aime, mon fils. Toujours.

Lucien opened his eyes and looked into a moonlight-washed night sky, his temples throbbing, his heart aching.

He'd severed the bond he'd shared with Dante and survived. But a cold, lightless hole had been ripped into the fabric of his being; a hole that seemed to rip wider with each breath he drew.

Had his child survived? And if so, was Dante's sanity still intact?

"Would you like more tea, Samael?"

Lucien sat up at the sound of his former name. The blue marble terrace whirled for a moment, then stilled once more. Pain flickered, faded. But dread gripped his stomach. He didn't recognize the woman who met his gaze. A spy for Gabriel?

She sat curled on a cushioned bench, her beautiful oval face full of concern. Her hair, pale as moonlight—silver with just a hint of blue—framed her face in wavy tresses, while artfully arranged curls were piled on top of her head in ancient Grecian style.

Something about her itched at the back of Lucien's mind, seemed familiar, but it was an itch he couldn't satisfy.

She regarded Lucien with solemn violet eyes. "You don't look well," she said. "Perhaps you should lie back down." She rose to her feet, tall and willowy, her hyacinth blue gown swirling around her ankles just above her bare feet.

"No, I'm well enough," Lucien said, planting his feet on the marble floor. "But I *would* like more tea, please."

The woman walked to a small table laden with pomegranates, limes, oranges, walnuts, and a simple white teapot. She studied Lucien, head tilted, her violet eyes curious, then she turned and poured tea into a handleless cup.

Lucien took in his surroundings—blue marble; tall pillars sculpted with scenes from Gehenna's long past; luxurious couches, chairs, and graceful tables; soft, glowing lamps; and standing at either side of an arched doorway leading into the aerie proper, a pair of guards.

The Royal Aerie.

A long cry from the smoldering embers of Sheol and its hooks. A quick flex told Lucien that his wings remained banded.

"You never answered my question," she said, swiveling and handing him the filled cup. He caught a whiff of her scent: apple blossoms and cool, shaded water.

Lucien frowned and wrapped his fingers around the porcelain cup, its heat warming his palm. "I don't remember the question." He sipped at the tea.

"I asked if you knew where my mother might be," she said. "I heard that she'd spoken to you in the pit when the *creawdwr* announced himself and . . ."

"Your mother?"

"Lilith. I'm her daughter, Hekate."

Lucien lowered his cup and stared at her. That pale, pale hair, those intense violet eyes—of course. Lilith and the Morningstar's daughter. No wonder she'd seemed familiar. His muscles knotted when he thought about how he'd shared Dante's existence with Lilith, yet never once had she mentioned her own child.

But the words Lilith's never-before-mentioned daughter had just spoken iced Lucien to his core. "Why can't you contact Lilith? Is she blocking you?"

"She isn't blocking me. It's more like . . ." Hekate looked away, trailing a finger along one of the delicate snake heads on the braided silver torc encircling her slender throat. "It's as though she no longer exists. Our bond hasn't been severed. It's like it never was."

"And the Morningstar? Has he been able to reach your mother?"

"He tells me he's too busy to worry about Lilith and assures me that she's fine."

"But you don't believe him."

"No."

"So is he still in the mortal world?"

"Yes." Hekate sighed. Her hand slipped away from her torc and returned to her side. She left the table and crossed to the terrace's white marble balustrade. She paced its length, her fingers trailing over the railing.

Lucien tossed back the rest of his tea, his heart drumming hard and fast. Lilith might be out of touch to protect her daughter, especially if the Morningstar was attempting to find her and the *creawdwr* she sheltered.

At least, Lucien hoped that was the case. Other darker possibilities—Dante in the Morningstar's hands, Lilith dead; Lilith dead at Dante's hands, his sanity slipping, and hunted by the Morningstar—flashed through his mind in quick succession.

Lucien shoved those nightmarish possibilities away. No.

"I've never heard an *anhrefncathl* before last night," Hekate said. "Never known a *creawdwr*. Never thought I would. The *creawdwr*'s song was so beautiful and wild, so savage; it poured through me like liquid night, dark and pure and primal. I've never felt anything like it."

"Was the Maker found?" Lucien asked, his fingers tightening around his cup.

"Hard to say," Hekate replied, "since there's been no contact with any of the emissaries Gabriel and my father sent. No one can reach them either. It's as though they've ceased to exist too."

Each word from Hekate's lips intensified Lucien's suspicion that something had gone terribly wrong. He didn't want to risk trying to contact Lilith or Von out of fear that it would lead Gabriel or the Morningstar straight to Dante. Which raised another question.

"Why am I here and not still in Sheol?" Lucien asked.

Hekate stopped pacing. She turned to face Lucien.

"Because you were once my mother's partner, her *cydymaith*, and I thought—" Her gaze skipped past Lucien and she stopped speaking.

"Because I ordered it, Samael." Gabriel's honey-smooth voice snaked through the air. He strode past Lucien's couch to stand beside Hekate in a bloodred kilt and braided gold torc.

Hands gripping the railing behind him, waist-length caramel-colored hair plaited down his back, Gabriel tilted his head toward Hekate as if to whisper a confidence.

"Your mother's former *cydymaith*, yes, and the murderer of our last *creawdwr*," he said. "I don't think you should rely on anything he might tell you, little dove. Samael is a liar."

"I no longer use Samael as my name. I prefer Lucien."

Gabriel laughed. "And your preferences matter to me, of course."

"Said one liar to another," Lucien retorted.

Gold light sparked in Gabriel's moss-green eyes. "You think you've been very clever, no doubt. But I know you sent Lilith to fetch the *creawdwr* you insisted didn't exist."

Surprise rippled across Hekate's face. She stared at Lucien.

"No one can *send* Lilith anywhere," Lucien replied. "And certainly not to *fetch*."

Gabriel pushed away from the balustrade. He wagged one finger in the air. "Ah, but *you* did, didn't you? Did she promise to keep this young Maker from me? Did she vow not to bond him? You're not a complete fool, so you must've realized whatever she agreed to, she lied. Yet you sent her anyway."

Seeing no point in continued denial, Lucien said, "Yes."

Hekate's fingers knotted in her gown. "You lied to me," she said, her violet gaze indignant.

"No, I didn't. I never answered your question."

"See?" Gabriel murmured. "What did I tell you, little dove?"

"So answer my question now," Hekate said, her attention still fixed on Lucien. "Where is my mother? Why can't I reach her?"

"You can't reach her," Gabriel said, sauntering to the fruit-laden table and plucking out a pomegranate, "because she and all of the others we sent to greet the *creawdwr* have been turned to stone."

Lucien sat up straight, cold frosting his spine. Even Lilith? His thoughts rolled back to Loki crouched in St. Louis No. 3, Dante's dark and chiming blossoms cupped within his stone hand.

"That can't be true," Hekate said, her face paling.

"Oh, it's true. The Morningstar witnessed it," Gabriel said as he slit the pomegranate open with one gold talon. Red juice trickled down his finger and along his hand, dripping onto the marble floor. "As for how—the *creawdwr* was responsible."

"But . . . why?"

"He's unbound and untrained, little dove. His sanity is failing."

Dante's words, low and taut, blazed through Lucien's mind: *If they find me, they ain't binding me. They're gonna hafta kill me.*

Lucien's hands knotted into fists. His child was stubborn enough to make that statement fact. Drawing in a quiet breath, he uncurled his hands, hoping Gabriel had missed that display of emotion.

But Gabriel's wink said he had, indeed, noticed. "Samael kept this young Maker away from *aingeals* who would guide and teach him. Kept him away from Elohim who would bond him and keep him sane. Kept him away from Gehenna and all those who would love him."

Hekate's violet gaze searched Lucien's eyes. "Why would you do that?"

"I know nothing about this *creawdwr*," he said, meeting and holding her gaze. "I slayed the last Maker. Why wouldn't I do the same with this one? The Morningstar is playing games with Gabriel."

"And with me," Hekate murmured, a dark and bitter note breaking her melodic voice. She spun around, her gown rippling like water, and gripped the balustrade's railing. "He told me my mother was *fine*."

"Ah, little dove," Gabriel said, "it's not your father who's playing games here. Samael just agreed that he'd sent your mother after the Maker, then told you he knew nothing about the *creawdwr*."

Hekate said nothing, her attention fixed on the night beyond the terrace.

Gabriel sat on a purple-cushioned bench beside the table. "Well then, I think you should know, Samael, that the Morningstar is following the *creawdwr* even now. He's studying him, learning the best way to get him under his wings."

"So he says," Lucien said, keeping his tone bored.

"True. But the Morningstar's given me a few interesting facts about this child-*creawdwr*. For one, he's a mixed blood—*Fola Fior* and Elohim." Gabriel glanced at Lucien from beneath his tawny lashes. "And he's been injured—perhaps by a severed bond. Hard to know for certain, but interesting."

"It sounds like the Morningstar has created an elaborate fiction to entertain you with," Lucien said. "*Fola Fior* and Elohim? As a Maker?" Lucien snorted.

"*You* lost consciousness in the pit last night after the *creawdwr* announced himself," Gabriel said. "You even bled from your nose."

"Because I cut my link with Lilith. I'm a tad diminished

these days thanks to a certain spell." Lucien paused, as though something had just occurred to him. He met Gabriel's amused gaze. "Are you actually suggesting that *I'm* the *creawdwr*'s father?"

"Given the Maker's mixed blood . . ." Gabriel spread his hands out, palms up.

Laughing, Lucien shook his head. "The Morningstar is feeding you very entertaining fiction, indeed. Now who's the fool?"

The amusement evaporated from Gabriel's face. Gold light sparked in his moss green eyes. "I can have you returned to the pit. And leave you there until you fade into nothingness."

Lucien pushed up onto his feet. "I think I'd prefer that over this boring conversation. Why *did* you have me brought to the palace, Seat-Warmer? Do you need instruction on how to rule?"

"I brought you here so you can watch as the Morningstar and I bond the *creawdwr*," Gabriel replied, a sly smile curving his pomegranate-red lips, "and become his *calon-cyfaills*. Bonded to him, heart and mind. We'll be the ones he whispers to in the night, the ones he trusts with every confidence, the ones he'll listen to. And we'll teach him what it is to be a Maker, Samael, we'll teach him well."

"Why should I care?" Lucien said, pleased his voice remained level.

"If all you've said is the truth, then I suppose you won't." Gabriel tossed the pomegranate rind over the balustrade with a casual twist of his wrist. He rose to his feet, meeting Lucien's cold regard. "But on the other hand . . ."

"Will the *creawdwr* restore to flesh those he turned to stone?" Hekate asked.

"Yes, all will be well, little dove, once the Maker has been bonded," Gabriel murmured, gold light sparking in his eyes. "In the meantime, I ask that you continue to tend to Samael. Keep him alive."

"If I must," Hekate said.

Striding to the balustrade, Gabriel kissed the curls coiled atop Hekate's head, then turned away and unfurled his golden wings. Without another word he launched himself into the night, his wings stroking through the jasmine-and-myrrh-scented air.

Hekate watched until he disappeared from view, then she swiveled around. She looked at Lucien for a long moment, her face composed, her gaze speculative.

"Do you need help sitting?" she asked, voice cool.

"Hardly."

Lucien had used the last of his strength to force himself onto his feet. Sweat beaded his forehead and his heart tripled-timed against his ribs. Thighs shaking, he managed to drop semigracefully onto the couch.

"More tea?" Hekate asked, picking up the teapot.

"Wine would be better," Lucien said, lying down on the couch. He draped an arm over his eye.

"I agree," Hekate murmured.

Lucien listened to the gentle *clack* as she returned the teapot to the table. A few moments later he heard the sound of sandals on marble as a summoned servant brought a pitcher, heard the liquid sound of wine poured into glass.

Why had Dante turned Lilith to stone? Had Dante refused Lilith's protection because he was still angry with Lucien or had she never had the chance to speak to him?

Despite Gabriel's threat to force him to watch as he bonded Dante, Lucien had a sneaking suspicion the puffed-up *aingeal* hoped that the *creawdwr* wouldn't be found until *after* Gehenna and Lucien had faded from existence.

Otherwise Dante's energy would feed the land, restoring its and Lucien's vitality. Gabriel would then either have to kill Lucien outright to be rid of him or convince the *creawdwr* to unmake him.

Gabriel no doubt believed that Dante could be persuaded to create a new Gehenna, one shaped by a young and powerful *creawdwr*, one that wouldn't bear the stamp and quirks of *creawdwrs* past; a new age for the Elohim.

Gabriel's words rolled like thunder through Lucien's mind: *And he's been injured—perhaps by a severed bond.*

How badly had he hurt his child in his effort to protect him?

The warm scent of apple blossoms and fruit-laden wine curled into Lucien's nostrils. He lifted his arm from his eyes and accepted the moisture-beaded glass Hekate offered him. "Thank you."

She nodded, then sipped from her glass of ruby red wine. She gave Lucien a sidelong glance, long silver-and-frost lashes shading her eyes. "My mother hated you for ages," she murmured. "And Gabriel worked hard to make sure I'd despise you."

"And you don't?"

"'The enemy of my enemy is my friend,'" Hekate quoted, holding Lucien's gaze.

Lucien chuckled. "You are your mother's daughter." He took a long, cooling swallow of wine, tasting the clean bite of lime beneath the pomegranate.

"No, I'm nothing like Lilith. I have no desire for power. I don't understand why anyone would crave to rule a dying land anyway."

"It wasn't always dying," Lucien said softly.

"But that's all I've ever known—a dying land, a stagnant people, endless wars."

Disappointment curled through Lucien. A spy for Gabriel, after all. Albeit a radiant and alluring spy, even if a bit clumsy.

"And all you'd need to fix that is the *creawdwr*," he commented, voice flat. "I don't know where he is, nor do I care."

Rosy color blossomed on Hekate's cheeks. "That's not what I meant," she said.

Lucien laughed. "Tell me, what *did* Gabriel mean for you to say? Perhaps you should've practiced a bit."

Indignation and chagrin chased across Hekate's lovely face. "I am *not* speaking for Gabriel," she said, chin lifted. "Only for myself."

Yes, very much Lilith's daughter. And yet . . .

Hekate crossed to the purple-cushioned bench and sat down, her back straight. She cupped both hands around her stemless wine glass. "I've been Gabriel's hostage for most of my life," she said, her voice low. "Well-treated, yes. I've lacked for nothing. Except my freedom. Oh, Gabriel never would've stopped me from winging to the mortal world to see its wonders. But he would've hung my parents from hooks in Sheol until I returned."

Lucien sat up. "I didn't know."

A hostage to ensure the good behavior of Lilith and the Morningstar. But that still didn't explain why Lilith had never mentioned Hekate.

A dark possibility brewed in Lucien's mind. *Maybe she never told me because she hoped to trade my son for her daughter; every word uttered from her lush lips a lie.*

Lilith of Lies.

Anger smoldered deep in Lucien's belly. He tossed back the rest of his wine.

"I think the *creawdwr is* your son," Hekate said, her violet eyes searching Lucien's. "I think everything you've endured in the pit and from Gabriel has been for your son's sake. I think you've been protecting him from *aingeals* like Gabriel and my father. And I think you severed your bond with him to keep Gabriel from following it."

Lucien said nothing.

Hekate finished her wine, then set the glass down on the marble floor. She rose to her feet, her hyacinth blue dress flowing like liquid silk along her curves, and walked to the balustrade.

"My *calon-cyfaill*, Jvala, was among the emissaries who went to greet the Maker," she said. "She's now silent, just like my mother."

"Why are you telling me this?" Lucien asked.

Hekate swiveled around to face him, one slender hand still holding the carved marble rail behind her. "I would do anything to find and free my *calon-cyfaill*. I would do anything to see my mother restored to flesh—despite all the harsh words between us."

Lucien forced himself to his feet. His heart kicked hard against his ribs once, then calmed. He walked across the terrace and joined Hekate at the balustrade. She lifted her gaze to his, and Lucien saw steel in the depths of her eyes, a heart-rooted resolve.

"I believe you."

"So if the *creawdwr* is your son, you would know where to find him, how to reason with him," she said. "If he's injured from the severed bond, you can balance him again. All I want is my mother and Jvala."

"Whether or not the Maker is my son doesn't matter," Lucien said gently. "I am captive here, bound to Gehenna. I can't help you."

"If you help me find Lilith and Jvala, I will help you escape," Hekate said, urgency edging her musical voice. "You'll still be tied to Gehenna's fate because of Gabriel's spell, but at least we'll be free."

"Hard for Gabriel to punish Lilith or the Morningstar with both of them in the mortal world," Lucien murmured. Tilting his head, he studied Hekate.

Perhaps she was more skilled in subterfuge than he'd first thought. Maybe she'd only played at being clumsy.

"How do you know I wouldn't abandon you the moment we arrived in the mortal world?" Lucien asked.

"Good question, and blunt." Hekate regarded Lucien, her index finger tapping against her chin as she considered. "I think I would have to place a *geis* upon you."

Lucien nodded. "And since I would need to be sure of your intentions as well, I would need to place a *geis* upon you too."

Hekate's eyes widened. A smile flickered across Lucien's lips. She hadn't thought things through all the way. A true schemer would have. A point in her favor.

Lucien shrugged. "How else can I trust you?"

Holding his gaze, Hekate drew in a deep breath of myrrh-scented air and lowered her shields. She lifted her chin again, daring him to refuse her gift—her unguarded mind.

But he couldn't delve into her mind. Not with his weak and fading shields. If he did, Hekate might see Dante in his thoughts, might see all his fears for his child.

"Name your *geis*," Lucien said.

"You would be forbidden to leave my side. And yours?"

"You would be forbidden to lead anyone to my son or reveal his location."

"Accepted," Hekate said breathlessly. "Your son. I knew it."

Lucien pressed a finger against her lips. "Never say or think that again."

Hekate pushed Lucien's silencing finger aside. "I won't."

"Then I accept your offer and your terms."

A radiant smile illuminated Hekate's face, then she gasped. Wonder blossomed on her lovely face, illuminated her violet, gold-flecked eyes. Her wings untucked and fanned out—creamy white, the smooth undersides pale lavender.

"*Anhrefncathl*," she whispered, voice trembling. Tears glinted in her eyes. "So exquisite. So haunted."

Lucien felt like his heart had turned to stone. The glass slipped from his grasp and shattered on the floor, wine spraying the blue marble like blood.

He neither heard nor felt Dante's song.

And severed bond or not, he should've heard. For whatever reason—Gabriel's spell, the severed bond—he'd lost Dante as son *and creawdwr*.

The hole inside of Lucien ripped wider.

19

EVENTS BEYOND THE SCOPE OF MORTALS

Teodoro Díon harvested the last image from Sheridan's unraveling mind, then withdrew—but not before causing, then rupturing, several arterial aneurysms within the fed's brain. No choice; the FBI agent's mind had been too fragile to wipe.

Teodoro rose to his feet and smoothed the wrinkles from his Italian-style charcoal slacks as Sheridan's vitals monitors flatlined. An urgent and steady *beeeeeeep* filled the room. He arranged his face into a proper expression of concern and touched his fingers to the cold metal of the bed rail with just a dash of hesitancy.

A female med tech in blue scrubs dashed into the room. Teodoro stepped back from the bed and the dead man nested within its beige blankets.

"Can I do anything to help?" Teodoro asked.

The med tech shook her head, her razor-cut blonde shag sweeping across the back of her neck. "Just keep outta the way." She lowered the bed railing.

Several more med techs hurried into the room; one pushed a crash cart, his mustached face calm and focused. Swarming around the bed, the med techs went to work, shouting out instructions and observations as they worked to resuscitate Sheridan.

Teodoro walked from the room and into the corridor, the high-pitched *beeeeeeep* declaring game over fading behind him with each step away.

His report to Purcell would be interesting, to say the least.

An image from Sheridan's mind played behind Teodoro's eyes: *Light flares in the sky. Waves of intense blue, purple, and green light shimmer through the night—a dancing aurora borealis.*

The statues had once been flesh.

And Dante Prejean was not what he seemed to be.

PURCELL WAS A NARCISSISTIC dickhead.

Looking all offended when she'd sparked up one of her clove cigarettes and ordering her to put it out. And what was up with his little speech to Emmett—the *never presume to know what Prejean would or wouldn't do* bullshit?

Man had one seriously big honking bug up his squeaky-tight ass.

Closing and locking the door to her temporary quarters, Merri swiveled around and looked the place over. Twin bed, nightstand, little trash basket, two-drawer dresser, easy chair—all in varying shades of beige—along with a small bathroom and closet.

Not bad for an overnight stay, all considered. The recycled air stank of ozone and fake pine. Ozone. Even though she knew the odor was due to the air filtration system, a cold finger traced her spine. She thought of blue sparks skipping along white stone.

I need to let Galiana know what we discovered in the woods outside Damascus. Maybe she has some ideas about what the hell is going on.

Merri tossed her overnight bag, ugly floppy-brimmed hat, and leather gloves onto the easy chair, then flopped onto the bed. Pulling her pack of Djarum Black cloves from the pocket of her suede jacket, she lit one up and took a long, delicious drag.

Merri exhaled spiced smoke into the air and thought of her *mère de sang*, Galiana al-Qibtiyah, strolling the evening-drenched streets of Savannah, tall and regal in a long, gauzy, sunset-shaded dress that showcased her chocolate brown skin and wavy, black hair. Tapping ash from her cigarette into the trash basket, she sent to Galiana.

<*Merri-girl, what's wrong? Exhaustion edges your thoughts.*>

<*Stupid stay-awake pills. Had a job to do during daylight hours.*>

<*Ah. I still don't understand why you want to work for mortals.*>

<*Sometimes I don't either.*>

Merri laid down on the bed and rested her head on the pillow. She described the Fallen Stonehenge circling the cave in the pine-, oak-, and elm-forested hills outside Damascus.

Blue sparks. Ozone. Heart beating within stone. Smooth wings.

<Fallen magic, girl. But on this scale . . . I think something huge is taking place.>

<Like what? How were so many of the Fallen transformed at once?>

<I'm not sure. Maybe this is the beginning of another war for power among the Elohim, or maybe it's a return of the Fallen en masse to the mortal world, but . . .>

A return? Merri wasn't sure she liked the sound of that. *<But what?>*

<Something went wrong.>

<They're the Elohim, the Fallen. What could go wrong? How?>

<You showed faces frozen in many different expressions— some ecstatic, others surprised, disbelieving, afraid. You think these fallen angels were all caught off-guard but for one, yes?>

<Yes.>

Merri's thoughts flipped back to the angel kneeling among the trees, knowing her *mère de sang* would receive the image.

The fallen angel's wings curve forward as if in an attempt to shelter herself, her eyes closed, her hands clenched into fists in her lap. A supplicant for mercy unreceived.

<She knew what was coming and why,> Galiana sent.

Merri felt the heat of provocative possibilities simmering in her *mère de sang's* mind. *<Why there?>* Merri sent. *<Why did the Fallen show up in Damascus, Oregon, of all places? Who or what turned them to stone and arranged them around a newly formed cave?>*

<Who took you to Damascus? Who were you seeking?>

<A couple of mortals and a vampire.>

<Research their histories. Maybe one of them is the key to this mystery. But please, Merri-girl, be cautious. I have a suspicion that events beyond the scope of mortals or even vampires might be unfolding.>

Uneasiness snaked through Merri, coiled cold in her belly. She sat up. <*Beyond the scope of vampires? What the hell does that mean?*>

<*I need to speak to the* llygaid *and look into this more. Research those histories like I asked and, Merri-girl?*>

<*Yeah?*>

<*Promise me you'll be careful.*>

With Merri's promise, the conversation ended. She stubbed her cigarette out in the bottom of the metallic trash basket beside the bed. She rose to her feet and her vision grayed. She sat down on the bed again, the springs only giving slightly beneath her, and lowered her head.

Damned stay-awake pills. It'd take several nights of natural Sleep before she was truly back on her game again. After a moment, Merri eased back onto her feet. Her vision remained clear. An excellent sign.

Rummaging through her overnight bag, Merri palmed the flash drive Gillespie had given them before she and Emmett had headed out for Portland, the flash drive containing all the pertinent data on the Rodriguez case and its suspects.

She'd learned quite a bit about both Wallace and Lyons, but Dante Prejean's history had been slim—frontman for Inferno, a bunch of arrests in New Orleans, all misdemeanors—so she hoped she could put a little more meat on its highly classified TSP bones tonight.

Merri tucked the flash drive into her jacket pocket. Unlocking the door, she slipped out into the empty and after-hours-quiet corridor. She looked at the door across from her own, Emmett's room. Probably in the cafeteria or snoozing. No need to bother him unless she found anything worthwhile.

Like why Gillespie had lied to her and Emmett about Prejean being enhanced.

Enhanced, my ass.

Opting for the stairs instead of the elevator to reach Prissy-Ass Purcell's office two levels down, Merri *moved* down the corridor for the door marked EXIT/STAIRS at its end. She hit the door's bar and breezed down the stairs, a blur on the security cameras stationed at each exit landing.

Yanking open the door on level five, Merri *moved* down another empty hall. She stopped outside Purcell's office. Light off, door closed. Mr. Prissy-Ass wasn't in. A small green light winked from the security keypad in the wall, indicating Purcell's door was unlocked.

Must mean he's coming back and soon.

Twisting the doorknob and cracking the door open just wide enough for her to slither through, Merri entered Purcell's darkened office. A hint of clove-scented smoke lingered in the air along with a faint trace of Purcell's cologne—a blend of ginger, green tea, and bitter orange.

Merri paused, waiting for her eyes to adjust to the near-total blackness of the underground office. Using the thin light filtering in through the door's frosted glass panel and the yellow and green telltales on Purcell's computer and printer, she padded over to his desk.

She tapped the mouse and the sleeping monitor flickered to life. A picture of the Fallen Stonehenge, white stone glistening in the rain, filled the screen. A chill touched the back of her neck.

Events beyond the scope of mortals or even vampires . . .

Fishing the flash drive from her jacket pocket, Merri inserted it into a USB port on Purcell's Dell and went to work downloading copies of files. She grabbed pretty much everything available. She'd check them out on her laptop once she'd returned to her room, and separate the wheat from the chaff.

The sound of footsteps in the corridor grabbed her

attention. Merri paused and listened. Two sets of footsteps. Two heartbeats, one a mortal's fast patter, the other slow enough to be vampire.

Prissy-Ass and a kissy-ass, no doubt. Time to go.

Disconnecting the flash drive from the Dell, Merri straightened, then stumbled as dizziness spun the room around her. She grabbed the edge of the desk to keep from falling. Her vision faded.

Oh, hell no! Goddamned pills.

Sucking in a deep breath of air, Merri lowered her head. Her jackhammering heart drowned out all other sound—including the approaching footsteps.

The room twirled to a halt, and the black flecks stealing her sight vanished. Shoving the flash drive into her pocket, Merri bolted for the door. The footsteps were closer, but she still had time to split without being seen.

Merri slid through the cracked-open door, then eased it shut. Given that Purcell seemed to be in a vampire's company, she tightened the shields around her mind. She hoped her frantic heartbeat hadn't already given her away.

Merri *moved* into a side hall and stopped inside a darkened office doorway, tucking herself into its shadows.

A few moments later, two men strode past the hall juncture in quick strides. The man walking with Purcell wore a slim-cut suit and was very tall, around Emmett's six three, with golden-brown hair razor-cut in a hip, European style. With his tanned olive skin, he sure as hell wasn't vampire. She caught a whiff of vanilla spice and dandelions and, laced underneath that, a hint of ozone.

No vampire. But not mortal either.

"And you're sure what you saw wasn't just madness? Delusion?" Purcell said. He opened the door to his office, flipped on the light, and went inside.

His companion paused at the threshold, then looked

back toward the juncture he'd just passed and tilted his head. His eyes—a startling violet—gleamed, full of captured light.

Merri held her breath and quieted her heart. Sank deeper into the shadows.

What the holy living hell is he?

After a moment that stretched out into decades, the man stepped inside Purcell's office and shut the door.

Relief curled through Merri. She had no idea exactly what Purcell's buddy was, but she didn't intend to hang around and find out. She'd do a little digging later.

She *moved.*

When she reached her room, Merri relocked the door, then fetched her laptop out of her bag. Plunking down onto the bed, she retrieved the flash drive from her pocket. She inserted it into one of the laptop's USB ports and started scrolling through files.

One titled Bad Seed caught her attention.

What kinda TSP was Prejean a part of?

HQ's playing this one real close to the vest. All I was told was that it was a joint project—us and the feds—devoted to the study of sociopaths.

In other words, their monster slipped its leash and they want us to fetch it.

Monsters. Sociopaths. Bad Seed.

Merri clicked open the file and began reading.

MERRI CLOSED THE LAPTOP, fire smoldering in her heart, an unholy image from the Bad Seed file etched into her mind.

In a blood-spattered straitjacket, Dante is suspended upside-down from a huge hook in the ceiling, chains wrapped around his ankles. He hangs above the bodies of those he's killed—including the body of his princess, his Winnie-the-Pooh-loving Chloe.

ADIC Johanna Moore enters the room—its walls a Jackson Pollock–worthy masterpiece in high-velocity blood spray—and bends over Chloe's body. With a touch of her fingers, Moore pushes the child's eyelids open. Makes sure Chloe's empty gaze remains fixed on Dante.

Setting the laptop aside on the bed, Merri rose to her feet. Her muscles felt hand-cranked-wire tight. A True Blood. Not an "enhanced" vampire. But a *True Blood* wrenched away from his mother at birth.

And the things done to him from that moment to this . . .

A muscle flexed in Merri's jaw. It looked like all the minds behind Bad Seed were the true sociopaths.

Oh, let's not forget Purcell. He'd participated in Bad Seed as Wells's errand boy. Seemed to delight in all the nasty things done—especially to Dante.

Merri lit up a Djarum Black and paced the small room while she smoked it, Prissy-Ass Purcell's words still ringing in her ears.

Fucking little psycho.

She needed to let Emmett know what she'd learned. Given Dante Prejean's programming and where he'd ended up—the Wells compound—she wondered if he'd been deliberately triggered and used to murder Rodriguez.

A sense of unease rippled through Merri as though she'd jumped into a lake and found the water too cold and too deep and too dark. Found herself sinking while a leviathan rose beneath her, jaws open.

Talk to Em. Get some perspective. See if you can make sense of this shit.

Merri walked into the bathroom and tossed her cigarette in the toilet. As she turned around, the room dipped and twirled. Black spots speckled her vision. She reached for the wall to steady herself, but missed. Her flailing hand grabbed at empty air.

She fell, crashing onto her side across the bathroom threshold, her damn-near lacquered ponytail lashing her cheek. Sleep poured into her like a waterfall, tumbling her consciousness away in a roaring rush of unstoppable black.

20

A SHALLOW GRAVE

THE SUV'S TIRES HUMMED along the interstate, a steady, hypnotic sound. With Dante doped and Sleeping, his head cushioned in her lap, her fingers stroking his hair, Heather decided to close her eyes. Just for a moment. She rested her head against the window. And dreamed.

OCTOBER AND THE AIR *is crisp. But she's not cold, she's on fire and alive and flying. Heather's birthday is coming up. She'll be twelve. Twelve going on forty. She sees too much and maybe not enough.*

Have I lost her?

I'll make her birthday special, bake her a chocolate cake with butter-cream frosting. I'll decorate the house with red, blue, and yellow balloons and string a HAPPY BIRTHDAY banner across the dining room archway.

Shannon stumbles, her heel catching on the asphalt's ragged edge. She giggles. Good thing she isn't driving. Point in her favor. She licks the tip of a finger and strokes an imaginary line in the air. Sliding off her shoe, she peers at the heel.

Headlights pierce the night. Shannon sticks out her shoe instead of her thumb, cocking her weight onto one hip and smiling. The headlights glow, twin moons filling her vision and dazzling her sight.

The car pulls over, tires crunching on gravel, the muffler streaming a plume of exhaust and the heady smell of gasoline in the air. The engine purrs.

Headlight-blinded, she wobbles as she tries to put her shoe back on. She hops backward before sprawling on her ass. She throws back her head and laughs. Good thing she isn't walking the line for a cop. Another point in her favor. She draws another imaginary line in the air.

Slipping off her other shoe, damned heels playing havoc with her balance, well, that and all the booze, Shannon climbs to her feet, stumbling only a little. She's brushing the dirt off her rear end when the driver's door opens.

A man slips out of the purring car, and something gleams in his hand.

"Need help, Shannon?" he asks.

Shannon shades her eyes from the headlight dazzle with the edge of her hand. Recognizing the tall figure with its tousled dark hair and tight smile, she mutters, "Crap."

Her good humor, her joie de vivre—as her drinking buddies at the Driftwood Bar and Lounge call it—evaporates. "Whatcha doing out here, Craig? Jim send you?"

"Jim? Only if you're on the Most Wanted list, Shan." Craig chuckles, but Shannon thinks she hears a bitter note in his laughter and wonders if something's come between her husband and his best friend. "Been helping a buddy work on his car. Just on my way home."

"That why you're holding a hammer?"

Craig looks down as if he just realized that he is, indeed, carrying a hammer. His fingers white-knuckle around the handle. Lifting his gaze back to Shannon's, he says quietly, "Get in the car. I'll take you home."

Shannon shakes her head. Her husband's friend and coworker seems strung tighter than a tennis racquet, for whatever reason. Maybe he needs a drink. She swallows back the giggles bubbling against her lips.

"Thanks anyway."

Craig sighs. "You aren't going to let me give you a ride, are you?"

"Bingo!" Shannon says. "Give the man a prize. No, I'm not going with you. No matter what you say, I know Jim sent you. I'll just go back to the Driftwood and call a cab."

Shoes in hand, Shannon manages an about-face and keeps her balance. Score. She draws another imaginary point in the air. She feels her joie de vivre catching a second wind. She steps onto the smooth road to spare her bare feet bruises from pebbles.

"Tell Jim he can go to hell. And you can go right with him."

"I have a feeling you're going first."

Behind her, Shannon hears a familiar sound. A sound that freezes her in midstride like a blast of frigid Arctic air: the ka-chunk of a round being chambered.

"Just get in the goddamned car, Shannon."

HEATHER TRIED TO FORCE her eyes open, tried to wake herself up, but couldn't. It felt like unseen and heavy hands held her in place. Paralyzed her. The dream shifted. The lonely highway housing an idling car, two people—her long-ago murdered mother and her recently KIA mentor in the FBI—aimed on destroying themselves, and a tavern gleaming with warm light . . . all of it pinwheeled away, the images getting smaller and smaller until they vanished altogether.

Something tugged at Heather, tried to yank her down into the dark. She gasped as pain scratched and clawed behind her eyelids. An inner borealis, streamers of undulating light—red, violet, blue, and green—accompanied the pain.

The unseen hands pressing down on her disappeared.

And something else hooked her and dragged her into darkness.

NIGHT-SHADOWED CYPRESS *and twisted old oaks surround two men standing behind a rust-pocked old Chevy, eyeing the contents of the trunk they've opened. One man holds a shovel.*

"A shame you killed dem, for true," one says.

"Dammit, I tole you it was an accident. Now shut the hell up about it, you."

"Why we burying dem? Next blowdown will wash dem bodies right outta the ground. We should feed 'em to the gators."

"Tais-toi, fool. Just dig."

The high-pitched and rhythmic scrubbing-against-the-washboard song of katydids fills the hot, humid night with natural music as the men—both of equal height, but one heavier than the other, and both in jeans and sweat-stained T-shirts—pull the bodies out of the trunk one by one and dump them onto the sawgrass.

Teenagers. Hands cuffed behind their backs.

One has black hair and pale, pale skin that seems to

gleam in the moonlight. Blood glistens at his temple. Heather's heart hammers against her ribs. Dante. Maybe thirteen or fourteen. This isn't in the Bad Seed files—at least not the ones she's viewed.

One of the men kneels and pushes Dante's hair back from his face. "I don't tink dis one's dead, Cecil."

"'Course the boy ain't dead, you fool. He's the best moneymaker I got or ever had, for true. I just held him under in the tub until he sucked some water into his lungs, then I pulled him out. Mighta knocked a few things off-a his skull too for good measure."

"Den why the hell we drag his ass down here?"

A smile curves Papa Cecil's lips, sharp as an icepick and twice as heartless. "Boy needs a lesson. Boy always needs a lesson."

Papa and his friend take turns digging a hole in the moist ground, tossing shovelfuls of sawgrass and dirt into air thick with the smells of moss and rotting wood and brackish water.

Once Papa judges the hole deep enough, he wipes sweat off his forehead with a bandana from his back pocket. "Fetch him," he pants, pointing at Dante.

"But he ain't dead."

"Fetch him anyway and toss him in the goddamned grave."

Papa's buddy sighs, then drags Dante to the edge of the impromptu grave. After glancing at Papa one more time, he rolls Dante into the hole.

"Now fetch the dead one," Papa says. "And drop him in too. Den start shoveling the dirt back in."

Dizziness twists through Heather. Nausea wrenches at her stomach. She spins, the cypress and old oaks whipping around her, the star-flecked sky wheeling above. She tumbles into the open grave.

She falls in slow motion. And even though the grave

*is only five feet deep, she falls forever and ever. Dante lies
sprawled at the grave's bottom. Water seeps up from beneath
him, turning the dirt into dark and stinking mud.*

Just before Heather slams into Dante, his eyes open.

"Où suis-je?" he whispers.

THE BEAUTIFUL SLEEPING REDHEAD'S eyes flew open.
Panic rimmed her twilight blue gaze. Sweat beaded her
forehead. "You're with me," she whispered, answering
Dante's question.

"And who are you?" Even as Dante voiced the words,
even as he reached up to protect her from the shovelfuls
of dark, damp dirt flying into the hole—*ain't a hole, it's a
grave*—he realized he knew her. He just didn't know when.

"Heather," he breathed. Her sweet evening scent—sage
and rain-wet lilacs—curled around him, filled his lungs.

A smile flickered across her lips. She nodded. "Here,
Baptiste."

Shovelfuls of dirt cascaded down on them, peppered
her hair. Mud and swampy water sucked at Dante, soaked
through his T-shirt and jeans. Electricity crackled along his
fingers, pooled in his hands. Wasps droned. Voices murmured and capered and insisted.

Boy always needs a lesson.

Dante-angel, run, run, run!

You'll fail, you know.

"Roll over," Dante said, "and let me up. I ain't gonna let
fucking Papa bury us."

Heather cupped a warm hand against his face. "You're
not in that grave, Baptiste. That happened a long time ago,"
she said. "You're here on the road to New Orleans with me.
I won't let you fall. I won't let you go."

A high tide of white silence rolled through Dante,

sluicing away the droning wasps and the poison they needled into his veins; drowned the goddamned voices. Everything stopped. The world spun white and silent around him—except for the North Star pull of Heather's voice.

"STAY HERE AND NOW, Baptiste," Heather said. "Stay here with us."

Fear twisted icy knots through her guts. She stared at Dante's glowing hands, Violet's transformation beneath those same hands playing behind her eyes.

Black hair ripples into red tresses, golden skin lightens to freckled and fair, life-sparked blue replaces empty jade green eyes.

A transformation Heather believed he hadn't intended. But lost to his past, he was also losing control over his Fallen magic.

So you trust him?

With my life.

Bending her head, Heather whispered into Dante's hoop-rimmed ear, "I'll never leave you behind, Baptiste, so you do the same for me. Come back."

Dante's tension-taut body quivered for a moment, then he unclenched his blue-fire engulfed fists. Closing his eyes, he visibly forced himself to relax muscle by muscle. Blue flames danced along the rings on his fingers and thumbs. Gleamed along the thighs of his leather pants.

"Holy hell, am I seeing blue in the rearview? Need help, doll?"

"Shit!" Annie cried. "Toss him out before he touches anyone!"

"Pull over in case I need to move real fast. Don't wanna do that at eighty plus."

"You got it."

The SUV slowed as Von eased up on the gas and steered the vehicle into the emergency lane, blinkers flashing.

Heather brushed the backs of her fingers against Dante's pale cheek. His thick, black eyelashes deepened the blue smudges under his eyes. "I'm here," she said.

"*Moi aussi*," he said.

Heather's breath caught in her throat as Dante's song, a beautiful and haunting aria, arced between them, heart-to-heart, crystalline and strong. It strummed across the deep-threaded strings composing her soul; a wild song, burning and passionate and tender.

Fire blazed through Heather's veins, torched her heart.

Dante opened his eyes. Gold flecked his deep brown irises, but his hands no longer glowed. He touched fevered fingers to Heather's face and traced a molten path along her jawline to her throat.

"*Je t'aime*," he whispered.

"*T'es sûr de sa?*" she said, her voice husky. " 'Cause I love you back."

A smile tilted Dante's lips. "Yeah?"

"Yeah."

Dante lifted up on one elbow as she brought her face down, his hot hand sliding around to the back of her neck. He kissed her long and deep, his lips burning against hers; kissed her breath away. Tasting amaretto on her tongue, her lips, Heather deepened the kiss, her fingers twisting in his silky hair. Heated flutters rippled through her belly.

When the kiss ended several breathless minutes later, Dante traced a finger along Heather's lips. He searched her eyes, his own unguarded. His pale, beautiful face was quiet, thoughtful.

"As lost as I get, I will find you, Heather. Always."

"You'd better," she whispered, throat tight.

Dante pulled her down into another long kiss.

21

ON MY WAY TO HELL

"SHIT."

Heather stared at the headline of the newspaper showcased in the vending machine in front of Rolling Rick's Stick-to-Your-Ribs Eats.

TRAGIC MENTAL ILLNESS CLAIMS FBI STAR PROFILER.

So Rutgers had made good on her threat. And hadn't wasted any time doing so either. Only three, no, four days had passed since their meeting in the Seattle field office.

Heather shivered in the predawn chill. She dug in her jeans pockets for change, but came up empty. "Shit."

The low thunder of idling truck engines rolled through the night and diesel fumes fogged the air, pungent and heady. Even so, she still caught a whiff of frosted earth and burning leaves as Dante stepped up beside her.

"What's wrong, *catin?*"

Heather pointed at the vending machine. "More CYA by the Bureau. This time it's aimed at me. You got any change?"

Dante patted his pants pockets, then shook his head. "Nope."

Stepping past Heather, he wrapped his fingers around the vending machine's pull-handle and yanked. The door snapped off with a metallic *pop*. Dante fished out a copy of the *Idaho Statesman*. He propped the broken door beside the vending machine.

"You didn't need to do that," Heather protested. "We could've scrounged up some money."

Dante shrugged one shoulder. His brows slanted down as he scanned the article. "Mother*fuckers*," he muttered, handing the newspaper to Heather. "The assholes are also calling you despondent and delusional and in treatment at an undisclosed location."

"Sure. First they'll discredit me," Heather said. "Then see if that's enough."

The meeting she'd attended in Rodriguez's office along with her father, SA James William Wallace, and a webcast-projected ADIC Rutgers replayed through her mind:

Mental illness has claimed two members of your family so far, your mother and your sister, I believe.

That's false, ma'am. My wife was an alcoholic—

Bipolar. Mom was bipolar. Annie too.

It'll be made clear that you are the third member of the family to become ill. We'll express our regret at seeing one of our finest brought low by ill health. We'll also let it be known that we wouldn't hold you responsible for any delusional comments you might make.

Meaning: just in case you decide to turn into a whistle-

blower about Bad Seed and the FBI's involvement, we'll make sure no one listens to you.

Heather glanced at the paper, then folded it and tucked it under her arm. Should make interesting breakfast reading, as long as "interesting" meant blowing out a few blood vessels in the brain with a warp-speed rise in blood pressure.

Heather drew in a long, hopefully calming, breath. She focused on her mantra: *One thing at a time, Wallace.* But this time it didn't work; her pulse continued to fly through her veins.

Not only had the Bureau officially cut her loose and smeared her name and reputation—as promised—she'd dreamed about her mother's murder again, with even more disquieting details.

This time she'd seen the killer—Craig Stearns, her late mentor and the man who'd been more of a father to her than James William Wallace ever had.

She refused to believe that Craig Stearns had anything to do with Shannon Wallace's murder. He'd been a young and dedicated fed at the time, and the man who had eventually tracked down the serial killer who'd murdered her mother and twenty-three other women along the I-5 corridor.

Dante had crafted changes into Heather when he'd saved her life, changes he hadn't intended to make and didn't know any more about than she did; changes she would have to discover as they made themselves known.

Maybe the dreams were just that, nothing more, not visions from a woman twenty years dead; just a scenario tossed together by her overworked subconscious and not due to Dante.

Maybe. But every instinct Heather possessed insisted otherwise, insisted she was witnessing events from her murdered mother's perspective.

Gotta be wrong about Stearns, though. He never

would've hurt Mom. Must be a reason I saw him, though. Maybe someone who reminded Mom of Stearns?

And somehow she had become entangled in Dante's dream/memory as well. The image of him as a slender teen, cuffed and unconscious, dumped from a car trunk and into a shallow grave had seared itself into her heart.

What had actually happened after Cecil Prejean and his accomplice had dumped both boys into that grave?

She jumped when Dante's hot hands cupped her face, melting away the chill sinking into her bones. "You okay? You look like you're a million miles away."

"For a despondent and delusional lunatic, I feel pretty good, actually," Heather said, offering him a smile.

Blue and gold flames flickered like stars in the ink-black depths of Dante's eyes. "What ain'tcha telling me, *catin?*"

Heather drew in a deep breath. "What the Bureau's doing—that's just step one. Next they'll try to make it a reality, have me committed somewhere. Or make me a suicide, just to be safe."

Fire ignited in Dante's eyes, his body coiled. "*Try* being the key word, *chère.*" His hands slid away from her face.

"And it's not just the Bureau. The SB is playing some kind of game."

"I think it's called cat and mouse."

"Hey, little brother, catch," Von said, joining them on the sidewalk. He tossed Dante a pair of sunglasses, then lobbed a plain black hoodie at him.

Dante caught both with a quick flick of his wrist. "*Merci beaucoup,*" he said, sliding on the shades. He slung the hoodie over his shoulder.

Von nodded at the small pack of nomads at one of the truck stop's fueling stations. "Raccoon clan, on their way to Wyoming," he said. "I dropped by to say hello and they said they'd be more than happy to offer us blood."

"Yeah?"

"Yup. Dawn's a couple hours away, so there's time if you'd rather hunt."

Dante trailed a hand through his hair. "Nah. Should be fine. Ain't got time to mess around. Not when *we're* the ones being hunted." He glanced at Heather.

"True . . ." Von stopped speaking, his gaze flicking between Dante and Heather. A vertical thinking-deep line creased his forehead. "What's up?" he asked, shoving his shades on top of his head.

"The Bureau just stepped things up." Heather pulled the paper out from under her arm and showed it to Von. He scanned the headline, his expression speed-shifting from neutral straight into indignant.

"So now the bastards claim you're loony tunes," Von said, voice flat. The crescent moon tattoo beneath his eye glinted in the starlight. "And the media's eating it up with a big ol' spoon."

"The FBI's expert in manufacturing evidence when necessary," Heather said. Her hands knotted into fists. Learning that fact had been a recent and bitter lesson. "Wasn't always that way, though."

"For you it never was," Dante said. He reached for her hand and smoothed her fingers away from her palm. "Yeah?"

Heather felt a smile tug at her lips. "Yeah."

Von pulled a map out of his back pocket and handed it to Heather. "I've got our route marked out. Why don't you go over it during breakfast, make sure everything's okay?"

"Good idea. I will."

Von glanced at Dante. "Ready, little brother?"

"Yeah, *mon ami*, I'm ready." Squeezing, then releasing Heather's hand, Dante bent and planted a heated amaretto kiss on her lips. "Back in a bit."

Heather nodded, unsure of what was the proper thing

to say when one's nightkind boyfriend slipped away for a little breakfast. Somehow *bon appétit* felt more than a little wrong. She settled on, "Be careful."

A smile tilted Dante's lips as he backed away. "That'd still be a first, *chérie*."

"A woman can dream," Heather replied.

Laughing, Dante blew her a kiss, then turned and walked across the parking lot toward the nomads, a smoldering and sexy vision in snug leather pants and mesh-and-PVC-sleeved T-shirt. He paused to pull on his new hoodie.

"I'll keep close to him, doll," Von said. "In case anything goes south."

"Good," Heather said. "He's still struggling."

"I know," Von said quietly. He sauntered after Dante, catching up in just a few long-legged strides.

More than one trucker stopped what he was doing to stare at Dante as he passed in a graceful, easy stride, his beauty and pale, pale face unhidden.

Light from the fueling station's overheads glinted silver off the metal buckles on Dante's boots, off the studs on the belt slung around his hips, on the rings gracing his fingers and thumbs, and off the collar strapped around his throat.

Dante flipped up the hood and tugged the edges past his face.

Heather studied the nomads as they gassed up several different types of motorcycles—Harley, Kawasaki, Sucker Punch Sally's, Ducati—and family-hauling Jeeps decorated with swirling Celtic designs in bright colors; men and women in road-dusty leathers checked knapsacked supplies and chatted while children raced each other to the restrooms.

Annie shoulder-opened the gift store's heavy glass door, and walked outside, tearing open a pack of Camels. "When are we going to eat? I'm fucking starving."

"Go grab us a booth," Heather said.

"What are *they* doing?" Annie asked. "Are those nomads friends of Von's?"

"I think they just met, but nomads regard nightkind with respect," Heather said. "View them as part of the natural order of things."

"Oh sure," Annie said. "Like leeches and mosquitoes."

Heather chose to ignore her sister's comment. Annie was bored and hoping for an argument, as usual. Heather heard the click of a lighter wheel, smelled burning tobacco as Annie lit a cigarette.

"I thought you were going to get us a booth."

"After my smoke." Annie paused, then said, "Holy shit, are they gonna *feed* on the nomads?"

"The nomads offered," Heather replied, her gaze still on Dante. He stood beside Von, his weight shifted onto one hip, hands at his sides. Several nomads, two men and a woman, knelt in front of Dante and bowed their heads. Dante shook his head, bent, and pulled one of the men to his feet.

"Huh. So why you watching? You jealous or something?"

Anger flared and Heather turned to face her sister. "No, I'm *not* jealous," she said, just managing to keep her voice level. "I sure as hell don't want to be food."

Annie regarded her for a moment, exhaling a gray plume of smoke, a wry gleam in her eyes. "Sure, not food. But I'll bet anything you don't want his lips on another woman. Or his hands. Or his—"

"Shut *up*," Heather cut in.

"He told me he kills them sometimes."

"Just shut the hell up, Annie."

If Annie had a superpower it would be button-pushing, because she always knew which ones to push. Always knew if a little tap would do or if she needed to lean into it with all she had. Worse? This time Annie was right. She'd nailed it on the head. The hard, heated knot coiled around Heather's heart verified it.

Jealous, and not proud of the fact. As for Dante killing those he fed upon, Heather felt more than a little uncertain. He hadn't killed Cortini—even when Athena had encouraged him to finish his "meal."

"Oooo, Gorgeous-But-Deadly picked one. Boy or girl? Guess!"

A chilly breeze smelling of sagebrush and gas fumes swept through the parking lot. Shivering, Heather folded her arms over her chest. But she refused to look, refused to swallow her sister's bait.

"I'm going to get us a booth."

Heather grabbed the door handle, pulled it open, and warm air whooshed out as she stepped inside, the sizzling smells of sausage, green peppers, and eggs making her stomach rumble. Checking to make sure the Browning was still snug against the small of her back and covered by her pink Emily the Strange T-shirt, Heather walked into the restaurant.

IN BETWEEN BITES OF scrambled eggs, Heather studied the map Von had given her since she and Annie would be handling driving duties during daylight hours.

Von had bought a few supplies before arriving at the Happy Beaver Motel to pick them up, and once Dante was conscious again, he'd suggested they drive straight through to New Orleans.

We can't risk Sleeping in motels. It'll give the SB and whoever else is chasing our asses too much time and opportunity to fuck with us.

What Dante didn't say, but Heather understood, was that he didn't trust Annie either. Motel time would give her opportunities to run away and opportunities to betray them.

And Heather was pretty damned sure Annie would take advantage of those opportunities first thing.

So they'd stopped at a twenty-four-hour Walmart Supercenter and bought blackout curtains and sleeping bags.

Between the curtains duct-taped over the back windows and dividing the front of the roomy Mercedes-Benz SUV, and the mummy-style sleeping bags with their face-hugging snorkel baffles, Dante and Von figured they'd have enough protection to Sleep in the back during the day while Heather and Annie drove.

At night, they'd switch places.

The route on the map led through Salt Lake City, Utah; down to Denver, Colorado; then on to Wichita, Kansas; Norman, Oklahoma; and Dallas, Texas. Then they'd cross into Louisiana, through Shreveport, Baton Rouge, and ending in New Orleans.

It chilled Heather to realize that their route was almost identical to the one Elroy Jordan, the Cross-Country Killer, had taken on his serial killer vacation tour.

Stopping only for food and bathroom breaks, the goal was to reach New Orleans in another forty hours—give or take. And the sooner the better.

Before the SB reversed their mysterious decision to let them go and burned rubber chasing them.

Before the Bureau decided Heather Wallace needed to run away from treatment and throw herself off a bridge.

Before the Fallen winged down from the sky in another bid to claim Dante. If they'd learned from the last experience, they'd come equipped with tranks and a large net.

The Bureau, the Shadow Branch, the Fallen. Oh, my.

Just as Heather finished the last bite of raspberry jam–slathered toast, Dante slid into the booth beside her. He parked his shades on top of his hooded head. His autumn scent curled around her. "Hey, *chérie*."

"Hey, back," Heather said, smiling.

Even through his clothes and hoodie, Dante's heat baked against her and, for the first time since they'd arrived at Rolling Rick's, she felt grateful she wore only a T-shirt and not something heavier.

"Hey, how was the guy you chowed down on?" Annie asked.

Without looking at her, Dante flipped her off. The intensity of the relief melting through Heather at Annie's words almost embarrassed her. He'd chosen a male.

"Von's in the SUV double-checking the blackout curtains," Dante said, picking up the check. "You about ready?" He held a debit spike—one of Von's—in his other hand.

"Definitely."

Heather and Annie visited the restroom one more time while Dante paid for the meal. When Heather walked outside into the wind-chilled night, she noticed Dante standing in the parking lot between the sidewalk and the SUV, his hood pushed back and his head tilted to one side, his gaze on the clear sky.

She hurried across the parking lot. "What is it?" she asked, gut-sure she knew the answer. His words validated her instincts.

"One of the Fallen."

"Does he know you're here?"

Dante considered, then shook his head, his gaze still on the fading night sky. "I don't think so. But, his song . . . a part of me wants to answer it." He shivered suddenly, then lowered his gaze. Curled his hands into fists.

"Maybe you should," Annie said, her voice low and urgent. "You'd be happier with someone like you. Someone who could take you to your true home."

"My true home? Someone like me?" Dante looked at

Annie, his expression half amused, half exasperated. "Ain't no such things. Trying to get rid of me, *p'tite?*"

"Excuse me for trying to help." Annie marched around the SUV to the front passenger door and climbed inside.

"Do you still hear it?" Heather asked, walking with Dante to the rear of the SUV.

Dante nodded, his gaze traveling back up to the sky. "He's hoping I'll answer."

And Heather would bet anything that Annie was hoping Dante would too.

Dante looped an arm around Heather's waist and pulled her up against him. He burned against her, his body fire and steel, his dark eyes dilated with coming Sleep. Hooking a finger through the ring on his collar, she pulled him down into a deep and lingering kiss.

"*Bonne nuit, catin,*" he whispered against her lips. "See you tonight."

"Sweet dreams, Baptiste."

Heather stepped back as Dante climbed into the back of the SUV and joined Von. All of the SUV's seats were folded down flat except for the two up front. She closed and locked the door, then walked around to the driver's seat and hopped in.

Heather held her breath, listening for the rush of wings, but she only heard rumbling diesel engines and the throaty roar of kick-started motorcycles.

And the hard pounding of her own heart.

22

THE BEGINNING OF
THE END

OVER THE AIRWAVES
March 26

MIKE CARR: What is going on in Damascus, Oregon? For those listeners in the area, I hope you'll phone in your observations. For the rest of you, I'll fill you in on the government's latest misdeed.

JILL CARR: We're counting on you to give us the true-blue scoop as always, Mike.

MIKE CARR: Well, here it is. Yesterday, state and federal authorities announced that due to a natural disaster—a sinkhole emitting toxic fumes—a large area outside Damascus is now off-limits to the public while the fumes are being contained and the sinkhole filled in or repaired or what have you.

The official word is that an entire family died when the sinkhole swallowed up their home. Word is that a couple of neighbors perished from the fumes as well. I also learned that a handful of nearby residents went through the whole *Silkwood*-shower-and-scrubbed-raw scenario. They also had to endure all kinds of blood tests and lab work.

JILL CARR: Scary, that.

MIKE CARR: It gets scarier, Jill. When I was reading the *Oregonian* yesterday, I caught a small article tucked away in the back pages.

JILL CARR: And what was this article about? Please enlighten us.

MIKE CARR: Well, it was about the shimmering light seen in the sky before dawn on day one of the sinkhole, waves of color like the aurora borealis—the northern lights, for our more down-to-earth listeners.

JILL CARR: And is that unusual for Oregon, Mike?

MIKE CARR: Thanks for asking, and the answer's hell, yes. Even though the northern lights can *sometimes* be glimpsed

	from Oregon if the conditions are right and the clouds don't block the view, this wasn't one of those times.
JILL CARR:	What made it different?
MIKE CARR:	It was raining, for one thing. The sky was full of clouds that early morning. So this "light anomaly" wasn't an atmospheric magnification of the aurora borealis. It was a *new* aurora borealis.
JILL CARR:	New? Is that possible?
MIKE CARR:	Anything is possible, I suppose. But if it was simply a "light anomaly caused by toxic fumes rising into the air" as the authorities claim, then why have they turned the area outside Damascus into a forbidden zone? I even tried to access the area through Google Earth and it's blocked off. D'ya hear that, people? The satellite image is *blocked off*!
JILL CARR:	Sounds like we have a new Area 51, Mike. What are they hiding? Could the lights have been caused by a spaceship landing or crashing?
MIKE CARR:	Or a new military weapon? Who knows, Jill? But whatever it is, both the Oregon state government and the federal government don't want *you* to know!
JILL CARR:	I've heard rumors that the SB— the supposedly nonexistent Shadow Branch of the U.S. government—is behind the cover-up taking place

right now in Damascus, Oregon, in the US of A! A part of this great nation!

MIKE CARR: You said it, Jill. And if the secretive SB is behind something, you know it's gotta be shady. In Nazi Germany, the SB might've been called the SS.

JILL CARR: The SS in our own country, making people disappear, making entire events disappear. Turns my blood to ice.

MIKE CARR: So let's open up the phone lines and see what our callers have to say about the Damascus mystery. Go ahead, Caller Number One, you're on the air and speaking to Mike Carr.

CALLER ONE: Hey, Mike, a big fan here. You always tell it like it is!

JILL CARR: Thanks, it's a dirty job, but someone's gotta do it. Am I right?

CALLER ONE: Damned straight, man! I live in Portland, but a good buddy of mine lives just outside Damascus and he saw them northern lights just before dawn on March 25. He grabbed his digital camera and took pictures too!

MIKE CARR: Fantastic! Is there any way your buddy can send us the photos?

CALLER ONE: I'm sure he wouldn't have a problem with it, Mike. I think he'd be honored! As soon as he gets back from his vacation, I'll let him know you'd like him to e-mail the pictures.

MIKE CARR: Vacation? In March?

CALLER ONE: Yeah, well, he and his family usually take their vacation the end of summer so as to avoid the crowds, y'know? But I guess they decided to go early this year.

MIKE CARR: Did your buddy tell you this?

CALLER ONE: (*hesitates*) No, not exactly. He had a message on his answering machine saying they were all on vacation.

JILL CARR: I have another caller on the line.

MIKE CARR: Stay on the line there, partner, okay?

CALLER ONE: Okay . . .

MIKE CARR: Let's see what Caller Two has to say. Go ahead, Caller Two, you're on the air and speaking with Mike Carr.

CALLER TWO: I saw what was going on that night, Mike. It wasn't a UFO or a secret weapon. It was a rip in time.

MIKE CARR: A rip in time? How many beers didja have tonight?

CALLER TWO: I ain't drunk, man, that's kinda mean, y'know? I'm not a whacko like a lot of your callers.

JILL CARR: Now who's being mean?

CALLER TWO: Sorry, ma'am. I saw things flying in the sky during that aurora borealis. Things too big to be birds. Unless they were a flock of condors, maybe. They were big and they were singing. I think they were pterodactyls.

MIKE CARR: Ah, the rip-in-time factor. Everyone knows that ancient pterodactyls sang and chirped and flew in flocks.

Caller One, did your friend mention birds or anything else flying in his pictures?

CALLER ONE: He did, Mike—wow, I forgot about that! He didn't say they was pterodactyls or anything like that. He thought it was birds attracted by the northern lights. Big birds, he said.

MIKE CARR: Very interesting. Thank you for joining us, Caller Two.

JILL CARR: We've another caller, Mike.

MIKE CARR: Stay on the line, Caller One. Caller Three, you're on the air and speaking with Mike Carr.

CALLER THREE: They was angels flying and singing, not pterodactyls. Christ! Sounds like someone needs to get back on their meds.

MIKE CARR: Sounds like he isn't the only one. Angels? Seriously?

CALLER THREE: I've taken my pills tonight, so it ain't that. I saw the lights and I saw the angels flying and singing. I also saw blue lightning bolts zip up from the ground and knock them outta the sky.

MIKE CARR: Blue lightning bolts? Whatcha you taking, partner? I sure could use some!

CALLER ONE: My buddy mentioned blue fire too, Mike. And he said whatever was flying plummeted to the ground like ducks blasted with shotgun pellets.

MIKE CARR: And you *just* remembered these little bits of info, Caller One?

CALLER ONE: Well, I didn't want you to think I was
                nuts, y'know?

CALLER THREE: I've heard that all pictures of the
                lights and angels from that night are
                being seized and destroyed by the
                government. I also heard that people
                are disappearing too. Evacuated be-
                cause of the toxic fumes.

CALLER ONE: Maybe that's why my buddy took an
                early vacation.

MIKE CARR: What else have you heard, Caller
                Three?

CALLER THREE: They ain't being evacuated. Some
                are getting their minds wiped—

MIKE CARR: Like in *Men in Black*? With the
                flashy-thingie?

CALLER THREE: Haven't seen the movie, Mike. But
                some are getting their minds wiped
                and others are being snuffed alto-
                gether. That's what's happened to
                your buddy, Caller One.

CALLER ONE: Oh, Jesus! You're fucking nuts! My
                buddy's on vacation!

MIKE CARR: You just earned me an FCC fine,
                Caller One.

CALLER ONE: Sorry about that, but this guy's a
                loon!

CALLER THREE: I'm not crazy, but I wish I was. Your
                buddy and his entire family are get-
                ting their minds wiped or they're
                being dumped in unmarked graves.
                Hell, maybe they'll make it look like
                a car accident or something.

CALLER ONE: You can just go to hell!

MIKE CARR: Can you back up your claims, Caller Three?

CALLER THREE: Just visit Damascus, Mike. Take a look around. Homes near the sinkhole are empty.

MIKE CARR: Do you have friends who've disappeared, Caller Three?

CALLER THREE: No, no friends. Safer not to have any.

MIKE CARR: So let's say for argument's sake that angels fell from the sky. Are you saying this is the end of days?

CALLER THREE: Naw. That happened a long time ago. We're all living in the thousand-year span before the final battle.

MIKE CARR: Of course, silly me.

CALLER THREE: You can make fun of me all you want, Mike. Fact is, angels fell from the sky—no, they was *knocked* from the sky and the government is *using* them.

MIKE CARR: Wait, hold on. You saying the government *lured* angels with a manufactured aurora borealis? Lured them, then *captured* them?

CALLER THREE: I ain't saying that, you are.

JILL CARR: I have another caller.

MIKE CARR: Hold a moment, Jill. Maybe I *am* saying that, for argument's sake. You said the government is using the angels. What would it use them *for*?

CALLER THREE: Any number of things, from using them to communicate with God, to using their powers against their enemies.

MIKE CARR: Why wouldn't God rescue them? Just smite the government?

CALLER THREE: Because God doesn't realize He's God yet, of course. He's still growing up.

MIKE CARR: (*laughs*) Of course. When do you think God'll realize He's God?

CALLER THREE: How the hell would I know?

MIKE CARR: Sounds like you know everything else that's going on, just figured you'd know that too. Hold on there, Caller Three, we've got another caller. Caller Four, you're on the air and speaking with Mike Carr.

CALLER FOUR: (*Woman's voice*) My sister disappeared. She lived in the area near the sinkhole and I've been trying to reach her to see if she's all right, but I haven't had any contact with her.

MIKE CARR: Maybe she was evacuated.

CALLER FOUR: That's what I thought too. But she doesn't answer her cell phone.

JILL CARR: Maybe she left it behind.

CALLER FOUR: That's what I've been hoping. I contacted the emergency number listed online for information about my sister and I was told she was in a secure site and not to worry.

MIKE CARR: So evacuees aren't being allowed to contact their families?

CALLER FOUR: That's the way it sounds to me. My question is why? If it's just a sinkhole, why are people being taken away and not allowed to contact anyone?

MIKE CARR: Maybe the toxic fumes are actually radioactive waste.

CALLER FOUR: But that wouldn't be a reason to block all communication!

MIKE CARR: It would be if people had been exposed. Especially if some of those exposed died or are dying.

CALLER FOUR: Oh my God.

CALLER THREE: He doesn't know that He's God yet. Give Him time.

MIKE CARR: Keep trying to reach your sister, Caller Four, okay? Contact the media, raise a big, stinking fuss over her whereabouts.

CALLER FOUR: But . . . if I draw too much attention, will I disappear too?

MIKE CARR: No, not if you draw public attention. They wouldn't dare touch you then. They'd be forced into answering your questions.

CALLER FOUR: Okay. Thank you.

CALLER THREE: You know they'll come for each of us now.

MIKE CARR: Thanks for all your . . . insights, Caller Three. Good night.

CALLER THREE: I wish you well, Mike and Jill. I'm going underground. I advise you to do the same.

MIKE CARR: That's all we have time for this early morning edition. Until tomorrow at the same time, same place, keep digging for the truth!

23

ILLUSIONS

WITH NIGHT-WOVEN AND STAR-PIERCED illusion wrapped tight around him, the Morningstar glided through the sky, following the forest green SUV as the *creawdwr*'s fetching and flame-haired lover steered the vehicle from the truck stop and onto the interstate.

Heather, the older sister of pliable and more-than-willing Annie.

He'd gleaned more than a little information about Dante from *both* minds.

Wybrcathl silenced, the Morningstar wheeled higher into the sky. Ice crystals hissed and steamed against his heated skin and beaded like diamonds in his white hair.

Annie's miswired mind had allowed her to see past his illusions. Had left her immune to his Word . . . ah, but not to his touch, his suggestions—especially not when she desired both. Without her willingness, he couldn't have planted careful little seeds in her subconscious.

You won't hurt him, right?

Of course not. He will be cherished.

Good. Um . . . you ready to go again?

Vicious and urgent in her coupling, Annie had worked hard to punish them both. She'd only half succeeded. Her tears afterward had puzzled him, as did her self-loathing, but even after millennia, he still couldn't claim to truly understand females, mortal or otherwise; a part of their allure.

The Morningstar's wings stroked through the dying night. Breathing in the crisp scent of frost, he reworked his illusion to match the coral sunrise streaking the mountain-peaked horizon.

Annie's knowledge of Dante had been sparse, however. So after she'd returned to her bed and had curled beside her sister, pretending to sleep, the Morningstar had delved into Heather's dreaming mind.

A treasure trove, lovely Heather.

When he finally winged down into New Orleans, the Morningstar would become the father and mentor missing from Dante's life and help this misused and tortured *creawdwr* fulfill his destiny.

CELESTE UNDERWOOD FINISHED HER coffee, barely tasting the Sumatra Mandheling's sweet roasted-caramel flavor, then rinsed the cup out in the sink. She gripped the counter's polished granite edge and stared out the kitchen window. Heavy, gray rain clouds hid the sunrise, stealing color from the horizon except for a lighter shade of gray.

She knew how to work gray, used it often in her job. Indeed, she was required to think in shades of gray instead of absolutes like black or white. And she even enjoyed it.

But Director Britto's call last night had muddied gray into black.

Call your people off S and Wallace. Immediately.

Bill, what's going on? I don't have a problem with letting Wallace or Lyons slip away, but I suspect S has been triggered and used. We absolutely need to bring him in and assess—

Celeste, listen to me, and listen carefully.

All right, Bill.

S is not to be brought in. He and Wallace are free to go wherever they damn well please, understand? Surveillance can continue, but it's essential your operatives aren't spotted.

I understand, but what happened? What's changed?

You mean aside from a missing house, an enigma of a cave, and a circle of stone-sculpted angels that are, even now, on their way to HQ?

But that's the point. S and Wallace must know what happened, how and why those things occurred. Interrogation would—

No. No interrogation. No pursuit. No arrest. Am I clear? Call your people off right now. If you turn up Lyons, make sure he truly becomes an official casualty of the sinkhole/toxic fumes cover story. S and Wallace are no longer your concern.

Ironic choice of words, given that she'd delivered the same orders to the Bureau's ADIC Rutgers. But officially or not, Prejean very much remained Celeste's concern. Especially since her former daughter-in-law might vanish with her granddaughters, her Stephen's girls.

What troubled Celeste even more than the director's command was the fear she thought she'd detected in his voice. Controlled, yes, but still present.

Who had the juice to put the squeeze on the director of the Shadow Branch?

What galled her to no end was the fact that Gillespie

and his agents actually had Prejean and Wallace in their gun sights when this goddamned order came down.

Sighing, Celeste pried her fingers away from the sink's counter. She crossed to the center island and finished putting together her lunch on the gold-veined green granite. She had a feeling that today would be an eat-in kind of day.

The curry, tuna, and tomato salad she prepared quickly filled the kitchen with a welcome and spicy odor. A few Ritz crackers and a generous slice of apple pie completed the meal.

Carrying her insulated purple lunch sack into the living room, Celeste rested it on the sofa. She picked up the report Gillespie had e-mailed her late last night. Some of the things it contained disturbed her, to say the least.

Gillespie claimed that Prejean had transformed a child shot in the crossfire into another child entirely. If not for the forwarded statements from witnesses to the event, including field agents, the motel manager, and the child's mother herself corroborating Gillespie's claim, Celeste would've assumed he'd had a six-pack too many.

As it was, she had no idea what to think of the transformation claim or how such a thing could be possible. Perhaps a mass illusion cast by a True Blood? Provided they possessed such an ability.

Should she pass the report on to the director or just sit on it for the time being? After all, S—Prejean—was officially no longer her concern.

Celeste slid the report into her briefcase, then latched it shut. Might be best to study it for a bit first. Look for any discrepancies. In truth, it sounded like the director had other worries on his mind.

Her cell's ringtone—a sophisticated and European trill—ended the silence. The ID named the caller as Purcell. Celeste flipped the cell open and said, "A bit early for you, Richard."

"Yes, ma'am. I'm afraid I have bad news. Sheridan died last night."

Celeste rubbed her forehead. *Of course. When it rains, it goddamned pours.*

"Before or after debriefing?"

"During, ma'am. An autopsy was performed right away and his death was due to multiple aneurysms in the brain. Possibly due to traveling with a bullet wound."

"Did Díon get anything useful from him before he died?"

"No, ma'am."

"Dammit," Celeste sighed. "Well, I would leave out the flight bit when you inform Monica Rutgers at the Bureau about the loss of her agent. She's going to be unhappy in any case, but no reason to give her ammunition for her I-told-you-so shotgun."

"Will do."

"And meet me at my office in two hours. We have a few things to discuss."

"Yes, ma'am."

Ending the call, Celeste slipped her cell into the right-hand pocket of her black blazer. She wondered how quickly Purcell could get to New Orleans. Bringing Prejean to Alexandria was out of the question now, but maybe Purcell could make other arrangements. Maybe somewhere closer to where Valerie worked.

An image from a crime scene photo—*the* crime scene—developed behind her eyes, an image she'd forced herself to remember in every heartrending detail.

Sprawled facedown in a pool of his own blood on the gray slate entryway floor, one shoe—a brown tasseled loafer—behind him like he'd stepped out of it, one hand bent underneath his chest, Stephen looks like he never knew what hit him.

But Celeste knew better. Her son's murderer had

confessed to a cellmate that Stephen had pleaded for his life and had offered his wallet before the bastard had shot him in the head. Then he'd placed the gun muzzle against Stephen's temple and fired again.

Stephen, her only son, her intelligent, creative boy, snuffed because his wife feared a divorce would cost her more than she cared to part with.

And the cost to arrange a murder? Abundant sexual favors, false promises, and five thousand dollars.

Cheaper than a divorce, true, but a murder trial really racked up the dollar signs.

Celeste would make sure that Purcell had everything he needed to trigger Prejean's programming one more time. Due to Director Britto's concerns, Purcell could no longer kill the vampire after he'd finished Valerie.

Unfortunate, but one couldn't have everything.

Scooping up her lunch bag and briefcase, Celeste left her town house for work.

GILLESPIE DRAINED HIS LAST beer, wishing for a bottle of Black Velvet or Jack Daniel's or even Grey Goose to chase it down. But he had a feeling that no matter how much booze he poured down his throat, he'd never kill enough brain cells to forget the images the security-cam footage had just etched into his mind.

The energy surrounding Prejean shafts into Johanna Moore's body from dozens of different points. Explodes from her eyes. From her nostrils. Her screaming mouth. She separates into strands, wet and glistening. Prejean's energy unthreads Moore. Pulls apart every single element of her flesh.

Unmakes her.

Johanna Moore spills to the tiled floor, her scream ending in a gurgle.

Well, the million-dollar question—where was Dr. Johanna Moore?—had finally been answered. She was still in the Bush Center for Psychological Research. Dead. Her remains most likely in a mop bucket.

Prejean's beautiful face is ecstatic. He closes his eyes and shivers as energy spikes from his body, flames from his hands.

The same blue flames that had surrounded Prejean's hands when he'd transformed that poor little girl. Medics had sedated her mother. The girl kept talking about the beautiful angel with black wings—Prejean.

I was a balloon with a broken string floating up to the stars, then the angel caught me and wrapped my string around his wrist and pulled me back down. It tickled in my tummy.

Now, after viewing the disk he'd confiscated at the site, those words chilled Gillespie to the bone.

A figure moves into view—waist-length black hair snaking into the air like night-blackened seaweed caught in a current. His wings, black and smooth, arched up behind him, half-folded, as he kneels on the floor and reaches for one of two figures crumpled together on the tile.

"Avenge your mother. And yourself."

And Prejean rises from the speaker's arm—from the fallen angel's arms—bathed in dim red emergency light, his body tight and coiled, blood smeared across his breathtaking face.

Prejean wasn't just a True Blood vampire—he was much, much more.

Fallen angels. Jesus-fucking-Christ! Gillespie would bet every last dollar he had in his pathetic 401(k) that the angel statues now rolling along the interstate to Alexandria hadn't started out as statues. But Prejean—*Name ain't Prejean*—had fixed that pesky flesh problem, now hadn't he?

Maybe Underwood had just discovered the truth about

Prejean herself and that was the reason he'd been ordered to stand down last night.

Wallace's words, a calm and clear warning, nudged Gillespie's memory.

They're lying to you. Ask about Bad Seed.

I know about Bad Seed. I know what Prejean is.

I doubt that.

She'd been right; he'd had no idea, and he knew very little about Bad Seed.

In all honesty, given what Prejean was or, more to the point, what he could *do*, Underwood had probably saved all of their lives with that order—no matter the reason. As it was, two agents had been medevacked to Legacy Emanuel in Portland in critical, but stable, condition.

Another thing Heather Wallace had been right about?

They're lying to you.

And they had no reason to stop.

Gillespie dropped his hands from his face, padded to the bathroom, and hit the shower. Once he'd shaved, splashed on a little Jōvan Musk, and dressed in fresh clothes—matching gray trousers and jacket, white shirt, blue tie—he repacked his suitcase.

Gathering the empty beer bottles, he racked them back into their carton slots, then placed the refilled sixer on top of the dresser. He powered down his laptop and switched it off, the pilfered security-cam footage of Prejean in its disk drive like a hidden and deadly cancer.

Gillespie stared at his reflection in the mirror. Noticed the extra pounds around the middle. Noticed the gray pallor of his skin. Noticed the fear in his eyes even behind his glasses.

It'd never been the booze.

He was a coward, plain and simple. His lack of heart had lost Lynda, had cost lives under his command, had drained away all respect—from his wife, his kids, his co-workers, and from himself.

Even drinking was cowardice.

Of course, Gillespie's thirsty brain insisted otherwise. Claimed he thought better, reasoned sharper, with a few brews under his belt.

Gillespie splayed his fingers on the dresser and leaned closer to the mirror and his sagging and aging reflection. Most people would probably guess his age a good ten years older than his forty-six.

He had a choice to make.

Option one: He could check out of the motel, get in his rental, drive to FedEx and Next Day Air the disk detailing Moore's death at Prejean's unearthly hands to Underwood, then putter back to the Wells compound and continue processing the site.

He could leave the fate of Prejean to his higher-ups as ordered. Wipe all thoughts of the bloodsucker from his mind. Or, more likely, booze them away.

Option two: He could check out of the motel, get in his rental, drive to Portland International and book a flight to New Orleans. Wallace had told Prejean that they were headed home. Home had to be New Orleans. Once Gillespie arrived, he would finally be able to do something that mattered.

Gillespie knew he'd never win Lynda back. Knew he'd never win back all the respect he'd pissed away. The lives lost on his watch due to his poor judgment, his cowardice, were his to carry forever. He just needed the courage and strength to do so.

He had an opportunity to do the right thing.

A chance to make the world safer. A chance to slay a true monster.

And all he wanted was a drink.

Pushing away from the dresser, Gillespie shrugged into

his Gore-Tex jacket, grabbed his suitcase, tucked his laptop into its sleek black bag, and walked out into the rain.

PURCELL'S WORDS—PROPER AND SYMPATHETIC and less sincere than a hooker's smile—still rang through Monica Rutgers's memory.

He came through surgery just fine, so we were all completely caught off guard by his death. SOD Underwood asks that you accept her condolences, ma'am.

She couldn't take the time to extend them to me herself?

I apologize, but she's in a meeting this morning.

I'm sure Sheridan's family would understand how a meeting would take precedence over Brian's death.

With a jab from one rage-trembling finger, Rutgers had ended the call. She couldn't stomach hearing Purcell's smooth voice for one more second.

SA Brian Sheridan was dead.

Rutgers rubbed her aching temples, her pulse throbbing hard and fast beneath her fingers. Underwood's words from the day before echoed through her memory:

You sent him into the line of fire. These are the consequences of action you spun into play and your agent will pay the price.

Rutgers had ordered Sheridan into the deep, dark woods and had promised to guide him out again; a promise she'd failed to keep.

The microwave beeped. Even in the midst of sorrow and disaster, everyday mundanity kept chugging along.

Sighing, Rutgers pushed away from her desk, and, rising to her feet, crossed to the beverage cart. She fetched her lavender mug out of the microwave and dropped two tea bags into the heated water it held, then carried the mug to her desk and set it on the cup warmer.

Vanilla-and-blueberry-fragrant steam curled into the air, unable for once to soothe her senses or quiet her restless mind. She knew the tea would remain untasted.

Rutgers tapped her assistant's button on the intercom.

"Yes, ma'am?"

Rutgers stared at the intercom, her heart kicking hard against her chest. For just a second, Ellis's voice had sounded like Sheridan's. Grief tightened her throat. Haunted by a voice. And by all that would never be said.

What would turn out to be her final conversation with Sheridan ghosted through Rutgers's mind:

And Brian? Be careful. Do you have your rifle?

Yes.

Use it.

Such Spartan words, efficient and to the point. And now—a cold and hollow eulogy. Sheridan had deserved so much more.

"Ma'am?" Ellis repeated.

Rutgers drew in a centering breath, then said, "Brian Sheridan died last night while in the care of the SB. I need you to send me the address and phone number for his parents."

"Brian? Shit. I mean, yes, ma'am, of course. Flowers to be sent?"

"Absolutely. And hold all my calls."

"Yes, ma'am."

Rutgers leaned back in her chair, her gaze on the cherry blossoms outside her window. Thanks to the SB, Sheridan was dead and Dante Prejean very much alive and free to continue to murder and corrupt.

Through unofficial channels Rutgers had heard about last night's shoot-out in a motel parking lot outside Damascus, Oregon, between Prejean and Wallace and Underwood's on-scene agents.

Section Chief Gillespie had been forced to let Prejean and Wallace walk while two of his men had landed in the hospital with bullets in places they didn't belong.

Rutgers felt a hard smile tug at the corners of her mouth. She would bet anything that had been a bitter pill for Gillespie to swallow. *Wonder how many bottles of beer it took to wash it down?*

An early morning breeze rippled through the cherry blossoms. A few of the pink flowers fluttered to the winter-sered lawn, delicate splashes of color.

The words Heather Wallace had written on her admissions application, words the former agent had once lived by, fluttered like cherry blossoms through Rutgers's mind.

I want to be a voice for the dead.

So do I.

For Sheridan. For Rodriguez. For all who'd died at the hands and fangs of Dante Prejean. Even for the woman who'd once been the dedicated and compassionate special agent named Heather Wallace.

Through Bad Seed, the Shadow Branch—no, be honest, the Shadow Branch *and* the Bureau—had created Dante Prejean. Had brutally shattered a child, then pieced him back together with misaligned edges, the cracks still showing. Just to see what would happen.

Prejean would never, ever stop killing. Whether on his own, or being used as a weapon by people in the know like Alexander Lyons, Prejean would never stop.

And, even after last night's fiasco in Oregon, the SB planned to step out of his way with a genial smile and an after-you-please wave of the hand, and allow him to continue spilling and drinking as much innocent blood as he desired.

Rutgers shifted her gaze from the window, blinking dazzling light from her eyes.

So much to do. And not enough time to do it all. Prioritize.

Turning to her computer, Rutgers composed a letter of resignation, printed it out, and signed it. Sealing it inside an envelope, she wrote the deputy director's name across the front in elegant, flowing script, then placed the envelope on her keyboard.

If you even feel the urge to pull another stunt like this, just tender your resignation and do it as a private citizen because you'll be done here.

Understood.

She'd never again order someone else into the deep, dark woods.

She would enter them alone.

24

VIOLENCE IN MY HEART

Gigeresque wasps crawl along Dante's mud-streaked arms, burrow under his skin. He feels the tiny metallic bodies scraping along his muscles and veins on their way to his nest-combed heart.

Droning reverberates within his skull. Fills his fucking head with noise.

Perry's weight pushes Dante deeper into the wasp-squirming mud. Like tiny sewing needles or a rose's ruthless thorns, stingers lance into his back, his ribs, and his neck again and again. Venom burns like spilled gasoline beneath his skin.

Perry makes a choked kind of gurgling sound and Dante realizes he isn't dead, that Papa plans to bury them both alive.

Fuck that fi' de garce Papa. Fuck him hard and sideways

until he screams for mercy. Then fuck the bastard a little more.

"*Perry?*" Dante whispers. But the furious droning in his head keeps him from hearing Perry's heart, from knowing if his foster brother really is still alive.

His handcuffed hands numb and pretty much useless, Dante twists in the cold, fetid mud, trying to wriggle out from under Perry's body, but manages to push himself deeper into the muck instead.

Shovelful after shovelful of dirt flies into the grave and, slowly, it fills. Dante shakes dirt from his face. And keeps up his effort to work free of Perry's dead weight. Sweat and dirt sting his eyes.

Just as Dante slithers, mud-greased, out from under Perry, he catches a flash of peripheral motion from up above and something hard and edged slams into his temple.

White light strobes across Dante's vision like heat lightning, then pain slams him back down into the mud. Blackout.

"LITTLE BROTHER?"

The low, urgent voice pulls Dante up from the mud. A familiar voice. One he can't quite place. He slivers open his eyes and pain pierces his head. Sledgehammers a red-hot spike behind his left eye. Dizziness spins him like a bottle in a kissing game.

How do I know that voice?

Not how, Dante-angel. When.

Dante stops spinning with a hard lurch. When bounces around his skull like a ricocheting bullet, sparking images from his memory with each hit.

Spark: A tall nomad pulls off his leather jacket and tosses it onto the chair. Unbuckling his double shoulder holsters, he shrugs them off and places them, along with his guns, on top of his jacket. He touches fingers to one bare, muscle-corded wrist.

Spark: A crescent moon tattoo beneath a green eye.

Spark: A wicked, mustached grin.

"Von?"

"You got it. I don't know how I got here, but let's getcha outta that grave."

"I was just getting comfortable."

"Getting whacked in the head with a shovel will do that to ya."

Von's strong hands loop around Dante's shoulders, pulling him free of the squelching mud and lifting him out of the grave and onto the sawgrass beneath the deep cypress shadows. Dante rolls to his knees, vision swimming. He closes his eyes and lowers his head, pain throbbing in his temples.

"What about Perry?" he whispers. "He still alive?"

"Who's Perry?"

"Mon ami. In the grave with me."

"You were the only one in there," Von replies.

"You sure? Cuz he was on top of me and hurt bad. Dying, maybe."

"Yup. I'm sure."

Maybe Papa took Perry with him when he left. Maybe Perry's still alive. A warm flicker of hope eases the chill from Dante's heart. "We gotta look for him."

Dante feels a hard tug on the cuffs, feels the cuffs bite deeper into his wrists. Feels hot blood slick his skin.

"Well, hell. These cuffs are nightkind-proof."

"Nightkind?"

"Yeah . . ." Von's voice trails off, then gentles. "Where you at, little brother?"

"Right here. In the grass beside an open grave," Dante says, puzzled. He opens his eyes and winces in the moonlight filtering through the trees overhead. He twists around to look back over his shoulder.

A good-looking guy in a white wife-beater and faded jeans

is kneeling behind him. Tied-back dark brown hair, mustache framing his mouth. Moonlight sparkles along the crescent moon tattoo beneath his right eye—concerned and familiar green eyes.

"Who are you again?"

Almost in answer, words whisper through Dante's memory and tug at his heart: A spoken thing or a wished-hard thing takes a shape within the heart, man. Takes shape. Becomes real.

Pain raps sharp knuckles against Dante's mind. "Von," *he breathes.*

A smile slides across Von's lips. "You got it." *He reaches up and wipes mud from Dante's cheek.* "We'll meet in a few years when you're grown up. But right now, I think somehow you've pulled me inside a dream you're having—no, make that a fucking nightmare. Or is this a memory, little brother?"

Uneasiness loops through Dante, coils along his spine. "Man, this feels fucking real to me so I ain't got an answer for that." *He turns back around and stares into the deep, still shadows pooled beneath the trees.* "There a difference between nightmares and memories?"

"Yeah, little brother, there is," *Von says, his voice low and tight.* "For most of us, anyway. But they fucked with you."

"They?"

"You'll kick their asses later. Forget it for now. Let's just concentrate on getting you outta these cuffs." *He pauses for a moment, then says,* "Hey, you think you could imagine a key? Or even just imagine that the cuffs are gone?"

"'Cuz this might be a dream or memory?" *Dante mulls it over, thinking he has nothing to lose.* "Yeah, d'accord. Why the hell not? I'll give it a shot."

"You're a Maker, little brother. Ain't nothing you can't do."

Another voice, deep and rumbling, rolls through Dante's

mind: Creawdwr. You're a Maker. The only one in existence.

Raw-edged grief squeezes Dante's heart and his breath catches in his throat.

Lucien. I abandoned him.

But then the name slides away, and Dante can't catch it, can't bring it back, can't even remember the feel of it upon his tongue. But the grief, barbed and prickling, remains.

"Make a key," *Dante whispers and closes his eyes.*

He visualizes the key Papa uses to unlock the cuffs from his wrists when he wakes up at twilight. Visualizes cramming key and cuffs down Papa's throat.

Forget Papa and focus. Make that key, get outta here, and find Perry.

Wait. I'm dreaming, yeah? I can't find Perry. He's long gone.

But Dante knows that's not right. He still feels Perry's weight against him, the heat of his body, still hears the gurgle choked from his throat.

"Make a key, little brother. I know you can do it."

Music ignites within Dante, blazes within his haunted heart, and soars burning into the night, an aria composed of fire. Something snaps and buzzes around Dante's captive hands.

A click. Then the cuffs fall away, thudding onto the ground.

"There ya go," *Von says, clapping him on the shoulder.* "I've never heard music like that before—ever. Fuck, Dante, it's . . . beautiful *ain't enough or right. Maybe celestial . . . ? But you gotta stop your song so you can stop the magic.*"

Dante opens his eyes and swings his hands around. Blue fire flickers and dances around them. He stares, a sense of déjà vu rippling through him, warring with the sense of soon-to-be sweeping across his mind.

"You gotta let the song go," Von says quietly.

Dante shivers, then without even thinking about what he's doing, he stabs his flaming fingers into the moist earth beneath the sawgrass. The song raging inside of him dims down to embers, then vanishes.

Von stands and moves in front of Dante, grasps his arms around the biceps. Helps him up onto his feet.

"Merci." Dante offers Von a tilted smile. He rubs his bruised and bloodied wrists. His healing wrists.

Von circles him, his face thoughtful despite the mischief winking in his eyes. "So this is you as a teenager, huh, little brother? Grimy little bastard, ain'tcha?"

"Hold on, got mud in my eyes," Dante says, rubbing the middle fingers of each hand beside his eyes.

Von laughs. "A grimy little bastard and a smart-ass. Yeah, that's my boy." He circles to a halt in front of Dante. "You're gonna grow a few inches taller and put on more muscle, and you're gonna strop a keen edge on that attitude." He rests a hand against Dante's muddy T-shirt, above his heart. "And this? Your heart, your compassion, and strength—that never stops growing, little brother. No matter what, your heart's true."

Pain coils through Dante's mind like a snake across water, trapping the words he was about to say in his throat. He squeezes his eyes shut. Voices whisper up from the wasp-riddled depths within.

Little fucking psycho.

Threeintooneholytrinity . . .

Boy needs a lesson. Boy *always* needs a lesson.

Dante's eyes fly open. Papa stands in front of him, sweat beading his fucking whiskered, double-chinned face and staining the pits of his T-shirt. And he's swinging a shovel like a baseball bat, mud-grimed blade up in the air and aimed at Dante's head.

Dante moves.

He wrenches the shovel from Papa's grasp and whips it around in a whistling arc aimed for Papa's balding head.

Turnabout is a bitch, yeah?

In the split second before the shovel connects with Papa's shocked face—guess who that grave's for now, fi' de garce?—another face overlays it, like a flickering frame in a film reel stuttering up and down.

Dante catches a glimpse of a dark-haired and green-eyed guy, a crescent moon inked beneath his right eye, someone familiar, someone he loves—mon cher ami—but the shovel whistling through the humid night air is beyond all recall.

The shovel smacks into the Papa/Von flickering face, slamming his head to the side, and toppling him into the sawgrass. The shock of the contact shudders up Dante's arms to his shoulders. The shovel drops from his nerveless fingers.

Dante falls to his knees in the blood-wet grass, whispering, "No."

CRUISING THE SUV AT a steady seventy-eight miles per hour on I-84 East, just outside of Brigham City, Utah, Heather straightened in her seat as the skin prickled along the back of her neck.

Had she just heard something from the back of the SUV? She touched the car-stereo mute control on the steering wheel and listened.

"Hey," Annie protested. "What're you doing?"

"Shhh."

From the other side of the blackout curtains, Heather heard thrashing sounds. Her blood turned to ice. She steered the SUV into the emergency lane.

"What's going on?" Annie asked. "Is it another seizure?"

Drumming sounds joined the sleeping-bag thrashing noise. "Yes, dammit." Heather slowed the SUV to a stop, turned off the engine, and switched on the hazard lights.

She grabbed the black zippered bag out from under her seat. Heart drumming in time with the rapid and violent rhythm behind her, she plucked a prefilled syringe free from the bag. She turned, preparing to slide between the blackout curtain panels and into the back. She hesitated. It'd be too dark for her to see.

Hold on, Baptiste. Just hold on.

Glancing at Annie, Heather said, "Get me a flashlight from the glove box."

Without a word, Annie yanked the glove box open and slapped a small flashlight into Heather's palm. "Need anything else?" she asked.

Heather shook her head, turned on the flashlight, and ever so carefully parted the blackout curtains just enough so she could slip through. A bar of bright morning sunshine slanted through the gap and slid across one of the sleeping bags—Von's.

Heather's heart jumped into her throat. Had Dante and Von switched places when they'd bedded down? Because otherwise the thrashing and twisting bag held the nomad, not Dante.

Heather closed the curtain and the bar of light and the dust motes it'd illuminated vanished. Flashlight in one hand, syringe in the other, Heather crawled over to the violently whipping sleeping bag and knelt beside it. She tugged down the zipper, unlaced the hood, and yanked it open.

Von. Convulsing. Blood smeared across his face. His movements too violent, too fast, for her to jab him with the syringe.

"Shit!"

Heather considered sitting on him to hold him still, but figured he'd just buck her off. But maybe two bodies would be enough to hold him long enough to get the needle into a vein—anywhere.

"Annie, I need your help."

"Really? You sure?"

"Yes! Get your butt back here."

Another bar of light sliced across Von's sleeping bag, then vanished. Annie crawled between the bags and joined Heather.

"Fuck. Is that Von? What's going on?"

"I don't know, but we need to sit on him, see if we can hold him still long enough to get the morphine into him."

"Are you fucking kidding?"

"No. Now on a count of three, we sit on him or lay across him, whatever, but we get on him. Got it?"

"Yeah," Annie sighed. She scooted closer to the convulsing nomad.

"One. Two. Three."

Heather flung herself across Von's torso, syringe poised between her fingers. She felt Annie land on him too, pinning down his legs—at least momentarily. He twisted and arched and Heather grabbed a handful of sleeping bag to anchor herself. Then she jabbed the needle into the side of his throat and thumbed the plunger.

Within a few moments, his convulsions stopped cold as if a plug had been yanked. But, unlike Dante, Von didn't wake, doped and dreamy, before sliding back into morphine's grip. He remained unconscious.

"Can I get up now?" Annie groaned. "I took a knee to the chesticles."

"Yeah, you can. Thanks for the help."

Heather pushed herself up and off of Von. She swung the flashlight around until it rested on the bags of supplies they'd picked up at Walmart. She scooted over to the bags and dug through them for the face-cleaning wipes Annie had tossed into the cart.

"Why's Von having a seizure? Ain't that Dante's thing?

I mean, is this some vampire plague or something?"

"I don't know what's going on," Heather said, crawling back to Von's sleeping bag. "Wish I did. Could you get us back on the road? We'll draw the wrong kind of attention if we stay here too long with our hazard lights on."

"Hey, you say that like the wrong kind of attention is a bad thing," Annie said. "But sure, I'll get us going again." She crawled to the front and slipped through the curtains, another ray of light appearing, then vanishing.

Heather opened the wipes, pulled one out, and started cleaning the blood smeared across Von's face. The source seemed to be his nose. Her pulse pounded through her veins.

What the hell happened?

She turned Von's head to the side. Blood pooled in the cup of his ear. Her heart went cold. Just like Dante, when his bond to Lucien had been severed. Fear pricked along her spine.

Swiveling around on her knees, Heather unlaced Dante's hood and pushed it away from his face. Blood trickled from his nose too. She stared at the tears glimmering on his dark lashes.

Another memory?

Brushing back Dante's silky hair, Heather checked his ears for blood and found none. But heat radiated from him in scented waves—burning leaves and deep, dark earth. Sweat popped up along her hairline.

Too hot. He's burning up.

Heather unzipped his sleeping bag, peeling the tight material away from him. She wondered if she should try to pull his shirt off, but decided opening the bag was risk enough in case of unexpected sunshine.

She shifted back around to Von. She touched his face. Sleep-cool. She placed her hand on his white wife-beater, fingers above his heart, and held her breath. After several long moments, she felt a strong beat against her palm. She closed her eyes in relief.

Yanking another face-wipe free from its box, she carefully cleaned up the blood from his ears, then wiped away more blood from his nose. Von's face seemed empty somehow, lax in a way it normally wasn't when he Slept.

And that scared her. Because it reminded her of how brain-damaged and comatose crime victims looked in the hospital. Missing, somehow.

Had he been attacked in his Sleep? But who could . . .

Her breath caught in her throat. She flipped her flashlight back over to Dante. Sliding the light along his tight-muscled length, she paused at his hands—clenched into white-knuckled fists. Her heart picked up speed.

Tears on his lashes. Fists clenched and ready to fight.

Just like when he lost Chloe.

A single heartbreaking thought chiseled itself into her mind.

Dante hurt Von and hurt him bad.

Heather remembered tumbling from the dream about her mother and into Dante's dark memory/dream, falling into that shallow grave on top of him.

Tumbled into or pulled into—she wasn't sure which, and when she'd asked Dante about it, he'd looked troubled and unsure too.

Maybe because the morphine knocked my shields down and we were both dreaming, but it ain't normal, catin. It worries the shit outta me. Maybe you shouldn't sleep too close to me until I get a handle on this.

What if something similar had happened to Von? And it went bad?

Von's words haunted her memory: *I'm really worried about him, doll. The images I got from him . . . his reality keeps shifting between now and then. He's fighting damned hard to keep himself here and now and with us. But . . .*

But . . . what if Dante lost his fight and his link to Von sucked the nomad into his shifting reality? Heather thought of Von's too-still face. Thought of the tears wetting Dante's lashes.

Feeling sick, Heather closed her eyes. Bad Seed was *still* stripping away everyone Dante cared about, one by one, and *still* finding ways to trick him into doing it himself.

I think he's had as much as he can take, doll. Heart and mind.

Losing Von would probably break Dante.

She refused to lose Dante, refused to let him slip away. She also refused to let either of them lose Von. Heather opened her eyes and switched off her flashlight. Crawling to Dante, she stretched out beside his fevered body and pressed close.

Not knowing if it would help, not knowing if anything could, she whispered into his ear, "Let me in, Baptiste."

25

THE GREATER GOOD

"SOD Underwood would like to debrief you as soon as you've finished lunch," FA Cooper said, a warm smile on her lips and in her whiskey-brown eyes.

Emmett finished chewing the last bite of his BLT—crispy, applewood-smoked bacon, but way too much mayo—and swallowed. "I thought that was scheduled for this evening when my partner's available."

Purcell's auburn-haired assistant nodded. "It was, but I think the SOD has a bit of unexpected free time in her schedule this afternoon. Shall I tell her you'll meet her in the interview room in fifteen?"

"Roger that," Emmett said, plucking a paper napkin from the metal dispenser on the table and wiping his fingers. "I'll finish my coffee and head down. Which level?"

"Four. Room 425. I'll let Underwood know you're on the way." Flashing another warm smile, Cooper turned and walked away, her curve-hugging gray skirt accenting her hip-swinging stride.

I think she's flirting with me.

Amused, Emmett wadded up his napkin and tossed it onto the table. He picked up his cup and finished his cooling no-frills-just-black java. Rising to his feet, he sauntered from the people-pocked cafeteria. He'd stop by his room, take a look in the mirror and make sure lettuce hadn't stealthed up between his teeth and boogers weren't dangling from his nostrils before greeting the SOD.

Another first.

According to the field-grunt grapevine, SOD Celeste Underwood was hard, but fair—a ballbuster only when deserved, needed, or required—and distant. Word through the grapevine also said that over the course of the last couple of years, Underwood had become even more distant.

Ever since the cold-blooded murder of her son, Stephen Underwood.

Emmett couldn't blame her for that. If anything happened to one of his kids . . . He shook away the thought, refusing to finish it.

Enough to turn anyone to stone.

After Emmett checked his reflection for potential sources of embarrassment, he raked a comb over his hair and brushed his suit for crumbs, then left his room. He slipped a note scrawled on a torn piece of yellow legal paper underneath his Sleeping partner's door.

He paused, touching his fingertips to her door. He wished he could talk to her, bounce a few thoughts around before heading in for debriefing. But it would have to wait until evening.

"Sleep tight," he murmured, dropping his hand.

Emmett turned and strode to the elevators. Stepped inside and punched the glowing button marked four. Despite a decent night's sleep, he couldn't shake the feeling that something was off-kilter.

Really? Fallen angels trapped inside stone and a cave where none existed before, and you have a feeling something's a teensy little bit off-kilter?

As his grandma would've said: Get your ass over here, boy, so I can knock some sense into that thick skull of yours.

Emmett chuckled. Grandma had never appreciated a flair for the obvious. But his amusement faded as he recalled how he used to feel when his grandmother had read to him from the book of Revelation—all goosebumps and dread.

He felt that now.

The elevator stopped. The doors slid apart, and Emmett stepped out into a corridor busy with agents hurrying along on various tasks. He joined the corridor flow, branching free when the frosted panel etched INTERVIEW STATION 425 popped into view.

Straightening the knot in his slim black tie, Emmett opened the door and walked inside. Three people—a black woman Emmett identified as SOD Underwood, Purcell, and another white male Emmett didn't recognize—sat in chairs on one side of a long, rectangular table, manila folders and Styrofoam cups of water or tea or coffee positioned in front of each pair of folded hands.

"Ah, Field Agent Thibodaux," said SOD Underwood. "So glad you could join us on such short notice. I appreciate it. By doing your debriefing now, I'll save time this evening."

"Not a problem, ma'am." Emmett walked around to the opposite side of the table and sat down in front of the single Styrofoam cup resting at his end. A quick peek confirmed water.

"You know my assistant, Field Agent Purcell," Underwood said. "On my left is Field Interrogator Díon."

Emmett nodded in acknowledgment.

Purcell inclined his head in return, his face calm and composed, unlike last night. FI Díon—broad shouldered, light brown hair, interesting violet eyes, maybe mid- to late-forties—offered Emmett a smile.

Emmett felt himself relax underneath the warmth of Díon's smile. He picked up his cup of water and took a sip.

"Shall we get started, gentlemen?" Underwood asked. After receiving their murmured assents, she leaned forward against the table and said, "Start with when you and your partner, FA Goodnight, arrived at the foot of the Wells's driveway."

Emmett led them through their discovery of Sheridan, the circle of white statues ringing the brand-new cave, of the headless body inside the guest cottage, and the long trip to Alexandria escorting the wounded and silent Sheridan. All standard. All routine.

He kept all of Merri's observations to himself.

I hear their hearts, Em. I hear their goddamned hearts.

"Thank you, Agent Thibodaux," Underwood said, a quick smile gracing her lips. "I think we're just about done here. I believe Díon has a few wrap-up questions, then you can go."

"Sounds good," Emmett replied.

Díon picked up the folder on the table in front of him, flipped through it, then stood up. As he walked around the table to Emmett's side, Emmett figured the FI to be close to his height, give or take. Tall man.

Díon paused beside Emmett's chair, another warm smile on his lips. Emmett caught a whiff of vanilla spice.

"We're going to try a new memory technique to make sure you haven't forgotten any details," Díon said, flipping the folder closed and sliding it onto the table.

"I don't think I've left anything out," Emmett replied, straightening in his chair.

"You'd be surprised," Díon said with a chuckle. "Memory's a tricky thing. Besides, the powers-that-be insist this new technique now be used at all debriefings."

Emmett felt an itch between his shoulder blades, like he was being lined up for a bull's-eye arrow to the back. He glanced at Underwood. She met his gaze, nodded.

Not liking it, but having no choice, Emmett returned his attention to Díon. Sympathy—*Man, I know just how you feel. Just the newest bullshit.*—lit the interrogator's gold-flecked violet eyes.

"Okay, then, let's get this done," Emmett said. "What do you need me to do?"

"Not much." Díon crouched beside Emmett's chair. "Just close your eyes and take a deep breath. We'll be done in a couple of minutes."

Easing his back against his chair, Emmett closed his eyes and drew in a breath of vanilla-spice-scented air. Something else danced beneath the vanilla, something green and smelling of sunshine. An image of a dandelion popped into his head.

"I'm going to touch your temples, but keep your eyes closed."

"Roger that."

Even though he knew it was coming, Emmett nearly jumped when Díon's fingers settled against his temples. Heated fingers, surprising, but soothing. Emmett's shoulders unkinked. He felt light-headed. Dizzy.

"Go back to the beginning," Díon whispered.

Colt .45 in hand, Emmett edges up along the passenger side of the travel-grimed SUV parked on the shoulder of the road, just past the steep driveway marked PRIVATE.

Even as the memory with its sounds—*the crunch of*

gravel and small twigs under shoes, a bird twittering in the pines—and pine and wet bark smells—filled Emmett's mind, it thinned like breeze-blown mist. Scattered, then dissipated.

Sudden nausea greased Emmett's guts and a cold sweat popped up on his forehead. Was it the mayo on his BLT? "Hold on, I'm not feeling so well. I think—"

A strong hand squeezed his forearm. "Just relax. It'll pass."

A thought as warm and soothing and thick as stove-top-heated maple syrup poured through Emmett's mind.

Everything's fine. You're safe. Doing your duty, then heading home.

Emmett felt his body relax, heard a soft sigh escape his lips. As he and Merri traveled up the Wells driveway, his thoughts and memories floated away on a summer breeze fragrant with vanilla spice and dandelions. Vanished.

But unseen and untouched, Grandma's goosebumps and dread settled into Emmett's heart and sank deep roots into his bones.

"I TAKE IT YOU'VE heard the rumors about ADIC Rutgers resigning?" Purcell asked, handing Celeste the ketchup bottle she'd asked for.

Celeste nodded. "I have my Bureau sources looking into the rumor." She squeezed a thick line of dark red Heinz on her sourdough hot dog bun running parallel to the line of Gulden's spicy brown mustard. "I have a feeling it's true."

"Why, ma'am?" Purcell asked, biting into his own doc-tored hot dog.

"Because she blames herself for Sheridan's death. She has an antiquated sense of honor. A shame, really. She's an intelligent and capable woman, but she allows herself to become too involved."

"Who do you think will be chosen to replace her?"

"Hard to say," Celeste murmured.

A breeze rippled through her hair, a bit chilly despite the early afternoon sunshine, but she'd chosen this outdoor deli, Blue Star Bistro, for their lunch so she and Purcell could speak without their words being recorded.

She'd been wrong about it being an eat-in day, but her lunch would keep in her compact office fridge for tomorrow.

Setting the Heinz bottle back on the glass tabletop, Celeste put her hot dog together and took a juicy bite.

"It went well with Thibodaux," she said, swallowing. "Hopefully it'll go as well with his partner. Do you anticipate any problems?"

"Possibly, ma'am. She's a vampire, after all. Díon won't be able to wipe her memory of the Wells site unless she lowers her shields."

"I doubt she'll agree to that—even with the 'new policy' story. How does he plan to get around her refusal?"

"Drugs in her water."

"And if she doesn't drink the water?"

"A trank gun, most likely. He could erase her memory of that too."

"I hope a trank gun isn't necessary," Celeste said. "Vampire or not, she's been a reliable field agent."

"Ma'am, if you don't mind my asking, why was the grab-and-detain order on Prejean and Wallace rescinded?"

"I don't know. The director neglected to enlighten me," Celeste said, pausing to take a sip of unsweetened iced tea. "So we need to work around the rescindment. Do you think you'll be able to isolate, control, and trigger Prejean if it's done in New Orleans instead of here? Without being seen?"

Chewing the last of his hot dog, Purcell's gaze drifted upward as he considered. After a moment, he nodded. "It's not going to be easy, ma'am, but I think I could. I'd need certain equipment and drugs, but yes."

Relief spiraled through Celeste. "Anything you need, you'll have."

"When would you like me to go, ma'am? Given what I'll need to take with me, it'd be best if I drove."

Celeste nodded. "Good point. Leave after you've finished with Thibodaux's partner. I'll officially list you as on surveillance duty."

"Yes, ma'am." Purcell dipped a greasy-looking fry in a pool of ketchup, face thoughtful. "Anything you'd like me have Prejean say to your daughter-in-law?"

"Yes, thank you. Have him tell the bitch that Stephen sends his regards."

"HAVE YOU HEARD ANYTHING from Beck?" Epstein asked. He rocked back in his nail-studded leather chair, the springs squeaking underneath him.

Caterina regarded her SB handler for a moment, frowning. She'd been anticipating this line of questioning regarding her partner on the Wells hit. Her *late* partner. "No. Any reason I should?"

"When and where did you last see him?"

Beck yanks his Colt free of its holster. Caterina squeezes the Glock's trigger. The bullet hits Beck between the eyes, and he's dead before his body crumples to the ground and rolls down the hill.

"I last saw Beck in his car when he dropped me off at my hotel in Portland after we retired Wells," Caterina said. "March 23."

Epstein held her gaze, his ice blue eyes charting her reactions like a human polygraph machine. "Immediately after you'd completed the job?"

Growing up as the only mortal in a vampire household had taught Caterina how to keep herself calm and cool, how to keep her heart rate and respiration as smooth as possible in order to survive *outside* of it. To avoid unwanted and hungry attention.

Panic will summon the beast to the feast, my little love.

"That's right."

"The two of you didn't stop for drinks? Dinner?" Epstein plucked a pink translucent square from the opened Jolly Rancher roll on his desk. Popped it into his mouth. Caterina caught a tangy whiff of watermelon.

"Dinner? With Beck? After spending hours in the dirt and pine needles with him during surveillance while he bitched about it? You've *got* to be kidding."

"I admit it does seem unlikely."

"What's this about, anyway?" Caterina asked, taking a sip of the caramel latte she'd picked up at Starbucks on her way into Alexandria. "Beck go AWOL?"

"Perhaps. We've had no contact with him since we sent him to meet you at Portland International on March 23."

Caterina shrugged. "Sorry to hear it, but not my concern."

"Fair enough." Epstein raised his arms and laced his fingers together behind his head. His white high-and-tight hair almost glowed beneath the overheads.

Caterina smiled. "What's the word? Got anything for me?"

Epstein studied her for a long, silent moment, his blue eyes thoughtful. Finally, he said, "We've worked together for quite a while, Cortini."

"That we have," she agreed, voice soft. "From my first day in black ops."

Like a patch of sunlight on winter-frosted metal, a brief smile sparked warmth into Epstein's icy eyes. "Unlike almost every other operative under my command, you've always known, always understood, what we did and why. Those other yahoos followed orders, yes. Plugged bullets into brains. Garroted. Good soldiers, all. But you—you *understood* it."

"With each life we end," Caterina murmured, "we alter the future, end possibilities; we become agents of destiny."

Epstein nodded. "Severing some, fulfilling others. A hard and honorable duty. And that's why the SB exists. To do the hard and honorable things that everyone else is either too lazy, too corrupt, or too afraid to do."

Caterina straightened in her chair, her slacks whispering against the leather seat, wondering at Epstein's uncharacteristic show of sentimentality. She wondered at his too-soft words and tight-jawed expression.

"What's this all about, Ep? Has something happened?"

Instead of answering Caterina's questions, Epstein asked, "Have you been brought up to speed yet?"

"No."

"After you retired Wells, his son—FBI SAC Alexander Lyons—accompanied by Heather Wallace"—Epstein arched an eyebrow and when Caterina nodded, acknowledging her former target, he resumed speaking—"put Wells's hard work into action and used Dante Prejean to murder SAC Alberto Rodriguez for reasons unknown."

"Are they still at large?"

"They are. Some of our field agents tracked Prejean and Wallace to a motel outside Damascus last night."

Caterina sipped at her latte, forced her muscles and posture to remain relaxed. "So Prejean and Wallace escaped?"

Epstein lowered his arms. Scrubbed a hand over his face. "More or less."

Man's bone-tired. But for Epstein to show it—another uncharacteristic display. A sense of uneasiness snaked around Caterina's spine. "More or less?"

"We were *ordered* to stand down and stay out of Prejean's way." Anticipating her next question, Epstein added, "Our illustrious Director Britto's order."

"Why the hell would the director order such a thing?"

"Good question. I might have a few answers." Pushing back from his desk, Epstein rose to his feet, one hand automatically smoothing his charcoal-gray tie.

Crooking a finger at Caterina, he walked to the oak four-drawer file cabinet across from his desk. He unlocked the top drawer, then slid it open. He reached in and withdrew a slim folder and what looked like an iPod classic.

An audio jammer.

Intrigue pulsed electric through Caterina's veins, tingled beneath her skin. Uncurling from her chair, she stood and joined Epstein at the file cabinet. Glancing at her from beneath his white brows, he placed the jammer on top of the filing cabinet and switched it on. The burbling and chirping device went to work, desensitizing all audio-recording equipment.

"I've been digging," Epstein said, tapping the folder against his hand. "Trying to understand why the director would allow Prejean to walk."

"And what have you learned?"

"I learned that Britto's son—sixteen years old and the only child—was dying of terminal brain cancer three years ago."

"Christ . . . Wait. Did you say *was*?"

A smile flickered across Epstein's lips. "I did. Seems like Britto's son is cancer-free and very much alive—especially between dusk and dawn."

"Britto made a deal with vampires for his son's life," Caterina said, leaning against the front of the file cabinet.

"Not just *any* vampires," Epstein said, his gaze holding hers. "Britto made a deal with Renata Alessa Cortini and she sent someone to cure his son."

"Sounds like her," Caterina said, kicking around that bit of information and tripping over it. "But I wonder why she never mentioned it to me."

"No need for you to know," Epstein said. "That'd be my guess. Especially since that deal meant your mother owned Britto. And I think she just called in a favor."

"To let Prejean walk? Why? Because he's a vampire? He's just one of many. She doesn't even know him, Ep." Caterina shook her head. "Sounds thin to me."

"I think the director fed Renata info from day one. Man's not only compromised his integrity for the sake of a son who's no longer even human, he's compromised everything the SB stands for: doing the hard and honorable thing."

"When no one else will," Caterina said. "I understand what you're saying, but maybe Britto's in more than one pocket. Who else would be interested in Prejean remaining free and out of our hands?"

Epstein chuckled. "Anyone still involved with Bad Seed. Maybe the missing Dr. Johanna Moore has a few things dangling over the director's head, as well." He looked at the folder in his hand. "The moment Britto agreed to order the release of a murdering, sociopathic fugitive, he altered his own destiny and that of the SB."

"Ep, where are you going with this?"

Epstein looked up, blue gaze level, and strapped-on-explosives resolute. "Bad Seed is over. A failure from day one, in my opinion. The only remaining subject is Dante Prejean. He's programmed in ways we'll never fully grasp because Wells kept a lot of secrets. Prejean's too dangerous to remain free, yet he keeps slipping away—with permission."

Caterina's pulse picked up speed and her calm began to fray. "Why are you telling me all this?"

A smile gentled the steel in Epstein's eyes. "I'm telling you all this because you understand, Caterina. And no one else would. That simple. Wells, Moore, Underwood, even Lyons, and now Britto, have all diverted Prejean's destiny from its true course time and again. We're going to set things on their proper paths again."

The uneasiness looping Caterina's spine squeezed python-tight.

Grasping her shoulders, Epstein said, "That's where you come into this. The SB needs to regain its honor. The director's your next assignment. Once you've finished with him, kill Prejean and put Bad Seed in the grave forever."

Feeling like a trap door had just swung open beneath her feet and plunged her into an icy and breath-stealing lake, Caterina stared at the folder her handler extended to her.

"Instructions on how to kill a True Blood," Epstein said.

26

SCARRED-UP KNUCKLES

No matter how lost I get, I will always find you, chérie. But that didn't seem to work in reverse; not lost, she couldn't find Dante. Pressed against his fevered body, whispering in his ear, she'd heard only her own thoughts.

Heather rolled away from Dante's sleeping bag and sat up between him and Von. She pushed her sweat-soaked hair back from her face. Exhaustion spiraled through her, dark and draining. Her throat ached from hours of whispering.

Let me in, Baptiste.

She didn't know if Sleep kept him from hearing or reaching for her; didn't know if he heard her just fine, but was refusing to let her in.

I don't need to be saved. Don't wanna be saved.

A chill rippled along her spine and, shivering, Heather

drew her knees up and wrapped her arms around them. Even as down-to-the-bone tired as she felt, she doubted she could force herself to sleep. Tension had ratcheted her muscles tight enough to sing.

And her heart pounded so hard that her body quivered with each painful pulse.

You're losing him. He's slipping, falling, tumbling past your reach.

Von too.

"Everything all right back there?" Annie called.

"No, not even close."

"A rest area's just ahead. Need to pee?"

"Yeah, but why don't you take the nearest food exit instead? Lunch would be good too."

"I'm for that."

Heather picked up her flashlight and switched it back on. Swiveling around on her hip, she centered the light on Von's face. His nosebleed had stopped. Gently turning his head, she checked his ears for more blood, but didn't find any. She released her breath in a low sigh.

A good sign, but that didn't necessarily mean the nomad had Slept his way out of the woods. He still didn't look right to her, his expression too lax, too empty.

Bending over and bringing her lips to Von's ear, Heather said, "You don't get off this easy, Mr. I'm-Still-Jailbait. I thought nomads were tough. C'mon, let's see those scarred-up knuckles of yours, lift 'em and fight."

Von's words slipped through her mind: *Keep close, doll. Keep close to your man until we can get him home.*

Heather shifted around to Dante, checked him with the flashlight beam. Blood still trickled from his nose, but tears no longer slicked his lashes. Rage and grief blazed like holy fire on his face. His body was as hard and tight as a brass-knuckled fist.

And if that fist was turned inward? Aimed at himself?

Heather thought of the blood cupped in Von's ears. Thought of Von pushing Dante's hood back at Sea-Tac International and cupping his face.

Let them see, little brother.

The never-ending Road.

Maybe she hadn't been able to tumble inside Dante's head because she needed to be asleep like before. Or drugged. Or maybe it'd just been a fluke.

Wait. *Drugged.*

Dante had been pumped full of morphine the last time. He'd told her that maybe it had lowered his shields and allowed her dreaming mind to slip inside his or maybe it had allowed his opium-soaked mind to reach into hers, and pull her into his nightmare.

"Annie," Heather called. "Toss me the morphine kit and a bottle of water."

HEATHER EMPTIED THE PLUNGER with a push of her thumb, then slipped the needle from Dante's throat. Tossing the syringe back into the black zippered bag, she watched as tension eased from Dante's muscles. As his hands unclenched.

Heather tucked herself against Dante again. His body felt as hot as sun-baked blacktop in August and sweat pooled in the hollow of her throat and trickled between her shoulder blades, beading on her face.

Fear coiled along Heather's spine. Fever that intense couldn't be good, nightkind or not. Twisting open her bottle of water, Heather splashed some of it on Dante's face, half-expecting steam to curl up from his skin and into the air. No sizzling or steaming, but the water evaporated within seconds.

She plucked open the collar of her T-shirt and poured water between her sweat-slicked breasts before wetting Dante down again with the last of it.

Heather dropped the empty bottle on the floor. She reached for Dante's hand and laced her fingers through his.

"Let me in, Baptiste," she whispered, closing her eyes.

Something hot and prickling—a thorned lasso—looped around Heather and cinched tight. Vertigo spun through her. Nausea squeezed her belly.

Dante yanked her inside and slammed the door.

27

WHEN EVENING FALLS

CURLED ON A CUSHIONED wrought-iron chair on her terrace, Renata basked in the moonlight. She drank in the night, the first breath of spring chilling her face. She imagined she tasted brine and surf-washed sand from the Mediterranean some thirty kilometers away.

Beyond her vined black railing, the city bustled in the gaily lit evening: beeping horns and screeching brakes; the high-pitched drone of scooters; voices lilting in laughter or spiked ire-sharp, or in greetings warm as a hug; the spicy odors of broiling shrimp, grilled garlic chicken, and baking pastries, saturating the air.

Renata sipped at her cup of espresso, dreaming.

A True Blood. And maybe a whispered bedtime tale come to life—a Fallen *creawdwr*. Ah, but if so, Dante

Baptiste belonged to vampires as much as he did to the Fallen—more, given that his mother had been vampire. Renata held to the ancient matriarchal belief that a mother's bloodline was the only lineage that mattered.

Giovanni padded onto the terrace, brushing both hands through his sleep-wild burgundy hair. Dark whiskers shadowed his face. "*Buona sera, bella,*" he said, slouching into a red rose-patterned chair. He wore tight black slacks and a white A-shirt, his feet remained bare.

Renata smiled. "Just the person I wanted to see."

Giovanni looked at her for a moment, then wagged his index finger. "I know that smile. You want something." He slouched deeper into his chair. "I'm not ready for requests. I just got up."

"*Ragazzo pigro,*" she teased. "You always say that."

A smile twitched up one corner of Giovanni's mouth. "True."

Florentina, plump and pretty in her white-lace apron, her hair pulled into a neat, dark chocolate–colored bun, walked out onto the terrace. She nodded a greeting to Giovanni—ignoring, as usual, his smoldering smile—then gave her attention to Renata.

"Wine this evening, *signora?*"

"*Sì,* Florentina, *grazie.* Merlot for both of us. And bring me my phone as well."

Nodding, the young mortal housemaid left the terrace for the kitchen.

A sour expression crossed Giovanni's face and he waved a dismissive hand in Florentina's direction. "She must be a lesbian."

"*Una leshica?* Because she's immune to your charm? No, Vanni *mio,* she has a boyfriend she loves very much. Her good common sense has told her everything she needs to know about you."

Giovanni now flapped a dismissive hand at Renata. "She knew what we were when you hired her."

"Not that." Renata laughed. "She knows how you play with . . . hearts."

Giovanni snorted. "With *hearts*. Delicate phrasing, *bella*."

Renata nestled her little white espresso cup into its rose-bordered saucer on the table. Rising to her feet, she stepped over to Giovanni and settled herself in his lap. Her knee-length blue toile dressing gown slid up to her thighs. She tipped his chin up with her index finger. The pout slipped away from his lips.

"Have you ever been to New Orleans, Giovanni?"

Amusement skipped like a stone across the surface of his hazel eyes. "No. But I have a feeling that will change soon."

"The jet will be ready for you tonight. I want you to speak to Guy Mauvais, the lord of the head household in New Orleans, see what he knows about Dante Baptiste."

"Ah." Giovanni straightened in his chair without disturbing Renata. "To get a feeling for the True Blood in his hometown, speak to those who know him, *sì*?"

"And to meet Baptiste once he's home again. I've made sure that he and his companions can travel unmolested," Renata said. "But before I approach the Cercle, I need to verify Caterina's statements. I don't doubt she believes every single word that she's told me. But . . ."

"But she's mortal," Giovanni finished for her, "and could be fooled by a True Blood with very little effort on his part, eh, *bella*?"

Renata sighed and trailed her fingers through her curls. "*Sì, esattamente, caro mio*. Given what Caterina told me about how Dante was tortured and twisted by mortal monsters . . ." She shook her head. "I need to be certain."

"How much is this Mauvais to know?" Giovanni asked, twirling one of her dark ringlets around his finger.

"You can let it slip that Dante is True Blood, but say nothing about the other. Mauvais doesn't need to know."

Giovanni nodded, face thoughtful. "And what do I say to Baptiste?"

"Tell him the truth—that you are Caterina's *frère du coeur*."

Florentina walked out onto the terrace, two half-filled wineglasses and a slim ruby red cell phone on a handled wood tray. Renata caught the tantalizing smell of black cherries and plums drifting from the glasses.

"*Magnifico*," Renata said, accepting a glass and her cell phone from the girl. Giovanni murmured his thanks.

Once Florentina had left the terrace, Renata said, "When evening falls in New Orleans, I will call Mauvais and let him know that you are on the way."

"*Buono*." Giovanni took a long swallow of wine. "I'll get ready to go."

Renata rested her hand against Giovanni's cheek. Felt the scratch of his whiskers against her palm. "*Grazie, caro mio*. When I hear more from Caterina, I'll pass it along." Leaning in, she pressed her lips against his in a tender kiss. "Just one thing, Vanni *mio* . . ."

He looked at her through his lashes. "*Sì, bella?*"

"Make sure that Mauvais understands that Dante Baptiste is to be guarded." She patted his cheek, allowing a wicked smile to play across her lips. "Oh, and be sure to shave. Those whiskers could be lethal."

28

THE GREAT DESTROYER

*H*eather hits the ground hard, landing on her hands *and knees in night-shadowed grass, the long, thin blades slick with moisture. She shifts one hand and it slides into nothing. She yanks her hand back, a quick glance revealing the shallow grave she fell into before. Empty now.*

She smells mud, swamp water, and the coppery reek of blood. Lots of blood.

A tornado of sound roars around Heather, sucking at her—whispering voices, droning wasps, the hypnotic rush of blood through veins and drumming hearts—plucking and pulling at her mind. Scattering her thoughts.

Fucking little psycho.

Dante-angel, Papa took down the curtains! Wake up!

Wantitneeditkillitdoitwantitneedit . . .

Heather throws her hands over her ears, but the noise and voices freight-trains through her mind, never slowing, smashing her concentration into tiny, spinning bits she can't grab, let alone piece together again.

Good thing he's restrained . . . fuck! What's he screamin'?

He's making a very loud, very clear, demand.

Kill me.

How does it feel, *marmot*?

Heather's heart kicks against her ribs and her mouth dries. She's here for a reason, in this place of graves and noise-storms. But the reason eludes her. A steady, pounding sound vibrates up through the dirt and grass and into Heather's knees. She looks for the source.

A black-haired teen in muddied jeans and T-shirt whacks a shovel blade against a body half hidden in the grass. Whacks it over and over. Blood spurts into the air with each strike. The muscles in his shoulders, arms, and back ripple beneath his T-shirt as he torques all of his strength into every downward swing of the glistening shovel blade.

The body jerks and twitches. Squishes.

Heather stares, nausea squeezing the pit of her stomach, and finds herself reaching for the small of her back. She pauses, wondering what she's reaching for. She's no longer certain, but her hand knows, so she allows it to continue its journey.

Her fingers wrap around the smooth grip of a gun. Pull it free. She arcs the gun around and aims it at the teen playing whack-a-mole with the body in the grass.

Moonlight trickles pale through the thick canopy of cypress and live oak trees and gleams on the teen's blood-freckled face, his blood and mud-spattered arms, the hands locked around the shovel's handle. He lifts it again.

"Hold it right there," Heather calls. "Put that shovel down slow and easy. Then step away from the body."

Droning and raging whispers whip around her. Dizzy her. She locks both hands around the gun to steady her grip, but still her hands shake.

I knew you'd come for me.

The prick thinks I'll murder everyone in their beds.

Wouldcha?

She trusted you, kid. I'd say she got what she deserved.

The teen swivels around to face her.

Heather's finger slips away from the trigger. She knows that gorgeous, pale face, has gazed deep into those dark brown, red-streaked eyes, has tasted those Cupid's bow lips.

Amaretto. His fevered kisses taste of amaretto.

Black light crackles around the teen, a blue-streaked nebula haloing his body, and his image flickers; shifts into the man he is/will be—leather and steel-buckled PVC, a bondage collar strapped around his throat; grown into his beauty, his strength, his pale moonlight-radiant skin.

Flicker: He shifts into the man-to-be—smooth black wings arch up behind him, fire patterns of brilliant blue and purple streaking their undersides. Blue flames lick around his clenched fists. Glimmer reflected along the thighs of his leather pants and sleek black latex, steel, and mesh shirt. A collar of braided black metal twists around his throat. And clipped to the steel ring at the collar's center, a leash, its silver-chained length leading down across his chest and abs, and disappearing into the right front pocket of his leather pants.

Tendrils of his black hair lift into the air as though breeze-caught. Gold light stars out from his black-rimmed eyes. He looks up as song—not his own—rings through the air. The night burns, the sky on fire from horizon to horizon.

The never-ending Road.

The Great Destroyer.

One or both or neither.

Possibilities stretch away like spokes on a wheel.

Flicker: *He's the shovel-wielding teen in torn, mud-grimed jeans and black T-shirt, gray duct-tape glinting around his sneakers. Small metallic wasps—distorted and stylized as if they've been crafted from polished steel by H.R. Giger (and she wonders where that thought comes from)—crawl along the teen's arms, into his lustrous black hair, and burrow into his skin.*

Flicker: *He's the man, coiled and wary, kohl-smudged eyes looking into her. His gaze brushes against her heart, a struck lighter tossed into a pool of gasoline. Wasps wriggle beneath his black-painted fingernails, rim the steel ring in his collar.*

His name forms on the tip of Heather's tongue, then vanishes before she can shape it. But she feels it burning within her heart, safeguarded from the tornado.

Flicker: *The teen lowers the shovel to his side, his mud-caked fingers white-knuckled around the handle. He stares at Heather, his head tilted to one side, and his eyes seem to widen with recognition.*

She wonders if her name is forming on his tongue.

His gaze slides past her. His dark brows slant down as fury ripples across his face.

He moves. A black-lit blur streaking straight for her.

She swings her gun up, pounding heart drowned out by the maelstrom of noise whirling around and through her. A chill creeps down her spine and she realizes too late that she's aimed her gun in the wrong direction.

A rough shove against her shoulder sends Heather stumbling into an oak as the teen pushes her aside. She grabs ahold of the tree trunk, the rough bark scraping beneath her fingernails, and catches her balance. Spinning around, she sees him slamming his shovel into the face of a balding, heavy-set man in a sweat-stained T-shirt.

Familiar, this man. Heather's fingers tighten around the gun's grip. She should know his name too, but the noise screaming through her skull obliterates it.

You don't need none of dat school shit for the work you do, *p'tit*. Waste o' time.

Boy needs a lesson. Boy *always* needs a lesson.

You wanna take her punishment, *p'tit*?

Holy, holy, holy . . .

Heather struggles with the urge to finish what the teen has started with his shovel and empty the gun's magazine between the man's eyes.

Blood spraying from the blade's deep bite into his throat, the man crumples to the ground, clawing at his wound. The teen beats the squirming, choking man with the shovel, pounding and hacking and smashing until the skull pulps.

"Fucker won't stay dead," he says.

Dropping the shovel, he bends and grabs the body by the ankles. He drags it through the night-wet grass, a gruesome wake of blood, brains, and moonlight-glinting bits of skull marking his path. He kicks the body into the grave. It hits the muddy ground with a wet thud.

"For Chloe," he whispers. "For Von."

Chloe. Von.

Heather grabs at the names, but the whispering/droning/ shrieking tornado rips them away from her. She shivers, caught in sound, held in a fist of noise. Gun down at her side, she walks to the grave and stands beside the teen. He stares into the grave, his face shadowed with exhaustion. He wipes at his bleeding nose with the back of one grimy hand.

"Who was he?" she asks.

He spits into the grave. "No one now."

"Who did you kill for?" *Heather asks, turning around.* "You said some names."

A wasp crawls beneath the collar of the teen's shirt. He

pushes his hair back from his face and motions behind himself with his head. He turns around, bends and picks up his shovel, then starts walking. Heather follows.

The teen stoops beneath the sheltering branches of a weeping willow and disappears beneath its green-leaved and sap-fragrant canopy. He holds the branches aside with the shovel's bloodstained handle as Heather ducks underneath. Night-cooled leaves brush against her cheek. She straightens, stops.

Bodies lie close to the willow's trunk — a little red-haired girl, a blood-smeared plushie orca tucked in her arms; and a man with dark brown hair, a crescent moon tattooed beneath his eye; a blond youth in a blood-soaked straitjacket, and snuggled against him, a brunette, a black stocking knotted around her throat, a black leather jacket draped over her body.

Heather's heart skips a beat. She knows them all—but knows the man with the crescent moon tattoo best.

Von.

She kneels in the tall, dewed grass beside the nomad and touches his cheek with shaking fingers. Cool, his skin feels Sleep-cool, not dead-cold.

"He's not dead. You can still save him."

The teen crouches beside her. "He's mon cher ami. And I tried to kill him."

She knows him then. Knows and loves the man the teen will become. She parts her lips, searching for his name, and finds it secreted in her heart, untouched by the whirlwind.

Safe from the whispers.

But before Heather can speak, someone else does instead, a voice rasping out of the darkness. "Beaucoup chaud tête-rouge," it says. "You'll be fun, you."

She catches peripheral movement just to her left and, pulse racing, she whirls around on her knees, lifting her gun.

But the teen—his name still shaping itself on her lips—has already moved. He stands over his cher ami *with the crescent moon tattoo, legs planted on either side of the nomad's body.*

"You ain't taking him," he says.

"You already did the taking, p'tit."

The stink of fetid mud and meat gone bad in the sun pinches Heather's nostrils. The balding man that the teen just dumped in the shallow grave rushes him, low and cannonball-fast.

But this time he isn't alone.

A man with graying blond hair and a blurred face saunters across the grass beneath the willow. He holds a syringe between his fingers, a bead of something pearled on the needle's end.

Barbed pain coils around Heather's mind and squeezes. Black flecks speckle her vision. She pulls the trigger and fires two bullets into each man. But she might as well have thrown water balloons for all the good it does.

Neither flinches. Or stops.

The teen swings the shovel between both of his attackers, the blade whanging from one face to the other. The shovel whistles through the night as he brings it down again and again. Blood jewels the air, a warm and never-ending rain.

And still bleeding they rise again and again and again.

Desperation edges the teen's face, tightens his fingers around the shovel's handle. Sweat trickles along his temples, plastering tendrils of black hair to his cheek, his forehead. The man with the film-stuttering blur of a face ghosts up behind the teen, needle poised.

Heather jumps up and shoves the teen. Music peals between them, untamed and ablaze, the moment her hand touches his shoulder. Chimes within her heart.

It's quiet when I'm with you. The noise stops.

Sanctus, sanctus, sanctus.

I'll help you stop it forever.

"*Let's see if you survive this, my little night-bred beauty,*" *a voice murmurs, breath warm on the nape of Heather's neck. Something pierces her throat. Fire scalds her lungs. Devours her breath.*

Heather falls, sprawling on her side across the nomad's body. The blood boils in her veins, the pain stealing her voice.

The teen whirls, shovel blurring through the air, and hammers the needle-plunging man into the ground. Blood splashes onto the teen's pale face. His gaze locks onto Heather. He sucks in a breath, face stricken. The shovel tumbles forgotten from his fingers.

"Heather," he whispers, voice rough. Dropping to his knees, he gathers her into his arms.

Shaped at last, his name spills from Heather's lips. "Baptiste."

Everything stops. Hushes.

The consuming fire inside her winks out. The pain disappears, never was. Dante flickers from the teen and into himself—here and now.

The raging noise- and debris-filled tornado sucks in Cecil Prejean and Robert Wells, then spirals up on itself and vanishes with a small pop.

A pearlescent light shimmers around them, cups them, shining and silent.

Binds them together.

Wasps drop from Dante's hair, from beneath his fingernails, from his arms, and fall into the grass, metallic bodies curled in.

He holds Heather close, holds her tight, holds her like he'll never let go. "What the fuck you doing here?"

Face tucked against Dante's heated neck, Heather laces

her arms around him, her heart drumming a deep rhythm. "I got a little lost inside your head," she admits.

Dante says nothing; just kisses her forehead, her eyelids, her mouth, his lips fevered and amaretto-sweet. Sleepiness spirals through her as warm and cozy as a familiar bed.

"Rêves doux, catin," he whispers, his burning leaves and frost scent wrapping around her like a blanket. He eases her from his arms and into the wet grass beneath the willow.

Heather curls on her side, her hands tucked under her cheek. She watches Dante from between her lashes as he goes to Von, wishing she could help him, wishing she could stay awake, but the need to sleep thickens within her.

Dante sits in the grass just behind the nomad, then pillows Von's head on his leather-clad thigh. Loss shadows his face, determination knots his body.

"A wished-hard thing takes a shape within the heart," he says, soft and low. "Takes shape. Becomes real." Raising his wrist to his mouth, he bites it, drinking in his own dark blood.

As sleep shutters her eyes and plunges her into a soothing darkness, Heather's last vision of Dante in the pearl-glossed air beneath the weeping willow is of him tucking a lock of black hair behind his ear as he lowers his face to Von's and kisses him with blood-smeared lips.

She hears a rush of wings.

29

A DIRTY MIRROR

Merri sucked in a long breath of air, opened her eyes, and got a stunning eye-level view of beige carpet. *Great. Lovely. Sleep knocked me on my ass before I could reach the bed. Damned stay-awake pills.*

Rising to her feet, Merri walked into the bedroom, peeling off her clothes as she went and dropping them behind her. She paused, her hands reaching for the back of her bra. A scrap of yellow legal paper lay on the carpet just inside the door.

A smile curved her lips. Looked like Em had left his usual, *I'm awake, you're not* note. An on-the-road tradition between them. Picking up the paper, she flipped it over. Yup. Emmett's sloppy scrawl—in felt-tip, no less.

HAHAHA! By the time you wake up, I'll already be debriefed and lounging in my spacious luxury room! You snooze you lose!!

"Lucky bastard," Merri muttered. Wadding up the note, she lobbed it into the trash basket beside the bed. She sat on the bed beside her laptop. Green telltales winked along the computer's slim edge, a flash drive still plugged into a USB port.

Before-Sleep memories sledgehammered through Merri's consciousness: contacting her *mère de sang* about the Fallen Stonehenge, sneaking into Purcell's office and downloading files.

Looking at those files.

"Let me hold him!" Genevieve screams.

Ice-cold fury frosted Merri's veins, so cold, she half-expected to see white mist pouring out from beneath her skin.

Dante *Baptiste*—not *Prejean*, no way that goddamned child-pimping bastard's last name should ever be attached to anyone, let alone a True Blood.

A True Blood—stolen at birth—had been shaped into the cold, murdering monster Bad Seed and the fucked-up minds behind it had yearned for. He'd been programmed, designed, to kill; those he loved hadn't been immune to that design.

Chloe lies in a pool of her own blood, her blue eyes empty.

But Baptiste *had* loved. At least once. Something true sociopaths were incapable of—except for self-love. Maybe that meant Baptiste could still be salvaged.

She needed to talk to Emmett and Galiana.

Unhooking her bra, then pulling down and kicking off her panties, Merri hurried into the bathroom and hit the shower. But not even the fresh and soothing scent of her English lavender body wash could ease her troubled thoughts.

I have a suspicion that events beyond the scope of mortals or even vampires might be unfolding.

Merri had a feeling Galiana might be right. And that scared the ever-loving shit out of her.

EMMETT OPENED THE DOOR and waved his partner inside with a grand, sweeping gesture. "Enter, She Who Is About to Face the Spanish Inquisition," he teased as Merri, her lavender-scented hair wet and slicked back from her face, slipped into the room. "Wanna grab some java before your debrief?"

"No," Merri said. She pulled her clove cigarettes from the pocket of her black suede jacket and lit one.

"What's got you all worked up?" Emmett asked, closing the door. He turned around to face her. Leaned one shoulder against the door. "The debrief was routine—"

Merri shook her head. "I'm not worried about the debrief." She reached into her pocket and grabbed the flash drive, then held it between her thumb and index finger for Emmett to see. "You need to look at this."

"I'll bite. What's on it?"

"Prejean's history. Beyond what we were given. *Way* beyond."

Emmett chuckled and pushed away from the door. "Okay. I'll bite again. What were we given about said Prejean?"

"Quit playing with me, Thibodaux," Merri said, exhaling clove-scented smoke. "Now's not the time. You remember all that enhanced vampire bullshit Gillespie gave us about Prejean and about him being part of some mysterious TSP? Well, that's exactly what it was—bullshit. He's a goddamned True Blood."

"Yeeaahh, right, a True Blood working in a government

TSP. Oh, hey. I know! He was teaching them how to keep things *really* secret, things like their existence."

"It's not like Prejean had a choice. And that's not his name, by the way."

Emmett's amusement faded. "I don't know what the hell you're talking about. Want to start at square one?"

Merri stopped pacing. She stared at Emmett. "What?"

"Exactly, sistah. What. But I'm listening, so enlighten me."

A cold lump of dread sank like a scuttled submarine into the pit of Merri's stomach. Her fingers curled around the flash drive and tucked it against her palm. "What did you discuss during the debrief, Em?"

"What the hell, Merri? You know we can't discuss that before you go in."

"Tell me, goddammit."

Emmett crossed the short distance between them and planted himself in front of her. "What's going on?"

A muscle flexed in her jaw. "The debrief, tell me."

"All right. We discussed the Rodriguez case, of course," he replied. "And how you and me discovered evidence that indicated Wallace and Lyons suckered some poor transient desperate for cash into whacking Rodriguez, then whacked the transient and made it all look like a burglary gone bad. "

"Yeah? And why did Wallace and Lyons want Rodriguez dead?"

"You know this, Merri. Why are you making me repeat it? They wanted Rodriguez dead because he'd learned they'd falsified evidence in several cases . . ."

Tears stung Merri's eyes. The motherfuckers had wiped Emmett. That's why they'd taken him into debrief early—to separate them. She wiped at the tears threatening to spill over her lashes with a furious sweep of her thumb.

Wipes happened to witnesses and perps, not to SB field agents.

What the hell had she and Emmett stumbled into?

"Merri, are you *crying?*" Emmett asked, voice low. "You're freaking me out."

"They've wiped your memory, Em. They fucking wiped your memory."

The color drained from Emmett's face. He stared at her. "No, that can't be. Why would they? They brought us here to congratulate us for . . ." He shook his head. "No. No."

Merri latched her fingers around his forearm, felt the hard muscle beneath. He looked down into her eyes. "I'm next," she said. "Part of the reason why is on that flash drive. Maybe what we discovered at the compound is another part of why."

"The compound? Shit! What compound? What did we discover?"

"If that's gone too, then I'm fucking right." Merri sucked in a deep lungful of smoke, then exhaled. She looked up into Emmett's eyes. "Have I ever given you reason not to trust me?"

"Nope."

"You need to trust me now, Em, okay?"

Emmett raked his fingers through his hair. Drew in a shaky breath. Nodded. "Okay. If you're next, then we've gotta get out of here."

"Truth, brothah." Merri squeezed his arm one more time before releasing it. "Leave behind everything you can't slip inside your laptop case or in your pockets. I'll do the same."

"Yeah, strolling along the corridor suitcase in hand might be a dead giveaway."

Merri nodded. "We've got a little bit of time. I'm not supposed to be in debrief until twenty hundred hours."

Emmett glanced at his watch. "Twenty minutes. Think there'll be problems getting out?"

"There's no reason for them to think we'd try to escape—we both believe we're doing a routine debrief." Merri strode to the door. "No reason for alarm or worry. No reason for us to be watched."

"Roger that."

"See you in five." Merri opened the door, then paused. She turned around.

Emmett grabbed his shoulder holster from the easy chair he'd tossed it onto and buckled it on, the leather creaking. Picking up his Colt .45, he chambered a round, then slid the gun into the holster.

Memory wiped.

A sick feeling twisted through her. Was her little data-theft adventure in Purcell's office part of the reason why? "Em?"

"Yeah?"

"I'm so sorry."

He looked at her, his gaze steady. "Don't be."

Merri slipped out the door. After she and Emmett escaped somewhere safe, she'd make sure he learned the truth. She'd make sure he learned the flash drive's contents inside and out, backward and frontward. She'd make sure no one would ever do another B&E gig in his mind and steal bits of his life, his reality, away again.

<GALIANA, I'M IN TROUBLE.>

Merri's *mère de sang* responded immediately, concern buzzing through her sending. <*I told you to be careful, girl. What's happened and how can I help?*>

<*The vampire I mentioned before? He's a True Blood and he's really young and in a huge amount of trouble.*>

A second of stunned silence pulsed through Merri's mind, then: <*A True Blood. By all that's holy, Merri-girl, that's good news.*>

<Not necessarily, but I'll explain all that later. They wiped part of Emmett's memory, and I'm next. We're going on the run.>

<Where are you going? I'll send help. You could come to Savannah.>

<No, first place they'll look for me. Once we're out of here, I'll let you know.>

<They hunt you, they'll be starting a fight they'll wish they never started.>

<Keep out of it for now, please. The True Blood's name is Dante Baptiste. He's from New Orleans and he's on the run. If he's still alive, that is.>

<I'll look into it. Keep safe, child. I'll be waiting to hear from you.>

<I will and thanks.>

Merri looped the strap of her laptop's black leather carrying case over her shoulder, then left her room. Emmett waited for her in the hall.

"You take the south elevators to the parking garage, I'll take the north," he said. "I'll meet you at the car."

"You mean *I'll* meet *you*," Merri said with a quick smile. She *moved*.

30

AT THE HEART OF
IT ALL

JUSTINE AUCOIN AWAKENED. SHE stared into the cabin's gloom. The riverboat creaked as the Mississippi lapped delicately against it. Beyond the curtained windows, the sun lingered just above the horizon. Evening had not yet arrived with its subtle, cool scents and its electric lure of mystery and danger; the world colored in shades of midnight blue, black, and deepest purple.

What had awakened her?

Uncurling from the silk sheets and velvet comforter, Justine sat up and listened. Creaking wood, splashing water, the babbling, unshielded thoughts of the servants and *apprentis*, the silence of Sleeping vampires.

She extended her senses out, searching for danger, for anything out of place, or for anyone who didn't belong. Nothing disturbed the spiderweb of security erected and maintained by Guy Mauvais's Sleeping mind. Ah, no longer Sleeping. Her *père de sang* was also awake.

Justine smoothed back her long hair and was about to turn around, a question on her lips, but it hit her then, like a spike through the heart, and her breath caught in her throat.

Once more, *absence* had awakened her. A void where once a Sleep-cool body had curled beside hers.

Justine closed her eyes. Even after a month, her grief whittled at her. She refused to swivel around and look at the empty bed. She wanted to keep the image of Étienne's black braids fanned across the pillow as he Slept, wanted to keep the image of his smooth café au lait skin showcased by her burgundy silk sheets.

She wouldn't look. She would pretend—as she had for the last month or so—that he still Slept, awaiting her kiss to reel him up out of dreams and into the night.

Before Dante Prejean had murdered him.

Smoothing back her long dark hair, Justine rose to her feet. She plucked her red silk bathrobe from the hook on the back of the cabin's door and slipped it on. Belting it at the waist, she sat at the polished maple vanity and picked up her brush.

Drawing it through her thick coffee-colored hair, she regarded her reflection in the vanity's mirror—white skin, full pale lips, large dark eyes still drowsy with dreams and shadows. Snow White before the apple. She touched her fingertips to the black velvet choker with the white rose cameo encircling her throat.

<Bonsoir, ma belle fille,> Guy sent, lacing warmth through Justine's mind. <*I have exciting news. Join me for tea.*>

<*The news? What is it?*>

Guy's amusement swept through her. <*Like a child before Christmas,*> he teased. <*So impatient. I'll tell you this much – it regards Dante Prejean.*>

Justine's heart leapt into her throat. She rested her brush on the vanity, her hand trembling. <*I'll be right there,* mon père.>

"I HAD A SUMMONS sent to Prejean's home," Mauvais said, shifting his gaze from the black water rippling past the *Winter Rose*'s bow to Justine's lovely moonlit face.

"He'll ignore it. Just like every other time."

Mauvais nodded. "Most likely. But this time, it'll cost him if he does."

He breathed in his *fille de sang*'s scent of wild rose— prickly and sweet—along with the river's odor of cold water, mud, and fish. Justine's scarlet gown looked nearly black in the starlight, its trimmed black lace curving around her full, white cleavage and shoulders.

"Why do you suppose Renata Alessa Cortini is interested in that defiant, murdering brat?" she asked.

Mauvais shrugged one shoulder. "Perhaps the defiant brat murdered someone else he shouldn't have."

He replayed his earlier conversation with Rome's leading lady and principal voice in the Cercle de Druide, examining it for hidden meanings and nuances he might've missed while listening to her enticing Italian-accented voice.

My fils de sang, Giovanni, will be paying you a visit, M'sieu *Mauvais.*

I am honored to play host to your son, ma belle dame. Will this be an official visit?

No, Giovanni is merely on a fact-finding mission.

I shall assist him in every way, Signora Cortini. *What information is he seeking?*

Everything you and yours know about Dante Baptiste.

Baptiste? I know of a troublemaking and unruly Dante Prejean, but no Baptiste.

Ah, sì, we've recently learned that his true name is Dante Baptiste.

An intriguing bit of information—Baptiste, not Prejean. A name change to hide other crimes, perhaps? A matter Mauvais intended to investigate further.

"I hope to find justice for Étienne," Justine murmured.

Mauvais looked at her. Justine gazed at the cloud-smudged night sky, her face wistful. Unable to stop himself, he brushed his fingers against her soft cheek.

"And if you don't?"

"Then I will settle for revenge."

"Is there a difference, *ma belle?*"

Justine sighed. "I don't know. Does it matter?" she asked, leaning against him.

Mauvais slipped an arm around her night-cooled shoulders. "Perhaps not."

Boards creaked beneath shoes as a servant hurried toward them. Ah, but not alone. Mauvais detected a slow and unfamiliar heartbeat edging the mortal servant's rapid patter.

<*Our guest has arrived,*> Mauvais sent.

Justine straightened, skirt rustling, and took her place at his side. The heady scent of roses perfumed the night air.

Victor, a white rose tucked into the breast pocket of his black butler's suit, ushered a man onto the riverboat's rear deck. Stopping beside Mauvais, Victor said, "*M'sieu* Giovanni Toscanini."

Dressed in crisp black jeans and a tight purple sweater, the handsome Italian with a proud Roman nose, wicked hazel eyes, and razor-cut burgundy hair sauntered forward.

"A pleasure to meet you, *signor*," Mauvais said, grasping the Italian's shoulders. He kissed both pale cheeks in turn. Giovanni smelled of the sea—of salt and sand and deep waters.

"And you." Giovanni returned the embrace, then released Mauvais, his light-filled hazel eyes dancing over Justine. She curtsied, her hands white blossoms on her bloodred skirts.

"My *fille de sang*, Justine Aucoin."

"*Bella*," Giovanni murmured, capturing one of her hands and touching it to his lips. "A true pleasure."

"*Merci*," Justine said, eyes amused. "*Vous êtes très aimable.*"

"Only when necessary," Giovanni said, a smile curving his lips. With a wink, he allowed her hand to slide free.

Mauvais stepped forward, gesturing for the others to follow. "Please, let's go below and make ourselves comfortable."

Victor had disappeared, already below, preparing drinks.

Justine led the way, her skirts whispering against the deck. Tendrils of dark hair had slid free of their pins and framed her pale face. She descended the wrought-iron staircase leading belowdecks.

"As I told Renata, I am happy to help you with whatever you need," Mauvais said, walking beside Giovanni. "But what is your interest in Dante Baptiste?"

The Italian glanced at Mauvais, a smile on his lips. "For one thing, the most important thing, we believe he is a True Blood."

Mauvais stopped walking. He stared at Giovanni. "Say again?"

"A True Blood."

"*Ce n'est pas possible*," Mauvais said.

"Are you telling me you've never even *met* Baptiste?"

"He refuses every invitation, every summons. He has been nothing but trouble and has been accused of murder—charges he still needs to face."

Giovanni shrugged. "We'll see, *mio amico*, we'll see. A True Blood can be forgiven many things, *sì*?"

Mauvais remained silent, knowing only one thing with absolute certainty: True Blood or not, Justine would forgive Dante Baptiste nothing.

Mauvais inhaled deeply, drawing calming night air into his lungs, and followed Giovanni down the curving metal staircase. His hand slid along the smooth railing, his feet soundless upon the steps.

And Justine would never forgive *him* if Dante Baptiste walked away untouched.

"A WISHED-HARD THING TAKES a shape within the heart. Takes shape. Becomes real."

His own whispered words guiding him up from Sleep, Dante drew in a deep breath of air. He smelled crackling frost and gun oil, tree sap and dewed grass, lilac-laced sweat, blood, and fear-spiced adrenaline.

Tasted his own blood.

Dante's eyes flew open. His heart kicked hard against his ribs. Whip-slender willow branches hung over the curtained windows. Grass cushioned his ass. Dante glanced down. Shock glaciered his heart.

Not lying down. Not in his mummy bag. Nope.

Ain't possible. Ain't no such thing as Sleep-walking.

Dante sat on the SUV's grass-covered floor, Von's head pillowed on his leather-clad thigh. Fading blue sparks winked along the nomad's body and face. And fear crackled through Dante like ice.

What the fuck did I just do to him?

Blood glistened on the nomad's lips. But dried blood streaked the skin beneath Von's nose and his mustache.

The shovel whistles through the night as he brings it down again and again. Blood jewels the air, a warm and never-ending rain.

Not a dream. Not a nightmare. He'd attacked Von during Sleep.

And had transformed the SUV's interior without a conscious thought. And Von?

"Fuck, fuck, fuck!"

Fear twisted, barbed and cold, through Dante's guts. The nomad hadn't stirred. Still Slept, despite the night's primal and arousing rhythm, a seductive drumming.

He's not dead. You can still save him.

He's mon cher ami *and I tried to kill him.*

"Takes shape, becomes real," Dante reminded himself. "Ain't losing you. Ain't leaving you underneath the willow tree." But pain pierced his head, slid like an ice pick through his left eye.

Heather, curled up against Dante's opened and abandoned sleeping bag, sucked in a sharp breath as though she'd felt the ice pick's touch too.

Dante stared at her. Remembered the music pealing between them, untamed and ablaze, the moment her hand touched his shoulder. Remembered the sound of his name spilling from her lips.

Baptiste.

Remembered the white silence, pearlescent and pure, descending over them, cupping around them. Sealing them together.

"What the fuck did you do?" a voice, low and shaky, asked.

Annie stood at the opened back door, her eyes wide and

ink-black, one hand still holding the door's edge. Dante realized she must've been standing there beside the open door ever since he'd awakened, pale moonlight pouring into the SUV and giving him more than enough light to see by.

Behind Annie, Dante could see a square building and parking lot lights glowing pink and orange. Rest area. The mingled odors of wet grass, dog shit, and oil-stained pavement wafted into the SUV along with night-chilled air.

"I don't know," Dante said, meeting Annie's stunned gaze.

"Grass and . . . are those *tree branches*?"

"Yeah. Think so."

"Is my sister okay?"

Heather's heartbeat, fast and steady, pulsed at the back of Dante's aching mind. He felt the rhythm of her chest rising and falling, felt the warm edge of the soothing sleep she'd tucked herself into.

"*Oui*," he said, voice soft. "She's okay."

But for how much longer, Dante-angel?

Dante didn't have an answer, but knew it was a damned good question.

Lifting his wrist, Dante bit it, filling his mouth with blood. It tasted thick and earthy—pomegranates and vine-ripened grapes. Bending, he pressed his lips against Von's, parting them with his tongue.

I won't lose you.

Pain trip-hammered against Dante's temples and another kind of pain squeezed his heart. Heather moaned in her sleep.

Von sucked in a breath, then his fingers brushed against Dante's cheek, entangled in his hair. He kissed Dante back, deep and hungry. Refused to let him go.

No matter what, your heart's true.

Breaking the kiss, Dante raised his head. Joy fluttered

through him, light as a moth, at the recognition glinting in the green depths of the nomad's eyes.

"I still believe that," Von said, pressing his hand against Dante's chest. "But that doesn't mean you don't scare the shit outta me, little brother."

"*Mon ami*," Dante whispered. "*Je re—*"

Von clapped a hand over his mouth. "Nuh-uh. Don't wanna hear it. You wanna owe me, then owe me. No apologies. Not between us. *D'accord?*"

Plucking Von's hand free, Dante said, "I owe you, for true. And if I wanna apologize, then I'm gonna fucking apologize. So—*je regrette.*"

"Like a goddamned mule."

"Mules apologize?"

Von slapped Dante's shoulder, then sat up. "Yeah, especially when they're not supposed to."

"Do you feel okay?" Dante asked. "I mean, do you feel . . . different?"

Von went still. Dante heard his heart pick up speed. "Did you do something to me, besides give me blood?" he asked, voice low.

"Ain't sure," Dante said. "But I think so."

Von nodded, then exhaled. "Ah, hell, little brother." He looked at Dante. "I'll let you know if anything odd pops up."

"I'll fix whatever I've changed," Dante promised.

"Well, if you've improved anything, I won't be complaining."

"It's you guys' turn to drive," Annie cut in. "I'm exhausted." But she remained outside, her face shadowed, her body language tense.

Given the grass and branches, understandable. Dante wondered if he should risk unmaking it, decided not to in case it went wrong.

He straightened and caught the car keys she tossed.

Tucked them into his pocket. *"D'accord.* Where are we?"

"Colorado, but we're getting close to the Kansas state line."

"That's good," Von said, smoothing his hair back from his face. "We should be home sometime late tomorrow afternoon." He touched fingers to his temple.

"You okay?"

"Just a little dizzy. Don't worry. I'm gonna hit the men's room. Wash up." Scooting to the door, Von hopped outside.

Annie climbed in. "This is fucking unreal," she muttered. "Dude, *grass?* Couldn't it be the kind we could smoke, at least?"

"Hey, it ain't prickly grass, so that's something."

Dante crawled over Von's sleeping bag to his own. Kneeling beside Heather, he checked her sleeping face for blood. He exhaled in relief when he didn't see any. Tendrils of sweat-damp red hair clung to her face. He brushed them aside, then bent and kissed her parted lips.

I got a little lost inside your head.

All heart and steel, his woman. Even though he'd yanked her into his nightmare, she'd fought beside him.

"Merci beaucoup, chérie," he whispered.

Heather's pink Emily the Strange T-shirt was soaked through and, spotting the empty Dasani bottle on the SUV's floor, he guessed water and sweat both played into the mix.

Then he saw the black zippered bag. "Another seizure?" he asked.

"Yeah, but Von had the seizure, not you."

An image strobed behind Dante's eyes: *The shovel smacks into the Papa/Von flickering face, slamming his head to the side, and toppling him into the sawgrass.*

"Merde."

Dante sat back on his heels, a hard knot burning in the center of his chest. Pain throbbed at his temples. He looked at Annie. She sat cross-legged on Von's sleeping bag, shadows smudged beneath her eyes, the line of her jaw tight. Moonlight glazed the piercings at her eyebrow and lower lip silver.

"Did I hurt Heather?" he asked. "I mean, a seizure or headache or nosebleed?"

Annie shook her head. "No. Not that I know of," she amended.

Dante nodded, throat tight. He returned his attention to Heather. Trailed his fingers along the curve of her cheek, down the line of her throat, and across her collarbone. Touched his fingertips to the collar of her damp shirt, then gently peeled the T-shirt off over her head.

"You got a dry shirt I can put on her?"

His gaze lingered on the curves of Heather's lavender bra–covered breasts. He imagined pushing the fabric aside, licking her nipple, then sucking the hardened bud into his mouth. His pulse quickened. He felt himself stir, stiffen. He wanted to trace his fingers along the soft skin over her taut, flat belly, the curves of her waist, down to the top of her jeans.

But he forced his hands to remain on his thighs. He wanted to be looking into her twilight blue eyes the next time he touched her, the next time he undressed her.

"You're gonna hurt Heather if you stay with her, y'know," Annie said softly. "You're gonna end up hurting everyone around you because you can't help it."

You're gonna hurt everyone around you.

Even if you don't mean to, huh, Dante-angel?

Watch over her, ma mère. S'il te plaît, keep her safe. Even from me.

Oui, princess. Even if I don't mean to.

"You don't need to waste that, by the way," Annie said, waving her hand at his crotch. "I'm awake. Unlike my sister."

Dante pushed his hair back from his face. "You got a dry shirt or not?"

"Don't get your panties in a twist." Annie swiveled around and grabbed her gym bag. She dug around in it, then pulled a shirt free. She tossed the bag back into its corner. She crawled across the grass and handed Dante the shirt.

"I know how you feel," she said.

"No, you don't."

"I've always been a fucking freak, different. I hurt everyone around me—especially the people I love."

"Do you wanna hurt them? Or does it just happen?"

"Both, sometimes." Annie's natural scent—vanilla and cloves—intensified, became smoky, but Dante caught something different underneath it, something he couldn't name. "Sometimes it's the only way to feel alive." She slid a hand up his thigh, hunger and heat shimmering in her blue eyes.

Annie's knowing touch reignited the smoldering embers of Dante's hunger for Heather. He locked his hand around Annie's wrist, stopping her hand just short of his crotch. "Ain't gonna let you hurt Heather."

"What she doesn't know *won't* hurt her."

"Yeah, it will."

Annie leaned into Dante, brushed her lips against his. "I know you wanna do this. You know it too." She reached for him with her free hand.

Dante *moved*. Only a couple of feet, but it was enough. Annie's hand swished through empty air. Dante dressed Heather in the Mad Edgar T-shirt and smoothed it over her belly. Fire flared. He drew in a deep breath and tamped the flames back down.

Want you, chérie. *Always will.*

"Interesting that you found that tee in your bag again, yeah, *p'tite?*" he said.

"I bet you'd fuck me if I wasn't Heather's sister," Annie said, shoving her blue/black/purple hair off her forehead.

"*Peut-être que oui, peut-être que non.* But since you are, it ain't happening."

"What *is* it with you? You piss me off and scare the shit outta me and get me hot all at the same frickin' time. Never met anyone like you." Annie knee-walked back to Von's sleeping bag and plopped down on it. "You know you don't belong here, right?"

"Yeah?" Dante asked, voice tight. "Where *do* I belong?"

"Someplace where you won't hurt everyone around you," Annie said, stripping off her pants and lobbing them into a corner. Purple panties peeked out from beneath the hem of her T-shirt. Panties she made sure he got a good look at before she rolled into the sleeping bag. "You say you don't want to hurt Heather, but that's hard for me to believe."

"Why?"

"'Cuz it's just a matter of time. You're going to hurt her and hurt her bad."

"Fuck you. That's between me and her."

"Just saying. Bet if you were with others like yourself, others who might understand all your blue-fire-mojo shit, they'd be able to teach you how to *not* hurt the people you care about, y'know, like Von?"

"*Tais-toi,*" Dante said, knotting his hands into fists. "Not another fucking word."

"Aw . . . he has buttons after all."

Afraid that if he didn't leave right now, he'd do something he would regret for a long time, Dante leaned over and kissed Heather's soft lips. "Sweet dreams, *catin,*" he whispered.

Dante climbed out of the SUV and closed the door. He leaned against it for a moment, waiting for his racing pulse to slow, for his hard-on to die down. Fire burned through his veins, torched his thoughts.

Pissed off at himself, most of all. He'd let Annie get under his skin.

Worse? The truth behind some of the shit she'd thrown at him.

Dante drew in a long, slow breath of air laced with the electric scent of impending rain, then pushed away from the car. He locked the SUV with a tap of the smart key, then strode across the parking lot to join Von in the men's room.

Watch over her, ma mère. *S'il te plaît*, *keep her safe. Even from me.*

VON LOOKED UP FROM the sink, water dripping from his face, when Dante pushed through the scratched-up metal door. "Hey," he said.

"Hey back. And whatta special smell in here. Eau de doo-doo." Dante walked over to a dripping sink, turned on the cold faucet and splashed water on his face.

"That doo-doo that you do?" Von drawled.

An appreciative smile ghosted across Dante's lips, but Von read the tension in his body, saw it knotted in the muscles along his shoulders and neck.

He ain't gonna forgive himself for what happened.

Von finished washing up, then walked over to the bank of almost ineffectual air blowers. Tapping one on, he crouched beneath it so it could blast air at his face and hands. He lifted his arms and angled his freshly scrubbed pits at the blower too.

The roaring *whoosh* of the machine made his ears and head ache.

<How do you stand the fucking noise?>

Dante's sending lanced through Von's mind, crisp and

clear, and sparked a chill down his spine. Normally a sending would filter in through his shields; now it was like nothing separated their minds, and that wasn't good.

"We'll meet in a few years when you're grown up. But right now, I think somehow you've pulled me inside a dream you're having—no, make that a fucking nightmare. Or is this a memory, little brother?"

"Man, this feels fucking real to me so I ain't got an answer for that." He turns back around and stares into the deep, still shadows pooled beneath the trees. *"There a difference between nightmares and memories?"*

That Dante even needed to ask a question like that . . .

The muscles tightened in Von's chest. What he wouldn't give to have some quality alone-time with the Bad Seed bastards who'd made Dante's life sheer hell from the moment he'd drawn his very first breath.

Nightmares. Memories.

Von needed to protect himself from the shifting realities inside Dante's mind—the lines blurring between dream, memory, and fluctuating time so he could help guide Dante, as both friend and *llygad*, along the dark and thorned path fate had unrolled beneath his feet.

Otherwise, Dante would probably kill him at some point—accidentally, of course. And that was the last thing either of them needed.

He's had all he can take for right now. Boy needs a break. Deserves a break.

"Von? You not answering me for a reason?"

Von swiveled around on his boot heels. Dante stood as far away as he could from the blowers, his hands pressed over his ears. His dark gaze searched Von's face. A muscle jumped at whatever he thought he saw in Von's eyes.

The blower clicked off. And some of the tension eased from Dante's face, but only some. Dante lowered his hands to his sides, his fingers curling in toward his palms.

"Let's go outside and talk, little brother," Von said, rising to his feet.

"*D'accord.*"

Outside, rain pattered onto the pavement, stirring the odor of wet blacktop into the pungent mix of diesel fuel and coffee. Von followed Dante to a picnic table on the other side of the parking lot, a good distance from the people coming and going from the restrooms and the coffee stand.

Dante straddled the picnic table bench and sat down. Beads of rain glistened in his hair and on his leather pants, jeweling the shoulders of his Saints of Ruin T-shirt.

On his bare white feet.

"Where your boots?" Von asked, straddling the bench so he could face Dante.

"Inside the car." Dante paused, trailing a hand through his hair, then said, "I fucked up. When I sent to you, I mean."

"You didn't fuck up."

"But it felt different, yeah? Like I'd just strolled into your bedroom without even pausing to knock, then realized there was no door."

"That's pretty much what it felt like, man. But all it means is that I need to strengthen and tighten my shields." Von tapped a finger against his temple. "Not a big deal."

"Yeah, it is. I pulled you into my dream, Von. Crashed your Sleep and your shields. No matter what you say, I'm responsible for hurting you. I think you should shut your link to me."

"I ain't gonna close off to you, little brother."

"Annie told me that . . ." Dante paused again, a muscle playing along his jaw. "That you had a seizure during Sleep."

Von stared at him, pulse racing. Holy hell. A seizure. A

real shovel would've fucking hurt, but wouldn't have damaged him. A realization chilled him: deadlier than reality, Dante's dreams.

He still didn't know how he'd landed in Dante's head in the first place, but suspected a part of Dante had realized he needed help and had instinctively reached for Von, pulled him inside.

To haul a struggling and bound boy out of a shallow grave.

"As long as you don't bash me with another shovel, I should be fine," Von said.

Dante cupped Von's face between his hot hands, the rain-chilled rings on his fingers and thumbs cold against Von's skin. "You ain't safe, not from me, and I ain't gonna lose you too, *mon ami*. Shut the link."

"Nope."

Dante held Von's gaze for a moment, his kohl-smudged dark eyes resolved. His hands slid away from Von's face. He stood. "Then I will."

<*You do, and I'm gonna kick your fucking ass.*>

But Von's thought bounced back unheard, the screened mental window between them closed and shuttered on Dante's side.

Von *moved*, tackling him around the waist and knocking them both over the bench and into the rain-slick grass. Dante exhaled hard in a startled *whoof*, his head bouncing against the ground. His black hair fanned across his face.

Von wrestled Dante—taut, corded muscles, faster-than-light reflexes, steel fingers and sharp nails; like wrestling a goddamned leopard—onto his back, pinned his wrists down at his sides, then sat on him, jamming knees into ribs.

Dante tossed his hair back from his face. Fury streaked his dark eyes with red. Corded the muscles in his neck. "Get the fuck offa me."

"Not until you open the link, you stubborn sonuv-abitch," Von growled.

"We ain't got time for this."

"No shit."

"Get the fuck offa me."

"And you know my answer to that." The muscles in Dante's wrists flexed. Von tightened his grip. "While I've got you here, there's a coupla other things we need to discuss."

"Fuck you."

"Stop being a dick and listen."

Fire blazed in Dante's eyes, but he kept his mouth shut, a good sign—even though his muscles remained coiled. Von nudged his knees deeper into Dante's sides.

"Here's a few facts you need to grasp: Just a month ago, a serial killer murdered two people you loved, then shoved a past you didn't even know about down your throat."

And I'll bet he did it with the same knives he used to slaughter Gina.

Dante went still. All expression vanished from his face.

Hating the necessity, Von continued, his throat almost too tight for words. "Just a couple of nights ago you were triggered and used by Lyons, then tortured. You lost your bond to Lucien and maybe, just maybe, you've lost Lucien himself."

"He ain't dead," Dante said, voice low and furious. "I'm gonna find him."

"And I'll help you. I'll be at your side every step of the way and we're gonna need that link to be open. Little brother, you don't have the faintest idea how important you are. Like it or not, you're a *creawdwr*. There ain't been one in thousands of years. Everyone's gonna want a piece of you, from mortals to nightkind to Fallen. And you ain't ready to face any of them."

"I wanna face them," Dante said. "Torch 'em. Burn 'em

to the fucking ground. I ain't running. The FBI's smearing Heather's name and rep and setting her up to be a future suicide, and the SB wants to take her apart to see what makes her tick—because of me."

"You. Ain't. Ready. To. Face. Any. Of. Them." Von released one of Dante's wrists so he could emphasize each word with a hard-fingered poke to his sternum—each poke slashing another stripe of red through Dante's brown irises. "You have power like no one else in this world. And if you don't learn how to use it, how to control it, you'll destroy the world and everyone on it—including Heather."

Dante's muscles bunched, flexed, then he *moved*, Von's hand still locked around his right wrist, his knees still in Dante's ribs. Von hit the ground hard, back first, then found himself staring up into the rain cloud-paled sky, Dante sitting on top of *him*.

Holy hell—boy's got a few moves I didn't know about. He felt a pleased smile curl across his lips.

"I. Ain't. Running," Dante said, poking a black-nailed finger into Von's chest with each word. "And I sure as hell ain't hiding."

"You're *making* things in your Sleep, little brother, without meaning to. Changing things. People, too. Do you even remember the little girl you transformed at the motel?"

Dante sucked in a breath as though gut-punched. He closed his eyes, a muscle ticking in his jaw. "Fuck," he whispered. "I thought I'd dreamed it."

"No dream, Dante," Von said, voice soft. "You saved her life, but she looks like someone else now. Because you don't know what you're doing and you don't have any control over your gifts, your power."

"My responsibility," Dante said, opening his eyes. "I get it, *mon ami*. I'll have Trey find out who she is and where she lives so I can make things right again for her."

"When things die down," Von pointed out. "But you need to realize, to expect, that things may never be right for her and her mom ever again. Think hard about that."

"*Bien compris*," Dante said, his expression troubled and weary. He rubbed a hand over his face, wiping away rain. "I'll think about everything you said, *d'accord*?"

Relief flickered through Von. "Fair enough."

The shutters on the window inside opened and Von felt Dante's warm, intense presence, followed by his thought.

<*I'm listening, llygad, but I promise you – I ain't running.*>

<*Understood. Wish I'd sat on you months ago, Hell, years ago.*>

Dante snorted, then offered Von the double-bird flip-off, before rising to his feet and pulling Von up with him. He paced in his bare feet in front of the bench. "Heather," he said, voice low. "She ended up in my dreams also, and—I don't know how it happened—but she's bonded to me now. I'll always be able to find her—no matter where she is, and she can reach me without touching me or being near, but everything in here"—Dante tapped a finger against his temple—"is gonna pour into her."

"Holy hell," Von breathed. "I'll teach her how to shield herself from you. So she don't get overwhelmed or—"

"Hurt," Dante finished. Emotion shadowed his dark eyes, knotted up his body.

"Yeah, little brother, that too. She'll be okay—we'll see to it, you and me."

Dante pushed his hands through his rain-wet hair, nodded. Then his eyes unfocused, turned inward. Von waited, wondering who was sending to him. After a moment, Dante refocused on Von, a smile tilting his lips.

"Simone," he said. "Mauvais sent a summons to the house. I guess his lackey promised dire fucking consequences if I don't show tomorrow night."

Von chuckled. "Wonder what passes for dire in that old Creole's mind? Not receiving an invitation to tea and a duel?"

Amusement gleamed in Dante's eyes. "The last thing he'll be expecting is for me to actually show up."

"Ah. True. Does that mean you will?"

"Maybe, yeah."

"Shall we grab a coupla towels outta the back of the SUV so we can dry off and get this show on the road?"

"I'm driving," Dante said. As he turned and trotted across the grass for the SUV, an image flashed into Von's mind, staggering him with its intensity.

Smooth black wings arch up behind Dante, fire patterns of brilliant blue and purple streaking their undersides. Blue flames lick around his clenched fists. Glimmer reflected along the thighs of his leather pants and sleek black latex, steel, and mesh shirt. A collar of braided black metal twists around his throat. And clipped to the steel ring at the collar's center, a leash, its silver-chained length leading down across his chest and abs, and disappearing into the right front pocket of his leather pants.

Tendrils of his black hair lift into the air as though breeze-caught. Gold light stars out from his black-rimmed eyes. He looks up as song—not his own—rings through the air. The night burns, the sky on fire from horizon to horizon.

The never-ending Road.

The Great Destroyer.

Von's mouth dried. He watched Dante climb into the driver's side of the SUV. *Think hard, little brother. Think long and hard on everything I just said.*

31

WITHOUT A RIPPLE

A TRUE BLOOD. AND right under his nose all this time.
Mauvais stalked the river's edge, the *Winter Rose* some distance behind him. Moonlight shivered across the river's sleek surface. Red lights winked as freighters glided upriver, sluicing through the black water.

Perhaps True Blood was the reason the Fallen, in the imposing form of Lucien De Noir—the Nightbringer—had chosen to stand beside Dante Baptiste.

Mauvais halted. He breathed in the Mississippi's scent of mud, moss, and fresh rain. He recalled Giovanni Toscanini's accented voice:

A True Blood can perhaps be forgiven many things?

Perhaps, perhaps not. But Mauvais was willing to be persuaded.

The Mississippi slapped against the rocks lining its banks and against wharf pilings. Mauvais caught a faint whiff of decaying wood.

And the world decays around us.

He resumed walking, hands clasped behind him.

The mortals destroy the planet that nurtures both our species and we do nothing; we who move through time, but are forever lost to it. Our society stagnates.

Dante could be a force of chaos, of change. He might divide us, awaken us.

Mauvais increased his pace, blurring past mortal strollers; gone in the blink of an eye. He abandoned the river for the beating heart of his beloved New Orleans: *le Vieux Carré.* Like a cool gust of air from the river, he breezed past streets choked with honking cars, past sidewalks thick with mortal crowds reeking of alcohol, lust, and abandon—and underneath, faint but present, the lingering odor of decay.

Mauvais strolled past the throng in Jackson Square, its iron fence decorated with colored lanterns. He walked Pirate's Alley, still amused after all these years at the name. Pirates had never congregated along that cobblestoned stretch except, perhaps, to urinate. He flew past Dumaine Street, then on to Chartres stopping at last beside the haunted walls of the Ursuline Convent.

Gaslit streetlights flickered orange on the rain-wet cobblestone street. Down the block, a horse's hoofs clopped as a carriageful of tourists headed back to Jackson Square. For a moment, Mauvais almost believed he'd stepped back in time to the New Orleans of two centuries ago. Back when the streets had never been this clean. A smile touched his lips.

He'd discovered Justine here just after the Second World War when he'd returned to the city after abandoning it for nearly a century. Beautiful Justine, a French refugee, heartbreakingly young and all alone.

Mauvais's heart contracted; his love for his *fille de sang*, his only blood-daughter, was a physical anguish at times, as sharp as a knife. With her white skin, dark eyes framed by thick black lashes, her cherry-red lips, he'd never known a moment of regret for her making. He couldn't say that for most of his *fils des sangs*.

But Justine had threatened to contact the Conseil du Sang if Giovanni and the Cercle de Druide allowed Dante Baptiste to walk away from his crimes unpunished—True Blood or not.

In truth, Mauvais doubted most members of the law-enforcing Conseil du Sang had ever laid eyes upon a True Blood. He had, centuries before, when he was quite young, and he'd never forgotten the intoxicating taste of a born vampire's blood. Or the strength it'd given him, for a time.

True Bloods, few as they were, seemed to be solitary creatures, rarely longing for the company of others. Dante was different even in this with his band and his Club Hell; not so solitary.

Perhaps True Blood aloofness could be attributed to the fact that they'd never been human. Never suffered the doubts and agonies of a newborn vampire remembering what it was to be mortal. Never experienced the anguished realization that draining the lifeblood from those they loved wasn't at all difficult.

Defiant and disrespectful, his every action brimming with anarchy, Dante might very well be the chaotic and violent infusion of life that their decaying societies–mortal and vampire—needed in order to survive.

The sound of hurried footsteps drew Mauvais's gaze. A young woman wrapped in an old-fashioned black cloak sprinted down the sidewalk. As she passed beneath the streetlight, the flickering flame etched gold light into her blonde hair. Shadows danced across her anxious face.

Small hands held her black and purple lace skirt up as she ran.

As she drew near him, Mauvais stepped forward. "May I be of assistance, *m'selle*?"

She stopped. She met Mauvais's gaze with deep green eyes outlined with kohl. Her crimsoned lips curved into a hesitant smile. She smelled of lavender and lilac. An exquisite doll.

"I'm so late," she said in the clipped tones of a Northerner. "The ghost tour, I mean. We're supposed to meet at Lafitte's Blacksmith Shop and I— Could you point me in the right direction?"

"I can do better than that, *m'selle*," Mauvais said with a courtly half-bow. "I shall escort you."

The girl's lovely face lit up when he offered his arm. All trace of her previous anxiety vanished. She looped her arm through his.

"A real live Southern gentleman," she murmured. "I'm April, by the way."

"*Enchanté, M'selle* April," Mauvais said, smiling. "A lady should never walk the streets alone after dark."

She looked away, cheeks flushed, dazzled. "And why is that?"

"It is the vampires, *m'selle*," Mauvais whispered. "You see, they are everywhere in this city."

She giggled. "Then it's really good I ran into you."

"I'd call it destiny, *m'selle*."

Her sweetness, her darling white face tugged at him. For a moment, he thought of giving Justine a sister. But only for a moment. He'd offered to escort her and so he, as a gentleman, would. She would never be safer.

Once April had been delivered to the candlelit tavern, Mauvais strolled the Quarter's sidewalks, listening to the mercurial heartbeat of the crowds filling the streets, listening for the single rhythm that would both drum up his hunger, then end it once more.

As he walked and listened, his thoughts looped back to Dante Baptiste, possibilities sparking like fireflies through his mind.

One: Win the favor of the holy Cercle de Druide and Renata Cortini in particular by doing everything that she and her *fils de sang* asked in regards to Dante.

Two: Allow Justine to voice her complaint to the Conseil du Sang and sow a few seeds of chaos, enough to rip open the rift of antipathy between the holy order and rigid vampire law—a rift the Elder judges of the Parliament of Ancients would be called upon to bridge. And in the confusion?

Possibility number three: Keep the True Blood for himself.

A heartbeat, as strong and as fast as a dragonfly's transparent wings, caught Mauvais's attention. He looked up.

She stood in front of the voodoo museum, a plastic Hurricane cup in her hand. A smile lit April's face when she saw him. She waved.

Destiny.

Mauvais waved back, amused that he'd lost two hours or more to his restless thoughts. He crossed the street to join her. "Did you enjoy your tour, *m'selle*?"

"Very much," she said. "It was totally awesome. I love this city."

"As do I. Would you grace me with your beautiful presence, *m'selle*, and accompany me on a walk along the river?"

Deep rosy color blossomed on April's cheeks. "I'd like that, kind sir."

Arm in arm, they ambled to the banks of the Mississippi. There Mauvais wrapped his arms around April—such a fragile and fragrant spring bouquet—and embraced her.

She never struggled and her body went into the black water with hardly a ripple.

And the world decays around us.

Yes, perhaps it *was* time for a change. Perhaps it would be a change he could direct and control. Perhaps.

But not until after Justine had her revenge.

32

IN THIS TWILIGHT

HEKATE SLIPPED OUT OF the golden and gleaming hall and into the starlit night. A complicated and trilling chorus of *wybrcathl* rang behind her; a melodious and heated debate regarding the future of the unnamed *creawdwr* still eluding the Elohim, free and unbound in the mortal world.

Hekate glanced over her shoulder, her pulse winging through her veins. Beyond the glittering hall's wide mouth, Gabriel walked before the gathering in a royal blue kilt, his golden wings fluttering in emphasis as his smooth and honeyed voice detailed his plans for the *creawdwr* and the Elohim.

Plans that didn't require the *creawdwr*'s consent.

"We need both—tradition and a new age—and we need

a sane *creawdwr* to achieve them," Gabriel said, his voice carrying above the tumult of song.

"The *creawdwr* has turned our emissaries to stone!"

A smile touched Gabriel's lips. "So the Morningstar claims. I find it intriguing that he, out of all of them, managed to remain flesh."

"It's a sign. The *creawdwr* is saying things need to change. Gehenna should die and so should all the old ways. It's time to begin fresh, to join the mortal and vampire worlds, and craft a new and golden age with a young Maker to lead us."

"A *creawdwr* who's already insane?"

"Soon this very young Maker will be bound and stabilized by strong and caring *calon-cyfaills*, and ready to take his place on the Chaos Seat," Gabriel said.

Wybrcathl quieted. The burring buzz of *chalkydri* wings echoed through the hall as the little demons helped the *nephilim* servants fetch and pour iced pitchers of wine.

"But," Gabriel continued, "perhaps it *is* time Gehenna was allowed to fade away." His golden wings fluttered, capturing attention. "And a new Gehenna created."

Shocked and outraged songs pealed through the air at Gabriel's words. Hekate unfolded her gleaming white wings and launched herself into the fragrant spring evening.

She hoped her plan would work. She hoped that Gabriel and his high-blood old guard debated the *creawdwr*'s and Gehenna's future late into the night.

Her wings cut like blades through the chilly air, each stroke bringing her closer to the Royal Aerie's east terrace where Lucien awaited her. Ghost-pale moonlight rippled along the mouths of the aeries she flew past.

As she kited down to the terrace, Lucien tipped his face up from the balcony he leaned against. A handsome face, but each passing day siphoned away more of its vitality, dimmed the heat in his black eyes to embers.

She saw the golden coil of her *geis* looped around his mind: *You would be forbidden to leave my side.*

And felt his snaking warm around her thoughts in return: *You would be forbidden to lead anyone to my son or reveal his location.*

Hekate's sandaled feet lit on the marble floor and she fluttered to a stop, folding her wings behind her. Lucien saluted her with his glass of plum purple wine.

"Very pretty," he said. "I enjoy watching you fly."

She joined him at the balustrade. "A debate is taking place at the Hall of Voices," she said. "We should leave as soon as I have you disguised."

Lucien nodded, then tossed back the last of his wine. "Do you need anything from me?" he asked, swiveling around to face her.

Weariness etched his face, pooled dark beneath his eyes. At times, his skin seemed almost translucent. Gabriel's punishment—binding Lucien's fate to the dying land— seemed cruel to her. But perhaps it was deserved. Lucien was a murderer, after all. *Calon-cyfaill* to the *creawdwr* he'd slaughtered. A chill shuddered along the length of Hekate's body; it was an unthinkable betrayal.

"No," Hekate said. "Just hold still and keep quiet until I complete the illusion."

Lucien set his empty glass on the balcony's edge, then straightened, head high. Hekate plucked energy out of the air, shaping it and weaving it around Lucien, chewing on her lower lip in concentration.

A quick bending of light rays finished her illusion. Lucien looked nothing like himself, his hair red, eyes green, his build slimmer and his face angled and sharp, his wings golden.

Hekate blew out her breath, then nodded. "Hold still," she said, stepping behind him. She sparked blue flame into the bands on his wings. Seals melted and they fell apart, clinking onto the marble floor. She scooped the pieces up and tossed them into the night.

"Ah," Lucien sighed, unfolding his wings. He flexed and fluttered them, tested their strength.

"Are you strong enough to fly?" Hekate asked.

"If I'm not, let me fall."

"Not very helpful," she said, turning away from him. She touched Menakel's waiting mind and the dark-haired *nephilim* servant padded past the guards and onto the terrace.

Hekate nodded at the couch. Without a word, Menakel went to it and laid down. She crossed the terrace, the *nephilim's* eyes drinking in each stride, then knelt beside his couch. She bent, kissed his lips, and murmured, "Thank you."

"Just don't get caught," he whispered.

"I won't," she said with more confidence than she felt. Drawing in a deep breath, she gathered more night energy and wove another illusion. A few minutes later, Lucien, wings banded, regarded her from the couch with dark eyes.

Joining the true Lucien at the balustrade once more, she said, "Shall we?"

A smile curved his lips. "Try to stop me." Walking to the terrace's open edge, he threw himself into the star-pricked sky.

Hekate's heart skipped a beat when he dropped from sight, but he rose a moment later, his false golden wings stroking through the air.

With a final glance at Menakel on the couch, Hekate snapped out her wings and followed Lucien to Gehenna's gate.

* * *

GABRIEL WALKED AWAY FROM the symphony of debate in the hall, seeking fresh air out on the terrace, seeking a glimpse of Hekate's white wings slicing through the night.

He wondered if she was even now flying from Gehenna and into the mortal world with an illusion-draped Samael winging at her side.

He rested his forearms on the cool stone balcony. He'd glimpsed the *geis* she'd placed upon the murdering *aingeal* and had known what she intended to do.

Search for her mother and her *calon-cyfaill*.

Ah, but Samael would search for the Maker and would, no doubt, find him. As would the agent Gabriel had tasked with following the pair.

Another part of him insisted that he *not* allow Samael and Hekate to escape, to have them captured at the gate and both tossed into Sheol.

But doubt chained his mind. The Morningstar claimed to be following the *creawdwr*. Claimed him to be *Fola Fior* and Elohim. Claimed him to be injured. But honesty had never been the Morningstar's gift.

Samael had said the Morningstar played games. True. But they all were guilty of that charge—games within games within games.

Insanity hadn't caused the *creawdwr* to turn Gehenna's emissaries into stone. No, Gabriel was quite certain that it had been done at Samael's command. And it was just as certain that Samael had sent Lilith into a trap, knowing what awaited the Elohim who answered the Maker's *anhrefncathl*.

Samael was guilty of the very thing he'd accused Gabriel of—chaining a *creawdwr* to his will. But what did he hope to accomplish? Could he be planning to reclaim Gehenna's Black-Starred throne?

Of course, if the *creawdwr* couldn't be located until

after Gehenna and treacherous Samael had faded out of existence, he'd no longer need to worry about Samael's possible plans.

<As you warned, the Lady Hekate has left with the prisoner Samael,> the captain of the royal guard sent. <Do you wish me to pursue?>

Gabriel studied the star-flecked night. Good question. A *very* good question.

Despite their centuries together, despite the fact that he'd never denied her anything, Hekate had sought help from his enemy—an *aingeal* who would trick and use her, despite her *geis*, instead of simply asking for Gabriel's assistance in searching for her loved ones trapped in the mortal world.

A child's game. A foolish girl. But useful.

Gabriel's talons bit into his palms. He felt the hot trickle of blood.

<Yes. Pursue and capture them. Shroud them both in chains and drop them into Sheol.>

<Both, my lord?>

<Both.>

Perhaps the Morningstar would be more forthcoming once he learned his daughter hung chained in Sheol's embered guts.

Games within games within games.

33

THIS TIME IS ALL
WE HAVE

BROWNING IN HAND, HEATHER surveyed the night-drenched yard, searching for anything out of place, for a sign of anyone watching since she'd pulled the SUV into the house's circular drive at 4:30 that afternoon.

She'd studied the house and yard then too, before locking up the vehicle and tucking herself against Dante's fevered warmth for a nap until his nightkind household awakened.

Dante draws in a deep breath and opens his dark eyes. Heather says, "We're home."

A warm, almost happy, smile curves his lips. "C'est bon, yeah?"

"*Definitely.*"

Heather bends and kisses his lips. Everything she sees in his eyes, she also feels. Ever since her journey through the dark forest of his mind, she feels connected to him in a way that reminds her of the temporary blood-link she shares with him whenever he drinks a little of her blood.

Bonded, he explains to her. Connected mind-to-mind and heart-to-heart.

"*I can feel you,* catin, *and you can feel me—no matter if we're together or not.*"

Dante returns her kiss passionately and heat ripples through her belly – hers and his. This is going to be interesting.

"All clear, doll," Von said, joining her on the cracked and root-tilted sidewalk. He slid his Browning back into its holster.

"Good." Heather tucked her gun into the back of her jeans, automatically tugging the hem of her shirt over the Browning.

Need to get my own gun.

"Cool house," Annie said, stopping beside her, gym bag in hand.

"No one watching, not from cars parked on the street, anyway," Dante said, slipping back into the driveway through the partially opened wrought-iron gate.

The front door flew open, smacking against the house, and Simone raced down the steps, her long blonde spirals bouncing against her back. She stopped in front of Dante and threw her arms around his neck.

The sweet smell of magnolias permeated the air.

"*Mon ami,*" she cried, kissing first his lips, then his cheeks, over and over again.

A radiant smile lit Dante's pale face. He laced his arms around her waist. "Hey, *chère,*" he said, Simone's kisses muffling his words. "Missed you."

"Hey, sugar," Von said, tipping Simone's face toward him. "Plant some on me."

Grinning, Simone loosened her hold on Dante and kissed Von thoroughly.

Annie arched an eyebrow and glanced at Heather. Heather forced a smile to her lips and tried to relax, reminding herself that Simone and Dante's relationship was one of friendship. At least, she thought so. All the same she itched to pluck the blonde away from Dante.

Silver, his Midnite Purple hair anime-styled and gelled, leaned in the doorway in black tee and jeans, a mischievous smile on his lips, streetlight gleaming in his silver eyes.

"Hey, Annie."

"Hey back." Hoisting the strap of her gym bag onto her shoulder, Annie climbed the steps to the front porch. Silver pushed away from the doorway and led the way into the house.

"Let's take this inside," Von said. "Might not be safe out here in the open."

Dante kissed Simone's forehead, then eased free of her embrace. "He's right."

Von snorted. "That goes without saying." He slipped an arm around Simone's waist. She looked at the nomad for a long moment, then face stricken, she leaned into him. She glanced at Dante, concern in her dark eyes. Von shook his head.

Heather had a feeling Von had just told Simone about Dante's loss.

Dante stretched a hand out to Heather and she grasped it. Lacing his fingers through hers, they walked up the sidewalk and into the house.

Home.

*   *   *

GILLESPIE WATCHED THROUGH HIS binoculars as Prejean, McGuinn, the Wallace sisters and the other two vampires—the gorgeous blonde and the slinky teenager—disappeared inside the house.

He'd also watched as Prejean had prowled the street and neighboring driveways looking for surveillance vehicles. Moonlight had glinted in his hair and along his leather pants, seemed to flow beneath his white skin.

Gillespie had pulled back from the window, heart pounding, wondering if the True Blood could sense him even across the street and through walls.

When he'd looked again, no one walked the street's edge and he'd suffered a bad moment imagining Prejean climbing in through the laundry room window.

He'd remembered Rodriguez's savaged throat in vivid detail.

Lifting his binoculars with shaking hands, he'd seen Prejean inside the gate, the blonde vamp draped over him and Heather Wallace looking none too pleased.

Gillespie rested the binoculars on the windowsill and went downstairs to fetch a couple of Pacificos from the fridge of the house he'd broken into when he'd learned the owners were on vacation.

Trudging back up the stairs, Gillespie settled into his chair again. He glanced at the sniper rifle in its case. When the time was right. No matter how long it took for that time to come around.

Through Prejean, he finally had a chance to redeem himself, to do something that mattered. Through Prejean, he had a chance to remove an evil from the world. An evil that unmade people and murdered others; an evil that had transformed a little girl into someone else.

An evil partially created and released by the SB itself—Dante Prejean.

Taking a long swallow of the lime-laced and frosty brew, Gillespie picked up his binoculars and went back to watching.

HEATHER DRAPED THE CLOTHES Simone had given her—panties, black bra, purple tank top, black leather pants, socks—on top of Dante's rumpled bed. The bra would be snug since she and Simone wore different cup sizes, but it'd work until she could buy clothes of her own.

Leather pants—a first. But Simone apparently didn't own a single pair of jeans— just a few pairs of leather pants and a closetful of skirts and dresses.

Mewing, Eerie inspected the clothes with delicate sniffs, decorating them with orange fur.

"Hey, you," Heather said, rubbing his head. "Quit helping."

Closing his eyes, Eerie stroked his jaw against her fingertips. He purred.

Dante had offered her and Annie rooms of their own, an offer of personal space that Annie had snatched up immediately.

Don't want you to feel like you hafta share a room with me, chérie. Until we get things figured out—

Do you want me in your room?

He answers her with a kiss that steals her breath away and weakens her knees.

Then shut up, Baptiste. There'll be time to figure things out later.

Heather stepped into Dante's bathroom and turned on the shower. A sense of loss shafted through her heart. Tears prickled in her eyes. Bewildered, she shut off the water. Then it hit her—it was Dante's grief, not her own.

She walked from his room and into the hall. She

peeked in each door she passed until she found him two doors down and across the hall. He stood at the closet of a neat, Spartan room, a white tailored shirt in his hands.

A shirt that had to be Lucien's, given the size.

Dante rubbed his ringed thumbs back and forth across the material. He blinked hard and fast several times.

Heather swiveled around and walked away, a lump in her throat. If she'd said anything or had stepped into the room, he would've put his grief aside. She couldn't do that to him.

Returning to the bathroom, Heather turned the shower back on and pulled off the Mad Edgar T-shirt. Steam curled into the air. As she reached to unfasten her bra, her hands brushed against hot fingers already working the bra hooks. Even hotter lips kissed her neck. Her bra dropped to the floor with a quick push and then those hot hands slid around and cupped her breasts.

Heather gasped, pleasure fluttering through her belly in intense waves.

Fangs pierced her flesh, a quick-vanishing sting at her neck. Dante drank her in with a low growl, his fingers squeezing and teasing her nipples. Pleasure spiraled through her in quick, ever-tightening loops.

She felt him hard against her, his erection pressing against her ass.

His hunger, his need, poured through her, stealing her breath and weakening her knees. One hand trailed away from her breast and down her bare belly to the top of her jeans. Heather moaned low and leaned into Dante—wanting his touch more than she'd ever wanted anyone's. She reached back, grabbed his ass, and pulled him closer still.

Dante's questing hand unbuttoned her jeans and wormed its way inside, slipping underneath her panties.

Her breath caught rough in her throat as his fingers found her—circling and dipping and tracing. Pleasure rippled through her with every touch.

His breathing quickening, Dante kissed her neck, then trailed moist, fevered kisses along her throat. Heather turned her face toward him so he could kiss her lips; she *yearned* for his kiss.

Hunger gleamed in Dante's eyes, a dark and ravenous fire. He slid his hand free of her jeans, then stepped around in front of her. He pulled off his shirt and dropped it on the floor. Hooking a finger through the ring on his collar, Heather reeled him in and down.

He kissed her long and deep—hot, bruising kisses—as he backed her up against the bathroom wall. Fire burned through Heather at the touch of his tongue, at the heat of his tight-muscled body pressing against her. She cupped her hands around his beautiful face and kissed him even deeper, devouring his sweet amaretto lips and savoring the grape-and-copper tang of her own blood on his tongue.

Working a hand between them, Heather grasped his hard length through his leather pants. Dante growled against her lips. His hands tore at her jeans, breaking the zipper in his effort to get them off of her.

Trailing wet kisses from her nipples to her belly, Dante dropped to his knees and yanked her jeans and panties down to her ankles. Heather stepped out of them, kicked them aside as Dante's hot, hot hands slid around to cup her ass. He licked her, kissed her, his tongue and lips molten and soft and knowing.

With each touch of Dante's hands and lips, music pulsed hot and liquid between them, a sensual and un-tamed song.

Struggling for breath, Heather came, pleasure rippling

through her in mind-blanking waves. Her eyes fluttered closed.

She heard a belt buckle jingle and her eyes flew open. "No! Not this time. *I'm* taking those goddamned pants off."

Still on his knees, Dante looked up at her, his fingers paused on the snap of his leather pants. A smile tilted his lips. He eased to his feet, his hands moving to her hips.

"They're all yours, *catin.*"

"Finally."

Heather knelt and peeled Dante's pants down, kissing his pale thighs as she went, each kiss eliciting a sharp intake of breath from him. Tracing her fingers, then her tongue along his hard, satiny length, she took him into her mouth. Dante shivered and a low moan slipped past his lips. His fingers entangled in her hair.

Like a match tossed onto a trail of gasoline leading to a bonfire, Dante's pleasure blazed through Heather, ignited and merged with her own, raging hotter with each passing minute, with each touch of her lips and tongue and hands. Blue light filled the bathroom, danced along their bodies. Dante's breath caught ragged in his throat as he came.

Heather blinked. Came, but still hard. So very much she needed to learn about him yet, about each other—especially in the sex department—but she was looking forward to the learning.

Dante pulled Heather to her feet and into a wild and fevered kiss. He lifted her up and onto him, resting her bare back against the wall. Gasping against his lips as he entered her, she wrapped her legs around his waist and her arms around his neck.

Dante drove into her, hard and deep. Music and hot, honeyed pleasure poured through Heather with each hungry thrust, a primal and earthy rhythm. Sweat slicked their bodies. His lips slid from hers and down and closed over her nipple, sucking it into the heat of his mouth. Her fingers entangled in his silky locks, her half-lidded gaze fixed on his beautiful, burning face.

Panting, she met him thrust for urgent thrust, closed her eyes, and abandoned herself to their hunger for each other, their need.

This time was all they had.

"IT'S GONNA TAKE PRACTICE, doll," Von said. "A lot of practice. And when—if—things ever quiet down, me and Dante will be able to sit down and really teach you."

"So the main thing is visualization and focus, right?" Heather said. She sat at the kitchen table, finishing a cup of rich French roast coffee while Dante went over urgent Inferno e-mail with Trey in the computer room, stuff the web-runner felt couldn't wait.

Heather wished she and Dante'd had more time to just linger together skin-to-skin and lips-to-lips, but the same urgency pushing her—*fresh outta time*—was pushing Dante too.

"I feel like time's running out for Lucien, catin. Can't explain it, but I feel it here." Dante touches their clasped hands against his bare chest over his heart and the little bat tattoo inked into his pale skin.

"You don't need to explain to me, Baptiste," she murmurs. "I understand."

"Is that dreamy expression for me, doll? I know I can be distracting, but—"

"What? Sorry. Hi, Von. Been sitting here long?" Heather offered the nomad an innocent smile.

"Ouch, woman."

"So, visualization and focus, right?" she repeated.

"*Focus* is key. Yup. Picture steel walls or whatever feels secure and safe to you, impenetrable, y'know?"

"Like a vault for your mind?" Heather asked.

"That'll work, yeah. Hey, take a walk outside with me," Von said, pushing back his chair and rising to his feet. "Got something to show you."

"I've seen your boxers. Sorry."

"No, woman, get your mind outta the gutter. And you ain't seen *these* boxers."

"Oops. My mistake." Heather finished her coffee and stood.

"Look at you—all sexy and bad-ass in leather pants."

Heather arched an eyebrow. "But not in jeans? Thanks, I think."

"I mean, sexier and bad-assier."

With a wicked grin, Von led Heather outside to the black van parked in the driveway—the van that she'd seen Lucien drive during her last visit to New Orleans. A pang pierced her heart. She hoped Dante was right and that he'd find his father and bring him home again.

The nomad unlocked the side doors and slid them open. "Gotta surprise for you, doll. Take a look."

Climbing into the back of the van, Heather discovered boxes and a duffel bag occupying the seats and floor space. Familiar boxes with a musty smell. Excitement curled through her. Her fingers skipped along the edges of the cartons marked WALLACE, SHANNON, CASE NO. 5123441.

"How did you do this?" she asked, glancing over her shoulder at Von.

"It was me and Trey, actually," the nomad said. "I saw your stuff and Dante's in your living room when I was looking for you two at your place, so after the shit in Damascus, I contacted Trey and he made the arrangements for a courier service to pick your stuff up before the feds could seize it."

"I can't thank you enough, Von. Seriously." Heather climbed out of the van and cat-bumped Von with her shoulder.

The nomad nudged her back, his leather jacket creaking. "I know how much you wanna find the bastard who murdered your mom."

"And this is going to make it possible. Again, thank you."

Von glanced toward the house, then lifted his shades on top of his head. "Dante say why he wants to start his search for Lucien at the cemetery?"

"He said one of the Fallen is there—Loki—one who Lucien turned to stone with some kind of spell. Dante's hoping that if he can free Loki, then he'll show him where Gehenna is."

"Yeah, I remember," Von said. "We saw the statue just before we left on tour. I hope Dante's right. If he can free Loki, the bastard might only play games with him. His name's Loki, right? Norse trickster god?"

"I don't think Dante's in the mood for games. Loki could find himself stone again in a heartbeat."

"True enough. Just remember what I told you about shielding. And you might need these." Von handed Heather a couple of morphine-filled syringes.

Heather slipped them into a pocket of her trench coat, another rescue from Von. He'd grabbed up her coat and personal stuff from her Trans Am before ditching it.

"You're Dante's lifeline, doll," Von said. "I'm sorry you had no say in getting bonded to him, but you quiet the storm inside-a him. And that's a damned good thing."

"When I was inside his head, all the noise, the pain, the constant fight to keep my identity . . ." Heather looked away, searching for the right words. Her gaze settled on the ivy-laced river rock wall. "Is that what he deals with every moment?"

"Yeah, doll, I think it is. Or just a taste of it. But I hope we can change that."

"I feel like time's running out," Heather said, half-afraid

of making the words come true by saying them aloud. "That he's slipping past my reach."

"I have a feeling a part of Dante thinks so too," Von said, voice low. "And that's why he reached out to us. Grabbed ahold. Stubborn sonuvabitch is fighting to hang on."

Dante's whispered words beneath the willow tree as he knelt beside Von's unconscious body curled through Heather's memory.

A wished-hard thing takes a shape within the heart.

Heather returned her attention to Von. Moonlight frosted the crescent moon tattoo inked beneath his eye. "Boy's got a destiny," he said. "One he can't walk away from because he *is* the future."

"The never-ending Road."

"Yup. And I think you're a part of that destiny, doll. Don't ever let him walk away from you."

"I can quote Dante for you on that one," Heather said, feeling a smile brush her lips. "Ain't asking permission."

"My advice? If he gets outta hand, sit on him. Works like a charm."

Laughter, low and warm and inviting, drew Heather's gaze to the front porch and the open door beyond it. Dante stood at the threshold, one arm laced around Simone's waist, Eerie nestled into the crook of his other arm. Eerie batted a paw at a low-fluttering moth, insisting it flutter straight into his open mouth.

The sight of her Eerie-kitty making Dante laugh untangled a few knots from around Heather's heart. An amused smile on her face, Simone touched her fingers to Dante's face and drew him down into a kiss.

And retangled the knots.

"Here, darlin', more magazines for your gun—just in case."

"Useful thing, paranoia," Heather said, gratefully shifting

her gaze away from Dante and Simone. She scooped the pistol mags from Von's extended hand. Dropped them into the trench coat pocket opposite the syringes.

"I wish you were coming with us," she said. "I could use an extra pair of eyes on lookout. Dante's going to be busy seeing if he can undo Lucien's magic and release Loki."

"I hear ya, doll. But some things a man's gotta do alone. If anything goes south or unexpected bad guys pop up, he'll give me a shout."

"Did he promise?"

"Did who promise what?" Dante asked, as he trotted down the porch steps. "My ears are burning, so must be me, yeah?"

He paused on the sidewalk to brush Eerie fur from his mesh-sleeved NIN T-shirt and from the front of his low-slung black restraint pants. Small chrome buckles edged the side of each leg from top to bottom.

"Yeah, you, and no." Von sighed. "He didn't promise, now that you mention it."

"Promise what?" Dante stopped beside Heather, a smile on his lips. Simone's magnolia scent clung to him like a cobweb. He shrugged on a black hoodie; red letters safety-pinned to the sleeves read: NOT DEAD—DO NOT TAKE TO MORGUE.

"To give a shout if things go south."

"Said I would. Ain't that a promise?"

Glancing at Simone, Heather wrapped her arms around Dante's waist and kissed him thoroughly. His burning autumn leaves scent coiled around her, whipped heat through her belly. Annoyed with herself for acting like a possessive get-your-eyeballs-off-my-man kind of lunatic, she ended the kiss.

Dante watched her with dark, smoldering eyes. "Feel better?"

Heather stared at him, then heat flushed her cheeks as she realized he could feel strong emotions from her too.

"Shields, doll, shields," Von murmured.

"Um . . . which car are we taking?" she said in a desperate attempt to change the subject.

"We ain't," Dante said, sliding on shades. "Von's loaning us his Harley. Wanna drive, *catin*?"

"I'd love to learn, but for now, you drive."

A few minutes later, Heather sat behind Dante on Von's Harley, her hands on his hips, her body cupped against his, the humid night whipping through her hair and his as he steered the rumbling and powerful bike toward New Orleans and St. Louis No. 3.

34

DARK AND AIRLESS HEARTS

DANTE LED HEATHER DOWN the cemetery's central path, past the moon-washed white crypts and the dead cradled within their dark and airless hearts, to the tomb marked BARONNE.

She studied Loki's crouched and stone-spelled form, shifting her weight onto one hip. Dante noticed her keen gaze drinking in every detail: the moonlight twinkling along faint designs swirled into the smooth wings, primal and stylized designs like tribal tattoos. Frozen waist-length hair framed Loki's screaming face. He was nude except for a thick torc twisted around his corded throat and a bracelet around one bicep.

The smell of vanilla and wax from the small candles burning in front of Loki's taloned feet mingled with the sweet scent of cherry blossoms and the dank scent of decay.

Dante noticed that the chiming black blossoms he'd created within Loki's cupped hands had vanished. A few shriveled black stems left behind told him that the flowers had been uprooted.

Heather fingered a string of plastic Mardi Gras beads—one of many—looped around the stone angel's wings and throat. Folded scraps of paper—prayers, words from the heart —littered the sidewalk in front of Loki. And chalked good-luck *x*'s in blue, yellow, and pink decorated the path.

"Why did Lucien turn him to stone?" Heather asked.

Lucien's words rolled through Dante's memory.

I trapped him to protect you.

I thought I could keep you safe in silence. I thought I could hide you, help you heal from all the damage done to you.

But I was wrong.

"To keep Loki from finding me," Dante said.

Heather let go of the strand of beads and it fell back, clicking against the stone. She turned around to face Dante. "Do you think releasing him is a good idea?"

"Probably not, but he's my best chance at finding Lucien. He can tell me how to find Gehenna. Hell, I bet he'd volunteer to take me." Dante pushed his hands through his hair. "Maybe Lucien ain't there, but I gotta know."

"Let's give it a shot," Heather said. Pulling the Browning free of an interior pocket of her trench, she clasped it in both hands and backed up so she could better watch the surrounding area.

Dante knelt on one knee in front of Loki's trapped form. The blood glyph Lucien had traced on Loki's forehead had faded almost completely away. The blue spark of Fallen magic that had leapt between the stone and Dante's fingertip a couple of weeks ago was only a pale flicker.

Frowning, Dante touched his fingers to Loki's stone chest. A faint, desperate song scratched like little squirrel claws beneath the cool, white stone. Dante trailed a finger along the blood glyph and imagined *unwriting* it, imagined the blood flaking away, swept along by the March breeze.

Blue fire crackled unbidden along his fingers. Black moss suddenly sprouted on Loki's forehead. A tiny song tinkled along the moss's rounded edges. Not what he wanted. Heart pounding, Dante clenched his hands into fists. The fire guttered out.

"We're not alone," Heather said, voice taut.

Her words snapped Dante up from his contemplation. He heard the slow beat of vampire hearts—multiple hearts. He rose smoothly to his feet and swiveled around.

Heather backed toward him, gun extended and swinging from left to right as nightkind dressed in expensive and Euro-stylish suits glided across the cemetery paths and from the shadows pooled between crypts.

Encircled them.

Dante figured he could take several down and maybe outrun the rest. He couldn't risk using his *creawdwr* power—not when whatever might pour out from his fingertips could affect Heather as well as nightkind.

"Perhaps you forgot about *M'sieu* Mauvais's invitation," a blond and well-coiffed nightkind said. Dante recognized him as Lackey *Numéro Un*—Laurent.

"Nope. Didn't forget. Just ain't interested," Dante said. "Now if y'all don't mind, we've got stuff to do."

"Listen, you piece of shit," a tall, Gold's Gym beefy nightkind with buzz-cut hair said, each word juiced with spittle. "You and your pretty little pet get into the limo Mauvais so thoughtfully provided or I'm gonna tear her apart in front—"

Dante *moved*. Stretched Tall'N'Beefy out on the stone path with hard-knuckled jabs to the fucker's throat and balls. TNB curled into a ball, coughing and gagging.

"Ain't tearing no one apart, motherfucker."

Dante heard a quick step behind him. He whirled and went low, slashing Laurent across the gut with his nails, feeling cloth, then flesh beneath his fingers. He breathed in the heady tang of nightkind blood and kept *moving*.

A gun fired, the sound cracking though the air like a hammer against glass. A second shot. A third. Dante risked a glance. Heather stood beside the Baronne tomb, her lovely face shadowed, the set of her jaw determined. Fire blazed from the barrel of her gun.

Several head-shot nightkind were sprawled on the path near her, dark pools of blood glistening on the cemetery path.

He needed to get her out of the fight before Mauvais's idiots killed her or, worse, fed on her. Dante darted for Heather, *moved* with everything he had. Blurred past nightkind stumbling to intercept him, wove around others. Heather gasped as he grabbed her by the waist, swung around, then raced for the cemetery gates.

<*Hold on*, chérie.>

She locked an arm around his waist, his blood-linked message received. The cherry blossom and blood-scented night whipped past him.

Nightkind hunting whoops and shouts cut through the air right behind him; Mauvais's hounds on his heels. Dante stopped at the foot of the locked wrought-iron gates and boosted Heather up and over. He lobbed the Harley keys over the fence.

<*Von, Heather needs you. Mauvais. Ambush. Cemetery.*>

<*On my way.*>

"Baptiste!" Heather cried. "Hurry!"

"Von's on his way. Go!" Dante backed away from the gates. He planned to keep his pursuers so occupied they would forget all about Heather.

But hands seized Dante at the shoulder and neck before he could whirl around and give them something to chase. Dante jabbed back with his elbow. Someone grunted in pain and the hand fell away from his neck. Spinning, he slammed his fist into the temple of the asshole gripping his shoulder. And knocked him back into two more well-dressed nightkind as they rushed forward. All three tumbled into Loki's stone form.

The statue teetered, then fell over onto the paving stones with an echoing *craack*. Plastic beads bounced along the pavement. Candles flickered, went out.

White stone cracked and crumbled away from Loki's body in patches, revealing glimpses of the flesh underneath. But the Fallen angel remained on his side, unmoving, and unnoticed, so far, except by Dante.

Had he succeeded in unwriting Lucien's spell or had—

More hands grabbed him and Dante stomped on the instep of the nightkind holding him from behind. Bone crunched. Then he swung to the side and sliced his nails across the throat of another. Blood sprayed his face; hot and pungent. Dante licked it from his lips. Throwing himself forward, he rolled onto his shoulder, then sprang to his feet.

A hand latched around his ankle and yanked.

Dante felt himself going down. He tensed, preparing to curl and roll again as soon as he hit the path. But someone fell on top of him, and he hit the pavement hard. Fangs pierced his throat; his blood pulsed into a greedy, cool mouth.

Heart hammering against his ribs, Dante pounded his fist against the drinker's temple until the bone dented and the mouth tore free of his throat with a wet pop. Several more bodies dropped onto him, knocking the air out of his lungs and pinning him to the ground like wrestlers in a grudge match.

Muscles straining, Dante tried to twist free, and managed to stamp a bootprint into someone's face. Then something smashed into his temple. Fiery light sparked through his vision. A second hard-driving blow. The light went out.

HEATHER STOOD AT A bus stop a couple of blocks down from St. Louis No. 3, watching as the first vampire Dante had taken down—his gait a bit stiff—carried Dante slung over his shoulder to a shining black limo edged up against the curb. He flung Dante's unconscious body inside.

Inside her pocket, her fingers flexed around the Browning's grip. If she did anything to call nightkind attention to herself, then everything Dante had done to get her free and clear would've been in vain.

Her pulse thundered at her temples. She had no idea why the nightkind—*M'sieu Mauvais*—wanted Dante or where they were taking him.

The rest of Mauvais's crew, a bit battered and torn, piled into the limo. The vehicle pulled out into traffic, as smooth and predatory as a shark.

Knowing the drive from Dante's house to downtown was a good twenty minutes, she could only wish Von clear roads and green lights.

Hurry, Von.

35

THE *WINTER ROSE*

THE LIMO GLIDED TO a stop. Tall'N'Beefy, or Payne, as Laurent had called him, opened the door and stepped out onto the wharf. Dante glanced past him to the docked riverboat. Painted crimson red with a white, twilight-dewed rose at its center, Mauvais's traveling home and casino gleamed in the moonlight. The river flowed beyond, dark and vast. Several figures stood on the riverboat's deck, slender silhouettes in the deepening night. Lanterns strung above the deck winked in the breeze.

"Out," Payne said, bending to glare in at Dante. His fingers curled around the door's edge. "I'll catch you if you run," he added with a fanged smile.

"You'll *try*, anyway," Dante said. "But running ain't on my mind."

Laurent shoved Dante, pushing him halfway across the seat. "Move your ass."

Dante whirled, seized a fistful of Laurent's blond hair, and yanked his head back until his pale throat stretched taut, the blue vein in his throat exposed. Pressing one black-painted fingernail to the throbbing vein, Dante leaned in close.

"Only gonna tell you once," he whispered. "Don't touch me."

Fingernail flicked. Blood trickled. Laurent's eyes widened. Point taken.

Payne was just beginning to react when Dante released Laurent and slid out of the limo. Dante felt Payne's gaze as he straightened. Smelled him: adrenaline-sharp and blood-hungry.

<Little brother, you okay? Where are you?>

<I'm good. Is Heather safe?>

<Yeah and worried sick about you. A little pissed too.>

<I'm on Mauvais's riverboat, but I can handle this,> Dante sent. < I need you to check Loki. I think Lucien's spell might be wearing off.>

<After we get you.>

<I'm fine. Check on Loki.>

Laurent's hand hovered above Dante's shoulder.

"Only once," Dante murmured, gaze still on the *Winter Rose*.

Laurent snatched his hand back.

Dante walked down the wharf to the riverboat's metal steps. He felt Payne on his left side and lovely Laurent on his right. Stepping up from the weather-warped dock onto the *Winter Rose*, Dante halted. Several guards patrolled the main deck, pistols holstered at their hips or tucked into shoulder harnesses.

Their body language, stiff and slow, told Dante they

were mortal long before he caught their scent on the night breeze, berry-tart and tantalizing. Hunger awakened.

"So what's the deal?" he said as Payne and Laurent drew up alongside him. "Anybody trying to slip in without paying the cover gets shot? Or is getting shot a bonus?"

"Below," Payne growled.

Dante shook his head. "Gotta sign you up for the Nightkind Without Humor support group." Sliding his hand along the cool metal railing, Dante climbed down the circular stairs.

At the bottom of the steps, a narrow, lantern-lit hall led to a large open room. The low murmur of voices and minds lapped rhythmically against Dante's thoughts like the muddy Mississippi against the riverboat. Slots chimed and rang, lights flashed, and laughter, high and light like champagne bubbles, drifted into the hall.

Dante closed his eyes and breathed in, deep and slow. Using energy as mortar, he bricked his shields up tight, then opened his eyes. Ignoring Payne and Laurent, Dante sauntered down the hall to the *Winter Rose*'s casino. He stepped through the open doors into a roomful of gorgeous, graceful nightkind dressed in everything from corsets and Levi's to ball gowns and leather.

Mortals walked among them, gazes lowered, carrying trays of drinks and pastries. A few didn't carry trays, offering instead a turned wrist or canted throat to any nightkind beauty who craved a blood treat.

Gaming tables, couches, and plush easy chairs were scattered throughout the room. A bar stretched along one wall. Clove and opium smoke curled into the air like thin gray dragons. Dante felt the heat of attention as some of Mauvais's partiers focused on him.

Payne and Laurent escorted Dante across the room and through the door at its end into a small library containing two mahogany-brown leather chairs—one occupied. The warm smell of a roses-drenched summer evening sweetened the air. The door latched behind them with a solid click.

Dante stopped a couple of yards from the chairs. He shifted his weight to one hip, folded his arms over his chest, and shook his hair back from his face.

"So where's Mauvais?" he asked.

"On his way," the woman in the chair said—a gorgeous chick in a long, sleek black dress. Her hair fell in dark waves to her bare shoulders and a black velvet choker with a white rose cameo at its center encircled her slender throat. "But I couldn't wait to get a look at the murderer."

"Mauvais?"

Her cold, dark gaze settled on him like a block of ice. "No, you, you prick."

"You'll hafta refresh my memory. Who'd I kill?"

"Would you like a list?" she replied. "It's time to answer for your crimes, Dante Baptiste." Her black-cherry-glossed lips curved into a smile. "I plan to watch you burn just like you watched Étienne burn."

"*Oui*, I did," Dante said. "And it was over too fast."

The memory of Jay's death—*mon cheri ami*—washed through Dante's mind in a black and violent tide.

Étienne's arms lock like steel bands around Dante. Yank him onto his ass. He struggles to break free, twisting, and driving an elbow back into Étienne's ribs. Dante scrambles to get his feet under him. Étienne digs in his fingernails, piercing latex and skin.

The blood flowing from Jay's slit throat has already slowed. It spreads in an ever-widening pool around him, staining his hair red. Jay's half-lidded gaze fixes on Dante.

Dante strains to pull free of the limbs holding him, strains to lower his mouth to his wrist. A sigh escapes Jay's lips. His heart stops. The light winks out of his eyes.

A hand brushes Dante's hair aside. Warm lips touch his ear. "*How does it feel*, marmot?" *Étienne whispers.*

"And I'd do it again," Dante said. "No regrets."

A glacier of black ice stretched behind the woman's eyes. "Trust me, I'll make sure you regret every breath you've ever drawn." Her gaze flicked past Dante. "Put him on his knees."

MAUVAIS SLIPPED AN ARM around Giovanni's shoulders as they strolled together along the *Winter Rose*'s main deck. "I regret that I need to cancel our get-together this evening. A matter has come up that requires my attention."

"Nothing serious, I hope," Giovanni said.

"Just a matter of discipline long overdue," Mauvais said. "We'll meet tomorrow evening, *oui*?"

Giovanni took a sip from his flute of bubbling champagne, then nodded. "*Sì*, tomorrow. Have you any word on Dante?"

"I'd heard rumors he was back in town, but my people haven't been able to locate him yet," Mauvais said, stopping at the starboard railing. "I'll let you know the moment I hear anything different."

Giovanni finished his champagne, his thoughtful gaze on Mauvais's face. Resting the emptied flute on the railing, he said, "You understand that Dante Baptiste is to be treated with the utmost respect once you *have* located him, *sì*?"

"No matter his crimes?"

"For now," Giovanni said. "But I will take his crimes before the Cercle de Druide for consideration, I promise."

"Ah. Consideration." Mauvais shifted his attention to the night-blackened Mississippi flowing past, breathed in its odors of fish and muddy brine. "And if he still refuses to recognize my authority?"

Giovanni's amused chuckle scraped along Mauvais's nerves. "You have no authority over a True Blood, *mio amico*. None of us do. We just need to make sure—young as he is—he doesn't realize that truth."

"I'll do my best," Mauvais said.

"Buono." Leaning in, Giovanni kissed each of Mauvais's cheeks in quick succession, his lips cool. "Now I will leave you to your matter of discipline, and I shall explore more of your beautiful city."

"Bonne nuit et bon appétit."

Laughing, Giovanni strode away and Mauvais went below decks to meet—at long last—the defiant and disrespectful True Blood brat named Dante Baptiste.

Justine's justice was finally under way.

ON YOUR KNEES, P'TIT, *hands behind yo' back. Gotta surprise visitor for you.*

Red-hot pain skewered Dante's left eye and the memory unthreaded. His song burned through him, poured molten from his heart.

He caught peripheral movement and whirled, blue light prickling warm and electric around his fingers, just as Laurent's hand locked around his left bicep.

Laurent froze, uncertainty flickering across his face. Tiny reflected blue flames glowed in his eyes.

"Toldja," Dante said. And grabbed Laurent's hand.

Gotta surprise visitor for you.

But the past reached out from behind the walls Lyons and Gone-Gone-Gone Athena had shattered and seized Dante; sucker punched him over and over again with images and whispers and the hard bite of handcuffs ratcheting shut around his wrists.

Sucker punched him with Jeanette's soft sobs.

You figured I didn't notice you playing under the sheets with Mark and Jolie Jeanette, huh, boy? Oh, I noticed, p'tit. I noticed for true. Here, let me turn this monitor thingie on and we'll watch.

A baseball bat of pain slammed into Dante's mind. His song shattered into thousands of jagged discordant notes. Fell away.

A fist rocketed into his temple, exploding red and orange light behind his eyes. His vision rippled like he was looking through water. On her feet in front of her chair, the chick with the black-cherry-painted lips stared at him.

Hands snagged Dante, and wrenched his left arm up hard behind his back, corkscrewing pain into his shoulder. More hands—another asshole or two summoned to the party—forced him down onto his knees. Another fist smashed into his ribs. Pounded the breath from his lungs. Dante tried to twist away from the punches and kicks falling against him like a hard rain, but he couldn't break free.

"How did he do that?" someone whispered. "Laurent's hand? It's gone."

"It'll grow back," Laurent said, voice shaking. "Right?"

"I . . . don't know. I don't know how or what he did . . ."

"He's a True Blood, Justine." An unfamiliar and assured voice joined the conversation. "He's capable of many things."

Dante looked up.

A man appearing to be in his mid-thirties, his slim body draped in an elegant charcoal-gray evening suit, stood beside the chick, the now-named Justine. A black ribbon gathered his long wheat-colored hair at the nape of his neck, allowing an unobstructed view of his sharp-angled aristocratic features and penetrating blue eyes.

Fucking Mauvais.

An amused smile brushed the old Creole's lips. "I see

you've been busy charming everyone. A shame you waited so long to grace us with your presence."

"Yeah, about that—fuck you."

"Ah. As I said, charming. Apparently, a lesson in manners is needed. If you would, Payne?"

Boy needs a lesson. Boy always *needs a lesson.*

Payne knelt behind Dante and wrenched his arm up even higher, then leaned into him with everything he had—and given his Tall'N'Beefy nickname, that was substantial. Dante felt his shoulder muscles tearing, white-hot pain needling the joint. His teeth sliced into his lower lip as he clamped his mouth shut. He tasted blood.

"Enough," Mauvais said quietly.

Payne eased back, but kept Dante's arm twisted up hard. Sweat beaded Dante's forehead. Mauvais looked at him for a long moment, his intent blue gaze traveling from head to knees and back again.

"Such a singular beauty," he said. "In truth, stunning."

"And a murderer," Justine pointed out. "He *admitted* that he killed Étienne. Said he didn't regret it."

"I killed the fucker, yeah. *Ça y revené.*"

"And what of his household?" Mauvais asked. "Did you set his home on fire and murder his entire household as well?"

Dante's heart kicked hard against his ribs. Étienne had tossed that particular accusation at him several times before over the last year, but he had no memory of that night—except for a dream of fire raging against the dying night sky and joy winging through his heart.

Might be guilty even though I had no beef going with Étienne at the time. Wish I knew the truth.

"I don't know," Dante said. "*Peut-être que oui, peut-être que non.*"

Mauvais tilted his head. "What an odd answer."

Bitter fury and grief burned in Justine's eyes. "He's lying."

"I've heard rumors that the boy never lies," Mauvais said, his tone thoughtful. "But that seems rather unlikely." He grasped Dante's chin between his fingers. "But maybe with beauty like this everything he says *sounds* like the truth."

Dante jerked free of Mauvais's cool touch. "Is this conversation part of the torture?"

The amused smile flitted across the Creole's lips again. "You refuse to recognize my authority."

"Authority over what? Wharf-rats? Compulsive gamblers?"

"You're disrespectful, defiant, and rude. You even break *our* laws."

"Fuck your laws," Dante said.

Bending, Mauvais touched a finger to the steel ring on Dante's collar, flicked it. He leveled his gaze with Dante's. "But given this bit of decoration, perhaps you crave discipline. Instruction. Perhaps you yearn for your role in things to be defined."

A smile tugged at Dante's lips. "You ain't got any fucking idea what I crave."

"Perhaps not," Mauvais murmured. He sliced a long, sharp fingernail into Dante's skin just above his bondage collar. Blood trickled hot down Dante's throat.

Mauvais took a deep whiff, his eyes closing in pleasure. "Time for me and mine to flood our veins with your strength, *mon joli*."

"I've got a better idea. Why don't y'all blow me instead?"

Chuckling, Mauvais opened his eyes. "Hold him tight."

DUCKING BEHIND A LINE of crates waiting to be loaded, Heather crouched beside Von, her gaze on the red riverboat at the wharf's end. Waves slapped against the pilings, while distant laughter, honking horns, and the high-pitched shriek of a saxophone echoed from the street behind her.

"We might need more ammo," the nomad muttered, his attention focused on the lantern-lit riverboat and the silhouetted figures strolling the deck.

No, make that *patrolling*. Posture too alert, steps too purposeful to be anything but security. The place was an exclusive casino, according to Von, but the security seemed excessive.

"Is it always like this?" Heather asked.

Von shrugged. "Ain't sure, doll. Don't have many reasons to visit the place, but I have a feeling they added a few bodies to the payroll for our benefit."

"That's what I thought," Heather said. She pulled the Browning from her trench pocket and checked the magazine—full—then chambered a round.

A *ka-chunk* from beside her told her that Von had done the same. He looked at her with moonlight-glinting eyes. "You ready, doll?"

"Ready." She stood.

Von wrapped an arm around her waist, his leather jacket creaking against her trench. She caught a whiff of motor oil and frost. "Guns blazing, darlin'. Shoot anyone who tries to stop you."

"I take it we're not going to try for stealth?"

"We'll try, yeah. But even the best-laid half-assed plans, yada yada . . ."

"Gotcha."

Swiveling around, the nomad hurtled over the crates, landing them both without a sound on the other side. He *moved* down the dock to the gangplank, the night streaking past in a cool, Mississippi-scented blur. Heather tightened her fingers around the Browning's grip.

Vaulting from the gangplank onto the riverboat, Von brought them to a stop on the deck away from the lanterns and near the steps leading belowdecks.

Heather's heart jumped into her throat when a pair of security guards stopped and turned, hands diving inside jackets.

She swung up the Browning and squeezed the trigger.

MAUVAIS LICKED AT THE blood trickling from Dante's throat, then, with a low moan, his lips fastened to the wound. Dante tried to jerk away from the Creole's hungry mouth, but pain ripped through his shoulder with every movement he made. His vision grayed.

"Keep him still," Justine snapped.

"Why don'tcha come over here and keep me still yourself, *chienne*?"

"If he says another word, hurt him."

"Here's a couple of my favs—Fuck. You."

A fist knuckled into Dante's aching ribs, but he held Justine's gaze and forced a smile to his lips. "Fuck you twice."

Fingers seized Dante's hair and yanked his head back. He tried to calm his racing pulse, not wanting to make anything easier for fucking Mauvais and his merry little crew, but his furious heart refused to listen.

Mauvais drank deep, his hands resting on Dante's hips, fingers kneading the leather beneath them like a contented cat. From above, Dante heard the muffled *pop-pop-pop-pop* of multiple gunshots.

Mauvais lifted his head. "Sounds like we have guests."

"*Oui.* A vampire male and mortal female," Justine said, a tight smile on her lips.

Her smile and Mauvais's calm sent chills down Dante's spine. They'd been *expecting,* maybe even *planning,* for someone to come for him.

<Keep away,> he sent. *<It's a trap.>*

More gunshots *pop-pop-pop*ped outside.

<No shit, little brother.>

<Keep the fuck away!>

"Friends of yours, I presume," Mauvais said. "That is, providing you're able to make and keep friends." He rose gracefully to his feet. Pulling an embroidered cream handkerchief from his breast pocket, he dabbed at his lips.

Several sets of hands released Dante as a couple of the nightkind holding him trotted out of the library to join the fight above. Felt like two remained holding him.

Send the pain below and fucking move.

White light flickered behind Dante's eyes. Pain hacked at his skull like a dull-edged axe. Seizing the pain, he used it, burned with it and, briefly, transcended it.

With a quick inward twist, Dante yanked his right arm free of the kneeling nightkind asshole holding it. Then, teeth gritted, he reached over his left shoulder and snagged the rim of Payne's ear. A hard jerk and the bastard's face slammed into Dante's shoulder, dislocating it with an audible *pop*.

"Fuck!" Pain poured molten through Dante's shoulder, collarbone, and chest. The room whirled.

Blood from Payne's nose or mouth or where-fucking-ever splashed hot across Dante's cheek. He heard a thud as Payne toppled to the floor behind him.

"Ouch. Well, hell," Von said. "Dante wasn't the one in danger, after all. My mistake."

"And *you* call *me* stubborn," Dante muttered. He rose to his feet, muscles coiled, burning up inside.

Justine's gaze slid past Dante, surprise rippling across her face. "Guy—a *llygad.*"

"You okay, Baptiste?"

Dante smelled lilac and evening rain, then felt Heather's

fingers brush against his cheek. "Better now, *catin*. You?"

Heather's mingled emotions, the butter-soft warmth of relief and rose-thorned anger, flowed into Dante through their bond. "I would've been better if you'd followed me over that wall. But we'll discuss that later."

"D'accord."

"An honor to have you with us, *llygad*," Mauvais said, extending his arm across his waist in a half-bow. "But this isn't an official . . . meeting." He pursed his lips as he straightened, his gaze reflective.

Dante knew just what he was thinking: *What the hell is a* llygad *doing storming a riverboat, gun in hand? Choosing a side and taking action—it ain't done.* He smiled. *Until Von, that is. A new breed.*

Von stepped up on Dante's left side. "You're wrong about that, Guy," he said. "The moment your people nabbed Dante it *became* official. I'm here as friend and *llygad* both. And I'll never just stand aside where he's concerned unless he asks me to—so you might keep that in mind."

A deep frown creased the skin between Mauvais's pale brows. "What you're saying goes against all precepts of *llygaid* law."

Von shrugged. "What can I say? Times are changing."

Mauvais's gaze shifted to Dante. "Indeed they are." He sat in one of the leather chairs and casually crossed his legs. "Since I have no desire to have my entire crew and staff slaughtered—at least, not tonight—please feel free to leave, Dante."

<This is too easy,> Von sent. *<They're up to something.>*
<I know, but I ain't sure what.>

Justine moved to stand behind the Creole's chair, her black gown clinging to every curve. Her body language and expression were wary despite the glimmer of excitement Dante caught in her eyes.

A danger alarm prickled along his senses, intensifying the chill he'd felt earlier. Something was off, wrong. Maybe not a trap, after all, maybe something else altogether.

"You wanted my attention?" Dante said. "You've got it. This ain't finished."

"And it won't be until you've paid for your crimes in full," Justine said.

A smile tilted Dante's lips. Extending both middle fingers, he stepped backward several paces before turning around. He met Heather's deepest-cornflower-blue gaze.

"You thinking there'll be an ambush?" she asked in a near whisper.

"Ain't sure. But maybe, yeah."

Heather nodded. She loaded a fresh magazine into her gun, then chambered a round. "Okay. How about your shoulder? I know you can't use it and—"

"We'll take care of it outside," Von said. "Once we're in the clear."

"*D'accord.*" Dante looped his good arm around Heather's trenchcoated waist. They *moved* out of the library, across the crowded salon, up to the main deck, and off the riverboat without a single challenge. Dante's inner alarms flashed warnings.

A deafening whistle blasted the air, the sound echoing through the night like a monster's bellow. Pale steam geysered above the river boat. The *Winter Rose* edged away from the dock.

"Let's do this, little brother."

Dante leaned against several stacked crates on the wharf and gingerly lowered his arm to his side. His shoulder throbbed.

"Ready?" Von asked.

Bracing himself against the crates, Dante drew in a deep breath. He nodded and tensed as Von grasped his left arm.

Before he had time to blink, the nomad slammed his hand into his shoulder, popping it back into place.

Dante banged his head back against the crates as pain washed over him like a tsunami; washed over, then ebbed away. Sliding down the crates, he sat down hard. "Shit," he breathed.

Von crouched in front of him. "You okay?"

"Fuck you."

Von grinned. "Yup. You're okay."

Sudden images and sensations poured through Dante's mind: walls of roaring flames, skin-charring heat, and choking black smoke; panicked images sent by Simone, Trey, and Silver.

Fire scorches her lungs. Blackens her skin. Devours her with relentless teeth.

"Simone," Dante whispered. Not a trap, no. Mauvais had *detained* him, insuring that he was kept away from home long enough for . . .

How does it feel, marmot?

Heather dropped to her knees, her eyes dilated and brimming with all the dark emotions crashing into her through their bond. "What is it? What's happening?"

"The house," Von said. "They're burning the fucking house!"

Simone's anguished screams ripped through Dante's mind, his hammering heart. He bolted to his feet, then stumbled as pain exploded behind his eyes like a fiery Molotov cocktail. Then stopped.

Simone's link wisped away.

Dante saw his own shock mirrored on Von's face. "She's gone."

36

THE TASTE OF HIS TEARS

FLAMES ENGULFED THE HOUSE. A few of the old oaks in the yard burned as well, the searing heat from the house igniting their branches. Yellow and orange lights from fire trucks, police cars, and an ambulance strobed across the night. Firemen in turnouts striped with reflective tape worked powerful hoses on the intense blaze.

Heather slid open the van's door and jumped out before Von had brought the vehicle to a complete stop. Thick acrid smoke and the odors of burning wood and melting vinyl layered the air. Rumbling generators and engines vibrated the pavement beneath her Skechers.

Water misted the air like rain.

Several clusters of people stood across the street, watching. A couple of people sat hunched on the curb—Trey and Silver.

Another hard knot twisted up Heather's guts as she looked for Annie. Spotting her sitting on the ambulance's bumper, Eerie clutched to her chest, Heather exhaled.

"*C'est bon, chérie,*" Dante said, as he joined her, his husky voice echoing her relief. "Annie's okay. Eerie-*minou* too."

Heather felt just an edge of his raw grief. She had a feeling he'd secured his shields; both to protect her and to give himself some privacy. She clasped his hand.

"I'm so sorry," she said, meaning it and wishing she could say more.

Dante squeezed her hand, then released it. "I know," he said softly. "*Merci.*" He strode down the street to where Trey and Silver sat on the curb, shoulders hunched, heads lowered. Silver jumped to his feet when he saw Dante, his soot-smeared face devastated. Dante grabbed him up in a tight hug.

Von stared at the burning house, a muscle in his jaw jumping. Firelight and shadows flickered across his face and the lenses of his shades. His hands clenched into fists.

"I didn't tell her good-bye. No need, y'know? I was coming back and . . ." His words trailed off and he drew in a long, shaky breath. "Go see Annie, doll. I'm okay—well, ain't okay, but I can be left alone."

Heather hugged the tall nomad. "I'll talk to the cops for you," she said.

"Just tell them that Lucien is the owner, and that he's in Russia somewhere on business and he'll contact them as soon as he returns. If they ask about Simone, Trey's her only kin. Don't let them talk to Dante. He's too wound up and will probably say or do something to get arrested."

"Understood," Heather said. She released Von and hurried to the ambulance.

Eerie fixed his lambent gaze on Heather, his eyes

glowing golden beneath the streetlights, and mewed. Annie looked up. Soot streaked her too-pale face.

"Simone never made it out," she said, her voice raspy with smoke. "Trey and Silver tried to go back in for her, but the flames . . ." She shook her head. "It was so fucking bad."

Heather sat beside her sister on the ambulance's bumper. "Here, let me have Eerie so the medic can take care of your other arm." Scooping her kitty from Annie's embrace, she cuddled him on her lap. "How is she?" she asked the medic.

"A few first- and second-degree burns on her hands and arms," he replied. "Some smoke inhalation. Shock. But she's doing okay. You should take her to a hospital when we're done here."

"Will do," Heather said, another warm rush of relief pouring through her. She checked Eerie over. A bit of singed fur, watering eyes, and tender paws, but he seemed okay. She stroked his little head, eyes stinging. "How many lives have you used up now, kitty-boy?" she whispered.

He chirruped and bumped his skull against her hand.

"I've got to talk to the cops," Heather said. "Join the guys when you're done here, okay?"

Blinking hard, Annie nodded.

Heather looked over at the curb. Dante sat behind Trey, holding him tight against his chest, his legs stretched around him. They rocked together, Dante's face pressed against Trey's dreads. Silver sat knotted up beside them, his face buried in his hands.

Heather's thoughts reeled back to earlier in the evening when she'd kissed Dante out of jealousy after he'd given Simone a good-bye smooch. A lump formed in her throat.

She glanced at the remains of the burning house — Simone's funeral pyre.

I'm so sorry, Simone. Please forgive me.

* * *

Gillespie slipped his rented Nissan Sentra into drive and pulled out into the street, following the black van Prejean, Wallace, and the others had piled into after the fiery action had died down.

Looked like the gorgeous blonde vamp with the long, spiraled hair hadn't survived the blaze. Not surprising, given that he'd heard crashing glass and the *whoomph* of Molotov cocktails and other incendiary explosives. Just lucky that everyone hadn't died in the raging columns of fire that'd whipped through the house at all exit points.

Or *unlucky*, depending on your point of view.

It seemed like Dante Prejean had more than a few enemies out there. Good to know. For now, it was time to move camp.

Sipping on a Pacifico, Gillespie hung back, allowing the van to drive out of sight. Lovely things, GPS transmitters.

Once Prejean was settled again, Gillespie would resume his work, his patient mission. The one thing that would validate his wasted life.

Learning the proper way to kill a demon-spawned vampire and waiting for the right moment to do it.

Standing behind the long polished bar in Club Hell, Silver poured straight shots of bourbon for himself, Von, and Annie. He placed an unopened bottle of absinthe on top of the bar for Dante. The throat-tightening odors of smoke and singed clothing and hair curled into the air.

Annie darted a look at Heather, then tossed back her shot. But her defiance had been wasted since Heather had already decided that her sister had been through too much tonight to deny her a few drinks.

She could've died tonight and badly.

"You sure you don't want one?" Silver asked, lifting his shot glass.

"In a bit, maybe," she said. "I'm going to check on Dante and Trey."

Nodding, Silver downed his shot, then poured another. Von said nothing, his gaze on the glass between his hands.

Heather filled a wide-mouthed tumbler with water, then placed it on the floor at the opposite end of the bar for Eerie. He lapped it up with quick darts of his tongue. Stroking her fingers along his soot-covered back, she murmured, "I'll get you some food later."

Heather went upstairs, following the soft and soothing sound of Dante's voice, singing in Cajun, down the hall and past the room Gina had been murdered in just a month ago.

Trey rested on a bed, curled on his side, staring into the darkness with gleaming and unblinking eyes. Dante was spooned against him and up on one elbow. As he sang, he brushed his fingertips against Trey's temples.

Heather leaned against the room's threshold, not wanting to intrude. She remembered a conversation she'd had with Simone a month ago during a drive to the house.

A friend of the family turned me, just after Papa's funeral.

Was it something you wanted?

No. But she didn't offer me a choice.

And your brother?

He was all the family left to me. I gave him a choice. If he'd-a said no, I probably woulda set myself on fire.

Heather closed her eyes, throat aching. She wondered how Trey would survive without his sister or if he'd even try.

Dante stopped singing. Heather opened her eyes. He leaned over Trey, his hand on the web-runner's jeans-clad hip, whispering into his ear.

"You gotta stay alive, *mon ami*, for Simone. I wanna kill the assholes responsible for her death, but that's your right. Mauvais and Justine ordered it. I'll help you find them and their house-torching buddies, and I'll stand beside you as you kill them."

"Can I stop living after that?" Trey asked, voice hollow.

Dante swallowed hard and a muscle flexed in his jaw. After a moment, he said, "Ain't up to me, *cher*. But ask me again when they're all dead, yeah?"

Trey closed his eyes.

With tender kisses to Trey's temple and cheek, Dante rolled off the bed and to his feet. He wiped at his glistening eyes with the back of a hand. Stopping in the doorway, he wrapped his arms around Heather. His fevered heat radiated into her, bone-deep. His scent of burning leaves and deep, dark earth swirled around her.

Reaching up, she cupped his face between her hands and kissed his lips. Mixed in with his amaretto-sweetness, she tasted the salt of his tears. He kissed her back, long and deep.

"What now, Baptiste?" she asked against his lips.

He touched his forehead to hers. "Gotta go make something right."

"Side-by-side and back-to-back, remember? You're not going out there alone."

"*Oui, je rappelle*," Dante said. "We're in this together, *chérie*."

"Glad to hear it," Heather murmured, kissing his lips one more time. When the kiss ended, she asked again, "So what now, Baptiste?"

Dante lifted his head. Blue flames flickered in the dark depths of his eyes. Dangerous blue flames. "We go get Lucien back."

37

WYBERCATHL

D ANTE PARKED THE VAN behind Von's Harley and shut off the engine.

"At least it's still here," Heather said, opening the door and climbing out onto the sidewalk in front of the cemetery.

"Good thing, yeah," Dante agreed. He walked around the van and joined her on the sidewalk. "Nobody wants a pissed-off nomad on their ass, let alone a pissed-off *nightkind* nomad. Results ain't pretty."

And right now, that pretty much described Von—pissed-off. Convincing him to remain at Club Hell hadn't been easy.

I'm coming with you, little brother. That's fucking final.

I need you here. I gotta know everyone's gonna be safe and I trust you to do that.

Maybe if I'd stayed at the house, Simone would still be alive — is that what you're saying?

What? Fuck, no! That's all on me. Simone's dead because I killed fucking Étienne. I coulda lost you all.

Simone's death ain't on you, Dante.

Yeah, mon ami, *it is. S'il te plaît, stay here and sit with Trey, yeah? He needs to be watched.*

So I just get to worry about you and Heather?

I can reach you.

So could Simone. Didn't do her much good, did it?

Dante hadn't had an answer for that or the next words that had slipped, low and ragged, from Von's lips.

Her screams . . . fuck, Dante . . . ain't never going to forget.

Eyes burning, Dante grabs Von in a hard hug. The tension in his friend's knotted muscles vibrates into him, along with the thundering beat of his heart.

Dante hoped Von would eventually forget the intensity of Simone's anguished cries, folded into swatches of passing time. As for himself, he didn't deserve to forget.

"Baptiste?"

"J'su ici," he said, focusing on Heather's face. Pain prickled at his temples. Concern whispered through their bond, and beneath that, the promise of white silence. A hush he might need later on.

She searched his face, her expression solemn. "What happens if you can't free Loki or if he refuses to take you — us — to Gehenna?"

"Then we'll find another way to get there."

A sad smile shadowed Heather's lips. She kissed him. "For luck, then."

"For luck," Dante whispered back.

He helped Heather scale the black wrought-iron cemetery gates, then dropped down on the other side beside her. Even though several hours had passed since their dustup with Mauvais's nightkind, Dante still smelled adrenaline-spiced blood in the grass.

Hunger coiled through him, awake and very, very sharp. Dante focused on the moonlit path beneath his boots and shoved the hunger aside.

But he knew he'd have to feed, and soon.

At the Baronne tomb, he slowed to a stop, cold frosting him from the inside out. Loki was gone. Plastic Mardi Gras beads, crumpled scraps of paper, chalked good luck *x*'s all indicated the spot where he *had* crouched.

"Fuck," Dante said, pushing a hand through his hair.

Chunks of white stone that had encased the fallen angel lay scattered on the path, but not enough of it to indicate that he'd broken free.

"Shit. Where is he?" Heather dropped into a crouch and examined the pieces of gleaming white stone.

Dante swiveled around, listening for a frantic song, a distant and desperate scrabbling, but heard nothing but the slow shifting of bones in their tombs and the whisper of cypress and oak leaves in the cherry blossom–scented air.

Someone had *stolen* Loki. Carted him out of a locked cemetery.

"He ain't here," Dante said.

Holding a piece of Loki's stone shell, Heather looked up at Dante. "Plan B?"

Dante shifted his gaze to the cloud-streaked night sky. His pulse raced. "I'm gonna send out an invitation," he said.

Heather rose to her feet. The breeze fluttered through her red hair, drew it across her face. "I don't know if that's a good idea."

"Probably ain't, but it's the only one I got at the moment."

Heather sighed. "I was afraid you were going to say that. What do you want me to do?"

"Send your silence through our bond if I get lost to the music, *catin*."

Heather frowned. "My . . . silence?"

"The thing you do that stops the noise in my head," Dante said. "And keep outta reach, yeah? No matter what happens, don't let me touch you when . . ." He circled his hands in the air.

"When they're glowing," Heather finished. "Oh, no problem there, Baptiste."

Lucien's words—spoken in this very spot almost two weeks ago—whispered up from Dante's memory.

Your song, your anhrefncathl, *drew me. Just like it drew Loki. Just like it will eventually draw the rest of the Elohim . . .*

Dante scooped up a piece of Loki shell, played it through his fingers. His song rose from his heart like a wild autumn storm, a dark and dangerous aria gusting through the New Orleans night.

Energy crackled along his fingers, engulfing the stone in blue flame. Reshaping it. Infusing life. It squirmed hot against Dante's palm. Strings of DNA vibrated like guitar strings beneath his fingers. He closed his eyes, ecstatic and shivering, caught in the song's molten rhythm.

You can create anything and everything. Your song carries the chaos rhythm of life. And you can unmake as well.

He hears a rush of wings.

Hears the metronome of another heartbeat. One he doesn't know.

"Silence the song, child," an unfamiliar voice urged. "Silence it before others find you."

Pain lanced through Dante's temples, and his breath caught in his throat. His song stopped, unfinished, a jumble of harsh notes tumbling away into the night.

Blood trickled from his nose.

Dante opened his eyes and looked at what he held cupped in his hands. A little white-furred, blue-eyed mouse blinked at him. Twin rows of small gossamer wings whirred along its back, music—like tiny bells—tinkled with each flutter.

"Go, you," Dante whispered. He tossed the moth-mouse into the air. It buzzed away, its tinkling song trailing after it.

"A beautiful creation, but what does it do?"

"Fly, for now," Dante said, wiping at his nose with the back of his hand and turning around.

The fallen angel facing him stood nearly as tall as Lucien, a belted cobalt blue kilt hanging to his knees. His short, white hair gleamed incandescent in the starlight. Folded white wings arched up behind his back. He regarded Dante with gold-flecked blue eyes, his handsome face radiant.

"Beautiful *creawdwr*," he said, inclining his head. "You seem to be injured."

Dante wiped at his nose again. "I'm fine. You know my name?"

The angel nodded.

"Then use it. Who are you?"

"I am called the Morningstar."

Heather, Browning gripped in both hands, stepped up beside Dante. "The Morningstar? As in Lucifer?"

The fallen angel tilted his head, a knowing smile on his lips. "Ah, the lovely and beloved Heather Wallace. A pleasure to meet you."

"How the hell do you know her name?" Dante asked, his hands clenching into fists. "Wait. You were the one who broke into our motel room, yeah?"

The Morningstar shrugged. "I've been keeping an eye on you for your father."

"Then Lucien's still alive," Dante said, relief unknotting his hands. "Is he in Gehenna?"

The Morningstar sauntered closer, his kilt swinging against his thighs. His scent, thick tree sap, bitter orange, and wing musk, wafted through the air. Dante caught a flash of peripheral movement as Heather lifted her gun higher. An amused smile danced across the fallen angel's lips. But he stopped.

"Alive?" the Morningstar said. "Yes. But not well. Lilith betrayed him to Gabriel, and Gabriel used a blood-spell to bind him to Gehenna's fate."

A chill touched the back of Dante's neck. "Gehenna's fate? What does that mean?"

"After enduring thousands of years without an infusion of energy from a *creawdwr*, Gehenna is fading away. Without you—without your touch—Gehenna will vanish. And your father with it."

Fury pounded through Dante, drummed up his hunger. "Why the hell would Gabriel do that to him?"

"Lucien never told you?"

"Would I be asking if he had?"

The Morningstar arched a frost-pale eyebrow. "I suppose not. Your father murdered the last *creawdwr*, a maker known as Yahweh, then fled Gehenna."

Heather sucked in a breath. Dante felt like a bucket of ice-cold water had been tossed into his face. "*Menteur*," he spat. "You're just another goddamned fucking liar."

All expression vanished from the Morningstar's face. He held up his hands, palms out. "I'm not lying about that, Dante," he said, his voice low and level. "I can take you to Lucien and you can ask him for the truth."

"Ain't going anywhere with you," Dante said. "Lucien warned me about the Fallen, and he sure as hell woulda told me if there were exceptions to the all-Fallen-want-to-bind-and-use-you rule. Since he didn't, you're a liar."

"He didn't know any of us would be on his side," the

Morningstar replied. "There was no way for him to know. So much has changed in his absence."

"Yeah, ain't buying it." Dante stepped across the stone path to stand in front of the now-wary fallen angel. "I need you to show me how to get to Gehenna."

The Morningstar backed up a pace, hand to his chin as if contemplating Dante's words, but Dante knew he was trying to get out of touching range. "I have to take you there," he said. "The gate is in the sky—"

"No, *show* me." Dante tapped a finger against his temple. "Let me see Gehenna, the gate, the way the place feels."

The Morningstar stared at him, his expression perplexed. "All right, I'll show you, but I don't know how that will be any help. You need to lower your shields."

Dante laughed. "You fucking kidding? No, just project—I'll pick shit up."

A look of indignation crossed the Morningstar's luminous face. "I'd never try to bind you without your permission," he said. "Elohim free will is the principle I've built my life around."

"Maybe, but I ain't taking your word for it."

"I believe you are even more stubborn than your father," the angel muttered.

"*Merci beaucoup.*" Dante turned to Heather. "I know bullets can't really harm him, but they *do* hurt, so if he tries anything that looks even slightly suspicious to you, empty the gun into him."

Heather nodded. "I will. You be careful, Baptiste."

"Truly, your concerns are unnecessary. I can give you all the information you're seeking in my *wybrcathl*."

"Is that your song? Like the ones I heard on the hill a few nights ago?"

"Yes. It sounds like your father has neglected much in your education."

"*Tais-toi*, you're talking about something you know nothing about."

"Then I will give you something I do know," the Morningstar said. He closed his eyes, long silver lashes curving up from the lids, and fanned out his wings, snapping the mingled scents of smoky incense and bitter orange into the air.

Song pealed through the night, a complex rhythm, brimming with information as its melody and crystalline chorus chimed images, locations, and star maps into Dante's mind: the golden gate whirling in black skies, Gehenna's bleeding life force an aurora borealis where none belonged; Gehenna itself, aerie-pocked cliffs and mountains and wild, frothing seas; the blue-marbled Royal Aerie and the warbling *aingeals* ringing its black-starred throne.

The Morningstar's trilling song ended.

Pulse racing, Dante struggled with the urge to unleash his song in response. He closed his eyes and studied the images lingering in his mind, the feel of fading Gehenna, its heat and pale skies. Thought of Lucien, visualized him.

"*D'accord*," he murmured, opening his eyes.

"You still need me to take you to the gate," the Morningstar said.

Dante shook his head. "Maybe not." Turning, he walked to the Baronne tomb and rested his palms against the smooth, night-chilled stone.

He heard light steps treading across the stone path behind him, caught a whiff of lilac and fresh rain. He looked up from the weather-stained tomb and into Heather's twilight gaze.

"What's the plan, Baptiste?" she asked.

"Ain't gonna know until I do it," he said. "I want you right beside me, *catin*, yeah? My gut says you're gonna be safest touching me this time round. Maybe loop your hand through my belt."

A line creased the skin between her eyes. "Should I be worried?"

"Probably, yeah."

"What about him?" she asked, nodding at the Morningstar.

"He should probably be worried too."

The Morningstar studied Dante for a long moment, the radiance beneath his skin dimming a few degrees. Uncertainty shadowed his face, an expression Dante had a feeling the fallen angel rarely used.

"Perhaps I'll wait in the sky," he said.

"*C'est bon*. 'Cuz you ain't looping a hand through my belt."

The Morningstar's white wings unfurled, their opalescent undersides glimmering in the starlight. Wing-gust extinguished the few candles still lit as he winged up into the night.

"Ready, *chérie*?"

Heather slid her gun into the inside pocket of her black trench. "Side-by-side," she said, slipping her hand beneath his belt and locking her fingers around it. "Back-to-back."

Dante closed his eyes and sucked in a deep breath. Held the image of Gehenna, of its sense of *place* firm in his mind. He drew back his left fist. His song cut into the air, thorn-edged and violent, crackling with electric rhythm.

Dante opened his eyes.

AND PUNCHED HIS BLUE-GLOWING fist into the tomb.

Whoomph.

A blast of heated air whipped through Heather's hair and sucked the breath from her lungs. Hammered at her ears. Blue light exploded out from the tomb in a massive razor-thin shock wave that vibrated through her core and shot throughout the cemetery, throughout the city, in an ever-expanding circle, rippling through the night at light speed.

Heather squeezed her eyes shut and tightened her grip on Dante's belt, her heart kicking against her ribs. Icy fear froze all of her thoughts, except for one: *What just happened?* She tucked her face against Dante's tensed shoulder in case of more nuclear-style fireworks. The ground beneath her Skechers trembled and quaked.

Genuine earthquake or . . . ?

A cacophony of noise filtered back into Heather's bruised ears as her hearing returned. Trees creaked and crashed, stone crumbled to the pavement, iron clanged against concrete. Car alarms beyond the cemetery walls screeched and beeped and whooped, and windows shattered, glass tinkling into the street. Dogs howled.

The prickling odor of ozone filled the air.

Distant, frightened voices buzzed into the night like disturbed wasps.

"Holy Jesus, did you see that?"

"An explosion in the cemetery—terrorists."

"Where's the fire? The smoke? What kinda explosion's that?"

"Dear Lord, oh, it's the end of days—a ring of fire!"

Dante collapsed to his knees, pulling Heather down with him. She landed ass-first on the paving stones, her jaw clicking together. Her eyes snapped open. As she took in the destruction surrounding her, she felt the first ice-cold touch of true fear.

Throughout the cemetery, tombs, crypts, and statues had been cut in half, their contents spilling onto the ruptured stone paths; the sliced-off tops of cypress and oaks had tumbled onto chunks of broken stone and masonry, their leaves aglow with blue flames. The cemetery walls had been smashed into blue-flickering ruin.

And in front of Dante, smoke curled from the molten edge of a huge circle in what remained of the Baronne tomb. On the other side of it, pale night skies stretched. Pale night skies full of rustling wings.

"By all that's holy," the Morningstar whispered.

Dante had opened his own gate.

38

THE END OF ALL
THEIR DREAMS

Fluting *chalkydri* song mingled with joyous *wybrcathl,* music cascading through the night skies like water into a deep bowl. Jumbled thoughts and emotions whispered against Lucien's thinning shields. But none of it made sense.

Gehenna is saved! The creawdwr!

He has found his way home!

Holy, holy, holy!

Lucien lifted his head; pain tore through his shoulders as the barbed hooks screwed deeper into his muscles. Above the mouth of the pit, winged figures flew, casting shadows across its glowing, embered floor.

"What's happening?" he asked. "Have they found Dante?"

Hekate hung across from Lucien, her beautiful white wings banded, hooks piercing her shoulders. Dried blood streaked her gold and black gown.

"No," she said, her gaze also on the sky above. Wonder eased the pain from her face—wonder and hope. "He's here."

Lucien's heart thundered. "What?"

"Your son is here. And so is my father."

Lucien closed his eyes. Dante in the Morningstar's hands. He'd failed once again.

ON YOUR KNEES, P'TIT, hands behind yo' back. Gotta surprise visitor for you.

Nah, Papa, I think I gotta surprise for you.

Pain hammered red-hot at Dante's temples. A cool, white stream of silence spilled through his mind and doused the hurt. He sucked in a breath.

Focus, goddammit. Gotta stay here and now.

"With me, Baptiste?" Heather asked, voice low and right beside him.

"*Oui, chérie. J'su ici.*" Rising to his feet, he ducked in through the tomb's smoldering hole, then turned and offered a hand to Heather.

She held his gaze, twilight blue eyes looking in and looking deep. Annie's words, mocking and oh-so-true, punched into Dante's memory: *It's just a matter of time. You're going to hurt her and hurt her bad.*

"It might be better if you stayed here," Dante said. "You aint gotta do this. In fact, I wish you'd—"

"Shut up, Baptiste," Heather replied, grasping his hand. Bending, she stepped through the tomb's hole and straightened beside him on the sky blue marble floor. "It's a good thing I love you, because you officially just scared the shit out of me."

"A good thing, yeah," Dante agreed, squeezing her hand before releasing it.

"She's not alone in those sentiments," the Morningstar said, wedging his tall body through the flame-coaled gate. "Except for the love. I make no claims there yet, little *creaw*—Dante."

Music swirled through air thick with the smoky scents of incense and flowers—jasmine, maybe—a thousand-voice choir warbling and trilling songs and desires to Dante, crooning, coaxing, greeting.

Welcome home, young creawdwr! *The Chaos Seat awaits! Welcome home!*

Holy, holy, holy!

Dante tried to close his mind to them, but there were so many—too many. Sweat beaded his forehead. He felt hollowed by hunger, his strength nearly gone. Exhaustion burned through his muscles.

"What part of Gehenna are we in?" Dante asked.

"The Royal Aerie," the Morningstar replied. A smile twitched across his lips. "I have a feeling Gabriel won't be too pleased about the gate you created within the palace."

"Yeah? Like I give a fuck. Where's Lucien?"

"I last saw him in the pit, so that'd be a good place to start," the Morningstar said. "But since we're here, wouldn't you like to meet Gabriel?"

Dante felt a cold smile stretch his lips. "Oh, I'm gonna be paying the fucker a visit, all right, but I wanna get Lucien first."

Heather grasped his hand again. "You're dead on your feet," she whispered. "So let's grab Lucien and head back. Leave Gabriel for another time."

"I can't, *catin*. He's gotta break the spell he placed on

Lucien." Dante laced his fingers through hers. "Keep close, I don't wanna lose you."

"Same here," she said softly. She pulled her gun from inside her trench, held it down at her side.

"How far away's the pit?" Dante asked.

"You can't walk there," the Morningstar said. "There are no streets in Gehenna, just landing terraces. We head for the nearest terrace, then I'll fly you."

"*D'accord.* Let's move."

Much as he didn't like the idea of entrusting himself and Heather into the Morningstar's embrace, Dante felt he had little choice. Not if he wanted to reach Lucien.

The Morningstar led the way down the sky blue marble corridor, past glowing lamps fragrant with sandalwood and hyacinth oils, and past fluted black columns flecked with gold.

As they walked, Dante caught glimpses of people ducking into shadows, then peering at him from around columns, their expressions a blend of wariness and hope. Several dropped to their knees as he passed and pressed their foreheads against the gleaming floor.

Dante wanted to tell them to get up and knock that shit off, but had a feeling it wouldn't do any good. "Who are they?"

"Servants. *Nephilim*—mortal/Elohim half-bloods."

"Servants, huh? Nice fucking system you got here." Song wormed at Dante's shields, pried at his mind, plucked at his heart.

Holy, holy, holy!

Welcome home! We shall love and serve you and you shall feed Gehenna.

Dissenting song slashed across the choir's voice.

Only feed Gehenna if you desire, young Maker. You can begin a new age for all.

Threeintooneholytrinitythreeintoone . . .

Boy needs a lesson. Boy always *needs a lesson.*

Papa swings the shovel up . . .

Pain jabbed a cold spike behind Dante's left eye. Heather's fingers knitted tighter through his. She squeezed his hand. "Hold on," she whispered. "Stay here."

"Working on it," Dante said, pushing the pain and the voices deeper below.

"Almost there," the Morningstar said. He swung left into another corridor, striding toward a gold-columned archway. Hand-in-hand with Heather, Dante followed him through the archway and onto a wide balconied terrace open to the star-jeweled sky.

Dante saw figures flying through a night shimmering with intense blue and purple and green waves—streamers of aurora borealis color—their wings stroking through the air in powerful sweeps as they homed-in on the terrace.

"They gonna be trouble?" Dante asked.

The Morningstar frowned. "No, but they'll delay you, try to chain you up in their songs and keep you here since you're just a child in desperate need of care and guidance."

"Child, huh?"

The Morningstar flashed Dante a knowing smile. "Most definitely. What are you? Twenty? You should still be in a playpen."

"Twenty-three and fuck you."

"Ah. And in desperate need of manners. Another thing your father neglected."

Pain skewered Dante's temples, flecking his vision with black.

Boy needs a lesson. Boy always *needs a lesson.*

"Again, you're talking about shit you know nothing about," Dante said, blinking to clear his vision. Hearing the sandal patter of multiple footsteps behind them, he swiveled around, unlinking his hand from Heather's.

"Welcome, young Maker, I am thrilled that the Morningstar has guided you home," the fallen angel said. Thick waist-length hair the color of good whiskey, a blood-red kilt, and confident—nah, make that smug—smile. Someone used to being in charge.

The Morningstar sighed. "Well, that's Gabriel, and he isn't going to be happy when you ignore him to go to the pit for your father." He looped an arm around Dante's waist. "Time for us to go."

Gabriel. The fucking asshole who'd locked Lucien's fate to that of a dying land.

"Hold on," Dante said, slipping free of the Morningstar's heated embrace.

Gabriel strode toward Dante, his golden wings folded at his back, moss green eyes gleaming. Other Fallen, guys and chicks, walked on either side of Gabriel, their faces lit, their wings—black and gold—fluttering with excitement.

Hunger sliced through Dante, carving at his thoughts. Song and voices and whispers battered his mind, inside and out. Beneath his skin, wasps droned. Above, the sky rustled. He started walking toward Gabriel.

"What are you doing?" the Morningstar asked, voice low.

"Changed my mind," Dante said.

Gabriel's stride slowed, then stopped as Dante approached. He stared at Dante, lips parting, his expression a familiar and irritating mix of surprise and lust. His scent—amber and pine and deep, dark earth—intensified.

"Beautiful little *creawdwr*," Gabriel breathed. "Welcome—"

Dante *moved*. He slammed into the fallen angel, knocking him onto the slick floor, flesh squeaking against marble. He sat on Gabriel's chest and jammed his knees into the fallen angel's ribs. Shoving his head to one side, Dante slashed into Gabriel's taut throat with his fangs.

And fed.

Blood, pomegranate-sweet and heady, poured between Dante's lips and down his throat, strength threading into him with each ravenous swallow. Gabriel struggled underneath him and Dante burrowed deeper into his throat. Blue light flared behind his closed eyes, song, wild and demanding, pulsing with each beat of his heart. Energy tingled along his fingers.

Gabriel gasped, then went still. Voices cried out. But no one grabbed Dante.

No one dared.

Wybrcathl hammered at Dante's thoughts, insisting he listen to its praise, its instruction.

Holy, holy, holy.

Quiet the song, young Maker.

Voices shoved and moshed through Dante's mind, knocking his thoughts out of sync and out of time. Here and now slipped away.

My little night-bred beauty. You'll survive anything I might do to you.

I'll help you find them and their house-torching buddies, and I'll stand beside you as you kill them.

Can I stop living after that?

Dante-angel, can I sleep with you? I'm cold.

Papa swings the shovel up, then down . . .

Pain raked along Dante's back—molten claws ripping through flesh and into muscle, tearing into him bone-deep. The sharp scent of his own blood saturated the air. Fire scalded his spine and ashed the blood in his veins.

Dante lifted his head from Gabriel's bleeding throat and screamed.

HEATHER RAN, PELTING THROUGH the terrace archway and down the corridor, Dante's anguished scream reverberating in her mind. A fiery aura of blue fire blazed around him, glinting from the horrified faces of the Fallen surrounding him, and from the fallen angel shoving him aside and rolling out from underneath.

Gabriel scooted away, a hand clasped against his bloodied throat. He stared at Dante with stunned, dilated eyes. "He's already mad," he whispered.

"No, he's not," Heather said, dropping to her knees beside Dante on the bruising marble floor.

On his knees, Dante had doubled over, his arms wrapped around himself. Sweat plastered tendrils of black hair to his face. Pain shut his eyes, bared his fangs, and strung his muscles wire-tight.

Dante hissed, the sound low and raw, a warning only a fool would ignore. Heather went still. Heat raged from him, heat so intense, her breath caught in her throat.

"What did you do to him?" Heather asked, snapping her gaze back to Gabriel.

"I . . . ? Nothing. I would never harm the *creawdwr*," the fallen angel said. Then his gaze locked with Heather's and indignation flared in his green eyes. "Who are *you* to question *me, mortal?*"

"She's the Maker's *cydymaith*," the Morningstar replied. "I'd advise a tad more respect."

"A mortal? He'll find worthier *cydymaiths* among his own," Gabriel said.

Heather tuned the fallen angel out and focused her attention on Dante. Blood soaked the back of his NIN T-shirt, glistening in the lamplight. His back *rippled*. Something poked up from beneath his shirt, stretching the fabric, then disappeared.

Heather stared, heart in her throat. *What the hell?*

Sucking in a pained breath through his teeth, Dante rocked forward, his fangs sinking into his bottom lip. Blood oozed down his chin.

Heather struggled with her urge to pull Dante into her arms, yank his shirt off and seek the source of his pain. But the blue light enveloping him kept her hands knotted on her leather-clad thighs.

"Baptiste, can you hear me?" she asked.

Dante's back rippled again and this time something ripped through his shirt, dark and wet with blood. Heather's thoughts came to a screeching halt as she took in what the something was: a wing tip crackling with blue sparks.

Dante cried out, the sound a ragged growl of mingled pain and rage, as his back undulated yet again. The other wing tip, gleaming with blood and blue flames, sliced through his shirt—shredding it. He fell forward onto his forearms and knees.

As if by reflex, Dante's wings fanned open, flinging droplets of dark blood onto the marble floor and walls and across the staring Fallen. Hot blood spattered Heather's face. She wiped at it with the backs of her trembling hands.

Black, Dante's wings, and edged in deepest crimson, the undersides streaked with fire patterns of brilliant blue and purple.

A sense of déjà vu whirled through Heather, keeping pace with her racing pulse.

The never-ending Road. The Great Destroyer. Both or neither or only one.

But still Dante, still the man she loved—if she could anchor him in the here and now. His pain and burning thoughts scorched Heather's thin shields. Voices melted through:

She trusted you, kid. I'd say she got what she deserved.

On your knees, p'tit, hands behind yo' back.

It's just a matter of time. You're going to hurt her and hurt her bad.

What's he screamin'?

"Kill me," Dante whispered.

His words icing her spine, Heather said, "Stay here, Dante, stay with me."

Dante staggered up to his feet. He stumbled, off-balanced by his wet and glistening wings. His red-streaked gaze locked on Gabriel. "Hey, Papa, your turn in the grave, yeah?"

Heart drumming hard and fast, Heather closed her eyes and imagined a lake surrounding her mind. Then, sucking in a deep breath, she dove into the storm raging inside Dante's head.

DANTE WRENCHES THE SHOVEL *from Papa's hands and swings it whistling through the air. The blade slams into the* fi' de garce's *face, stoves it in with a crunch of bone. The pungent scent of fresh blood wafts into the night. Without a sound, Papa keels over into the dark and muddy grave.*

Dante waits for the fucker to rise again, his fingers white-knuckled around the shovel's smooth handle.

Furious wasps drone, stingers burning venom into his veins.

I'm scared, Dante-angel, but I'm glad I'm with you.

No escape for you, sweetie.

I'll be your god and you'll love me.

Ice shivs Dante's heart. He whirls, too late. The shovel vanishes from his hand and he's stretched-out and cuffed in the back of Perv's van—hurtling through the night.

"Looks like you shoulda been worried about me, sexy, not Papa." Elroy Jordan grins and drives a shiv into Dante's chest. "Name the one you love."

Pain punches the air from Dante's lungs. "Still ain't you," he gasps.

A voice from another time, another place, whispers through Dante's mind.

Imagine a key, little brother.

Lust scorches the Perv's eyes nearly black. Another shiv arcs through the air.

A key of blue flame clicks into the keyhole of the handcuffs latched around Dante's wrists. The cuffs fall away and Dante—grabbing two handfuls of the Perv's shirt—falls with them, smacking shoulder-first into cold, stinking mud, the Perv on top of him; falls into a shallow grave lined with upright shovels, their blades buried in the sawgrass above.

Mud-slick, Dante slithers out from under the Perv and straddles him. Rips into the bastard's throat with his nails. Blood fountains into the air and drenches him, hot and heady. The Perv's sneaker heels thump and squish into the mud.

A shovel vanishes from the lip of the grave.

Where you think you're going, *p'tit*? Think you're walking away from me, you?

Silence descends into the shallow grave on white wings and curves around Dante, sheltering him within pale shadows as cool as winter rain.

It's quiet when I'm with you. The noise stops.

Sanctus, sanctus, sanctus.

I'll help you stop it forever.

<Baptiste.>

Everything hushes. Everything goes still.

The firestorm of pain in Dante's head gutters beneath a wind smelling of rain-wet lilac and sage—gutters, but doesn't go out.

<We need you—I need you—here and now.>

A beautiful woman with red hair kneels at the grave's edge and extends a hand.

His beautiful woman—all heart and steel.

Dante grasps Heather's strong, warm hand and hauls himself up and out of the grave. Crouched on the sawgrass, he flicker-shifts from the muddy, blood-soaked teen and into himself.

Dante opened his eyes and looked into Heather's deep blue gaze, feeling her promise inside of him, a sacrament of silence. "*Je t'aime, chérie,*" he said, his voice low and husky. The blue light dancing around his fingers shivered, then winked out.

Heather's hands cupped his face. She brushed her lips against his. "I know," she murmured. "A good thing too." Releasing him, she studied him. "Do you remember what happened?"

"Happened?"

Heather nodded. "Your wings."

Dante stared at her. "My . . . ?"

Pain throbbed at his back, between his shoulder blades, burning like spilled gasoline down his spine. His muscles twitched, spasming fresh pain along his nerves, and wings—*his* goddamned wings—rustled behind him.

Dante didn't know if he'd accidentally transformed himself or if Gabriel's blood had birthed something that had always been curled up inside of him, waiting. But he planned to find out when he had time.

"*Holy* fucking shit," he muttered, pushing a hand through his hair.

"Exactly," Heather agreed.

"Beautiful wings," the Morningstar said. "Unlike any I've seen before. As you are unlike any *creawdwr* I've ever known."

Dante looked past Heather to the Morningstar. Reflected light from his radiant face danced along the corridor's polished walls, and from the decorations gleaming . . .

Dante's heart kicked hard against his ribs as he realized just what he was looking at—not decorations, but blue-bladed shovels rooted to the marble walls on each side of the corridor.

Ready for use.

Cold fingers latched around his heart. One night, one way or another, he would be free—his life, his own. But if this, shovels on the walls of a palace he'd punched a gate into, equaled the first step onto that path, then so fucking be it.

"Unlike any *creawdwr*, yes," another voice said—Gabriel—a voice winding tighter and tighter with anger. "But also a misguided and naïve child. How could you allow him to chose a mortal for his first *calon-cyfaill*, Star?"

"She balanced him without even a touch," the Morningstar replied. "That speaks for itself, don't you think?"

"I'm right here. Talk *to* me, not *about* me, assholes." Dante's wings automatically fluttered, fanning the scent of burning leaves into the corridor. Pain rippled along his muscles.

Gabriel's Fallen companions had dropped to their knees, their gazes fixed on the marble floor, all color drained from their faces.

"Y'all should stand up," Dante said. "Don't know why the fuck you'd kneel for anyone—unless it's in the bedroom—otherwise it's annoying as hell."

One pair of eyes, golden and curious, darted a look up, then away again. The other Fallen remained motionless as if they'd already been turned to stone.

Dante sighed. Returning his attention to the Morningstar, he asked, "What's a *calon-cyfaill*?"

"A bondmate," the Morningstar said. "A heartmate. The strongest and most profound relationship among Elohim."

"One that should never be shared with a mortal," Gabriel grumbled.

Dante *moved*, but this time the fallen angel, adrenaline peppering his scent, leaped out of reach before Dante could snag him. But then he tripped over his kneeling companions and sprawled ass and elbows onto the hard floor.

Dante crouched beside him, his wings fanning, then closing, and nearly unbalancing him in the process. "I'll share whatever I want, with whoever I want," he said. "We clear?"

Sweat popped up along Gabriel's hairline, but fury slashed across his face. "You're too young to know what you want," he said, pushing himself up onto his knees. "Or even to know what's in your best interests. You *can't* be bound to a mortal."

"Why the hell not?"

"It isn't done. Simply not possible." Gabriel's gaze flicked past Dante to Heather. "Or shouldn't be, anyway."

"Anything's possible," Dante said. "For instance, you're gonna break the spell you placed on Lucien—my father—and you ain't gonna send anyone after me again."

Gabriel's gaze flew back to Dante. "Your father," he breathed. "I *knew* it." He frowned, replaying Dante's words. "After you again? Are you saying that you're *leaving*? But your place is here in Gehenna on the Chaos Seat."

"Ain't interested. I'm only here for Lucien."

"Perhaps you might consider infusing new life into the land," the Morningstar said, voice low and smooth, "once you've taken your father home and gotten him settled."

Gabriel looked at the Morningstar, his head tilted.

"Maybe, yeah." Dante pointed down the corridor to the cooling hole/gate in the marble wall, capturing Gabriel's attention once more. "You wanna talk to me, just ask nice. But it's gonna be on my terms, my time. Ain't gonna play games."

"I don't think you understand," Gabriel said. "You are all we've dreamed about for millennia. We can't just let you walk away. You need to be bound—"

"Ain't binding me. Not now. Not ever." Dante reached out and pushed Gabriel's whiskey-colored hair away from his ear and whispered into it. "If you wanna push things, you wanna fight me, call me out, and I'll be right fucking here." Blue flames pinwheeled along his fingers. "We clear *now*?"

A muscle jumped in Gabriel's jaw. When he spoke, his voice was pure frost. "Very clear."

"Now break that fucking spell."

WINGS FANNED THE PIT'S sulfurous stench and smoke into the air and through Lucien's fevered dreams. Hot hands pushed his hair back from his face. Held him as others unscrewed the barbs from his shoulders and unclipped the bands from his wings.

Held him tight. Held him close.

Lucien dreamed of Dante. Smelled him, burning leaves and evening frost.

Heated lips kissed his forehead, his eyelids, his lips. Lucien awakened and looked into eyes of deepest brown, blue flames flickering in their depths.

His son's eyes.

"Found you, *mon cher ami, mon père,* and I ain't never losing you again," Dante said, voice husky. "We're going home."

"I'd like that, *mon fils,*" Lucien whispered. "I'd like that very much."